Mystery and Horror, LLC

Tarpon Springs, FL

HISTORY AND HORROR, OH MY!

Copyright 2014 Mystery and Horror, LLC
Edited by Sarah E. Glenn

"Someone to Watch Over Me" was originally published in *Summer Thrills* (Dorothy Davies, ed.) by Static Movement.

ISBN: 978-0-9915825-5-6

Published in USA by Mystery and Horror, LLC
Tarpon Springs, FL

TABLE OF CONTENTS

DEDICATION

This book is dedicated to the memory of my big brother Donald Gene Mayo (1951-2014). Don saw more real horror in the 63 years he lived than any one person should ever see. I hope that wherever the afterlife takes him, he finds more peace and comfort than he was afforded in his time with us.

- Gwen Mayo, Publisher

INTRODUCTION

History and Horror, Oh My! is the first volume of a two volume collection of historical genre fiction. Its companion book, History and Mystery, Oh My!, is in the editing process as I pen this introduction. We realize that there are many definitions of *historical*. Mystery and Horror, LLC defined *historical* as meaning stories set at least fifty years before publication of this book. In answer to that definition, authors sent us stories ranging from the early 1960's to tales set in ancient times.

The majority of our authors reside in the US, Canada, and Europe. However, both volumes hold stories from exotic locations. Join our authors on a dark trip through time.

Turn the page and step into a tale explaining the destruction of Atlantis, or find out what happens when an unexpected sneeze calls Anubis. Walk with zombies through the trenches of France and journey through America's Dust Bowl with a vampire.

Mystery and Horror is always on the lookout for talented authors from all walks of life. We love short speculative fiction and believe it still has a place in our modern world. Mystery and Horror welcomes LBGTQ, multiethnic, multinational, nontraditional, and unusual fiction. We are concerned with well-written stories involving well-developed characters.

- Gwen Mayo

EKDIKISI

BY AHIMSA KERP

On any other day, Piraeus was the same as any port city in the ancient world. The crowded, meandering streets were swollen with people, goods, and animals from the world over. Piraeus bordered Athens, of course, and acted as its port, but instead of shining columns and beautiful structures, it featured swaggering sailors, drunken barbarians, and grubby wine shops. The great docks were busy during all hours of the day as grain shipments from Egypt, camels from Africa, and spices from the East flowed in, while amphorae of wine or olive oil, along with an abundance of fish, were shipped out. There was art, almost, in the chaos.

This was not, however, a day like any other. Xenophon drank deeply from his *kylix* and slammed a few drachmas onto the table. He was late. The tide was already flowing out, and with it would go the doomed old man. Standing up too quickly, he stumbled as he misjudged his steps. He rarely drank unmixed wine and it was affecting him already. But his sobriety was finding it hard to overlook his anxiety.

He stepped into the streets and felt somewhat invigorated by the salty breeze. The busy port always confused him; he hardly knew his way around Piraeus. He made it to the docks after a few false steps and sighed deeply in relief. There was still time; the old man remained on dry land. There were people everywhere, waiting to witness this ultimate ostracism. It was supposed to have been a secret, but something this momentous could never have been hidden from so many people.

He slipped closer to the docks, pushing through slaves and citizens alike. Finally, he stood at the front, next to three large, blond warriors who reeked of butter. Xenophon wrinkled his nose at the unpleasant warriors and then forgot all about them as five *phroureo*, city guards, nervously herded their prisoner onto the ship. He did not appear to need so many guards. He did not appear to need any guards.

The old man wore a filthy toga. His feet were bare and blackened with dirt and red clay. His muscles were frail and, though otherwise lean, the paunch in his stomach bulged noticeably. His beard was long and untrimmed and, like his hair, was too dirty to be called white any longer. He had no strength and even from several meters away Xenophon could see the gleam of madness in his once shrewd eyes. The only bit of pomp about him sparkled around his neck. It was a glowing, cloudy crystal of unusual angles that made up a *trapezohedron*, of sorts, though it was difficult to count the sides. There were an additional five *phroureo* on the ship; it seemed strange that the frail old man would warrant such precautions.

He needed them all, Xenophon knew. The old man was so dangerous, in fact, that an unprecedented step had been taken. For the first time, a trial was to be held outside Athens. His power had been demonstrated too potently for the citizens of Athens to forget. Too many had already died. Reluctant as he had been to admit it, Xenophon knew now: Socrates must die.

The old philosopher was on the plank now, and Xenophon hurried after him. The guards greeted him as he came aboard the sturdy trading ship named the *Conium*. The hardened ship had been in use for a generation and likely would last another. Four men could sail it and, fully loaded, it could transport more than four hundred amphorae. Today the hold was filled with a bounty of another nature. The ship was

—

2

loaded with books, papers, and pamphlets. Every copy of everything Socrates had ever written, or so they had said. Xenophon thought surely some must have escaped the net. There was no denying, however, that it was an impressive collection. It was almost a pity that it all had to be destroyed.

The ship held fourteen men; Socrates, the ten *phroureo*, Xenophon himself and four sailors led by Anytus. Anytus had discovered their destination and was the chief accuser of Socrates. Xenophon had the privilege of chronicling the madman's trial. It had been an honor to be chosen, but now as he stared at the cold, uncaring sea he began to feel doubt. He wondered if he'd ever see Athens again.

The island had no name, not that Xenophon knew. It was an ancient place, long uninhabited. It had only recently been discovered by Anytus and he remained the only man who knew how to sail to it. It was an utterly strange place, but Xenophon understood now why it had been chosen.

There had been a city here once, and it had been built not by Atticans nor Spartans nor Phoenicians but an older, forgotten people. It was a place of sepulchers and mausoleums, an ode to another time. The buildings were strangely shaped and reminded Xenophon of the stone around Socrates' neck. They shared its lack of angles. It was spooky, alien, and strange, to be sure, but it didn't seem to be dangerous.

"Why am I here?" the old man asked suddenly. He was looking directly at Xenophon. His eyes were clear, and his confusion genuine. Xenophon hated these moments of clarity.

"We are arrived, Socrates," he said to his one-time mentor. He was not sure how much he was able to say. The last thing he wanted to do was awake the philosopher's insanity. The old man was powerless without it.

"That's nice," the old man agreed amiably. He walked away, his blackened and leathery feet clacking against the brown stone. Together, they walked through the abandoned city, all ten *phroureo* ringing Socrates and alert for any danger. Their footsteps intruded upon the silent streets, until they reached a large temple. The trial of Socrates was to begin.

Anytus stood before the assembled group, on a dais of sorts in an enormously large chamber. There were guards by the door, four on either side. Two remained by Socrates. He sat on the floor, his leathery fingers playing with the stone around his neck. A snail of drool slipped from his open mouth. The three sailors and Xenophon sat on heavy slabs that were strangely cold.

Xenephon was diligently writing everything down, but there was little new to be said. Anytus detailed how the impious acts of Socrates corrupted the youth, namely Critias and Alciabiades, with *asebeia*. He mentioned that Socrates followed his *daimonion* to the point of madness.

Xenophon reluctantly agreed. He had written extensively of madness. He knew that some madmen feared nothing, others had no sense of decorum, and others completely lacked respect, even for temples and god. Socrates, he feared, fit all three descriptions.

"Socrates, you deserve death for those crimes. But your deeds grow far fouler," Anytus boomed, his deep voice echoing in that vast chamber. The cold marble pressed into Xenophon's flesh. "In the war against Sparta, you unleashed He Who is Not to Be Named. One man in four lay dead, including Pericles himself, after The Tongueless Void strode through our city. At the time, we blamed your pupils Critias and Alcibiades; and they were put to death. We know better now. "

Xenophon felt his blood run cold. It was still hard to believe. He had lost a sister and his last living brother to the plague some thirty years ago. He had himself been in Sparta with the army, or he too would doubtless be dead. The only thing that made war look civilized, he thought, was something truly indiscriminate. Like a plague.

Socrates looked up. His eyes flickered wildly and his voice sounded strange, distracted. "I will obey the god rather than you," Socrates said. "I would have you know that, if you kill such a one as I am, you will injure yourselves more than you will injure me," he said.

Xenophon did not like the sound of that. It was suddenly very quiet. The sound of the sea filled the room, crashing to the shore with the rhythm of a heartbeat.

Anytus, too was troubled. He paused and looked to Xenophon and the sailors. But he continued: "Recently, we discovered an ancient tome in your possession detailing matters too horrible to speak of. You not only refuse to acknowledge our gods but seek to introduce new, terrible replacements--"

Socrates started laughing and stood up. He suddenly didn't seem so old, so frail. "New gods? New gods? Ha ha ha. These beings are older than Greece, older than Olympus, older than time itself. New gods? You Athena lovers and Zeus buggerers are the only ones guilty of worshiping new gods."

"As I say, you admit to the guilt yourself," interjected Anytus. His voice was shaky and he had grown pale. The tension in the room was at pre-storm levels. "You are sentenced to death."

Socrates laughed again. "You have doomed me to death? Is that what you think? We are all of us doomed to die. All of us." He laughed harshly as he strode toward Anytus. His body moved with a macabre rhythm.

Something wet splashed at Xenophon's leg. He looked down, uncomprehending, at the vast stretch of steel-cold sea water filling the room. There was something wrong with the murky liquid; it was dark and oily and frigid beyond description.

Anytus moved to block the madmen's advance and something happened. Socrates' hand blurred and Anytus fell gasping into the dark water. He did not rise again. The philosopher moved back into the shadows of the chamber.

What happened next, Xenophon did not know; he leaped from his seat and splashed out of the temple, no longer interested in the madman's trial. His parchment fell unheeded into the water.

Xenophon stopped at the entrance to the temple, stunned and shaking. His mind refused to accept the hideous reality before him. The stars were bright in the day sky, shifting as if they were the plaything of some cosmic being. The entire island was sinking, quickly sinking. Buildings crumbled or sank sideways into the sea. The air reverberated with an amusical tone that rung heavily in his ears. Strands of whip-like darkness writhed through the churning water. They looked like ethereal tentacles, composed not of matter but of nightmares and insanity.

Xenophon fell to his knees and wished desperately that he had made a sacrifice to the Olympians before this voyage. He was shoved in the back as the guards pushed past him. They stopped as they realized it was only water before them, water for as long and far as they could see. The sailors and several of the guards jumped into the greasy, broiling water and swam towards the ship, but Xenophon knew better. Their fate had been written the moment they'd stepped foot on the island. This, he thought, this is something indiscriminate on a scale meant for the stars.

The water was up to his shoulders now. His body was numb and dying, but it was his mind that truly suffered as a repugnance so great and so vast crawled jaggedly from the temple and spread over the island. Xenophon felt something in his mind snap. Bizarrely, he thought of the books still on the ship. Who would know of Socrates and his great menace without the repugnant record of his writing? Then the cold sea water reached his neck and drove all such thoughts away. Doomed, he thought. We were all doomed when we set foot on this island. No, when we arrested Socrates. No, not that either. We were doomed the moment we were born into this cold, uncaring world. His last thoughts were of his long-dead brother and sister.

After consuming the Greeks, the horrible isle R'lyeh and its horrible creature sank horribly back into the sea. It was not seen again for many generations. Left only with the works of Socrates' pupil Plato, the wicked prophet received an undeserved reputation of greatness. The puzzled Athenians sent out search ships but nothing save a few waterlogged timbers from the Conium were ever found. It was then that the island of Atlantis acquired a mythical reputation.

Ahimsa Kerp is the author of the historical horror novel Empire Of The Undead *from Severed Press and co-author of the mosaic fantasy novel* The Roads To Baldairn Motte *from Reputation Books, as well as a contributor to many anthologies including* Cthulhurotica *and* Dead Harvest. *Ahimsa hails from the Pacific Northwest but has been living overseas since the aughts. Follow him on Twitter @ahimsakerp.*

ZUKA'S MISFORTUNE

BY CHANTAL BOUDREAU

It all began with a feather.

Zuka, a scribe who specialized in the Coffin Texts, had always served as a prime example of discipline. He considered his skills as essential to the various objects in the tombs where he worked as the people laid to rest there, decorating not just the coffins but masks, canopic jars and other ritual items used to usher individuals into the afterlife. That was why he had learned each of the one thousand, one hundred and eighty-five spells of the Coffin Texts by heart, having then to rely only on his pristine memory, his artistic hand and eye, and the finest of materials whenever he worked. He always kept the best of carbons and ochre on hand and even a small supply of precious gold leaf. Zuka was not just any scribe, he was a true master.

That day he had been charged with preparing the belongings of a lesser noble, making sure the man's coffin and accompanying paraphernalia would bear all of the necessary symbols required to deliver him safely into the afterlife. The fact that this was no pharaoh meant little to Zuka; he gave his all to every job, no matter how regal or lowly the subject. He rarely made preparations for commoners anymore, however. His skills were greatly in demand. His prices were high as a result, too much for the average man to afford.

Unlike other scribes, Zuka chose not to bring the items he was preparing into a workshop – he preferred to travel to their final resting place, for inspiration. He liked to work at night by candlelight, after all the other laborers, craftsmen, and artisans had returned home for the evening to be with their families.

Zuka had no family. His profession was his life and he felt he had no time to dedicate to securing a wife or raising children. His legacy would be passed on to those he apprenticed. Heirs were unnecessary.

Settling onto the cold dirt floor beside the sarcophagus he was charged with adorning, he carefully laid out the tools of his trade, his brushes glinting in the candlelight. His preparations included pulling out the pigments he used one by one, which he would scrutinize thoroughly before lowering them into their place, laid out in anticipation of their use. He always examined his materials before leaving home, but would do a secondary check before beginning - just to be sure he hadn't missed anything. For Zuka, everything had to be exact, as perfect as humanly possible.

Unfortunately, as diligent as Zuka was about maintaining the standards of all items he brought to his trade, including his own scribe abilities, he could not control everything. Because he insisted on working in the burial places rather than at home, a personal quirk, he was not able to regulate all aspects of his environment. And as previously mentioned, that day's mishap began with a simple stray feather.

Zuka completed his pre-work ritual and started into his task, nearing the end of the hieroglyphs required for the particular spell he was applying to the coffin. While he did shiver from the drafty airs moving through the tomb, he failed to notice what they carried with them into the chamber where he sat. Perhaps because of the dim lighting from his candle, or the rapt attention he was paying to every tiny detail, he remained oblivious to the miniscule feather blown in by the dank breezes – the downy fleck that settled atop his upper lip. He was not aware when he first inhaled it either, as he paused

10

mid-brushstroke to draw in breath.

It was only for the briefest moment before he sneezed, as his nose began to burn and tickle, that he realized something was not quite right. This moment did not prove to be sufficient warning as he started into the next stroke, unable to draw his hand away because of his momentum.

"Ah-choo!"

Tragedy struck for Zuka, who prided himself in his great finesse and steady hand. While he was able to restrain his response to his sneeze to some extent, enough of the jarring transferred to the fingers grasping the brush and marred his application of the hieroglyph.

In a knee-jerk reaction, Zuka yanked his hand back, gasping in both dismay and horror. Even in his apprentice days when his hand was somewhat shaky and less sure, he had never made such a blatant mistake. Recovering his senses, he fumbled about for water and a swath of cloth – one he had never had to use for this purpose, but which he always kept on hand "just in case". He hoped desperately that the unintended mark would not leave a stain once he had wiped it away in order to start anew. A sloppy hieroglyph could ruin his pristine reputation.

The consequences would prove far worse than that, however.

Before Zuka had even had the chance to daub at the mess, an unexplained occurrence drew his eye away from the necessary repair. The dirt floor started to rumble and shudder, crumbling away a few feet from where Zuka had perched himself. From out of the hole forming, there spilled a mass of writhing rats and scarabs, scrabbling and squirming, a sight so startling to the master scribe he nearly fainted. Instead, he made do with recoiling away, pressing his back up against cold hard stone. He also clapped his hands over his ears to shield himself from the flurry of clicking and squeaking. The rank stench of sulphur accompanied the swarm, all exits blocked as they scattered about the chamber.

But they didn't come alone.

Rising up from the now rather large hole in the dirt floor was a majestic black jackal head, adorned with auspicious jewelry made from gold and an assortment of precious stones, its dark eyes glinting with a divine but frightening red glow. The head topped a well-physiqued body of a man, far larger than average, bedecked in clothing befitting a pharaoh along with more golden finery. Zuka wondered in awe if this were Anubis himself.

It was.

"Why have you summoned me, mortal? Your offering had better be significant to demand my presence. Normally I only come at the call of royalty and high priests."

The deity's words were loud without being loud, their echo ripping through Zuka's flesh almost as if they had physical substance. Anubis's question caused the coffin scribe's entire body to quake painfully, making it much more difficult for Zuka to take in everything that was happening at that moment. He knew he had to concentrate, choosing his response carefully. He wasn't very successful with this endeavor.

"Summon you? You're mistaken. I didn't summon you," Zuka insisted. He could barely speak over the chattering of his teeth and the knocking of his knees.

"Your spell requested my presence to accept your offering. I decided to come on a whim. I rarely have this opportunity. I'm oft overshadowed by Osiris, despite the fact that I rule over death."

Zuka didn't understand how this could have happened. The coffin spells appealed to Osiris to guide the special spirit present safely into the afterlife, not to Anubis. Scratching his head, he glanced at the smudge. If he squinted and looked at it with his head cocked sideways, it might read "death" rather than "the afterlife" and "safely" had been blotted out altogether. Did this mean Anubis had come anticipating a sacrifice, guiding someone into death, his sphere of control?

The only life Zuka had to offer the god was his own – and he certainly didn't want to do that. But how else was he going to appease the god for disturbing his peace and drawing him into the mortal realm? Zuka had a feeling Anubis would not be willing to leave empty handed. That meant he would have to come up with some sort of appropriate gift, and fast.

"That's true," Zuka said, thinking quickly on his feet. "And I had hoped to rectify that. Instead of texts dedicated solely to Osiris, there should be something that acknowledges you as well..."

"A Book of the Dead," the god rumbled, sounding less angry and more intrigued than he had before.

"Yes – yes, exactly," Zuka continued. He had never been much of a salesperson, but at that moment his life likely depended on it. He would sweeten his tongue as much as possible in hopes of charming the god. "I'm a master scribe, oh divine one. Who better to create such a tome to honour your place as god of the dead? It's time you received the recognition and reverence you deserve. It's time to rise up out of Osiris's shadow. This will elevate you to a place of higher status. I'm sure of it."

Zuka couldn't believe he was speaking this way to a god, but then again, he was amazed he had not fainted dead away at the awe and fear-inspiring sight of the deity. Better if he could live through such an experience and actually survive to tell the tale. Nobody would believe him; they would assume he had dreamt or hallucinated it. He couldn't be sure that wasn't the case himself.

"How do I know this is not some ploy to placate me while seeking glory for yourself? I came here expecting a sacrifice, not a disclaimer. This isn't living up to my expectations." Anubis took a threatening step towards Zuka where he was kneeling in the dirt at the foot of the coffin. Zuka's heart pounded and he trembled in the god's looming shadow, wishing he had the means to simply turn death away. Not even the most powerful of high priests had that ability. Zuka, therefore, would have to use a different tactic.

"Where is the sacrifice?" Zuka replied, his voice now little more than an anxious squeak. "I'll tell you where the sacrifice will be. It will be in the sweat and tears I shed while toiling away at your tome, slaving over it on a daily basis. It will be in the sleep I miss while I tend to the tiniest of details, not a single line out of place. It will be in the lack of recognition I earn for this work, because I will not borrow from your glory. I will remain anonymous, sharing this Book of the Dead with apprentices and scribes alike, without revealing the nature of its origin. Those pages will be spread far and wide, but nobody will know its creator. The distinction shall be all yours."

Zuka hoped that would be enough, an offer of servitude rather than giving up his life as sacrifice. Considering how Anubis valued death, the master scribe wasn't sure if he would consider the offer fair exchange. With nothing else to lose, Zuka hoped the idea would appeal to the god's ego. He didn't think it was fair he would have to pay such a high price for a mistake that was not truly his fault – more of an accident than anything else.

"And my book, it will have more spells than the other texts? There will be illustrations depicting me specifically? The book will offer me praise?"

Zuka nodded eagerly. He would have said almost anything to Anubis at that point to gain further favour. The deity appeared to be leaning his way. "Whatever pleases you, oh great one."

"I accept your proposal then, a book to do me fitting homage. I expect you to work as hard on this as promised and if you fail to deliver, I'll return to fetch you myself. You do understand?"

Shivering at the notion of the god's return, Zuka attempted to clear his throat and rasped a barely audible "yes". An uncomfortable silence followed, as if there was a chance Anubis might change his mind. The ground then opened up and swallowed him again, as quickly as it had initially spit him out. The rats and the beetles which had not already scattered followed him into the hole before it closed. Even after the god was gone, the smell of sulphur continued to linger.

Zuka's hands shook violently for more than an hour after Anubis had departed and he found it hard to breathe, his heart pounding and sweat pouring down his clammy flesh. Unable to continue his inscription as long as the trembling remained, Zuka focused on cleaning off as much of the smudge his unfortunate sneeze had caused. As he had feared, there was a slight stain, in part because Anubis's appearance had delayed the cleaning. Zuka could only hope it would fade enough with time that when he finished with his work, it wouldn't mar the end product.

When he had scrubbed away as much as possible, Zuka sat back on his haunches and stared at the place where the god had stood, no sign of disruption left behind. Had it been all a fabrication of an overactive imagination, a waking dream of some kind, or had he actually come face to face with Anubis? He likely would never know, but a promise was a promise. Zuka would create that Book of the Dead as discussed. He would do so in complete anonymity, just as they had agreed, releasing it to his fellow scribes upon its completion so its use would spread. It would likely be his greatest work and nobody ever would attribute the masterpiece to him.

What else did it mean for Zuka? Well, aside from the fact that he would reap no rewards for that work, neither status nor wealth, he would likely spend every waking hour plying his craft until the book was complete – daylight hours dedicated to the books and evening hours scribing in the tombs. After all, he would still need to earn money to eat. Leisure time would be a thing of the past.

And if he failed to do this, the threat of Anubis's return would hang over him. If Zuka did not exist a slave of the book until it was done, the god would be back to claim his life...or rather his death...instead. Zuka wasn't quite sure which really would be worse.

It was a good thing his job was his life - and as fate would have it, now his greatest misfortune.

Relaxing into humble acceptance, Zuka sighed and returned to his original task, first making sure the chamber was clear of any other stray feathers come to plague him.

Chantal Boudreau is an accountant by day and an author/illustrator during evenings and weekends. She lives by the ocean in beautiful Nova Scotia, Canada with her husband and two children. In addition to being a CMA-MBA, she has a BA with a major in English from Dalhousie University. An affiliate member of the Horror Writers Association, she writes and illustrates horror, dark fantasy and fantasy and has had several of her stories published in a variety of horror anthologies, online journals and magazines. She has also published ten novels to date. Find out more at: http://chantellyb.wordpress.com.

OF BLOOD AND MEN

BY GWENDOLYN KISTE

The dust waltzed across the wheat field again. Alone in the open, I leaned against a desiccated redbud tree and observed the storm's three-step dance. Bear down to the earth, float up to the sky, and turn back the way it came. On a lyrical repeat, the silt spun into itself until the pattern almost made me dizzy to watch.

My left hand fumbled for my last cigarette. But as soon as I clutched the flaking tobacco between two calloused fingers, I didn't know why I bothered to wrangle it. No match could ignite under the weight of that afternoon wind.

I forced the smoke into my weathered jacket and removed a pocket watch. Somewhere around three. The exact time eluded me since I always forgot to wind the damn thing, but I guessed that was about right.

For the sodbusters, dust meant death. No food. No livelihood. No existence. But the storms meant something else to me. On days the breeze whipped the restless soil a mile into the sky, the sun disappeared altogether. For sometimes a week at a stretch, our little panhandle town lapsed into darkness. And the thick debris wasn't like an ordinary storm cloud that suddenly traveled on its way, exposing the light without a moment's notice. The gray dust would settle, one minuscule particle after another, and I could feel my skin start to boil hours before I was at any real risk.

Until I found Oklahoma, I hadn't spent a day outdoors in over a century. Now I cheated the afterlife as often as some people draped laundry from a clothesline.

I lifted my cracked guitar and shook out a stream of dirt. But when I set it back down, more debris rushed through the strings into the heart of the instrument. In under a minute, the dull contraption was once again as heavy as a sandbag.

The family of seven that owned and lost a farm along the Cimarron River secured the broken remnants of a hard-fought life onto the back of an overtaxed jalopy. In the waning dusk, I helped the patriarch and two of his sons attach a chain to the bumper.

"That ought to ground her," the man said. "Now the dust can try to short out the engine, but it'll fail." Proud that he managed one final insult to the weather, he shooed his progeny inside to say goodbye to the place as he and I loaded the last few pots into a splintered milk crate.

I was almost sad to see them go. Every summer, the kids invited me to their bonfires, and while I pretended to consume a bowl of homemade slop, I listened to the men talk of game hunting. The three boys and their father admired the beauty and cunning of their prey—the grace of the deer, the speed of the rabbit, the majesty of the buffalo. But when they needed to feed the family, they never forgot who possessed the advantage. So as I slipped a very grateful mutt my dried meat and salted broth, I realized my own pursuit was not so different from theirs.

But the wheat and corn died, and fate swapped bonfires for dust pneumonia. If the clan remained much longer, the children's fragile lungs would forget how to breathe altogether.

The father put his thumbs under his suspenders and stared across the forsaken field. "There ain't much left around here."

I shook my head and kicked a pile of dust in the air.

He turned and inspected me in earnest. "Why don't you come to California with us?"

"Too bright," I said and grimaced at the thought of those jovial leaflets the people passed around to each other. If the smiling yellow blot on the cover was any indication, I'd perish of terminal sunburn in a cellar.

He laughed. "You're an odd one, John."

"I've been called worse."

"Come another black blizzard like last year, and you might change your mind." He laughed through a tight, beaten smirk. "If you do, we're planning to settle in Monterey. You'll find us there."

But whether they reached Monterey or not, we both knew this was farewell for good.

His wife beckoned from the shell they once called a home, and the man nodded at me before he departed.

Hunger pinched at my bowels, and I glowered into the darkness that extended for a thousand miles. Oklahoma was an ugly state even before life abandoned it. Flat. Plain. Like some old-time European peasant always begging for scraps. I was born too late to witness the Black Plague but minus a few tumbleweeds, I figured it looked a lot like the Dust Bowl.

Jerome, the freckled and blistered middle son, wandered to the side of the car where I kneeled and tightened the bolts on the rear right tire.

He dug the toe of his boot into the loose soil. "I'm sorry I can't help you anymore."

I glanced to either side of me to ensure no one heard his remark. "Don't worry about me." I attempted a smile. "I survived before I met you."

Jerome bobbed his head a few times. "I'm sure you can find someone else for your transfusions." He crossed his arms and rocked in place. "How are you doin' anyway?"

"Not too bad." The tire looked secure, so I stood and surveyed the area. We were still alone, so I let him talk.

"But your sickness? What's it called again?

"Anemia." I said it slow and clear. If he ever repeated the lie I told him, I wanted the imaginary details to be correct.

"Anemia. That's a lifetime disease, ain't it?"

"My kind is."

Now he glanced around for eavesdroppers. "We need more cash for the trip. I thought maybe I could help you a last time, and you could help me."

There was only one derelict shack left on the property, but that was enough to conceal us. I used my fingernail to open an old dime-size wound on his shoulder and pressed my lips into the thin stream of blood. Because he stood a half foot taller than me, he hunched a little to ensure I could reach.

"My family's gonna miss the extra money. They think I've been doing odd jobs at other farms." Jerome liked to talk while I fed. He must have felt it assuaged some of the awkwardness.

"But I'll tell you something," he continued. "I'm not gonna miss lying to Mama about why the sores on my back won't heal."

Maybe he was naïve enough to believe me about my alleged illness, but we both knew the danger in being discovered. They wouldn't understand, I explained to him the first time, and he nodded and instinctively led me behind the barn.

As I fed, he shifted and winced. His blood, once sweet and smooth, tasted tangy now, and I wondered if the weather had rendered him anemic instead. I drank less than I needed and paid him more than I had to spare.

His mother called into the gloom and announced they were ready. Like his father, he nodded at me and marched with a pallbearer's gait toward the rusted car that smoked even when the engine wasn't running.

From in front of the shack, I waved to the seven phantoms spiriting off into the desolate night. If I'd had a shred of compassion, I would have broken all their necks just to save them the heartache.

The next night, I played a square dance inside the town

hall. Nobody conducted business there anymore, so the elected officials decided to use the place for something else.

The event hosted fifteen emaciated faces. When I first arrived in Oklahoma, these sorts of occasions would fill any venue. Dance floors practically buckled from the weight, and wayward couples spilled into every corner and crevice—the darker, the better. But if the emigration persisted, my audience would soon consist of a couple stray dogs and a curmudgeonly old timer who refused to leave, though his home and family had already gone.

A stocky, fair-headed kid of about twenty snaked through the meager crowd. His gaze flitted to me, and I knew what he wanted.

For two years, Jerome was my favorite. But in case he died or moved or refused, I secured backups. I told them my feeding was a kind of newfangled blood transfusion.

"Perfected in the south of Spain," I'd say and they'd usually believe me. Even if they didn't, they'd believe my money.

Killing was fun but drew attention. That proved messy and unnecessary when I could borrow a few confused kids instead. And each day or so, their blood renewed itself like some mythical spring. I often mused that if a single buffalo could provide a family with a new leg of meat week after week, people probably wouldn't be so eager for the slaughter either.

Gene stopped in front of me, unconcerned that I was working. Unlike Jerome who always acted a bit fidgety over the whole process, Gene seemed concerned simply with how fast and how often he got paid.

"You sound good tonight," he said and stared at my guitar. Earlier in the spring, he requested I teach him a few chords, and though I obliged, I knew he only asked to endear himself to me. The tactic failed, and I still felt as ambivalent as ever toward him.

I continued to play. The four dancing couples clapped

their hands out of sync.

"I was thinking after you're done, you and I might take a walk," he said. "Catch up a bit."

Gene was a clumsy kid who understood the basics of propriety but could never fine-tune the details.

"I've got another gig right after this one," I said and finished the song to little applause. "Besides, I'm good right now. Ask me again next week."

Jerome's final offering would slake me well enough for another few days, and I hated to gorge. I felt so sluggish afterwards.

Gene sneered. "I thought I might buy my family some flour and milk this week."

"Here," I said and passed him a dollar. "That ought to help."

The grimace melted into a grin. "Thanks, John." And he disappeared into the evening in search of the nearest hooker.

"Flour and milk." I scoffed at the fib and tuned my guitar for "Choctaw Waltz".

Gene didn't know it yet, but he'd be dead soon. His body looked strong on the outside, but I could taste the death in him. And blood doesn't lie. So if prostitutes were what he craved, I figured let him have them while he could.

Around eight o'clock, at least by my failing watch's time, the dust arrived, and the people scattered with it.

Guitar slung over my back, I started into the darkness after them. A musician with nobody to listen might be the one thing sadder than Oklahoma. A crackle of electricity—smaller than lightning but just as dangerous—flashed in the distance. I smiled to myself. On whatever road Jerome and his family traveled, that chain we fastened to the bumper protected them.

I lit a cigarette and thought how my one-man concert at the bar was probably canceled too. But since I had nothing else to do, I decided to stroll there and find out.

I opened the door and a pile of earth joined me.

"I'm here to play for y'all."

Four men with slack jaws and burnt faces sat inside the establishment, and from the worn-in look to the place, I assumed they'd been in those same positions for the last twenty years. I recognized the man behind the bar as the one that booked me a couple weeks back at a square dance. Miller, I remembered. I assumed that was his last name, but I never bothered to ask for his first. He only seemed like half a person anyhow.

An elbow on the bar, Miller studied me. "Where'd you come from?"

I pointed my guitar to indicate the direction. "The dance at town hall."

"That's almost two miles. How'd you get here?"

"By placing one foot in front of the other."

"How do you breathe out there?" said the man closest to me. His port-wine birthmark was the single remarkable element on an otherwise bland face. The stain started on his left cheek and wrapped around his jaw and onto his neck.

"I don't breathe," I said.

Another man leered at me. "Is this a joke?"

The heavy-lidded expressions belied their ruthlessness. If I failed to offer a sufficient explanation, they were ready to dust the rust off the pitchforks and pursue me in tandem.

"I've spent some time in foreign lands," I said and swaggered to the bar. "They teach you all kinds of tricks. Like holding your breath."

Miller tilted his head. "No shit?"

"No shit."

His hand extended toward me, and he shook an index finger at the air. "I could use a guy like you."

"Doing what?" I pretended to examine a large gash in the bar while I watched the birthmark in my peripheral vision.

"You could bring me supplies when the weather's bad. Whiskey and what not. Save me a lot of trouble."

To entice me, Miller pulled a bottle from a

compartment behind the bar and poured me a shot. Oklahoma never bothered to repeal Prohibition, so the place called itself a restaurant, though everybody including the sheriff knew better.

"I've got a job." I used my guitar to nudge the glass of liquor back to him.

"But those gigs aren't so easy to come by these days, are they?"

I shrugged and turned to stare at the men who might have threatened me with a wooden stake if they thought it would scare me.

Miller continued with his scheme. "I like to do business at night when the lawman won't bother you for details." He leaned toward me and squinted one eye closed. "You don't mind breaking the law, do ya?"

I grinned. "I've done worse."

"I don't trust him," the man with the birthmark said. "That sounds an awful lot like witchcraft to me."

"Maybe it is," Miller said, "but I reckon I wouldn't be against casting a spell myself if it stopped these storms."

And he was right about the music gigs. The opportunities had all but dried up, but as I soon learned, the liquor sure hadn't. I visited moonshiners and whiskey makers and every man and woman in the county who produced a drop of booze. With bottles on my back, I trekked across the dirt, against the dirt, at one with the dirt. After less than a week, my stamina left me, and I feared the undead might be susceptible to dust pneumonia after all.

Close to midnight one evening, I deposited my plunder onto the bar and stared at Miller.

"We need to discuss payment."

He shrugged. "How much do you want?"

"I don't want money."

"Then what do you want?"

"Anyone with a healthy body."

After a moment spent gawking at the statement, he

released a deep "Oh" and motioned for me to follow. I trudged after him, curious what he thought I meant. He led me through the back room, down an unlit hallway, and stopped before a door that creaked partway open.

"You're gonna love this."

The hinge shrieked and I peered inside. A dark-haired girl in her mid-twenties rested on a bed.

To Miller, a healthy body implied a woman, but my tastes usually favored men. And if I got the choice, I wanted them right after a long day in the field, when the flesh heated and the blood sweltered from the vein. My mouth watered at the thought.

"This is my daughter." Miller pointed to her as if I wouldn't know which one. "Try not to rough her up too badly."

I suddenly hated the brute and wanted to dine on him instead. And I might have been on the run from a murder charge before morning if the daughter's cheeks hadn't been so flushed. My gaze admired the tiny pink circles that swirled across her pores.

"What's your name?" But I didn't care what her name was. Her worthless father could have christened her Gladys or Eunice or Myrtle, and I would have still starved for that blood.

"Rachel." She bit her bottom lip.

"Have fun." Miller pushed me into the room and slammed the door behind me.

"I'm John," I said and felt foolish as soon as I did. She had no interest in who I was or why I was there. Her hair twirled around her fingertips as she pressed that beautiful ruddy face into a faded lace pillow.

"I told him before. I ain't some prostitute."

"I never accused you of being one."

She shook her head. "He tries this every week. Never works out for him, so I don't know why he bothers. But come Friday or Saturday night, he brings yet another guy in here for me to please."

"I don't want that kind of pleasure." My cavernous stomach convulsed, revolted at the very suggestion.

"Really?" The wide, expectant eyes studied me. "Then what do ya need?"

"Blood."

She hoisted herself onto her elbows and blinked at me. "Why blood?"

"Because," I said, "that's the deal. I do some favors for your father, and you do some favors for me."

"Why? What do I get?" The feisty negotiations reddened her complexion another couple shades, and I prepared to slaughter half of Oklahoma if she commanded it.

Though I had no need to breathe, I started to pant. "What do you want?"

"To leave this town."

I sighed. "Where do you want to go? And please don't say California."

"Why not California?"

"I don't like sunshine."

Her nose crinkled. "Is it related to the blood thing?"

"You could say that."

"You're an odd fellow." She reclined on the bed, tilted her chin to meet her chest, and examined me through a narrowed gaze. "But I guess I've met worse."

"How 'bout we compromise?" I said. "Let's say we leave for Oregon."

"When?"

"A year?" I figured by the following June, I'd have played the town every tune I knew and gathered plenty of booze for her father. I could buy some rundown Ford—one with a usable roof I could reinforce and sun-proof.

She shrugged. "Okay."

We shook hands to seal it, but the gesture was meaningless. Maybe I'd ditch her before the year was over. Maybe she'd ditch me. In the meantime, though, I enjoyed my regular meals.

Rachel chortled. "That tickles."

"Your blood's fine, you know that?" The clean, metallic scent overwhelmed me. The scores of starved Okies had made me forget how good blood tasted.

"Daddy runs booze," she said. "Everybody wants booze. We don't ever go hungry."

So neither did I.

On the days her skin looked too pallid, I'd fast another night or two, but for the most part, I fed a few evenings a week. My greatest fear soon shifted from finding a good meal twice a month to contending with my ever bulging waistline.

But as much as I valued his daughter — or at least what she could give me — my dislike of Miller compounded with each new assignment. His smugness disgusted me as did his inquisitive pals. I dreaded the conversations they tried to initiate with me when I entered through the bar en route to the bedroom, so after about a month, Rachel started to leave the back door unlatched.

"You're awfully obliging," I said.

She jockeyed for an almost empty bottle of clouded gold. "As long as you're visiting, my daddy won't try to force some other fool on me."

I pulled the nightgown off her shoulder and rubbed my fingers across her latest lesion until the scab sloughed off and a tiny tributary of red escaped.

She finished the jug and tossed it to the floor. "Who helped you with this before me?"

"I never ask for life history."

"But you called 'em something, right?"

I paused and searched for the name I'd nearly forgotten. "A kid called Gene."

Rachel flexed her shoulders and shifted on the bed. "He a greasy fellow? Blonde hair and dumber than life outta allow?"

I removed my mouth from her back long enough to snicker. "Yup, that's him."

"I know him too. He's friends with my daddy." Her hands fumbled for another bottle. "Who else?"

I drank for a moment and then pulled away from her skin to speak. "Jerome. He lived with a big family on the other side of the river."

"He left a few weeks ago, didn't he?"

"That's the one."

She sprawled her body onto the mattress, forcing my lips to search the dim room for nourishment. I found her and between sips, I tried to explain.

"Jerome helped me for a couple years." I suckled at the wound. "I thought for awhile things might become permanent." Another deep drink. "Even once he married and started a family, he could've still used the extra few dollars." Her blood tasted sweet. Almost too sweet. "Or maybe he didn't want a family. Maybe he could have joined me. Been like me."

I realized in my distracted diatribe that I drank more than I intended.

"Rachel? Are you okay?"

My hand groped across her neck and face. She didn't move.

"Rachel?"

I struck her cheek with several quick slaps.

"Rachel!"

I shook her. She flailed.

"Don't do that," she murmured. "You'll make me sick."

I sighed and collapsed onto the bed. "I thought you were dead."

"No, just sleepy."

A rivulet of blood trickled along her shoulder blade. I traced its path with my fingertip.

She turned her head and glared at me with only her right eye. "Are you done?"

"Are you awake?" I scowled, though she'd already looked away. "Rachel, I need you to tell me if you start to feel lightheaded."

"I'll tell ya. Don't worry."

We listened as the dust tapped upon the roof.

"I'd feel better if you weren't drunk when we did this," I said. "It's dangerous. You could fall asleep and not know I've taken too much"

I moved toward her back, and she jabbed me with the neck of the bottle. I swatted her hand. She laughed and quaffed another three shots.

"Don't you drink?"

"No," I said and buried my lips against her warm skin.

The man with the birthmark examined me as I waited for Miller to finish in the back room.

"Where'd you say you learned that breathing trick?"

"In my travels." I leaned over the bar and pretended to ignore him.

"But whereabouts exactly did you learn it?"

I shook my head. "I can't divulge all my secrets. I'd be out of a job."

Miller finally materialized and gave me the address where his next batch of liquor waited. The air was clear, which meant he was capable of claiming this cargo himself. But I enjoyed the walk. The stars pushed through the diaphanous sky, and for the entire seven miles, I lamented how much I took the constellations for granted before the storms.

When I arrived at the property, a tall, gray man kneeled in front of a beaten car and tried to change a tire. I told him who I was.

"Wait here," he said and wiped dirt and sweat from his shrunken cheeks.

I lingered a few yards from the porch, hands in my pockets. The field all around me started to shimmer as a few specks of dust skipped into the air. In response, the bootlegger's house shook and bowed. If this family ever lost the place, the bank men wouldn't need a bulldozer to level it.

A gentle breeze would do it for them.

A clamoring of glass chimed into the night, and the man emerged from a backyard hovel. He distributed a dozen bottles at my feet, and I dropped a handful of cash onto his liver spot-ravaged palm. He scowled and argued for more.

"That's all Miller gave me," I said. "Take it up with him."

While the bootlegger grumbled, the door frame rattled, and inside a voice chirped.

"Is that John I hear?"

As though he had waited all day for his cue, Gene appeared on the porch, a half smile on his face. "How are ya?"

"Doing well," I said. "You live here?"

"Naw." Gene waved his hand at me. "Just visiting my uncle." He motioned to the man who rolled his eyes, grumbled again, and retreated to his booze shack.

"I looked for you last week at the Smith's dance," Gene said. "You weren't anywhere around. Not playing much anymore?"

"No," I said and pointed to the bottles. "I've got another gig."

"Does it pay better?"

I thought of Rachel's writhing veins. "You could say that."

Gene shifted his weight back and forth, swaying like a guilty child. "You need anything for your 'nemia?"

I shook my head. "But thanks for checking on me."

"Do you maybe have some money though?" He swallowed air. "For the next time you do need something?"

"I haven't got paid yet," I said. "I'm sorry."

"Should I ask next week?" He spoke the question but there was no need. His gaunt face asked for him.

"Sure," I said, though I could see he didn't believe me.

I cut the route short that evening.

"Slow down." Rachel giggled. "You'll make yourself sick if you eat so fast."

I swallowed hard. "Who said I'm eating? This is for my condition."

"Yes, your condition called hunger. Just like this is for my condition called thirst." She raised a bottle of gin and chugged from it.

"Can you please not drink while we do this? I thought you died the last time."

"And were you worried you might miss a meal?" Another giggle.

My mouth pressed closer to her skin, and I drank until I was full and she was drunk. Then with nothing left to do, we slept. We slept without waking until the sun rose and fell silently through the dust.

Around midnight, Miller pounded on the door and announced I had another assignment. I struggled into my boots as Rachel squinted at me through the darkness.

"See you in the morning," she said and rolled onto her stomach.

In the pungent air, I trotted with no clear intention yet made the long trek in less than an hour. I could almost see the bootlegger's house through the dust lilting across the fields when a car rumbled past me and stopped in the middle of the road. The man with the birthmark opened the door and put one foot on the soil.

"I've got a surprise for you tonight."

"Yeah?" I lit a cigarette. "What's that?"

He reached into the car and removed Gene by his hair. The oily blonde squirmed and fidgeted as three other men stepped out of the vehicle.

"Genie here told us something interesting," one of them said.

Another drifted toward me. "He claims you cut open his veins. Drank his blood."

"Said it was some kind of Spanish blood transfusion?" The birthmark twisted and contorted and pretended to smile.

"How much did they pay you to lie?" I clenched my

jaw and glared at Gene.

"Not a lie," he said and returned the glare. "And you know it."

The men circled like ambivalent birds of prey uncertain if the wounded rabbit was worth their time.

"I've met people from Spain before," one said to another, "but I ain't ever heard of them drinking anything like that."

"I've got a book," I said with a shrug. "It explains the whole process."

"You ain't got no book."

"Sure I do. It's at the bar. Ask to see it next time you stop for a drink."

I maneuvered between them, but the marked man grabbed my shoulder and shoved me where they could all inspect me.

"What do you do to that girl?"

"Rachel?" I grinned. "You know. The usual."

"He drinks her blood too." Gene's voice quivered. "That's why he's left me alone for awhile. Because he's been after her."

"I'm not after anyone." I exhaled an elaborate sigh, hoping to intimate enough exasperation to convince them they were wrong. "Stop by later tonight and ask Rachel yourself."

"Maybe we'll do that."

They departed, grunting and grimacing as they went. I watched the jalopy turn at the end of the dusty road, and when I was certain they'd gone, I crossed the field and doubled back to the bar. Across the five miles that estranged me from Rachel, I ran.

When I reached the back door, I listened for voices. They weren't there. Yet.

"We need to leave." I grabbed a dress from the bedroom floor and tossed it to Rachel. "Now."

"Why?" She shimmied into the faded cotton.

"They're on their way. Or they will be soon."

—

32

"To do what? Kill you?" Her soft lilt never wavered. "Exactly how do you plan to get to Oregon? On foot?"

"I'll steal a car," I said.

Her laugh struck a shrill, unforgiving note. "What a plan."

"It's all I've got."

She plopped onto the bed. "It's not enough. We'll never reach the state line."

"So does that mean you're staying?"

She shook her head. "You shouldn't get too hopeful is all. We won't make it far."

She was right on that account. When I started toward the door, I collapsed to my knees.

"You all right?"

"Sure," I mumbled. "Just tired. I ran here. I ran for miles." My words disappeared into the air.

Rachel tilted her head. "You need to eat first?"

I nodded. She waved me to the bed. My fingernail glided across the last wound at the base of her back, and the blood broke through the skin with ease. As the warmth flowed across my tongue and circulated through me, Rachel emptied another bottle.

"Please stop that," I said and returned to my feeding.

"You eat. I drink. I think that's fair."

Another begrudging pause. "I need to eat to survive. You don't need to drink."

"Sure I do." She closed her eyes and rested her head on a mound of sheets. "Besides, I doubt you'll carry my bottle collection for me. And there's no way I'm leaving it for my dad."

She set the whiskey on the floor and inhaled softly. My lips pressed into her skin as I heard the men arrive. My gulps became deeper and quicker, and I waited for her to tell me to stop. Then when the voices entered the hallway, I realized Rachel wasn't going to tell me anything. She was no longer conscious.

"Don't do this." I moved around the bed and ran my hand across her damp face. "Not now. Wake up."

I held her by the shoulders and shook her body. She never stirred.

I didn't know if I'd imbibed enough to kill her or turn her. Fists pounded at the rusted hinges, and I doubted I would be around to find out which it was.

When the throng of men broke the door in two and found me cradling Rachel's corpse, all I could think was how I should've gone to Monterey.

With parents who married on Halloween and read her Bradbury stories long before she started kindergarten, Gwendolyn Kiste considers horror, fantasy, and all things strange to be her birthright. Her genre editorials appear regularly on sites such as Horror-Movies.ca *and* Micro-Shock, *and she is the resident "weird wanderer" for the travel-centric* Wanderlust and Lipstick. *Every year, she celebrates the fall season through her blog,* 60 Days of Halloween, *a collection of humorous essays chronicling her autumnal misadventures.*

With a background in cinema and theater, she has written and directed several feature-length and short horror films, and her plays have been produced as part of the Big Read, a program of the National Endowment for the Arts. Her short stories have also appeared in Strangely Funny II *and* Whispers from the Past: Fright and Fear. *An Ohio native, she currently resides in the wilds of Pennsylvania with her husband, Bill, and cat, McQueen.*

You can find her at www.gwendolynkiste.com and on Twitter (@GwendolynKiste)

AND IF THINE EYE OFFEND THEE...

BY JONAH BUCK

Political mutilations enjoyed a long history in the Byzantine Empire. Rebellious generals and disloyal governors were a fact of life for any emperor or empress. Successful traitors gained a throne. Unsuccessful ones were dragged in front of a bellowing crowd and red-hot iron stakes were driven into their eyes.

The practice was brutal, horrifying, and Isa Dragas approved of it immensely. Years in the service of Emperor Michael VII taught Isa to value two things above all else: a powerful crown and practicality.

Blinding rather than killing a particularly cunning prisoner allowed the emperor to exercise his official "mercy." A rebel commander required the loyalty of thousands of troops, support from the populace, and the tacit approval of dozens of powerful bureaucrats. Executing such a stalwart leader would enrage his lieutenants or send howling mobs into the streets of the Constantinople.

An enemy without eyes was no threat at all. The broken rival was banished to some quiet hole inside the capital, usually a monastery. There, the emperor could keep tabs on his defeated opponents like a stable of living trophies. Even if he escaped, an eyeless man couldn't direct troops or ride a horse into battle.

Given its value as a politically safe way to administer an object lesson, public maiming represented the best solution to many problems.

Then there was another class of problem entirely.

Isa watched unseen from a nearby rooftop as two squat, semi-human figures threw themselves at the advancing line of Byzantine infantrymen. One of the creatures wielded a scimitar while the other gripped a club in its webbed hands. Monks' cowls covered both monsters, compounding the obscenity of their existence. Many of the demons roaming the city were blasphemously dressed as Orthodox holy men. The Patriarch of Constantinople had given his blessing to wipe them out.

Lunging forward, the first monstrosity swung its sword at a trooper's head. The soldier expertly deflected the blow with his shield, and his comrades gigged the frog-like horror on their spears.

This same tactic, the *phalanx*, had allowed Alexander the Great and the Romans alike to conquer much of the known world. Even the forces of hell couldn't offer serious resistance to a mass of disciplined Byzantine infantry.

Marching forward, the column of troops trampled the first demon's remains into the cobblestones. The other creature retreated away from the wall of gleaming metal in a bandy-legged sprint.

Safely out of range of the spears, the malformed monk shouted something back at the unit of soldiers.

Isa was an imperial spy. He needed to be well-versed in the many tongues of the empire. Like any learned resident of the Eastern Roman Empire, Isa spoke Greek and Latin, but he also possessed a thorough knowledge of Syriac, Turkish, and Persian. For good measure, Isa knew some choice insults in Armenian, Magyar, and Macedonian.

Even so, he had never heard anything like this language. The noises sounded less like words and more like someone butchering ducks.

The column of troops marched down the narrow street, filling it wall-to-wall. More units moved down other roads in parallel, methodically flushing the city of the freakish deacons.

Leading the phalanx was the campaign's commander, Alexandrios Maniakes. Alexandrios was a preening playboy who openly coveted the throne. Isa would have preferred to see the man locked in a dungeon somewhere before he could cause any lasting harm, but Maniakes had cultivated far too many powerful connections.

Admittedly, the man was brave, but he owed his post to his social leverage rather than any martial skill. However, not even Alexandrios could ruin this operation. With glory to be had in battle against the forces of hell, he had mustered every soldier under his command and begun pushing the monsters back toward their point of origin, the Monastery of Hekatonus. There, heavy *cataphract* cavalry would run them down.

The plan was simple and vicious and therefore good.

From his rooftop position, Isa studied the remaining demon as it taunted the soldiers. It looked like a fishmonger's nightmare. Sharp, stubby teeth stuck crookedly from its meaty lips. Ropy drool hung from its mouth. Its skin was puckered and shiny, like someone who had survived a nasty fire. Really, it looked like a crude human armature covered in frog flesh. Sometimes the Hippodrome exhibited natural curiosities such as conjoined twins for paying onlookers. This looked like something that escaped from one of hell's sideshows.

Reaching into a pouch, Isa pulled out a tough hemp cable and an almond-shaped lump of lead. Placing the weighty projectile in the cord's cradle, he spun the sling over his head.

David slew Goliath with a sling, and ancient Greek peltasts wreaked havoc with the simple weapon. Slings did not require the brute strength of a sword, and they could be easily concealed where a bow could not.

Isa's lithe, scar-crusted body lacked the muscular bulk of the infantrymen below, and his light leather armor offered only minimal protection. Even so, the spy was deadlier than any three of the soldiers.

Twirling the sling like a lasso, Isa released one end of the strap and catapulted the tiny missile toward its target. The bullet hurtled through the air at an incredible velocity.

Crunch!

Enormous kinetic energy punched the projectile through the monk's sloped forehead. The creature wobbled, took one jittery step forward, and collapsed on the pavement. Blood oozed onto the cobblestones.

Below, Alexandrios whipped around in search of the projectile's source. Hallooing the troops below, Isa shot a curt nod to Alexandrios. *If you screw this up, you're next.*

Though he had the high, sweet voice of a castrato, and a boyish, stubble-free chin, Isa was the deadliest man in Constantinople. Yellow calluses rimmed the skin between his thumb and forefinger where his hand had become accustomed to the grip of a dagger. His dark features would have been handsome but for a twice broken nose and alarming, fiery eyes.

Isa served as a civil inquisitor, ensuring compliance with the emperor's will through bribery, misdirection, and murder. He had assassinated emirs, would-be crusaders, barbarian chieftains, and duplicitous bureaucrats. Still, killing monsters was entirely out of his bailiwick.

Top Byzantine agents worked for the *proedros*, the emperor's highest minister. Isa could act as a diplomat by morning, a spy by afternoon, and an assassin by evening, according to the emperor's will. Usually, that meant corralling imbeciles like Alexandrios, not battling hell's minions.

Because the *proedros's* detectives had such open access to the emperor, the spy corps consisted wholly of eunuchs. The procedure served two purposes. First, it was the ultimate test of loyalty. Second, spies couldn't start their own dynasties, reducing the chances they'd go rogue and try to place the crown on their own heads.

Isa was the adopted son of Konstantine Dragas, a

Byzantine general. During a campaign against the Seljuk Turks, Dragas and his faithful companion Nikephoros Botaneiates marched into a village near Edessa.

Cholera had wiped out every living soul except for a single malnourished infant. Konstantine took the child back to Constantinople, named him Isaakios, and raised him as his own. Growing up among the seething rivalries of petty aristocrats, Isa developed a keen awareness of the anarchy boiling just below the capital's surface.

Leading the empire was like shepherding tigers. Each wanted to go its own direction and might turn on the shepherd at a moment's notice. Regardless of how incompetent or cruel the shepherd might be, a pack of loose tigers would cause far more havoc and bloodshed.

Every guildmaster, governor, and general believed that he should truly be emperor, and many of them were willing to burn Byzantium down to meet that goal. Isa was like a gardener, nurturing useful plants and ferociously hoeing weeds before they could proliferate and choke the garden.

Today, that meant bringing Michael VII the head of Nikephoros Botaneiates, Konstantine Dragas's former partner and Isa's friend.

Strategos Botaneiates, promoted on Konstantine's death, simply disappeared several years ago. Constantinople's many wags assumed that he had been casually murdered and his body dumped in some anonymous cistern. Not even Isa knew where he went.

When he suddenly appeared at the gates of Byzantium with a sizeable army, few in the capital were overjoyed by his return. Isa in particular was shocked and disquieted by the change in his friend.

Nikephoros's army was grafted from the detritus of humanity. Somehow, he had fashioned a force from pagan berserkers, nomadic steppe horsemen, an obscure sect of heretical Muhammadans, and a band of excommunicated Italian mercenaries.

Forces loyal to the emperor quickly routed Nikephoros's stitched-together army. Cataphract knights ran down the infantry while the Byzantine phalanxes shredded whatever nuggets of resistance remained.

They paraded the captured *strategos* through the capital. All the while, Botaneiates spewed outrageous blasphemies at his captors. His ravings were not so much heresy as pure madness, and the emperor ordered Nikephoros blinded and banished to the walled Monastery of Hekatonus. Now, his crazed statements seemed to be coming true, and demons were loose in the capital.

No one had seen the monastery's acolytes in the daylight for decades, and how the order had not died out in such isolation was a mystery. The monastery's gates would not open for anything short of an imperial edict, and even then, only under the cover of darkness.

The monastery was a massive, rambling structure originally built as a fortress in the days when Rome still reigned supreme. The bounty of the river left the monks almost completely self-sufficient behind their ramparts. On the rare occasions they did require something from the outside world, the inhabitants traded gold trinkets with the shady boatmen merchants of the Bosporus.

Rumors claimed the monastery contained a massive collection of ancient texts and artifacts pilfered from the Library of Alexandria. Canopic jars filled with the organs of mad pharaohs, Ethiopian steles carved with untranslatable runes, and the pickled remains of creatures thawed from Siberian ice were all said to reside in the monastery's vaults.

Now Isa suspected the unthinkable. Nikephoros had engineered his own internment at the monastery. The rebellion had merely been a ruse to gain him access to the vile secrets behind its walls. Banishment to such a pit was supposed to be the ultimate punishment, but it was exactly what Nikephoros wanted.

The waterfront had always been a dangerous area,

especially at night. People had been disappearing regularly there for as long as anyone could remember, but the situation only recently spiraled out of control, immediately after Botaneiates arrived at the monastery.

People started to go missing in droves. Residents awoke to find everyone else in the building simply gone. Entire blocks vanished in a single night. Even militia patrols near the monastery evaporated into the shadows, never to be seen again. It wasn't until the regular military was called up that they discovered what was stealing residents off the streets.

Several of the soldiers who filed the first report had since committed suicide, and Isa had read a few rambling accounts from the other witnesses. The mutated monks and something else were responsible. Now, every soldier in the city was on the march to wipe out the source of the evil.

The monks seemed to serve the same dark forces Nikephoros had screamed about before he was blinded. Now the rogue general had his true army, the inhabitants of the monastery, and they were eager to do his bidding.

Isa slipped off the roof into an alley, his leather boots absorbing the sound of his landing. He unsheathed a pair of daggers. The waterfront was just ahead.

A large group of the demonic clerics stood in loose formation in front of the monastery gates. Several of them were holding curious staves in their clawed hands. Some of the unholy holy men wore patchworks of armor that looked like they dated back to the Punic Wars, no doubt raided from one of the monastery's curio vaults.

One of the creatures was more thoroughly inhuman than the rest, and it wore the best armor and robes. Isa surmised that this was the abbot.

He held his staff aloft like a street performer spinning a plate. All of the monks were completely absorbed in the odd little ritual, occasionally burbling grotesque laughter.

Where the hell were the *cataphracts*? They were

supposed to clear out any clusters of monks as the infantry pushed them into the open.

Isa quickly ducked into a small two-story shop fronting the square. It was a bakery with living quarters on the upper floor. The ashes of a fire lay dead in a nearby kiln, sad and lifeless in the oven's metal womb. Hardening dough sat nearby, probably left there from when the residents fled or were snatched by amphibious abominations.

An infinitesimally tiny sound reached Isa's ears. Something was moving upstairs. He tensed. Another nearly inaudible creak sounded from above.

Isa's eyes darted about for someplace to hide. The oven. A half-full flour barrel. Beneath a table. The bare shop provided few options.

Seconds later, two of the hideous fish men tore down the stairs brandishing crossbows. They swept through the bakery quickly and efficiently, searching for the intruder.

The bigger of the two was built like a war elephant and looked like a flounder with scabies. He sported an underbite bristling with a double row of shark's teeth.

His partner was less human. Greasy hair hung from his skull, but his face looked like an explosion at the fish market. Two lobster-like eyes rotated independently, searching the room.

They split up, overturning the table, throwing open the oven grate, and kicking the barrel. Flour spilled across the floor in white puffs. Nothing.

Isa clung onto the timbered ceiling overhead like a louse nestled into the folds on an aging whore's flesh, using his daggers as pitons. He swung his legs down behind the smaller monk's head and latched on with his boots.

Using the torque of his leg muscles, Isa twisted his feet and pulverized the fragile bones in the monster's neck. The demon's head crunched to an unnatural angle as bone and cartilage popped out of place.

Even as his partner slumped to the ground, the larger

frogstrosity whirled around, leveling his crossbow. Isa was already on the ground, but he was too far away for a lunge. The crossbow would nail him to the wall before he could get close.

Rolling diagonally forward, Isa scooped up a handful of flour and hurled it at the horror's face. With a surprised croak, the monk instinctively raised an arm to shield his bulging, vulnerable eyes. The crossbow swung away from Isa.

Isa brought his daggers down with a wet puncturing noise. With great effort, Isa yanked the knives down exactly like he was cleaning a large fish. Foul-smelling ichor jetted across the floor. The monk dropped to the floor and flopped spastically before going still. Sheathing his weapons, Isa briefly examined the two corpses, making sure they were dead.

The shorter corpse bore a small pouch made from freckled leather. Human skin. Isa slit the purse open with a knife so that he wouldn't have to touch it with his fingers.

Several small spheres rolled out, no larger than Isa's thumbnail. Curious, he picked one up. The object was perfectly smooth and clear, like rolled quartz.

There was a tiny fleck at the center. At first, he thought it was a minuscule imperfection, some natural flaw. Isa squinted, holding the object up the light.

The "fleck" was actually a tiny sigil.

Sinuous lines flowed together in an undulating orgy of geometry. The symbol was mesmerizing, twisting ever in on itself. Isa thought he could see something at the very center, where all the lines converged. His eyes followed the twists deeper. Deeper…

Isa snapped alert as he suddenly became aware of the sound of clanking armor outside. The blood on the floor was completely coagulated. How much time had passed?

Gathering the bizarre globes, he stuffed them in the oven. When this was finished, he'd come back and melt them to slag.

Dashing up the stairs, Isa stood on a low balcony and watched as several phalanxes converged on the monastery. They came from every street, converging like the spokes of a wheel.

The monks by the gate stood their ground. Their leader continued to hold his staff aloft, like a scaly Moses guiding his people to the Promised Land.

Isa pulled out his sling and laid his sack of bullets on the wooden railing, within easy reach. *Dekarchs*, the infantry sergeants, scrambled through the ranks, ordering bows at the ready. If the *cataphracts* were unavailable, the infantry could handle this easily enough. A rain of arrows would make short work of this lot.

Seeing the mass of soldiers prepping their bows, the monks readied their staves. One of them pointed the end of his staff menacingly at a rank of soldiers. Brave but suici—

The row of troopers splashed backwards as some invisible force rendered their bodies to red pulp. Isa blinked. A nearby lieutenant stopped bawling orders midsentence and gawped at the crimson mess.

Another monk gestured, and a row of men began screaming. Their skin contracted, splitting open like an overstuffed sack. The line of soldiers howled as their flesh sucked tight against their bones.

Elsewhere, a *dekarch's* skeleton violently disarticulated itself in a sudden crackle, as if the man's bones had suddenly turned to oppositely-charged lodestones and repelled each other in every direction.

Whipping his sling around, Isa slew one of the monks. What manner of devilry was this? Isa had met mystics from nearly every inhabited corner of the world. Sometimes he greeted them in the name of Michael VII and offered them lavish gifts. Sometimes, he slit their throats and threw the bodies in the Bosporus. Whatever the empire required, he delivered.

He had met sages, shamans, and spiritualists of every

stripe, holy men and heretics, but Isa had never seen anyone in tune with whatever grisly force these monsters commanded. His mind struggled to summon an appropriate term. Witchcraft? Magic? Sorcery?

He decided it didn't matter. These creatures represented the single greatest threat to Constantinople that the city had ever faced, and he would help end them. Nikephoros would pay for unleashing these monsters.

Isa rocketed a projectile across the square, cracking the skull of another fishy priest. Below, the archers were somehow standing steady amid the chaos, preparing a volley. A staff was pointed in their direction. The sky suddenly opened up and vomited snakes on them.

Even in the chaos of battle, the abbot continued to hold his staff aloft, seemingly unconcerned with the bloodshed all around.

Other groups were trying to advance on the monks, cursed forward by shouting *dekarchs*. They were relying more on numbers than strategy or organization. No one had prepared for this, least of all Alexandrios. Where the hell were the *cataphracts*?

Sprinting forward like men trying to escape a heavy rain, a cohort of soldiers disappeared as the earth tore open beneath their feet. They plummeted, screaming, into the hungry darkness below. The ground refolded on itself, erasing every trace the men had ever existed.

As Isa smote another of the demons with his sling, they suddenly became aware of his presence. One of the frog priests raised a staff in his direction.

Isa ducked back inside the bakery, not at all sure that its brickwork walls would offer any protection whatsoever. There was no time to snatch up his ammunition.

A split second latter, there was a vibration in the air, as if a huge bell was ringing somewhere nearby. All the hair on the back of Isa's neck stood on end. There was a warm, fetid puff, as if Polyphemus had just belched outside the window.

Then the wall began dissolving into spiders.

The bricks came alive with crawling, tumbling arachnids. Hairy arthropods fanned out in a confused swarm as the wall disintegrated into ever more furiously scrabbling bodies.

Despite the heavy casualties, the soldiers drew closer to the circle of monks. There were simply too many for the priests to fight them all, even with the aid of their infernal magic. One group of spearmen got within thirty yards before their intestines erupted out of their bellies and began strangling them.

Isa spotted Alexandrios leading a group of his personal guards forward. The *strategos* suddenly screamed as his armor glowed a merry red and began to melt. Steam bellowed out of the armor's gaps as the man's flesh boiled. Alexandrios's guards writhed on the ground as fist-sized flies crawled up their esophagi and out their mouths in a buzzing cacophony.

His boots crunching dozens of spiders to mush, Isa started to spin back onto the balcony to grab his ammunition. He saw the head priest finally lower his staff. The demonic abbot continued to stare skyward though, as if placating the heavens for manna.

Isa chanced a glance upwards to see what the abbot was looking at.

Good God.

He turned on his heels, abandoning his projectiles, and sprinted down the stairs. His feet barely touched the floorboards as his ears picked up a thin reedy sound. The noise increased in volume, resolving itself into terrified screams and whinnies.

Isa had found the *cataphracts*.

Without pausing, he hurled himself into his only hope for safety: the metal oven. He twisted around in the cramped space and slammed the grate shut just as an armored horse plunged through the timbered ceiling and detonated like a blood bomb.

Isa's sling worked by accelerating tiny objects to enormous speeds. Catapults operated in a similar fashion, taking a projectile with even more mass and demolishing a wall with it. The more mass an object had, the deadlier its impact.

An armored horse had a lot of mass.

The abbot had been levitating the *cataphracts* the entire time, and now he was letting them plunge to earth. There were panicked shouts and unspeakable crunching noises as an entire cavalry unit plummeted out of the sky.

Infantry gear meant to deflect a sword blow pancaked to almost two dimensional proportions when a horse fell out of the heavens on it. Soldiers squirted out of their armor as it instantaneously compressed. Men and horses smashed into buildings at terminal velocity, shattering masonry in great sprays of dust and organs.

The oven rang like a gong as a knight slammed through what remained of the roof and struck the metal covering, denting it. After a minute, the unholy bombardment ceased, and Isa clambered out of the oven. Half the district was destroyed, and the other half looked a lot worse.

There was no chance of finding his ammunition in the charnel house of bricks and exploded bodies. Isa looked around for replacement projectiles and grabbed the pouch of spheres he had placed in the oven earlier. Maybe he could put the blasted things to good use.

He felt numb. The few unscathed troops retreated in haste. Most of them didn't make it very far before their brains leapt out the top of their skulls or molten silver began spraying out their every orifice.

The monks cackled wildly. The abbot, who had been keeping the cavalry aloft through the arcane magic of his staff, had just annihilated the province's best troops. Their victory was assured.

Placing one of the orbs in his sling, Isa readied his attack. He had ten spheres, and he estimated that he could take down three of the demons before they zeroed in on the bakery and ended him. If he ran, he was dead. If he attacked, he was also dead. Might as well send some demons back to hell with him.

He took a deep breath. Eyes narrowed in concentration, Isa focused on the abbot. With a crack, he released the sling, sending the curious missile spinning through the air.

Isa's fingers were already groping for the next round as the projectile smashed into the abbot's face and shattered. He readied another bullet and cast his eyes around for the next target.

The sling went slack in his grip.

Smoke churned forth from the shattered sphere, engulfing everything in the square. Screams sounded across the boulevard for a second time. The scent of brimstone and sulfur filled the air. The deadly fog stripped the flesh off the monks, boiling it into the atmosphere.

Their clothes dissolved in sizzling strips. Their staves dribbled like oversized candles, puddling into goo. Their skin and muscles sublimated, transforming directly from a solid to a gas. Shrieks faded to ghastly gurgles.

In just a few seconds, the monks were nothing but pitted skeletons, and then even those were absorbed by the voracious haze. Even the cobblestones were melting. Isa watched in amazement as the street collapsed in on itself.

Tendrils of mist reached blindly about, as if searching for more organic matter to feast upon. After a few seconds of probing, the noxious vapors shrank back, compressing inward. Almost as quickly as it had appeared, the cloud condensed into a mere mote and then was gone.

Isa cautiously put the remaining orbs away, wanting nothing else to do with the enchanted objects. Half-expecting his flesh to explode off his bones at any second, he proceeded to the hole in the buckled street.

Dusty skeletons stared up at him, their mouths contorted open in silent screams. The pit led to the monastery's catacombs. Many of the skeletons weren't human.

The hole was also filled with fresher bodies, the recently disappeared waterfront residents. They were missing their eyes.

Scaly, hairless things that might have once been rats scrambled through the darkness. Isa hopped into the pit and crept forward through the tunnel. He needed to find Nikephoros and end this madness. Part of him grieved at the prospect of murdering one of his oldest friends. Most of him was merely sickened by the carnage Botaneiates had brought upon the city.

As Isa traveled further, he noticed a faint glow ahead. Light trickled in through the cracks of an overhead hatch. He was directly under the monastery now. There was a dragging noise overhead, moving toward the hatch.

Tensing, Isa prepared to lunge upward. Surprise and speed were his allies. The monks wouldn't be expecting an attack from below, not at the center of their sanctum sanctorum.

The door burst open, and Isa started to pounce...only to skid to a halt. Nikephoros's body tumbled into the darkness with a thump, an angry, clotted hole where his throat should be. His heart had been ripped from his chest. Empty eye sockets looked pleadingly up at Isa.

Staring up into the light, Isa blinked and wondered if he'd gone insane.

"Hello, Isaakios," Emperor Michael VII said. He was dressed in the purple robes of his office, draped in silken splendor. His hands were wet with blood.

Two of the monks flanked him like bodyguards. A curved ceremonial knife hung from the emperor's hand. "I'm sorry you had to see that. I know you and Nikephoros were close once, but I think you of all people would appreciate what's happening here."

"Your Majesty, I...You're..."

"It's all right, Isaakios. The monks are here to help."

"Help? Sire, they just wiped out a half a *themata* of your soldiers."

"No, they wiped out Alexandrios's soldiers. Alexandrios was a power hungry fool, and they were loyal to him. No great loss."

For the first time in his life, Isa was completely flabbergasted.

"You're owed an explanation. You know the rumors about this place. Why do you think this monastery is tolerated? Why do you think prisoners are sent here? I tried to explain this to Nikephoros years ago, but I was hasty. He would have made a valuable ally. Instead, he fled and gathered whatever forces he could against me, hoping to thwart the powers here."

"I'm not sure I understand."

"The priests of Hekatonus and I reached an agreement long ago. I allow them a certain amount of free reign to gather sacrifices near the ports. In turn, they are willing to bring vigor to the throne. They've been gathering their strength for years, and now they are finally ready to back me."

"So Alexandrios…"

"That's right. I'm bringing the empire into line. In exchange for my aid, the monks are willing to scatter the rat nests that have proliferated across the land. Those who would stand in the way, like Alexandrios and Nikephoros, are offered up to certain, ah, entities capable of aiding the empire. Finally, the political entropy plaguing Constantinople will be reversed for good."

Emotions crashed like waves inside Isa's breast. These things were…what precisely? Isa's new partners? If what the emperor said was true, it would be everything Isa ever worked toward, but it was still all wrong.

"You have been one of my most faithful servants, Isaakios. The monks still have human needs. They must keep their numbers strong, and they need fresh blood to keep future generations from reverting entirely. Normally, I would gladly reward you with retirement to watch the fruits of your labor fulfilled…on the condition that you mix your line with theirs."

Isa shuddered.

"Unfortunately, due to shortsightedness on my part, neither you nor your colleagues can truly aid them in this regard. So, there is one more request I must make of you. I'll need your eyes."

Rolling back his silken sleeves, the emperor revealed dozens, no hundreds, of eyeballs embedded in his flesh. They jittered around in confusion and horror. The waterfront residents. "The emperor sees all," Michael VII grinned madly.

Something shifted in the darkness with Isa. He glanced to either side. Shapes hunkered in the shadows, more twisted than anything he had seen before. The darkness mercifully hid their outlines, but shark-like rows of double teeth glittered in gloom.

Isa looked back up. "Goodbye, Isaakios. Your work is complete."

The emperor closed the hatch, and darkness descended on the catacombs.

Jonah Buck splits his time between studying law at the University of Oregon, performing stage magic, writing horror, and other disreputable pursuits. He is an avid historian, exotic poultry fancier, fossil hunter, and B-grade monster movie enthusiast. Special thanks to George Sheridan.

—

SOMEONE TO WATCH OVER ME

BY HENRY SNIDER

Moonlight and Roses echoed throughout the makeshift speakeasy, drowning out most of the conversations. Several couples clung to each other and swayed to the slow song. Hanging lanterns cast a sleepy amber glow on the patronage. Elsie Blancard stared into the shadows wreathing the far end of the great room. There, in the darkness, a solitary man drank from a tin cup. Behind him, shadows had their own momentum, shifting with the subtle movements of couples taking advantage of dim illumination.

"Is that him?"

"Easy, Els." Mary shook a bit of spilled bathtub gin from her hand. "This stuff's expensive."

Elsie leaned in close. "I said, 'Is that him?'" She pointed at the dark-haired stranger.

Mary nodded a confirmation. "Yeah, that's Charles Machon. Just got in a couple a' days ago. Old money. Had some problem during the war." Another song started up, this one enticing the masses into drunken renditions of the Charleston and forced Mary to speak up. "Nearly got blipped off during some battle and lost his noodle."

Elsie tapped her heel to the music but never took her eyes off Charles. Her flapper dress sparkled hypnotically. "He's a real sheik, you know?"

"Oh deary." Mary draped an arm across Elsie's shoulders, "Sheik's so yesterday." We're in the land of talkies now. Haven't you heard?"

—

She pulled away, skirting the crowd.

"Els! Where ya goin'?"

The blonde threw a wicked glance over one shoulder. "You can't expect me to bump gums with you here all night, now can you?" She slid between the masses, snaking her way into one corner of the designated dance area and narrowly dodged one couple kicking their heels up. A handful of steps later Elsie bumped into the intended quarry.

"I – oh...sorry." She giggled.

He looked down, eyes black in the limited light. "I assume you were looking for me?" His thick, British accent cut against her McKee's Rocks, Pennsylvania twang and left them both straining to understand each other.

Elsie feigned innocence. "No...I don't–"

"Well," he cut in with a somehow sad smile, "I don't think you were planning on going back there alone?" He nodded to the half-dozen or so couples clutching at one another, actions hidden by well-placed coats.

"Oh." She stood a little straighter. "And you think you're the man for the job, do you?"

Charles looked left, then right before settling his gaze upon her once more. "I think I'm the only man in the vicinity at the moment."

"Brazen." She smiled.

"Just observant." He took a long, slow swallow from the cup.

Elsie moved a little closer. "You're the talk-o-the-Rocks here, Chuck."

"Charles," he corrected.

"Charles. Sorry." She shifted from one heel to the other and looked down at his cup. "Offer a girl a drink?"

"Certainly. I believe–"

Elsie snatched the cup from his hand and took a swallow, making sure to lick her lips slowly and steal a glance to see if he paid attention.

He did.

"That's not gin." A new song started up and dancers cluttered the floor.

"No. I believe it's made from corn."

"Mash," she said over the increasing din.

"Of course."

"Do you wanna...?" Elsie motioned to the dance floor.

"I'm afraid that seems a bit active at the moment. Perhaps you would be content with a walk, miss?"

"You mean leave all this?" She waved an arm at the convention of law-breakers. "Elsie. Elsie Blancard. Now, lead on." Her hand grasped the crook of Charles' elbow. The flapper gave a devilish look, winking across the barn to Mary. This was met with riotous laughter.

The two walked past the dozen or so wagons and spattering of Fords that filled the otherwise empty field. A full moon lit up the night, making the hill country stand out like a minimalist painting.

"Look at that." Elsie pulled free and walked to the side of a newer convertible.

Charles sounded bored. "What about it?"

"It's yellow," she stammered.

"I like yellow."

She stared back at him, slack-jawed. "You mean this is yours? Is it new?"

He popped the door open for Elsie. "This one is a twenty-three. Only a couple of years old, but I still like it."

"But it's yellow," she repeated.

"I know."

"But they're never yellow."

"This one is. My father knows Henry and managed to talk the moose into making this one a color other than his obsessive black." Charles offered the last swallow from the cup to Elsie, which she took and downed in an unladylike gulp. "Now, about that walk."

"What about a ride instead?"

"You want to go for a ride? With me? A perfect

stranger?"

"You don't seem that strange to me. Maybe a little off your pill, but not all that strange."

"Won't your friends be worried about you?"

"Them? Nah. They're already trolling for beaus."

Charles stepped up onto the sideboard and slid behind the Model T's wheel. "Then a ride you shall have." He retarded the spark and throttled down before turning the ignition switch. A hard stomp on the starter and the car rumbled to life. The sudden noise disturbed the horses. "Direction?"

Elsie thought a moment. "Pull out onto the main road and go left."

"Toward the river?"

"Yeah. There's a place my granddaddy worked one summer called 'The Mound'." She flicked a lock of bobbed hair behind one ear. "It's an Indian burial mound."

The car turned in a tight circle and started down the muddy field's access. He cut a sideways glance at Elsie. "You want to take me to a cemetery?"

"Not a cemetery. A burial mound. It hasn't been used in ages. Some professor hired Papaw away from the mine to help on a dig." The flapper slid a little closer. "You know, like that tomb they found in Egypt."

"King Tutankhamen?"

She clapped Charles on the arm and he visibly winced. "That's the chap."

"Chap?"

"Sure." A devious grin crossed her face, makeup exaggerating it in the moonlight. "Isn't that what the British say? 'Pip, pip' and 'cheerio' and 'chap?'" Elsie adjusted her coat as a cut of cool air sliced the side of the car. "Besides, there's a beautiful view of the Ohio River there. We might be able to even see Brunot."

Charles slowed the Ford and navigated a handful of axle-busting rocks at the road's edge before the car turned onto the hard-packed earth. "Who's Brunot?"

Elsie laughed, then choked on a mouthful of dust. "No, no. Brunot's a little island to the south."

"And what's so interesting about this island?"

She shifted, uncomfortable with the jostling vehicle. "I dunno. I just like it. That's all."

Bugs peppered the windshield as they flew down the country road. Sounds changed when the car left the field behind them and entered a wooden grove. Trees whipped by with a repetitive thump-thump sound while scattered beams of moonlight broke the canopy and danced along the forest floor.

"You're going to want to slow down here," Elsie shouted, now unable to suppress an excited grin. A low branch whooshed by and almost snatched her hat.

Charles acquiesced and slowed the convertible to a more reasonable speed. A rough patch in the road jostled the car so severely Elsie almost lost the grip on the dash. The high bounces rode her dress up. Seconds later she realized this and caught him staring at her legs.

"Eyes on the road, buster," she said with a laugh. "It'd be a heck of a note to be killed because of my gams."

"Killer gams," Charles said with a smirk.

Elsie pointed to the right. "We're nearly there. It's just a cut in the woods. I'm not even sure we can get up there with this bucket."

A darker patch of woods appeared in the general direction she pointed. Charles stepped on the gas, shot off the road and down a slight embankment before spewing rocks as they skidded around a bend.

"Slow!" She grabbed a handful of his upper arm and he screamed, stomping on the brakes until the car skidded to a halt. Charles cradled his bicep, just over her grip. Elsie let go and leaned back. "I didn't mean–"

"It's not you," he managed through gritted teeth. "It's just an old injury acting up."

"Was it–"

"The war? Yes." Charles rubbed his arm through the jacket. "Isn't it always the war for anyone my age?"

Elsie slid closer. "You're not all that old. You're what...thirty?"

He managed a grim smile. "Twenty-three...nearly to the day."

"So you went in when you were...?" Elsie let the question drift off.

Charles sighed and looked up at the hint of moon visible through the lush greenery. "Fourteen. I stole my brother's papers and enlisted. By the time my parents sorted out what happened I was already neck deep at the Battle of the Somme under Sir Douglas Haig."

She returned a hand to his arm and mimicked the soft massage. He winced again and she eased the pressure. "What was it like?"

In lieu of a response, Charles turned and caressed the side of Elsie's face, trailing one finger under her jaw and tipping her head up in preparation for a kiss. Lips met, parted and released tongues to explore new territory.

They shifted, Elsie's hand slid across his body and around his neck, while his own slid from face to arm, to hip and rested on her coat-covered thigh. The time-immortal dominance dance played out in the front seat, Charles urging her to lie back. She pressed her own advantage by shifting and made access to anything other than her lips more difficult.

The kiss broke and left each flushed.

"Would it be more comfortable...?" He motioned to the back seat, but Elsie had already slid the car's width and gotten out on the far side. She turned and rested her forearms on the door.

"So are you coming or not?"

"I thought we were enjoying the evening here."

"We are, silly." Elsie backed away, illuminated by the car's headlights. "Up on the mound. I'm serious about wanting to show it to you."

Charles let loose a laugh. "You actually think you're going to entice me into following you into the night?"

Elsie grinned and lifted the hem of her coat and dress, flashing a glimpse of knee.

"You're incorrigible." The driver's side door swung open and he climbed out, alcohol making legs more wobbly than when they'd left the speakeasy. "Lead on, milady." He clicked off the lights and followed her through the foliage.

The couple ascended the low hill at a snail's pace. Undergrowth gave way to trees and dried remains of leaves. They peaked the crest and Elsie sat on rotted pile of lumber and looked down into a cone-shaped depression. The remnants of the dig spanned a good thirty feet and better than a third of that in depth. Just beyond the far side's lip lay a ledge. The Ohio River flowed past better than a tree's height below.

"My Papaw worked this with the archaeologist from some college. I grew up with him telling me and my brothers stories about what they found here."

Charles leaned against a tree and hunted for a match. "What, pray tell, did they find here? Gold? Jewels?"

She scrunched her face up as only a young woman still on the shy side of twenty could. "No. They were Indians."

A match bit back the darkness as it jumped to life. "Then what?" He drew deep against the flame, and the cigarette's tip pulsed yellow-red.

Elsie leaned back. "Over thirty Indians. Tools. Seashells. Pottery. They said this mound is probably full of bodies going back hundreds of years."

"Really?" Disbelief hung heavy in Charles' sarcastic tone.

"Yes, really." She stood, walked over and took his cigarette as her own. The ember glowed hot as she drew deep on the oily smoke. "They think there may be hundreds more deeper than what they dug out."

He reached out, put a hand on Elsie's hip and pulled to close the distance between them. "Fascinating."

"It is," she insisted. "The Hopewell Indians took this area over from the Adena." A schoolmarm quality overtook the flapper, her enthusiasm coming across like a lesson. "They don't know what happened to the tribe. From the artifacts they found, the Adena, at least this particular tribe," she corrected herself, "just died out and then the Hopewell were here."

"Hmm." Charles leaned down and nuzzled her neck. "Sounds like the Hopewell killed them off."

"No." Elsie stepped back a bit, wrapped up in sharing this all-too-well-known local story with someone new. "The Hopewell were peaceful for the most part. The last Adena found were buried like the Hopewell did for their own dead."

"Fascinating," he repeated. Charles closed the distance between them, mind still on the fumblings exchanged in the car. One hand met another and the cigarette changed partners again.

"Isn't it? Hey, there's Brunot." She pointed through a copse of trees to a split in the river a few hundred yards distant. The land mass lay as a dark patch of blue-green encompassed by a silver chain of water.

He dropped the butt and pulled her tight, lips searching. Elsie resisted for a second then leaned in, pressing herself against him. The couple found their way to the ground but never broke contact. Elsie wrapped her arms around to the small of Charles' back. His palm, hot in contrast to the night air, on her leg, rested just below where acceptable modesty placed this season's hemline. She shifted and felt a hand move up a foot before realizing it. Fingertips, softer than those of local beaus, danced at her stocking top, though stayed well below the garter belt's fasteners. Knees relaxed, then parted to allow better access. Nails drug upward and slid from silk to naked thigh. Hesitant caresses teased scant inches away from her *mons*. With no rejection, the journey continued under the short-bloomers and made quick work of her folds. As digits met target Elsie let loose a gasp and drew her own attention to just below Charles' belt buckle. Another hesitation for propriety's sake, then nature took over and she rubbed the front of his trousers, increasing pressure along his rigid length.

Minutes passed as they groped in the moonlight and Charles grew more aggressive with his ministrations. Elsie's pulse pounded in her ears. The flapper's stomach tightened and the forthcoming wash of pleasure made itself known. Then, just short of a quivering release, fingers slid lower, searching for her center. She stopped him short of actual penetration.

"Whoa," she said through the kiss, "I only pet."

A familiar sigh of frustration escaped Elsie's new suitor. She shifted her hand, allowing two fingers to slide past trouser buttons, through underlying fabric and actually touched his length in an effort to regain the enthusiasm he'd shown a moment before. He flexed, then pulled away and sat up.

"I...I need a moment."

"I'm sorry."

Charles patted her knee. "It's fine."

Elsie watched him rub at his shoulder. "How bad was it?" The question blurted out and she found herself adding, "When you got hurt?"

He rested elbows on knees and looked into the night. "You know, I knew I would end up out here in the woods tonight."

"With me?" She smiled and propped her head up on one hand.

"With someone."

The smile faded.

"It was a full moon in nineteen-sixteen. Jerry was coming into the trenches faster than the rain. A bomb went off nearby, but it wasn't the same as the others. Smoke and rain kept us from seeing it at first. Melburn saw the cloud at first – this dingy brown mess that covered everything."

She realized he wasn't really there anymore. The question put Charles back at that night almost a decade earlier. "I didn't think anyone called the Germans 'Jerry' anymo–"

"We heard the screams from the trenches as soon as it hit them. We thought Jerry was using the cloud for cover, but no one was shooting." His hands shook. Elsie reached out to comfort him, but he pulled away, still favoring the old injury.

"Chuck...Charles," she self-corrected.

"Then it got to us. This oily...it burned and we couldn't get it off. It itched at first, like when you don't get all the soap off from a bath."

Fear crept along Elsie's spine, raising hairs. "We don't have to talk about this."

He turned to her then, mask of kindness gone, now replaced with an anger she'd only seen in men her mother dated over the years. "Oh, but we do, Elsie. We do."

She straightened her dress and coat. "I think it's time you took me back."

"I remember running, jumping over my friends, getting away from the gas."

"Mustard gas." She pulled back into the story at the mention of the horrific weapon.

His look became a sneer. "Of course it was mustard gas! Another bomb went off nearby. Everything went black. The next thing I remember I'm wrapped up in bandages and lying in bed looking up at a doctor."

"I want to go back," Elsie said simply. The man she came here with was all but gone.

"I saw Jerries along with a few of my friends standing over by the window. They didn't fight each other. They just stood there looking at me." Charles held a hand out as if showing her where to look. He shook his head. "Of course there weren't any Jerries in the hospital and the friends I saw couldn't be there. They were already under mud and forgotten at the Somme."

Elsie rolled onto her side and got up, trying to understand what Charles said. A glance around reminded her just how truly alone they were at the moment. The occasional whisper of music echoed down from where everyone else drank, laughed and danced a mile or so away. She held a hand out and forced a smile. "Come on. Let's get us both a drink and get back to the party. You can drive me home later," she lied.

He looked at her outstretched arm, then disregarded it. "They said it was because I died that night. My mind must be hurt from the blast. I wasn't breathing when Walden found me. He pounded on my chest and I came to. I was dead. Docs, even the men, said it was a miracle."

"Well that's a good thing." She let the hand drop and decided to push the point. "Look, I'm heading back. Are you going to drive me or not?"

"The moon looked like it does here...just not as sharp." Charles stood, moving between Elsie and the makeshift path back to the car. "I found another two that could see. Both died like me." Moonlight caught his eyes and reflected a soft blue. "Died and came back on the full moon."

Panic nibbled at her. "You're just trying to scare me because I said no." She tapped a nervous foot and tried to stare the Brit down. "The sheriff's my cousin. Do you know what he'll do to you if you try anything?"

The threat fell on deaf ears. "They didn't see the same people I do. We talked about it for days, but never around the doctors. We knew they'd take us for loonies and place us in the sanitarium." She stepped to the left, and Charles mirrored the action. "It's only the dead that are around when you come back. None of us saw each other's audience, you see." He stepped forward.

"N-no. I don't see."

Spittle fell from his lips. "The people that came back

with us."

Elsie looked around for a means of escape and backed to the excavation's edge, glancing warily at the thirty foot drop to the water below. Charles closed the distance in two steps.

"Riley killed the doctor before he hung himself."

"Ch-Charles–"

He took another step. "Pulled the man's insides out like he was looking for something. I knew he was going to do it. He said that's what they wanted – for him to close the door that being brought back opened. I think...I think the doctor was just because he harassed the private so incessantly." His hands clenched and opened, clenched and opened. "Johnson...," Charles choked on his words for a second. "Johnson clawed his own eyes out so he wouldn't have to look at them anymore. But you know what?" Arms stretched out for her then jerked back. Elsie retreated, working her way around the narrow lip by the ledge. "Do...you...know...what?"

Her heel caught on a root and Elsie pinwheeled both arms, righting herself just short of disaster.

"It didn't help. He could still see them...still hear them." He stopped the advance. "I shipped home a couple of days later to recover from the burns the gas left on me." He took off his jacket and held it out to her. "Here. You look cold," he offered with a grim smile.

One shaky hand reached out and Charles snatched her by the wrist, jerking the flapper off balance. Elsie fell to her knees and he shoved her onto her back.

"And do you know what my audience says, bitch? My audience says little girls shouldn't tease." He climbed on top of her. Hands went to Elsie's throat and thumbs dug deep, cutting off her air. She kicked out, legs splayed on either side of the Brit in a perversion of the very act he'd striven for earlier. "You bitch," he screamed. "*Du dumme schlampe!*"

Her eyes teared and she beat at his arms, strikes against his right side brought a roar of rage and pain from Charles.

He squeezed harder.

"*Schlampe*," he repeated. He kept the grip around her throat, lifted Elsie a foot off the ground and slammed her head down against the rocks.

Lights danced.

"Bitch!"

Pinpricks of light winked before her eyes. Movement came from all around them. Figures in the shadows shifted. Then the lights were gone.

So was the pain.

She was flying.

Everything stopped.

Her entire body struck something and Elsie went rigid with a sudden bone-numbing cold. Her gasp came as little more than a wheeze and water flooded an open mouth. Feet found shaky purchase in mud and the flapper pulled herself first to the water's surface then to the river's edge.

"*Schlampe*," echoed a scream from upstream. Branches broke nearby.

Words, guttural and hollow, echoed all around her. Words that made no sense, but their meaning was clear. "Get up."

Elsie shook her head in an effort to clear foggy thoughts. What wasn't frigid from the river hurt. Her face felt like she ran into a door. So did her chest, but it ached deeper, all the way to the back. Though a struggle, a deep inhale passed blue lips. Words came faster, overlapping each other until a cacophony of verbiage rattled her eardrums.

"Bitch," Charles screamed again, but barely heard over the other voices. "Where are you?" The Brit kicked through a cluster of weeds. A speeding blur of gray caught his attention.

The fist-sized river rock struck home, impacting wetly against the would-be killer.

Her hands grabbed a broken branch, its raw end jagged and menacing. Elsie staggered over to the moaning form at her feet and stood over him. Moonlight caught her eyes, reflecting in a powder blue iris.

"Th-The Hopewell killed off the last of this...." She swallowed hard and took a breath. "...this Adena tribe. They'd gone inbred and the few remaining weren't right in the head." Elsie rolled Charles onto his stomach and squatted over him, one knee planted in the small of the man's back. A single jerk to the collar of his shirt ripped the fabric free and exposed a large patch of mottled, leathery scars blanketing the entire right side of his back, shoulder and arm. "You...you were right when you said the Hopewell killed them."

Charles didn't move.

"Are you listening?" Elsie smacked her palm onto his ruined shoulder blade.

He spasmed in pain. "*Schlampe*," he managed. "Bitch."

"They want...." Another breath. This one came with less effort. "They want...to know something."

"Who?"

"The Adena." She grabbed a handful of hair and turned his head so she could see his profile. Eye shine met eye shine as one predator recognized another. "They want to know what you taste like."

Henry Snider is a founding member of the award-winning Colorado Springs Fiction Writer's Group (1996-2013), and Fiction Foundry (est. 2012). During the last two decades he's dedicated his time to helping others tighten their writing through critique groups, classes, lectures, prison prose programs and high school fiction contests. Thirteen years to the month from founding the group, he retired from the CSFWG presidency in January, 2009. After a much needed vacation he returned to the literary world. While still reserving enough time to pursue his own fiction aspirations, Henry continues to be active in the writing community through classes, editing services and advice. Henry lives with his wife, fellow author and editor Hollie Snider, son – poet Josh Snider, and numerous neurotic animals, including, of course, Fizzgig, the token black cat.

Learn more about Henry at http://henrysnider.com and http://fictionfoundry.org .

THE CHINA QUEEN

BY SCOTT T. BARNES

The gossip buzzed around Newell's ears worse than Nevada's infamous bluebottle flies, plentiful on this desert sheep ranch. The China Queen, Benjamin Stanton's wife, was coming home from Boston. The gossip followed her theoretical passage along the Oregon Trail as far as Salt Lake City where she rested a week, then turned south towards the Stanton Ranch four hundred miles into Nevada's unmapped Great Basin.

"She arrived two years ago in San Francisco with the 1862 railroad crews, a real life Queen of the Orient," they said. "Stanton bought her for fifteen thousand sheep. Now the China Queen is the Mutton Queen."

If the chief gossiper wasn't his friend Jakome, Newell would have punched him in the nose.

"She's just crossing Salty Creek. She'll be arriving Thursday next." Jakome's hands--one holding the tail-docking knife--weaved curves worthy of a goddess. A blue bandana supplemented Jakome's typical Basque attire of round, brimmed hat, buttoned shirt and vest. He had narrow lines and an outthrust jaw like the plow of a train.

Newell was a bean-pole. He wore a miner's flannel shirt that barely covered his waist and a slouch hat. He spit a pair of prairie oysters in the half-full tin and released the wether. They hardly bleated during the castration, something Newell found incredible. "One gal and fifty-plus shearers.

Stanton must have her well protected."

Newell didn't bother to rinse--better to keep the canteen clean. He lunged after another lamb, caught it by the ear and flank, and flipped it onto its back. At 190 pounds of lean, Newell could flip lambs all day. "I'll get my pay and move on. There's a silver strike near Lake Crossing. Figure I'll go west. Keep my nose clean."

Jakome batted Newell's slouch hat over his eyes. "You'll want her if you see her."

Newell grabbed his friend's arm. "There are plenty of women ready to spend your gold in Salt Lake City, women who aren't protected by lead."

Jakome's leer told Newell more than he wanted to know.

The Stanton headquarters crouched against the western Monitor Range, a rugged teeth-edge of granite running North-South that bit through the desert sands to about ten thousand feet. A creek meandered past the ranch buildings nurturing a swath of green before the desert swallowed it further south.

They docked, castrated and sheared forty thousand sheep a year here. A bleating, dusty hell. Sheep droppings ground to dust over blood and matted wool. A half dozen barns scattered like dice on the valley floor sheltered newborn lambs. Two bunkhouses were fenced off from the bleaters, one for the Basques and one for Stanton's gunslingers. Newell slept outside in a triangle of fenced-off sand, freezing at night, broiling during the day, unwelcome in either crowd. Only Jakome had shown him any signs of friendship.

He hardly cared. The food was good, if you liked mutton and beans, the pay better. Two dollars a day. If you could keep from getting the sheep runs—a fever associated— it was good money.

Sure enough on the predicted day the party of three wagons and dusty, armed riders rattled into the yard. The China Queen hustled into the house and gunmen took up position on the porch. Just the little he saw, a flash of charcoal hair and a cobalt dress swishing against pale ankles, caused Newell's throat to tighten. He hadn't seen a woman of any sort since arriving in this dusty furnace thirty-nine days before, and while the mining camps had a sort of woman, they certainly didn't have ladies.

The China Queen hustled with poise. He'd bet she could dance those European dances that required a hoop skirt. She was without a doubt a lady.

The ram he'd been holding jerked its hind foot and scrambled free. With a curse he dove and snagged the animal by the right hock. The combination of the derisive laughter of the shearers and the ram's backside staring at him drove away his daydream of the China Queen.

That night Stanton declared a mandatory barbecue. Newell cleaned himself up as best he could, washing the creek-water brown with blood and manure. He groomed the horseshoe moustache that distinguished him physically from his brothers--not that he'd likely see them again, having left the three in Pennsylvania in the care of Union recruiters. He put on his clean linen shirt and rubbed orange peel on his hands to kill the lanolin smell.

Sunset turned the sand orange and the creosotes black. Newell approached the rambling, wooden house, enjoying the smell of roasting meat from afar. He figured he'd slip in and out without attracting attention. The single-story house looked more like a lodge than a residence, with room for half a dozen families. The wood planks had either come from several thousand feet above in the Monitor Range, or across 400 miles of sand. Either one a monumental effort. While he admired its sturdy lines, it was a rich man's house, and being near it made Newell uncomfortable.

The fat splashing on mesquite charcoal made his mouth water, and Newell relaxed as the cooks with their checkered bandanas slopped beans and a slice of lamb shank onto his tin plate. He declined the prairie oysters--he'd had his share of those--but the beer was welcome.

Jakome sat on an overturned barrel facing the house. He patted the space next to him and Newell joined him. He pointed a spoonful of beans at the wrap-around porch, lit now with yellow lamps. The underside of the eaves had turned black from years of lamp-smoke. "Look at what wool can buy."

Newell whistled his appreciation.

Stanton, a small man around 40 years old, stood on the porch with his thumbs in his coat pockets, his smile as wide as his pencil moustache. He wore a dark tail-coat and trousers with a white cravat. Gunslingers stood on either side of the front door, repeating Henrys ready.

From inside the house, a white ghost scooted behind the windows. Newell peered but couldn't get a good look. The men quieted down. A coyote yapped in the distance, and a sheepdog barked in reply.

"Gentlemen," Stanton said as the door opened, "may I present my China Queen."

The men burst into applause.

Her oval face beamed, lips painted bright red, cheeks feathered with blush. She wore a sleeveless Oriental silk dress, yellow-white in the lamplight and sheath-tight, with red leaves embroidered from the waist up. Hoop earrings jangled against her bare neck. A bracelet with an ivory bas-relief of some kind adorned her right wrist. The bas-relief looked too large; a man's, perhaps, or something intended for a frame in a house, with the black leather strap added afterwards. Her hair was tied in a bun.

Jakome hadn't exaggerated her curves, though her wasp's waist made them possible, her not having much buxom. The only thing was one lazy eye that seemed to pull her face to the left.

After the applause quieted down, the Queen pulled a deck of cards from the front of her dress. Newell couldn't have been more surprised if she'd pulled out a horned toad.

———

70

"Thank you for kind greetings. I like to perform magic now."

Stanton chuckled like he knew this was coming, and lickety-split a wooden barrel was set on end as a table.

She did a few tricks, first with cards, and then with silver hoops about five inches in diameter, clinking them together, tossing them into the air, locking them into chains. Close magic. She didn't banter like a carnival magician would have; maybe her English wasn't good enough.

Newell hadn't seen the rings before, but he knew cards. He watched the fingers of her empty hand, the way they curved just slightly, or sat a little off line. A skilled magician could palm a card and hold it with slight pressure from a single digit. His uncle Florian had taught him some tricks, enough to spot card counters and impress small-town girls. He could have been a magician himself if he'd had the patience.

"I've practiced that every day for the past 28 years," Uncle Florian had said of his best trick, "and I just about have it right."

Newell knew then magic wasn't for him. He'd get rich the easy way--gold mining. He'd done all right in Aurora in 1864. When his claim ran out of pay dirt he'd come to the Stanton ranch to castrate sheep for two dollars a day, enough to buy tools for the next strike.

The China Queen wasn't particularly good, but clever at diversion. No wonder, with that figure. And her lazy eye made it embarrassing to look at her. Uncle Florian preferred card counting; the China Queen relied on sleight-of-hand.

He allowed himself a smile. A fine evening. If only he had a smoke to roll.

For a finale she dropped a die under a wooden cup, lifted it, and three sat there. She put down three cups, shuffled and lifted them, one at a time, proving that the three dice lay together. They clinked each time she shuffled a particular cup. She lifted it. They had disappeared.

She didn't have sleeves, and she wasn't fast enough to have hidden them. Newell squinted. Was it a trick barrel?

With great flair Stanton whipped a liberty coin from his pocket and held it between index and middle fingers. "Ten dollars for anyone who can figure out how she does that."

She did the pass again. It got quiet. Five days' pay for a correct guess. Lamb grease crackled on charcoal. She lifted the noisy cup.

Nothing.

Newell bounced his heels on the wooden barrel, satisfied. That explained the oversized bracelet.

The Basques called for her to lift the other two cups. "You want me lift cups?" she said in a teasing lilt. "A silver dollar for your guess. A silver dollar each."

Several men volunteered. Hoping, no doubt, to brush her fingertips as the money exchanged hands.

"Well?" Jakome whispered.

"Magnet," Newell replied, "in her bracelet. The dice have iron cores."

The Basque hopped from his perch, strode forward and clomped up the three porch steps, ignoring Newell's warning. "They ain't there," Jakome said. "A magnet's holding them in the cup bottom." He pulled the China Queen's hand from the wooden cup and the dice dropped.

Stanton looked like he'd swallowed a charcoal canary.

The China Queen's lazy eye didn't look so empty just then. She asked Jakome something quiet-like, and he responded with "What do I know about magic? Only everything."

And the Queen steered Jakome into the ranch house by the elbow, plucking the liberty from her husband's fingers herself.

That broke up the party, all right. Newell figured Jakome owed him the liberty. The China Queen was giving the Basque some other kind of reward. But Newell 'd rather not have Stanton's glare on his back the way Jakome got it. No sir, Newell 'd collect his pay and be off on the next caravan. Keep his nose clean.

The next day a pair of sandaled feet parked alongside Newell's head among the bleaters, the toenails pink with silver flowers, trimmed perfectly. Newell looked up from a mouthful of wether.

The China Queen had changed out of her silks and wore sturdy white cotton. She smiled with very un-ladylike intentions. "You told Jakome about my charm."

Newell rose, conscious of the skin lodged between his molars. He cleared his throat, covering his mouth with his hand. "My uncle was a magician."

"Come to the house after you finish. You show me everything." She strode away, five-foot-one of lady. The sheep parted for her like water fleeing oil.

Newell had had a couple affairs in his twenty-four years. Married women seemed attracted to him, and given their looks, he figured he was doing their husbands a favor, mostly. But not this gal. She might have been too muscled for some, but Newell couldn't believe...well, any of it. The open door to the ranch house. The gunslingers acting like he was invisible. The black garter. Fishnet stockings.

He gained the stamina of three men, as if vitality poured from her thighs into his veins. He'd never experienced anything like it. The air around her tingled as if she radiated electricity, sort of like the static lighting around Nevada's dust storms. Sheep ranching felt pretty good just now. Stanton must be swell.

He didn't remember sleeping, but at one point he was on his feet hitching his belt and the sun had crested the windowsill. Behind the belt he slipped his curved docking knife. He nearly tripped on the steamer trunk chalked with Boston-Salt Lake City.

"What's your name?" he asked. "Your real name."

"Names not give you power over me." Her hand made a kind of warding gesture.

He shrugged.

"Jing-Wei. It mean Pretty Bird. Like your cardinal." She smiled.

Baubles lay scattered across a marble-topped dresser: a ceramic box with lid depicting dragons, hoop earrings, playing cards, black-lacquered hair combs with dragon-flies stenciled on them...the bracelet. He weighed it in his hand. It was far heavier than he had imagined. Its oval ceramic showed an Oriental woman's profile with a teardrop for an eye. The level of detail was uncanny.

Fabricated for one single high-stakes game, he wondered, or a long grift? Possibly both.

Jing-Wei pulled the sheet up to her chest. "You promised me something."

Newell returned the bracelet to the dresser. He whipped his shirt over his head. "It was magic, sweets."

Something like a mirage flowed over her body. She became less solid, like looking at the edges of a sandstorm.

The bottom fell out of his stomach. He hadn't really seen that, had he? "I...I guess you've seen that trick before."

"You tell, yes or no?"

"Yes, sure. No problem. What's your interest in magic?" What had he gotten himself into?

She leaned back and a pink nipple slipped into view. Her face resumed its soft polish. "In China magic everyday thing. Trees magic. Birds magic. Dishes are house spirits in disguise. But these western tricks are charming. Charming make me smile."

Superstitions, he thought, remembering his Uncle's advice, *are a magician's best friend.*

He took the card deck and began shuffling nervously, dropping aces to the bottom. Stanton could come in at any moment. Jakome could come in any minute now. How long did he have, anyway? What the hell had he been thinking?

"This is a little trick a Cherokee taught me," he lied. "We were sharing a watering hole in Oklahoma, and he proposed a guessing game, with a scalp for the winner. Terrible gamblers, the Cherokee..."

He did the quick pass, coming up with three aces in succession, kid's stuff, but one he knew like sin. If he'd had time to rig the deck he could have produced kings, queens and jacks to order. He showed her two passes more, counting games that didn't require a rigged deck, making up stories for each. He calculated that he knew six tricks total, so he was half done. Maybe he wouldn't come back, or maybe he'd show the other three tomorrow.

But even as he thought this he knew he'd come back again, and again if she'd let him. He'd show her one trick a night, and puzzle out another if he had to. She was irresistible. And the mirage thing intrigued him to no end. He'd like to see that again. And feel that electricity.

He unlatched the window and began to climb out.

Jing-Wei pulled her cotton dress over her muscled body, giving him one more glimpse of everything. "Use front door. Stanton knows you here."

He hesitated half in and half out. The Nevada heat already made breathing painful. "That just don't feel right." His boots made a grinding sound against the sand as he trudged to the flock.

"Tease." She leaned against the sill, her shoulders white as alkali soil. "Don't wash your mouth, lover. Come straight here. I want to taste mutton."

They found Jakome about a mile from the ranch house. Word went round that he'd been torn up by a mountain lion. It probably dropped out of the Monitor Range for an easy supper. Out here starvation was everyone's best friend, and creatures took desperate measures not to let him get too intimate.

The shepherds saw buzzards circling and investigated,

thinking to find the body of a stray lamb. Instead they found Jakome, so disfigured they only recognized him by his blue bandana.

The Basques dug the grave and buried him, then sang with voices trained on desert loneliness. They divided up Jakome's few possessions.

Newell chaffed about being shut out from the funeral. He'd been Jakome's friend. Not that anyone had real friends out here, a bunch of convicts and deserters for the most part, but Jakome had been sociable.

The enmity between him and the Basques grew, and he counted the days when the sheep would be processed and Newell on his way to the next mine. He could live without Jing-Wei's affections...after tonight.

Newell stared at her curtains. What had happened to Jakome? A bullet or a mountain lion? Both, the bullet first, the lion cleaning up?

A lantern went on. Like every night, two gunslingers sat on the porch, Henrys across their knees. Newell could stand it no longer. He walked straight to the front door. One gunslinger nodded, but not a friendly nod. Newell pushed and the door opened. A fire crackled in the fireplace, scenting the air with sweet smoke.

Stanton, in a red leather armchair, read *A Buckeye Abroad*, glasses on his nose, black cowboy hat pushed back.

The room was full of display cases, furniture and shelves covered with knickknacks. Newell approached Stanton. "Sir, I'm going into Jing-Wei's room. I'm going to spend the night."

The boss lowered the book. Only the briefest jiggle in his jaw betrayed anger. With a creak in the armchair, he rose to his five-foot eight-inches. "Son. Let me give you something to chew on besides prairie oysters."

As he crossed the room with a bowlegged gait, his fingers gestured absently at the collections. He said things like, "Lithuanian figurines from Klaipeda. Toy soldiers from Manchester. Belgium lace," and other things Newell didn't catch. They arrived at a wooden table with rosewood legs and a top inlaid with glass.

Stanton put it between himself and Newell and leaned on it with both hands. "Jing-Wei is an artist, Mister Newell. One of the best. And like all artists, she quickly tires of her fancies. Except one. Silver. And I can give her that."

Newell peered through the tabletop beyond the reflection of himself and Stanton. One hundred forty-four oval cut-outs in black matte velvet. About half were filled with ceramics. All but the five latest depicted Oriental men.

The final ceramic showed a Caucasian with an outthrust jaw wearing bandana and round, brimmed hat.

Jakome.

Newell and Jing-Wei were slick with sweat. Newell had no tenderness, and Jing-Wei met him and clawed back like a badger. Her hair writhed around him. Lit by starlight, he couldn't see anything clearly, but the dust devil edges of flesh produced the same electric effect as last time. It drove him to a frenzy.

He wasn't aware of exactly when they finished. His mind swirled a few times before crawling into focus. A petite woman lay beneath him. Gooseflesh raised on his back and arms as his sweat evaporated into the night. Her heart thrummed beneath her breasts. All as it should be...except for her husband in the next room, and Jakome dead, and a case full of ceramics that looked altogether too lifelike.

As she stroked his back, he fought to still his breathing. Could he steal a horse and outride Stanton's gunslingers along the road? Maybe. If he took the right horse. But horse thieving was a capital offence. He'd be condemned anywhere he set foot. No, he'd better come up with a plan for crossing four hundred miles of desert on his own, and fast.

The shepherds might be able to do it--did do it--but

Newell had come on a wagon and expected to leave on one. He didn't know the watering holes, the Shoshone, nothing. And those Basques wouldn't help.

Four hundred miles, that'd take roughly...one month. Head for Salt Lake City, lose himself in the travelers west. If he took ewes and a sheepdog he could eat the ewes one by one and drink their milk when he got thirsty. The dog would know the watering holes. What with shepherds coming and going the tracks would be garbled.

A plan. Finally.

Her hands stilled. She slept.

He rose and riffled Jing-Wei's dresser. He pocketed a few items. It felt like two combs, a worn silver dollar, and a lace doily. Things to peddle in the city. He couldn't survive without money, and Stanton owed him a month's wages. And ten dollars for Jakome.

His fingers touched a leather strap, slick and smooth. The bracelet. He jerked away, then reached out tentatively, not quite sure why it scared him. He traced the bas-relief, smooth as Jing-Wei's skin. What if it were a house spirit or something? That was fools' talk, superstition. But how had Jing-Wei made such a life-like ceramic of Jakome so quickly? He hadn't seen any artist's implements in the house.

He closed his fist over it.

She hadn't worn it since the barbecue. She wouldn't notice. Not right away. And if it had power, he wanted it in his pocket, not Stanton's. He took it, kissed her on the shoulder, and exited through the window.

The eight woolies trotted up the sloping valley, bleating at their receding comrades. Their wrinkled, shorn bodies looked ridiculous. Black skin showed where the wool had been cut close. Bluebottle flies gathered over the gouges where the shearers nicked them. They'd gained at least two thousand feet in elevation.

Newell ducked into the shade of an oblong boulder.

The collie sheepdog brought the woolies around in a tight crescent. The dog hadn't been particularly enthusiastic about leaving; it kept turning and whining, so Newell gave it one of the ribs he'd managed to swipe from the chuck wagon. It stopped to gnaw, holding the bone between its paws, and the woolies wandered around the boulder, seeking anything greener and softer than a cactus.

Jing-Wei would be up by now. She'd have discovered his theft, and a search would start. First they'd question the Basques. Then they'd search the barns and bunkhouses, the wagons and the ranch house. Finally they would send out trackers.

He'd spotted a party of horsemen traveling on the road towards Salt Lake City, which would confuse them for a time. They wouldn't know for sure how Newell had disappeared until they caught and questioned them.

A frightened bleating brought Newell and the sheepdog scrambling around the boulder. They arrived in time to see a black-faced ewe slide off a stone shelf and plunge into a crevasse onto a barrel cactus. It twisted there, bleating pitiably, wedged.

Newell slid feet-first down the adjacent slope, using chaparral for handholds, until his feet hit the ledge. The dog whined from above. He pulled the docking knife from his belt, intending to put an end to the ewe's pain, but couldn't draw it against its throat. Its wide, brown eyes pled. He reached around its belly, pricking his fingers on the cactus, and hoisted it free. Putting it onto his shoulders, he climbed the slope, hand over hand. Needles in the animal's belly dug into his neck.

He lay the ewe upside down on the hard ground. Its nostrils flared, and the sun traveled a good hour as he pulled needles from its belly and thighs. But when he had finished, he knew he had acquired a friend for life. It fell into step, limping bravely by his side, and he rubbed the knobs of its horns. "I'm sorry I took you, mama. Likely as not we're going to die of thirst."

It rubbed its head against his leg.

"I'll call you Gettysburg, in honor of my brothers. Like as not they died there."

The near part of the journey was up, up and up the Monitor Range. Not high peaks, but rugged slopes, crags and creosotes, with rattlers for company. Newell glanced back at the valley. The sheep resembled a cotton field around the rectangular house. The road to civilization curved northeast. He'd parallel that as much as he could, so as not to get lost.

He pulled the shirt away from his sweaty body and kept climbing.

The sheepdog deserted him at noon. Gettysburg nudged Newell awake from his nap to discover that the collie had the seven woolies barreling downhill at three times the rate they had come up, headed straight back toward the ranch house.

The valley floor was close enough to make out details yet, barns, wagons, sheep...and a posse. No mistake about it, nine or ten horses. If they hadn't known his direction before, the deserters would confirm it.

He knelt down and wrapped his arm around Gettysburg's neck. "You picked the wrong camp, sweetheart, but I appreciate it. Someone's got to root for the underdog." Its sour cud smelled downright friendly.

His canteen ran out the following day. Two vultures picked up his trail, spiraling the updrafts as if the white sand and gleaming granite were a light source and he and Gettysburg cast shadows overhead. Shots echoed off the hills. Probably the Henrys couldn't shoot this high, but Newell flinched with each retort.

"The wrath of a scorned husband knoweth no bounds," Newell muttered. He jangled the bracelet in his pocket. *If I get out of this I'll keep Gettysburg forever. I'll buy her a clover field with this bracelet.*

The bracelet. He pulled it out, wondering how much extra trouble it'd cost him. It showed Jing-Wei's profile with a teardrop for an eye. Watching him. He strapped it to his wrist.

He needed water. His tongue was swollen, making swallowing a chore. He couldn't go another step without a drink. He grabbed Gettysburg's thigh with one hand and her head with the other, flipping her. He crouched between her legs, feeling very odd not to have anything to bite off.

"She won't last another day, Newell." Jing-Wei approached on tiny feet. Naked and beautiful.

"You aren't real. You're a heat dream."

"I take it you out of magic and abandon me. Smart boy."

He wasn't having this conversation. His mind must have snapped. Well, with luck he'd be without wits when Stanton caught him. "I got three more tricks. But sadly, no cards."

Jing-Wei stopped a handbreadth away. The scent of her skin tickled his nostrils. Gettysburg squirmed. "Return the bracelet and I will lead Stanton in wrong direction." She offered her open hand and a smile. "For what we had."

"I think I'll peddle it in Kansas City and use the money to buy some ladies. I'll call them Jing-Wei. Each and every one."

Jing-Wei melted in a swirl of sand.

Newell slipped his mouth over a teat and sucked. Gettysburg's steady breathing, the lift and fall of her chest reassured him. The milk was sweet, and not at all spoiled by her breezy flatulence.

Sycamores alerted him to the oasis, wide, yellow-green leaves on white branches, a thick stand between high cliffs. Though midday, the bottom was dark. Newell guessed it never saw direct sunlight. He slid down the bank in a pebble cascade. His feet hit mud.

Gettysburg scrambled down beside him...and the mud

erupted from gunfire. Newell slapped the ewe on the rump and ran in the opposite direction. He dove behind a fallen tree. Bullets tore the top of it off, showering him with splinters. His ears rang.

It felt like minutes before the barrage paused.

"Newell. I know you can hear me. Play time's over." Stanton's voice echoed between the cliff walls.

One end of the log concealing Newell had snapped clean off. The other sprouted gnarled roots clinging to dirt clods, as if a tree had toppled in a flash flood and held back the torrent until the powerful drive of water and rock snapped it in half. Newell peeked between the roots, inhaling their earthy smell.

Stanton stood atop an outcropping about a hundred feet away and two hundred high, as easy to plink off as a barn...if Newell had had a gun. The rancher stared over Newell's head, perhaps unsure exactly where Newell was. He cupped his hands and shouted again. "You know what the Shoshone do to thieves? They stake them on ant hills. The ants crawl into your holes, Newell, and gnaw your insides out. Know what I mean?"

He knew.

"Yankee..." A whisper.

Newell started, nearly blowing his cover. Jing-Wei sat cross-legged behind his log. She wound a strand of charcoal hair around her finger. He felt no lust, despite her nakedness. All she inspired now was fear.

"This is most exciting part," she said, "where you fight gunslingers for me."

"I ain't fighting for you. I ain't fighting for nobody." Newell wiped the sweat from his moustache with thumb and index. He wondered what his docking knife would do to a heat dream.

"You there, Newell?" Stanton said. "We got stakes, and rope, and all the water in the world." He poured a canteen off the rocks. Newell listened to the water tinkling on the stones and felt hiccups coming on.

Water. Wasted.

"My husband, such a showman. He like be magician like you."

"You don't spook me, witch. You're a heat fever. A dream! But them bullets are real. If one of them hits me, I'm dead." He knew he was babbling. And why not? He'd not survive the day.

Maybe he could goad Stanton into killing him quick. Maybe, if he was lucky, he'd go down with a single bullet. He poked his head around the end of the log. "Come and get me, Stanton. Mano a mano."

Laughter pealed from the canyon walls to either side. More bullets, now more accurately aimed, drove Newell back into cover. They almost had his position now, and Newell couldn't find the courage--or cowardice--to reveal himself and end it. If he saw a chance of survival he'd grab hold with both hands.

He caught Jing-Wei staring at the bracelet. She met his eyes and tilted her head seductively, but too late. He'd seen her more concerned with the bracelet than Newell or the bullets from the blazing guns.

Gettysburg bleated from the sycamore grove, beckoning him to deeper cover. Newell tore the bracelet off his wrist.

Jing-Wei unwound her legs and climbed to her knees. "What you doing?"

"What I should have done a long time ago." He pulled the curved docking knife from his belt and jabbed the tip between the frame and bas-relief, trying to lever it free.

"You leave be. You leave be!" Static crackled in Jing-Wei's hair. Dust whirled in her lazy eye.

"Hold up, boys!" Stanton called. The gunfire rattled to a stop. "Sounds like my China Queen has found him. If you're squeamish, now's the time to be closing your eyes." Manzanita branches crackled and boots scuffed on rock as Stanton made his way towards the valley floor, slowing his descent with handholds of brush, chuckling all the way.

The tip of Newell's knife slipped, slicing his index across two knuckles. The white ball-joints gleamed; blood puddled down the finger into his palm. He dug in the knife-tip again, grinding his teeth, trying to hold on to the slippery ceramic. He dug hard and popped the ceramic free. He looked frantically for a rock to smash it, but the mud and rotten logs littering the oasis didn't give enough purchase. Jing-Wei rushed him. She grabbed his wrists and her hair slithered across him with bursts of static, jolts that made his muscles pop. She bit at his neck, mouth opening impossibly wide. The bas-relief dropped into the mud. Newell landed on top of it, barely able to keep the striving jaws from his larynx. With a twist he managed to free half his body from the squirming, naked woman.

"Here, witch, get it!" He flung the ceramic as far as he could through the trees. Jing-Wei stood and took off after, sprinting on the balls of her feet. She stopped about twenty feet away, turned, and stared at him with a puzzled expression.

Newell turned his hand over. He'd palmed the ceramic and thrown a glob of mud as a diversion. A magician's trick. He dashed to the canyon wall and dropped the bas-relief on a vein of quartz that protruded like gristle from the surrounding granite. Jing-Wei's scream reverberated off the walls of the canyon. The sycamores shuddered. Newell wrenched a fist-sized stone from the quartz vein and smashed the ceramic with a solid blow. Jing-Wei whirled into a storm of white sand which blasted his face. And then she was gone.

He turned to see a Colt 45 staring at him. The gun barrel dipped, then dropped from Stanton's limp hand. The rancher fell forward onto his face. His cloths sagged, as if his body had suddenly dehydrated. His facial skin crackled, disintegrated. Jerky-like flesh remained. His body, for surely he was dead, smelled worse than week-old offal. Gunfire erupted from above, ricocheting off the granite face, splintering the sycamore trunks, splattering mud and pieces of Stanton's body. Gettysburg bleated, and Newell sprinted into the shadows of the oasis.

He emerged three miles later to the brilliance of the day--thirst quenched, shirt drenched and canteen full. A new valley opened before him, glaring and white hot. He put his hand on the thin layer of lanolin-slick wool of Gettysburg's back.

"What do you think, Gettysburg? Are they going to turn back now that the China Queen and Stanton are dead? Some of them got to be thinking a raid on the ranch house would be a lot more profitable than chasing a sheep castrator across the Great Basin. They're like as me to run across a band of Shoshone."

Gettysburg bleated and bounded down from rock to rock, eager to be away.

"Right. Dehydration, snakes, and three hundred fifty miles of desert to cross. Another day in Nevada's Great Basin."

Newell followed the ewe.

Scott T. Barnes writes primarily science fiction and fantasy. His short story "Insect Sculptor" won second place in the Writers of the Future Contest, 2011. *Since graduating* Odyssey, the Fantasy Writing Workshop *in 2008, Scott's short fiction has appeared in over a dozen magazines and anthologies. A country boy at heart, having grown up on a California farm and cattle ranch, Scott adores the history of the west with passion that can be plainly seen in "The China Queen." His fourth-grade reader* Rancho San Felipe — A Story of California One Hundred Years Ago, *coauthored and illustrated by Sarah Duque and published in conjunction with the Olaf Wieghorst Western Heritage Center, is used as a textbook in several Southern California schools. Scott also edits the online magazine* NewMyths.com. *His website is* www.scotttbarnes.com.

GODLY

BY STEPHANIE ELLIS

The small group of men huddled around the fire on top of St. George's Hill. They had been promised salvation if they followed him, for surely William Everard was a Godly man. But William had left them three days ago.

The blaze provided little comfort, encouraging eyes to turn inwards, to recall long-buried nightmares. Visions of old atrocities danced in the flames before them. Memories they had fought hard to suppress as they tried to find their way in this new world order. Faith was their one certainty. Hadn't William told them God would show them the way? And He had brought them here, to a place that felt both cheerless and forsaken. Despite his reassurances, they did not believe William would be coming back.

The men had managed to clear only a small part of their chosen settlement and had been unable to build any shelter before the sun dipped beneath the horizon. Tonight they would be sleeping under the stars. The shadows deepened and they shivered as the spring chill started to seep into their bones.

Below the hill, the fields were empty. The last cattle had long since been slaughtered and farms had lain fallow where sons had left to fight in a war that pitted brother against brother, son against father. Bitterness and starvation, mingled with the tears of the mothers, was all that had been left behind. The King was dead. Long live the Commonwealth.

Stomachs growled in conversation, a stark contrast to the silence of the men. They had eaten the last of their supplies two days ago and desperation had begun to take hold. Each man sent an unspoken prayer into the night sky and as if in answer, a figure stepped out from the darkness. William had returned.

"Why so glum, gentlemen?" he asked, slinging a sack onto the ground. "I said I'd return and I have. I said I'd get you meat – and meat you have, courtesy of Parson Platt. A most generous man I found. I did not expect you to have such little faith in me. The parson has said that there is more where this comes from should you need it."

Shamefaced, they looked away; they had let him down. With a disappointed air, William proceeded to pull a haunch from the sack and started to thread it onto a spit. Ten pairs of hungry eyes were reluctantly drawn back to him, following his every move.

As the meat began to cook, the men returned their gaze to the flames, and this time they found comfort in what they saw. Their mouths started to water.

William smiled as he turned the spit. Feed the belly and control the mind. It had been so long since he had been accepted among a company of men. The time had never been right for his work. Now however, a new age had begun and conditions were perfect. The men were ripe for the picking. Tonight he would feed them and they would follow him anywhere. The hand that fed was the hand that ruled. He was ready for the parson.

Meanwhile, the man who occupied the thoughts of William Everard on St. George's Hill was attending to the business of his town of Cobham. Parson John Platt had seen the small beacon on the nearby hill and it had annoyed him. The Diggers had arrived. Platt had no intention of allowing dissenters to disrupt his little community. At least he had the militia to support him.

At his request, Captain Gladman had taken two of his

soldiers up to investigate but so far had not returned. He sighed. The spread of nonconformism across the country was a contagion, a disease which had to be cut out, root and branch, just like the bishops, just like the late King. Platt had embraced the Commonwealth, had been delighted that now they could live according to the Holy Word, free from the insidious Catholicism which had crept into religious life and the bishops who promoted it. Dissent had turned his world upside down, challenged his authority and allowed the uneducated to interpret the Bible according to their own limited understanding. They denied Platt his authority. It could not be tolerated.

He had other things to worry about too. The food crisis was worsening. Rationing was breeding resentment and suspicion. People were beginning to starve; the numbers of dying had risen. His appeals to Fairfax for aid at the last council had fallen on sympathetic, but unhelpful ears. The General's priority was to the stomachs of his men. A hungry army was more dangerous than a few starving rustics. Platt understood of course, didn't he? Fairfax could, though, spare a few soldiers to help maintain order. General Fairfax had shaken his hand and returned to the dinner that awaited him. He had not invited Platt to his table.

The parson had gone back to town determined to stamp his authority on the people. The lucky discovery of a hoarder and necromancer gave him the ideal opportunity; Elias Henry was expendable, his death would serve Platt's purpose. It was for the town's good. Tonight's execution would send a clear message. Even if they didn't agree, they would be cowed into submission.

However, he had had to make one change to his plans. The guilty man had initially been condemned to death at the stake, a method of execution increasingly rare but which he felt was the most effective at making his point. And even now, the stake stood in readiness on the other side of the town square. But there had been stories. Strange, disturbing tales had reached his ears, barely believable accounts of the horrors that one man could inflict on another. Revulsion had swept over him. He could not let the people weaken. Burning was no longer an option. Temptation had to be kept at bay.

Instead the gallows had been quickly prepared, standing ready; the noose an empty void waiting to be filled. The condemned man stood at the base of the steps leading up to his place of execution. Simply survival, Henry had said at his trial and shrugged his shoulders in resignation.

The crowd had gathered already. Platt recognised many of his parishioners but there were strangers amongst their number. There was something about their faces: the empty expressions, the pallid skin. Was plague to stalk the land too? That would be one trial too many.

Even though the night was cool, Platt could feel the sweat trickling down his back. He loosened his collar. He felt strangely separate, a spectator to his own life. Even his words did not seem to belong to him. He was speaking lines that someone else had written. The air was close and humid, oppressive, unnatural for a spring day. One hand searched a pocket for the small crucifix that he still carried despite his condemnation of the practise in others. The constable had announced the proceedings and the condemned was making a final prayer, although to whom, the Parson could not be sure.

The throng had grown. He could see friends and neighbours, yet their countenance scared him. There was an air of menace just below the surface. Those stories...

"We are hungry, Parson Platt." The voice belonged to Nathaniel Yates, a firebrand known to be of the Diggers party. He had been staying at The Swan and Gladman had been keeping an eye on him. The Captain had said that he was often in contact with the man known as William Everard, the leader of the Diggers' settlement. A man Platt had met but once and whom he thought had at last left the area.

"We are starving, Parson Platt." Another voice from somewhere at the back of the crowd.

The townsfolk nodded and murmured in agreement, a rare sign of dissent against their Lord of the Manor.

Platt raised his hand to silence the crowd.

"My fellow townspeople, you know we have taken steps to ration food and provide enough for all..."

"Rations that are greater for some." That dissenting voice again.

"I can assure you that all are treated equally," said the parson. "There is a meeting of the Council tomorrow. I suggest that if you have any concerns you present your case there. Tonight we must deal with this miscreant in the name of justice, in the name of the Lord. This man, Elias Henry, is the sinner who has denied you food, this man has admitted to consorting with the devil, this man is the enemy of you and of God."

The thunder in his voice silenced the onlookers who lowered their eyes, unable to meet his gaze. He had made them his sheep again.

"The soul must be cleansed, purified by fire. Why do you deny the sinner the Lord's will?" Nathaniel's voice was insistent, reasonable.

Again a slow murmur of assent started to rumble amongst the throng. How easily the uneducated are swayed, thought Platt.

"He has confessed his sins," said the parson. "He is to be shown mercy."

"No!" said Yates. "No mercy. He must pay for his crimes."

Platt's sheep became restive, low murmurings reached his ears; they wanted a sacrifice, something that would show God their true remorse, convince Him to return the land to fruitfulness, to feed his starving followers.

"Whatever his crimes were, he does not warrant such a death," said Platt.

The bleating of his flock became louder.

"Why the change of heart? Have you forgotten the

words of the Book? Did you not ready the stake?" demanded Yates.

Platt forced down his anger. Rarely was he confronted in such a public way. He needed to show the town his methods were reasonable, humane. Part of him still wished to see the man burn, to rid the world of the demon that lived inside but the stories he had heard stopped him. He wished Captain Gladman would hurry up and return. The people were becoming agitated and only the firm hand of the New Model Army was effective in subduing them. By now Yates had made his way to the front of the crowd and met his look in a direct challenge.

"Master Yates. Yet again it is you who seek to disturb the peace of this council. Your voice is becoming most discordant to my ears."

"I speak only the truth," replied Nathaniel Yates, refusing to drop his gaze.

"Nor do you remove your hat," mused the Parson, conveniently forgetting the pride with which he refused to remove his own when speaking to prisoners from the old aristocracy.

"We are all equal, no man is above another; that is the law of our Commonwealth."

He had to put Yates in his place. At a signal, two men from Platt's own household moved up behind Yates and brought him further forward, forcing him to his knees in front of the parson.

"True," said the Parson, leaning down towards the kneeling man, a friendly smile dancing on his lips. Those who knew that smile crossed themselves surreptitiously and waited. "Tell me. Why is it so important that this man must burn?" he asked.

"To show that you are truly a man of God. That you do not permit the devil that dwells amongst us the chance to infect the innocent. Only fire can prevent this."

"He is right, Parson."

Annoyed, Platt turned to the new speaker. Joseph Avery, the local smith. A man who lived amongst the flames every day of his life. Burly, stolid, respectable. Once he had spoken, others added their voice to his.

He thought quickly. Perhaps the stories were just that… stories. Did he really expect his friends and neighbours would perform such a heinous crime? He should have faith in their humanity. He must trust them.

Yet he could not allow Yates to undermine him; he would give the man what he wanted but he would make it very clear that it was his, Platt's, decision; a sign of his reasonableness, his humility, not of his weakness. Scripture would help him regain his flock. He chose his words carefully.

"Good people," he said, stretching out his arms in an all-encompassing embrace. "You are right. In my conceit I had indeed forgotten the words that I should have let guide me. Now I recall them, let me speak them now so that we are all in agreement … as brothers, as a community."

All eyes focused on him, ready to listen to the words of the Lord.

"Let us all remember the Gospel of Mark. 'And the scribes who had descended from Jerusalem said, 'For if a kingdom is divided against itself, that kingdom is not able to stand. And if a house is divided against itself, that house is not able to stand.' We have suffered much in recent times, families have been torn asunder, communities destroyed. Now is the time to rebuild and we must stand together in concord. Therefore, in agreement with your wishes, Elias Henry will die according to the original sentence of execution for 'he who will have blasphemed against the Holy Spirit shall not have forgiveness in eternity; instead he shall be guilty of an eternal offense. For they said: 'He has an unclean spirit.'"

A swell of 'Amens' reached his ears. They were his again. He looked at Nathaniel Yates in triumph. His adversary showed no emotion.

"Elias Henry will burn at the stake," continued Platt.

"For as is said in Revelation 'But as for the cowardly, the faithless, the detestable, as for murderers, the sexually immoral, sorcerers, idolaters, and all liars, their portion will be in the lake that burns with fire and sulphure, which is the second death.'"

At these words the condemned man was dragged towards the silent stake and bound under the satisfied eyes of the community. He made no utterance, no plea for clemency. Joseph Avery lit the faggots that circled the base and gradually the fire began to take hold.

Slowly the flames crept up Henry's body, clothes smouldering gently at first before erupting into a blaze that consumed and enveloped. Still Henry did not scream. He just stared at the church which rose up behind the Parson, his mouth continuing to move silently. Platt thought he recognised the words of the Lord's Prayer. He felt a brief pang as he recalled the nature of the evidence against the accused but swiftly brushed it aside. Henry had been found guilty, that was sufficient. The devil was often to be found within those who appeared to be the most innocent.

Eventually, the man's lips stopped moving, his face dissolved and flesh melted. He was no longer of this earth. Platt could not tear his eyes away from the sight. Then he discovered there was something else holding him transfixed, something that had also kept the crowd quiet, waiting … expectant.

The flames had begun to die down but the aroma of roasted flesh still hung in the air, tormenting them, teasing their senses with its relentless assault. The defenceless stomachs of the hungry townsfolk growled in response, mouths salivating as forbidden thoughts entered starved minds. Platt knew what they were thinking, what they were feeling, for he was experiencing it too. The stories that he had dismissed as unholy gossip came back sharply. He crossed himself, even as his own mouth started to water.

"We are hungry, Parson Platt," said William Everard,

even though he had so recently dined.

Platt was surprised to see him.

"We are starving, Parson Platt," said Nathaniel Yates.

"We need food, Parson Platt," said Joseph Avery, unable to deny the effect the smell of the dead man's cooked flesh was having on him.

"The grain houses are empty, Platt," said William. "How will you feed your people?"

"They have had no meat for many days now," said Nathaniel Yates.

"No," said Parson Platt. "I know your intentions even though you have not voiced them, but the eating of human flesh is an abomination against the Lord."

There was no shock amongst the crowd as he spoke these words. A few looked slightly shame-faced but hunger had pushed many to ignore the peril to their immortal souls; he could see that only earthly suffering drove them now. Had they too heard the stories? Had some here already indulged in such practises? Many had already died, a number had left. Were some of them unwitting victims? He doubted he would ever be able to find out.

"Where in the Scriptures does it say that, Parson?" asked William with a smile.

The parson remained silent.

"Nowhere," said William, answering his own question. Then he turned to the crowd. "You are hungry, you are starving. I see the bones and pale skin of your children. I see the weakness and increasing feebleness of your mothers. To eat flesh is not a sin, yet to waste the chance of sustenance surely is. Those who are dead or dying would surely wish their families to take whatever chances they had."

Neighbours cast secretive looks about them, searching the reactions of their friends and family. Still the smell of meat hung in the air.

A man stepped forward, a stranger to Platt. There were too many strangers, he thought. He wore the uniform of the

Godly; a plain collar, brown doublet, breeches, broad-brimmed hat. He was clean and well-shaven. His demeanour made all regard him with respectful interest.

"I am Daniel," he said. "I am a man of this county, although not of these parts. I have suffered just like you. Do not be afraid, good people. In times of trial we have to search for that which can sustain us. I have eaten such meat before and come to no harm. I have been to Church and not been struck down. I have prayed to the Lord and he has answered. I have been able to save my family. Provided the source of the flesh is not taken violently or against their wishes, there is nothing to fear. God has surely provided."

Then a woman moved to the front. "Who … who did you …?"

Daniel smiled reassuringly at her.

"Someone who had not long left for this world. He chose to gift himself to us; he even blessed us as he died."

William opened up the extra sacks that he had brought back with him when he returned to Cobham. They still retained that freshly cooked aroma.

"Remember, Parson Platt," said William. 'Matthew said that 'any sin and blasphemy shall be forgiven but blasphemy against the Spirit shall not be forgiven.' Let Henry do some good even in his death."

By now, Nathaniel had moved over to the stake and was cutting the remains of Henry's body down. Jeremiah Simon, the town butcher, had the long-unused tools of his trade ready. At a signal from Will, the butcher started to slice and cleave and Joseph Avery distributed the meat amongst the watchers. Nobody turned him down but nor did they look at each other and nor did the members of his own household refuse.

William selected the choicest cut and walked up to Platt. "For this reason I say to you, do not worry about your life, as to what you will eat."

Even as the hunger gnawed at his stomach, Platt drove

the feelings from his mind. He knew he was in the presence of a malevolent force. He could feel its foulness seeping into him, wrapping itself around his heart, slowing his pulse, feeding his fear.

"Yea, though I walk through valley of the shadow death, I will fear no evil," he murmured. "For thou art with me. Thy rod and thy staff, they comfort me."

A sneer crossed Everard's face.

"You call yourself Godly, William Everard?" said Platt. "You commit this crime and say it is in the name of the Lamb? You are damned William Everard, you are damned."

Platt turned his attention back to the townspeople. Some had already started to eat whilst others hesitated nervously, torn between survival and self-loathing.

"I repeat this is an abomination. Let no man amongst you eat the flesh of another for you will no longer be welcome in the Lord's house."

The crowd around the parson shifted nervously.

"And who are you to say who is welcome in the Lord's house?" asked William. "It is for every man now to read the Bible for himself, to interpret the Book according to his own understanding, not to listen to the words of priest or minister who turns the words of God towards his own ends. Man can worship in his own house or under God's own sky; he has no need of a church."

Again Platt wondered where Captain Gladman was. The man should have returned by now. His men would quell any dissent. Where were they?

His gaze ran over the people still devouring the remains of the dead man; a hellish scene that froze his soul. The devil was surely walking abroad tonight.

William still stood in front of him, meat in hand. Platt backed away, feeling for the solid comfort of the church behind him in the darkness. Holy ground was his only hope. He sensed the ancient stone building rising up behind him in the gloom, its square Norman tower a comforting Christian reassurance against this assault of wickedness.

Had he not served faithfully? He had stripped the idols from the walls, had rid the holiest of sanctuaries of adornments whose richness were more suited to a whorehouse, had removed the altar screens that had separated clergy from congregation, allowing all to celebrate the Lord as equals. He had re-established the simplicity and purity that was the Christian way. He had spoken to God in his own language, not of the false Roman. How could he be put to the trial like this?

William matched him step for step, never taking his eyes from the parson's face, not even faltering as the man finally stepped over the threshold of the holy building. Together they entered God's house. Nobody else followed.

Platt felt it immediately. A sense of wrongness that he could not quite place. The air of sanctity that usually hung over this piece of consecrated ground seemed disturbed. There was another presence. Something else had entered here, another door had been opened, one not of this world.

A few flickering candles illuminated the scene, serving only to exaggerate the sense of displacement that he currently felt. Casting his eyes around, Platt could not believe the horrors presented to him. His sanctuary, his point of reference in all things, his one certainty in the turmoil that had ravaged the lands during seven years of war had been destroyed.

Despair ripped through him at the sight of the upturned pews, the vile messages on the walls, the destruction of the pulpit, the desecration of the altar – the altar…

William said nothing. He ignored the parson and walked up to the altar, placing the executed man's cooked flesh on the table.

Platt stared at the devastation. Wondering how this man, if man he was, had the nerve to behave in such a manner beneath the cross that hung there. Then he raised his eyes. The cross had been moved so that now it hung inverted over the table. Platt slowly started to pray whilst William poured a particularly viscous looking liquid into a goblet. Then his adversary turned to him.

"You came here to be saved, old man?" he asked. "That is easily done. Take communion with me and you will be redeemed."

William's laughter echoed around the building.

"You are the devil," said Platt, crossing himself. An action which only served to increase Will's mirth.

"No..."

Whatever else William was going to say was cut short by the sound of the church door crashing open. A group of men moved up the aisle in the darkness. Platt could not make out their features but from previous descriptions he guessed that these were the remaining Diggers come visiting from St. George's Hill. He had not, however, seen them in the square that evening.

William had placed the goblet back on the table before the men closed in on them. Their timing was perfect. The message he had sent back had drawn them to him immediately. It was clear they had followed his instructions to wait until the square had emptied before they entered the town. The men knew they were disliked amongst the locals and had no wish to provoke any violence. It also meant that they had not witnessed the dispute between Platt and the townsfolk. Ignorance was such bliss, he thought.

"Gentlemen, you came," said William.

"We had to be sure," said one.

"You truly believe him to be a demon?" asked another with a smile. "I see no tail or cloven hoof. We are men of a new age, not believers in old wives' tales."

"The devil takes many forms," said William. "He walks amongst us and we must be on our guard."

"But the parson is a man of the cloth."

Doubtful looks were cast at Platt who had neither moved nor spoken since they had entered.

William sighed. It had been hard to convince them of Platt's apparent nature and even now, after they had seen the evidence with their own eyes, they were unwilling to accept his, William's, truth. He had a little more work to do.

"What man of God condemns the innocent to the flames?" he asked. "What man brings the flesh of another as an offering in this, the holiest of places?

Only then did Parson Platt know that this was to be his trial, the test of his faith. He looked at the five men, saw the uncertainty in their eyes. What was their background? he wondered. What had brought them here?

"You sent us meat when we were starving," said one of the five.

"Sent you ...? No, I ..."

"He sent us meat," said another looking at the altar table.

"What did you feed us?" asked a third.

Realisation dawned on the faces of all. But for each side it was a different truth. Platt knew it then. "Gladman..." he whispered.

The men looked at him in horror. Took this utterance as his admission of guilt. William moved back into the shadows.

"You have made monsters of us."

"You have corrupted us."

"No, no," said Platt, desperately trying to fend off their accusations, the words that turned to blows, to the glint of a knife. "I am God's servant. I preach only the word of the Lord. I am innocent..."

A blow to the head silenced his protests, sent him sprawling to the ground. The men had lost all sense of where they were. Their violence was calling his master, drawing him nearer. William could feel his presence.

He watched as innocent blood was shed on hallowed ground, seeping into the stone and the soul of the church, feeding the One that he served.

The attackers only stopped when all energy had gone,

slumping down onto broken pews, unable to look at each other, unable to speak.

William stood over the parson's inert body, now no more than a bloodied lump of flesh. Someone else to be hung in the town's larder. The dead man's eyes stared up at him in accusation.

"For even Satan, disguises himself as an angel of light," said William, as he bent down to close them.

"Satan's servant," said one of the murderers, finally summoning the courage to look at Platt's remains.

"No," said William coldly. "That honour belongs to me and now it has been extended to you gentlemen. I think you should welcome your new master. He has been waiting a long time for me to summon him."

Confusion and fear suffused their faces. And then came understanding. They had danced to the devil's tune and their misplaced faith, their misguided accusations had damned them. That was William's ultimate triumph. He savoured their terror, drank it in like the nectar it was. They rose, tried to move, found they could not run.

A roar swept through the church, cracking stone and smashing glass alike, opening up the ground at their feet. Fire took hold of wood and flesh. The screams of the men sang their song of death only for a short while until they too were silenced forever by the burning frenzy as it devoured everything that was holy, all that was human. It spared none except William, who stood, untouched, at the foot of his Master's cross.

This new Commonwealth will not be a place for the Godly, he thought. Then he turned and, smiling, bowed low to his Lord. The King is dead; long live the King.

Stephanie Ellis is currently a Teaching Assistant in a secondary school in Southampton, England, but before that worked as a Technical Author for a number of years.

She writes speculative fiction stories which have found success in Massacre Magazine (Issues 2 and 3) *and* Sanitarium magazine (Issues 15 and 24) *as well as in anthologies by a number of publishers, including:* Alchemy Press' *upcoming* Demon Rum and Other Evil Spirits, *KnightWatch Press'* Cadavers, *and Sky Warrior Books' upcoming* Vampires Don't Sparkle (Vol 2).

Her poetry has been published in local and national press, Far Off Places Magazine *and* What the Dickens *ezine.*

Stephanie can be found, together with her twisted nursery rhymes and flash fiction, on http://stephellis.weebly.com/ and on twitter at @el_stevie.

ANTIPHON

BY ZACHARY O'SHEA

The cart's frame clattered akin to bleached bones. Through quiet streets the rattle echoed for blocks, maybe even miles. The haunting sound redoubled off time-worn wood and windows which sat dark for weeks. With it moved a heavy miasma, punctuated by the pungent scent of death. Only the three men travelling with the tumbrel suffered the charnel stench. For his part, the grayed driver numbed to the fetor of putrefying flesh within the first few weeks. The red scarf over the lower half of his face merely kept the plague at bay. From under a wide brim, his fearful eyes kept watch on every shifting shadow as the mangy mule plodded forward. As far as the trio knew, most everyone of this district had either fled to the center of town, or been swept up into the tireless steps of the *danse macabre*. Nevertheless threats remained from lurking hold-outs to madmen who looked to add to the heaps of dead. Of course, looters remained a concern; there were always men who unwisely placed easy coin ahead of their health. Worst yet were the stories of carcasses which shambled in a mockery of life.

The cart sat just under half-full of cadavers; half-full of fathers and brothers, mothers and daughters, now all nothing more than mortal clay. Each succumbed to the Black Death in twisted agony, only to have their heads caved in by sledges. Two stocky men walked grimly along behind the corpse-wagon with their befouled tools of the trade hefted on broad shoulders. So far they'd not run into these supposed risen, but the night was young.

The ominous procession stopped beside another stack of human dross in the gutter. All of the nearby doors bore a red mark to warn that the Reaper had called on the occupants. Not even the foolish or desperate still remained on this extinct avenue. Therefore all the three needed to worry after were those like themselves, the greedy. The simple need to fill their purses with bits drove the trio out night after night to collect Heilbronn's dead no matter the risks.

The two attendants sighed and trudged toward the corpses, using their mallets to scare off festering rats that always swarmed to nibble on such sweet refuse. If it wasn't for the generous pay the Count gifted them each dawn, the pair would have quit a long time ago, but they were all too happy to take from the warlord's coffers. Rumors ran rampant that their new ruler was a vampire or similar ghoul. If they contained true at least he was a dead thing not actively trying to eat them. Färber, the wagon driver, didn't buy into the stories about their pale master's inhuman state. He figured the Count knew how valuable the trade route Heilbronn sat on was before the Black Death scythed its way through Holy Roman Empire, and knew once it passed the city would prosper again. Yet, Färber felt unsure that the contagion would end. In the dim dawn of morning he oft wondered if the rest of the world past the Schwarzwald's edge teemed with nothing more than the lifeless, walking or otherwise.

One of the two workmen, Hans, dragged the top body off of the pile. She'd been a pretty girl once, the sort that he'd stare at. Now her face was ashen save for terrible bruising around plush lips. He gave her a shove, and eyed one ripe breast that would never rise again after it rolled from her shirt. "Damn, what a waste of a fine body." He thought. Hans wondered after her soul, for surely such a creature had been endowed with the sweetest sort. At this moment did she sing with the angels at the feet of the Lord, or was her spirit consumed by the devils behind this pestilence? Would he live long enough to marry a comely little *fraulein*, or would the rented-out-thighs of the whores at the Red Door be the only ones he'd ever enjoy? With a sigh he brought the sledge down on the dead girl's skull.

The other, Jakob, adopted a cautious route. He prodded the next body with the edge of his implement before dragging the elderly man away from the stack by the foot. After another nudge he gave the corpse a good whack to the head too. Once he earned enough coin he'd apprentice with a travelling minstrel. Provided the Black Death waned and left the world with more than just carrion and scavengers.

"Don't forget to look them over for loot," the driver rasped. Not that he ever did any of the dirty work. But it was his cart, his mule, and his eyes sharpest in the dark. Still Färber failed to notice a pallid hand which twitched under the mound, grasped at dried mud, and the body attached sliding free until it was too late.

"*Mein Gott!*" Jakob screamed when the corpse latched onto his leg with two fingers, and pressed its face to his boot. Its maw split nearly to the back of each cheek, with gums receded until only bone white teeth remained behind. Thankfully the shoes he wore were of thick leather, to ward off vermin nips. He swathed himself in layers too, for not only a corpse's bite could pass on the plague, but merely the touch of one of the walking damned. He bore talismans also because the right gestures from one of Satan's many wives, or one of said witches' cat familiars rubbing against you, spread the infection. There were so many ways to catch the Black Death, so few to cure it. He recoiled and fell with a whimper as dead grip held tightly. Hans grimaced, muttered a prayer, and stepped into the fray. A lone corpse provided little threat so he eyed the remaining pile for movement even as the monster's mouth swallowed his partner's footwear.

"Do something!" Jakob kicked at the risen's head. Teeth tore from what little fetid meat remained, and clattered down the street. Yet the hungry cadaver held on. The driver sighed and looked away from them, over the empty avenue. He didn't seem that worried for the time being. Hans lifted his mallet high with a disgruntled snort and smashed not the monster's head, but where neck attached to shoulders. A second good whack got it free from Jakob's leg. A third stopped the risen with a spatter of putrid brain matter.

"You scream like a tiny girl." Hans said to the other man as he offered a hand up.

"Will you two stop horsing around!" Färber hissed and tried not to shiver. There was something else in the air tonight. Perhaps one of Satan's servants lurked nearby or worse yet, the Count's Pale Watch. The eerie men-at-arms, just as pallid as their master, had a habit of asking questions he'd rather not answer. He plucked a stray red thread from his black coat. As he strained the avaricious fool swore he heard faint music.

Bile dribbled from Jakob's lips as he managed to find his feet again. They almost immediately went right back out from under him, but he managed to keep from swooning. His hand practically convulsed as he pointed at the carcass. It still twitched!

"But," Hans protested "but I smashed its head in! It should be dead. It should be dead, right?"

Jakob torpidly fumbled at the handle of his sledge, which evaded all attempts to be lifted from the filthy ground. Everyone knew that destroying the brain of a risen laid it to rest, or a pious priest's prayers. All three men were most definitely sinners, so the second option proved useless. The trio made damn sure to track down all the lore they could about the carnivorous dead, and now confronted with their first shambler found it inadequate. The pair of brutes dumbly watched as the animate writhed obscenely for several seconds, and willingly waited for their doom as an exhausted rabbit would under a wolf's jaws.

Jakob noted the focal point of the undulation lay in the carcass's distended abdomen, and the horrid urge to know why proved the antidote for his fear. A sliver of his psyche wailed in protest as he edged closer to the flopping corpse, much like a child standing at door to a pitch black room wanting to know what horror lay beyond the threshold. In the end no such terror ever materialized, just insubstantial fears evaporated by rush-light. Yet in this case Jakob understood fresh fright awaited them within the bloated stomach. The man's midsection shouldn't be so full; perhaps it was the devoured arm tearing its way free. Rancid ichors oozed from several puckering postmortem sphincters formed between ribs. He snatched his truncheon.

"What are you doing?"

"Going mad," Jakob thought. He wondered if his own heart was going to tear free from its sinewy moorings at any moment. It certainly felt like it was coming up his throat. He shuddered out a hot breath, and lifted the hammer. Instead of prodding the vermicular tracks the cudgel head hung in the air as if the implement itself feared the aberrance it may unleash. The man swallowed dry, pushed past his fear, and jabbed the mallet against one of the seeping lacerations. A thick gout of creamy discharge covered his boots and he gagged, but prodded harder still.

"Jakob, what are you doing? Stop!"

He didn't, not until the gut ruptured. "No, bloomed is a better word," Jakob thought. Bloomed like red-petal flower with a deep-purple stigma. The fragrance produced defied easy classification, so very fertile and foul at the same time; like the vile perfume worn by crooked crones as they stole seed from unwilling male victims as they slept. Nothing as benign as a bumblebee traipsed on fleshy leaves, but rather a greasy mother rat slick with rotted blood and as large as a human infant. Her maw brimmed with teeth sharpened on human bone, tongue festooned with tumors. Around the she-rodent rolled her blind pale young, which reminded the men of colossal maggots save for discordant cries and deformed limbs.

The idea that these vermin utilized a human's cold clay for incubation proved too much for the pair. As he bellowed with blind rage Jakob smashed the fat matriarch from her perch. He followed after the rat, pounding hard until all that remained was a matted puddle of meat and hair. At the same time Hans cruelly stomped on the blind pups until the disgusting little things moved no more.

The two brutes panted hard, shared a look, and laughed. The shared strained sound echoed through the abandoned avenues. It dripped with an undertow of fracturing sanity. Hans clapped his friend's shoulder. "You thought it was a risen come to eat you! Hah!"

"But," Jakob wiped tears of false mirth from his eyes, "it was only flopping around because of the rats inside. Ugly little monsters."

"Yeah, just rats."

Their chuckling trailed off. The truth sunk in their guts that gestating vermin were no less terrible than ravenous ghouls. They shared a grim look, and then turned to the driver. Hans coughed, face flushed. "That's taken care of then. We'll just see to the rest of them, *Herr* Färber."

Atop his cart Färber simply bobbed his head, the wide-brim flopped. Clearly he was either too amused, or angry, to say anything. As usual he acted as if he were above the workmen. Both louts assumed he pocketed more of the Count's money for less risk. Hans and Jakob grumbled to one another as they prodded the mound of dead more aggressively this time. When none of the corpses moved they returned to bashing in heads, and now stomping on stomachs. It was barbarous work, but some of the best that could be found in this dark time. Soon enough one grisly task was done, and hammers set aside. The pair next busied themselves by tossing the abused cadavers into the dray. Both got dusted with foul fluids.

A cloud of bats flitted through the night sky hunting for their nightly meal. Their leathery silhouettes starkly contrasted against harvest moon. It was hard to tell if they were squeaking, or giggling in the distance.

After they finished the drudges took a moment to breathe at the back of the wagon. Jakob glanced at his boot and didn't fancy the bite marks, or the tooth left in it. But his skin hadn't been broken. He grunted at his good luck and tried to reassure himself he felt hot from the hard work instead of the onset of disease. Beside him Hans snorted in disgust at the mixture of rat-and-human blood on his shoes. Hans shifted and glanced at the driver who was staring ahead now, silently. The old bastard probably wanted to get moving again. The corpse caisson wasn't full yet, and their purses wouldn't be either until it was. Hans nudged Jakob before fetching his sledge.

"We're done here." Hans called out. While the mule snorted their supervisor didn't respond. That wasn't so strange. At times Färber liked to ignore them. After Jakob grabbed his cudgel the pair moved to the sides of the ghastly conveyance. Neither the cart, nor Färber moved.

"He said we're done." Jakob tapped on the wagon's rail once, then harder to try and get the driver's attention. The mule brayed. Färber didn't respond. The men shared a fresh look of creeping dread.

"Hey... let's get moving. Did you fall asleep," Hans coughed "*Herr* Färber?"

When there still was no response the pair sucked in thick gulps of vile air.

A chilled wind blew down the road. They shivered and scanned the streets around them while waste frolicked about their feet. Curtains twisted out of abandoned windows like ghosts beckoning the living to join in their lethal festival. The cold breeze stirred up both the stink of split bodies and a mournful sound, the source of which was difficult to place. Hans suspected it was only the wind winding through the forsaken buildings. On the other hand Jakob imagined it to be the skeletal musicians who followed the Reaper from fete to fete. The haunting draw of bow across violin strings sealed the vision for Jakob, though Hans blamed that sound on rusted hinges. Both men's heart thudded with equal fright. Färber remained listless. Eager to regain some face, Jakob was the first to advance.

He crept around the front of the cart, and readied his truncheon. The whole time he kept his eye firmly on the coachman. His knuckles went white gripping the handle of the gore-soaked tool. "*Herr* Färber?" Jakob squeaked. Hans followed on the other side. The miser's head drooped down. His scarf and hat fully obscured features. Jakob chewed on the side of his lip, and considered if he should climb up or not. He thought it better to give *Herr* Färber a good prod with the sledge first.

The driver toppled over the other side, and impacted without the hard crunch expected. Instead there came a small slough of viscera to precede an eruption of blood-anointed rats from the large coat. Both men shrieked and back-pedaled away. They stammered out prayers instead of prodding one another's lacking bravado. The spectral violin screamed while the debris dashed away from the scattering swarm.

Hans took a few swipes at the moist vermin when they got near him. The blighters triumphantly squeaked as they fled into the night. Within moments the swarm dispersed, and left the men wax-white and sweating. Jakob even crossed himself as he took the Lord's name in vain. He knew that his partner would never tell. From windows and drains dozens, then hundreds, of beady hungry eyes watched them. The deserted streets continued to conjure up unnatural tones like an orchestra comprised of the extinct. If anything the wind grew colder, as if the months until winter's arrival passed within moments. Jakob moaned as he drew up to Hans' side. Both men bled from at least a dozen small bites, but hardly suffered anything life threatening, yet.

"What do we do now?"

A shiver cascaded through Hans' bulk. "The Lord only

knows, Jakob. Though I fear this night His eye may be turned from us." He rotated slowly to seek an escape route. Everywhere the lug looked ravenous red gazes fixed on them.

Jakob tried to talk, only to find his airway restricted by anxiety. Any moment now the ever-rising tide of rodents would come for them, pull them down, and gnaw them to the bone while still alive. He trembled and wondered if waiting for such a terrible fate was perhaps worse than receiving it. Then there was the hell-born music. The aberrant rhythm bore its way toward the core of his being. Freakish strings now coupled with a howling chorus of the damned, flute whistles from hollowed femurs, and the percussion of bare skulls. The urge to dance pulled at his sinew as if some shuddersome puppeteer hovered over him even now! The tremble flourished into a fit, and perspiration trailed down his forehead only to be immediately cooled to rime. "Do you feel it? Do you feel it, the Dance?"

The frantic shrilling of his companion's voice twisted Hans' guts. He completed his ascertainment, but barely resisted the urge to twirl about akin to the scraps of waste in the air all about them. He brought the truncheon's head down hard onto the street, and hoped its extra weight would keep his psyche anchored. "I do."

"*Mein Gott*," Jakob sniveled.

"We need to get onto the wagon and--"Hans' suggestion was severed short when a raw scream tore from deep within him. The latest strongest gust cast Färber's fine coat into the air. It flared once as if it would be swept away, only to hover in defiance of all sense of reality several feet up. The apparel spun dramatically, and sprinkled the last drops of what had been their better across nearby facades. The wind spiked once more and blew the coat back into the nearest intersection where it floated down and bowed all on its own. One empty sleeve thrust forward and as if beckoned Färber's floppy hat lifted from the ground to cartwheel after.

Jakob understood that the fresh heat on his legs came

from involuntarily relieving himself, but consoled himself as he'd have room for more ale later. Surely if he survived this encounter he would need to drink himself to the edge of oblivion to ever sleep again.

Not much better off, Hans leaned against his tool and wheezed. All he wanted was the warmth of one of the local whores wrapped around him now. Hell, the brute might even make her honest if she kept this chill away every night going forward.

Voracious rats surged shadowed alleys. Streams of vermin flowed from a tainted well beside what was once an inn, and still more vomited from every shattered window and ill-hung door. Their screeching fell in harmony with the spectral music, not unlike godly folk singing psalms. Jakob gripped the side of the wagon with one hand, and discarded the sledge so he could pull Hans close with the other. The torrent of offal-caked scurriers washed around them, over their boots and legs as powerful as any spring runoff.

The animated coat took its place in the center of the crossway. The thin houses on each corner tottered into their neighbors to shy away from the spectacle. As the rats formed concentric circles around the floating apparel, Färber's hat caught an uneven stone and flipped up to where a hand would be if an arm filled the coat. From there it bounced off of the cuff and caught on the edge of the stained collar. This gave the headwear the appearance of being jauntily pulled down over a dancer's invisible head.

"In with the dead."

"What?" Hans couldn't tear his gaze away from the possessed coat as it lazily turned in the air with arms wide and welcoming. The music dimmed to a hush. The rats unilaterally fell silent and from front-to-back bowed low to their formless maestro. It wasn't until Jakob's grip started to really crush that Hans managed to look away for a fleeting moment. His friend had his face buried against the railing.

"We need to get in with the dead, bury our heads, and wait for this to pass." Jakob struggled against the compulsion to look. Deep down he knew if he relented he'd join the cavorting, this *danse macabre*. If he acquiesced he would end up worse than the headless stiffs in the back. "Hans, please. Whatever you do, don't watch. Don't listen. Don't dance."

"I..." Hans looked back, snared by the surging melody like Odysseus by the sirens. Save he only had his friend's hand to hold him, instead of being lashed to a mast. The rats gamboled elegantly. Each individual ring moved counter to those on either side, but still all perfectly in time. It recalled a maypole dance to his mind, but far better organized. In the center, the coat gestured to the left and then to right, before it clapped immaterial hands. The hat slid back, and hung on an equally insubstantial head. The circuits of vermin switched positions in some elaborate pattern he didn't wish to understand. Hans caught wisps of frost sketching a hint of femurs below the coat's hem and a ribcage between lapels. "It's like they are calling something forth, Jakob. Something wonderful. Something terrible. I…"

Hans' words perished when the frolicking wraith solidified. Ghostly guts writhed like agitated earthworms under the ribs; clawed hands gesticulated precisely in time with the terrifying tune, and under the hat's brim... Merciful Heaven! Under the hat's brim traces of a skull grinned, but in a distinctly inhuman manner. Its slim muzzle ended in two pronounced fangs with a narrower and small set beneath. The specter's cranium bulged back further than any man's would. The brute muttered what his brain had a hard time processing. For once he didn't envy Jakob an articulate nature. "Like a rat, a human-sized rat. But. I… I.. what has a head like that, but a god?"

Hans yearned no longer for carnal satisfaction. Rather he desired joining the vermin in their blasphemous revelry, to fall into their rhythm. He strained against Jakob's grip. His pitiful soul longed to raise his arms in unclean praise while the rodents gorged up to his fingertips. He craved to have the ruinous gaze of the pestilent phantom fall onto him and acknowledge his devotion before snuffing out the pitiful animus within. While the rats ached for human meat, their master desired the choice morsel of his essence. Worst of all, Hans was utterly willing to relinquish it. All he had to do was dance, and he took the first step toward his last.

A spike of pain shattered his entrancement when Jakob struck him where spine and skull met. The wave of nausea which followed washed away suicidal urges. While he stumbled, this time Hans complied with his friend's coaxing. The pair lurched into the back of the dray, too frightened to care about the putrid ichors coating their bodies inch by inch as they wiggled into the stack of headless cadavers.

A whine escaped Jakob's throat when lifeless fingers dragged across his face, and almost hooked on his lips. All around him the cold meat pressed, and blocked off the sight of everything but anemic flesh and spoiled cloth. The stench overwhelmed him, wormed its way into its gut and from there into the blood. Icy humors trickled through his hair, down the front of his forehead, pooled beside an eye. A careless blink could draw it all inside, but he didn't have room to swipe it away. He didn't stop burrowing. For the deeper into the dead he went, the more muffled the profane litany became. His heart nearly stopped as several corpses beside him wiggled seemingly on their own. He realized they didn't move because they were risen, or even because of rats breeding in their torsos, merely Hans crawled beside him. He tried to titter, only to gag on the taste of moist rot.

Thousands of rodents sung their praise into the darkness of night as the infernal harmony spiraled toward crescendo. So violent was the cacophony the men heard a nearby structure collapse. Jakob swore he made out words, but not from any sort of tongue humans spoke before or after Babel. Thus he did his best to ignore them, not to listen lest he might understand their meaning. Yet inklings chewed their way into his psyche. He worked his arms through the smothering corpses and clamped hands over ears. Several bodies slid up and over the side of the cart as Hans curled up in the fetal position so he could do the same.

Even as the men struggled to block it out the horrid sounds dug deep into their souls and wiped out every other sensation. So complete was the song's saturation into their very fiber that the two louts didn't immediately react to its sudden end. The silence lasted for several minutes before Jakob realized he could hear his own breathing, and Hans the fact he was sobbing softly. Still they waited for some time with their senses strained for any hint of the unearthly presence, or of its zealous tabernacle.

The press of frozen meat and damp noisomeness eventually became too much and the pair struggled to the surface. First their tallow-oiled hands broke free and struggled to attain a grip. Shortly their faces emerged, mouths wide in search of fresh air. They groped about before finding the wooden back of the driver's bench, and used it to haul themselves out of the fleshy quagmire. They stared at the empty intersection, well nearly empty. The tattered remains of the hat and coat lay in the center. First Hans began to giggle, followed by Jakob.

"Guess *Herr* Färber won't need the cart any more. What do you say we call it an early night? We only need to split the Count's coin two ways." Hans coldly suggested. His numb gaze drifted away from the empty coat. Part of his spirit had withered away. To let it die was the only way he could keep his sanity.

Jakob agreed via mute nod, but didn't look away. He couldn't fully fathom the truth of the rats' reverie and Färber's death. Likewise no conjecture was made to why the wagon's mule seemed idly bored, as if nothing was amiss. He did understand why the Lord answered no prayers to stop the Black Death. What was the power of their creator, compared to one worshiped by beasts who outnumbered humanity by factors untold? Man was fashioned in the image of a lesser god.

Hans claimed the reins firmly in his hands. Hands he was unsure would ever stop shaking. He needed a hot bath, and a woman to pass the night with. Jakob scrubbed at his hair, trying to get cadaver chunks out of it. His desire to be a minstrel disappeared, for he knew he'd be tempted to recreate the blasphemous symphony. Tonight he'd join Hans in having a bath and paying for feminine comfort. He took up the horsewhip and set the mule to moving. The quicker they struck this night from their minds, the better.

Unseen rodents squeaked within the surrounding buildings. With nightly services done they returned to breeding, eating, and spreading their deity's curse.

The cart rattled on.

Zachary O'Shea was born in the refinery belt of California and raised in the neon desolation of Nevada. When not avoiding one-armed bandits and tourists, he enjoys various activities: facilitating, designing, and occasionally playing table-top RPGs, reading, writing, and eating out too often with great friends. You can find him at www.lastslicestudios.com and follow @boxofteeth on Twitter.

SKOOKUM

BY BARB SIPLES

Last words? *Oui, monsieur,* I have last words. I have last words for *Monsieur* McLaughlin there, regarding the so-called justice of the frontier. And for you, *abbé*. And for all you people of Fort Vancouver, you trappers and traders, my so-called peers, you from Scotland and England and the Sandwich Isles and ah, *oui,* from my own Quebec, for I see a few *voyageurs* among you. And I have words for you dusky beauties, you daughters of the Chinook and the Quinault in your calicos and petticoats, you who have taken the white man and his ways to your bosom, words most especially for you, for if any have the right to judge me it is you. *Oui,* I have last words. But will you listen?

The factor here, *Monsieur* McLaughlin, he wants to be rid of me, rid of Jean-Batiste Micheau and the sorry tale that sticks to me like a stink, like a shadow. But I swear to you! I swear by Saint Anne, patron of travelers, who grants safe portages and gentles white water and keeps the tobacco dry and the fire burning through the night! I am blameless of these deeds, murders so macabre, so monstrous that only a monster could commit them. Will you hear me? Will you judge me as my peers? And you, *Monsieur* McLaughlin? Will you honor the will of the people who gather here so eagerly to see justice done? Will you set me free if, after hearing my tale, the good people gathered here are moved to find me innocent? Will you consider them a jury of my peers?

Très bon, très bon! You agree. Then take from my neck

this rope, for it chafes me. I have never been fond of neckties. Give me some room on this platform, *mon abbé*, and let me tell my tale.

I'm a man of the St. Lawrence, of the Wild River Micheaus, and never will you find a nobler line of *voyageurs*. *Mon grandpère* Henri Micheau put his X on his last contract in 1788 and never returned from the mountains. Algonquin thieves murdered *mon père* Amable Micheau not six years past, killed protecting his company's goods. *Mon oncle* Pierre is presently wintering at Connor's Fort on the St. Croix as an *engagé* with the American Fur Company, but were he here he'd speak for me.

Everyone on the St. Lawrence will speak for the Micheaux! Everyone knows us by sight. We're a stocky bunch, petite in the lower body so we may sit untroubled for hours in a birch bark *cannot*, but with mighty arms for rowing through rapids and for portaging goods and furs, and equipped with mighty hearts to send us thundering forward. No *voyageur* can row as long, shoot as fast, sing as loud or charm a war party like a Micheau! *N'est-ce pas?*

As for me, Jean-Batiste, I engaged with the Northwest Company last spring. Some twenty we were and a new man. I don't need to tell you people here. A new man is as welcome among *voyageurs* as a fart at a wedding—*excusez-moi, ma'mselle, madame.* He must expect the insults, the pranks that serve as his *rites de passage* from the other *voyageurs* and even from the agents, who sit all day eating pork and have not the bravery, the *coeur*, to go farther west than Missouri. So this new man, a Scotsman named Haley, he bore the brunt of our mischief — his tobacco robbed, his brandy plundered — but he bore it with ill grace.

Haley did not sing with the rest as we loaded the *cannots* and launched into the St. Lawrence. He did not doff his red cap on sight of the crosses that line the banks, memorials to the *voyageurs* whose ghosts still wander the rivers of the west. I did not think he would last the week.

We merged into the Ottawa and then the Mattawa and stopped only to unload-portage-reload, as quick as that makes it sound. And after twenty-one portages that first day, only then did we make our first *campement*.

This fellow, this Scotsman named Haley, he took a dislike to me in particular. The senior men sang around the fire and drank and Haley drank and kept silent and stared at me from smoke-reddened eyes. I scowled right back at him.

In the morning Haley's moccasins were filled with mud when he went to put them on. The trick was all in good fun and the men laughed, but not Haley. The next morning saw the guts of a fish in his shoes, and the next a series of thorns, arranged so that the eye saw nothing, but they pricked the man's toes when he slid them on. The *voyageurs* roared with good humor, though some of the more senior fellows shook their heads and frowned. Haley said I had done the deed, *oui*, done it out of malice. But he could prove nothing.

The morning after that my moccasins went missing. Gone. No moccasins, *monsieur*! Nothing between my feet and the thorny ground. There was no mystery to me who had done away with them. Haley would neither confess nor apologize. He only looked at me with his sly eyes and smiled. Nor was that the last of his attentions. I spent all of one cloudy day in a wet shirt because my pack had been submerged in the river. I grew angrier as the day wore on, determined to have satisfaction when we made camp. That was when I first glimpsed the skookum.

The skookum, *monsieur*? I'll get to that anon. Patience, *oui*?

We spent that night around the fire as was our habit. Only a few men sat up still, no one talking, the *parfum* of the pipe smoke stronger now than the smoke rising from the cedar coals. Haley was there, but as I watched he tapped his calumet against his palm and let the ashes fall. He rose and moved to the edge of camp and I followed him.

You, Haley, I said. He turned and his face changed

when he saw it was I. *Cease your torment of me or there will be consequences*, I said.

Go back to the fire, Micheau, before you get lost. And he turned and went into the trees. I lost sight of him before his last word faded but heard a sigh issue from the bracken, as if some sizeable creature swept the bushes with its pelt. And then I heard a shout.

I found Haley on his back, clutching at his side. When I came upon him he gave me a wild look, scrambled to his feet and ran to camp.

Micheau attacked me! he cried and the men pressed forward to see the blood ooze between his fingers where he held himself. A man took my arm, our captain Robert Llewellyn, and knowing him for a level-headed fellow I let him hold onto me and did not resist. At length Haley was compelled to lift his hand and raise his blue shirt and it was clear no man had made the mark that was etched into his flesh.

Bear, said Llewellyn and James Mason said, *Cougar.*

It was Micheau! the Scotsman cried, sticking to his tale like a fly in maple sap. I only laughed.

The next morning there was one man less in the camp, for Haley was nowhere to be found. We ate a cold bite and packed and still he was nowhere. We called and went into the trees and found no one, though we wandered into the thick of the wood. Coming back to camp I spied a lump of leather sitting on the cold hearth: Haley's moccasins. Blood stained them. The *voyageurs* called on Saint Mary and Saint Anne and crossed themselves but I, I picked up the shoes and claimed them as my own. That is justice, no?

There was no singing that day. We rowed in silence. But my heart was light as we portaged, for my feet were well kept. We never saw Haley again and good riddance.

We made good time for days and days, but then we met with weather. A fierce gale brought the rain that swelled the river. We cut trees and made a shelter of logs with a pine bough roof and drank and smoked. At the end of three days of howling winds a man named Toussaint sought a quarrel with me. I stood accused of besmirching his sweetheart, though I said only what everyone knows about Lorraine Colbert who lives on the St. Lawrence. But Toussaint would not rest until he had defended her imaginary honor with his fists, and so I must agree to fight him.

It is a testament to the strength of the storm that none of the *voyageurs* came out to witness the spectacle, though they were still laying wagers when we faced each other in the clearing our axes had made. Toussaint gave a shout and fell to. I defended myself with alacrity, I can assure you, *madame, ma'mselle.*

But Toussaint broke off all at once. He was quite frightened. Why do you make this noise? he demanded. The noise came again, low and haunting, not a growl so much as a moan. Stop it! Toussaint cried, backing away.

I looked over my shoulder and caught a glimpse of rough fur, brown-black and brindle, humping into the trees. When I looked back, Toussaint was running into the brush. I chased him, thinking to bring him back to our shelter, but he outpaced me.

I ran until my breath scraped my lungs raw, calling to Toussaint. All at once I stumbled over a fallen log and sprawled face forward onto a fresh carcass. And that is how the company found me, lying across Toussaint's mangled corpse.

The *engagés* had all come outside on hearing the howl that had unnerved the dead man, and had followed our path through the wood. They helped me to my feet and we inspected the place where our fellow had met his end. Trees had been shredded and splintered by the same jaws and talons that had mauled Toussaint. Great clots of soil and leaves had been loosened from the earth and spattered the branches beyond even the height of the tallest among us. No bear had done this. No cougar either. The men looked at me, foul with gore up to my elbows from where I had fallen on Toussaint. Looked at me and did not speak.

We packed and loaded and launched at once into the river, though it was folly. By some miracle we passed unharmed through the swollen current, though logs and debris choked the waters and knocked our *cannots* like a drum and the danger of capsizing was real. But the men would not stop to camp. There was a panic on them, like hares when the hawk's shadow touches them. George Washington, our half-breed, whispered something about a skookum. When pressed he only shook his head.

The men let me unload at Fort McGhee and carry the goods to the counting house alongside them. But once done they would have nothing more to do with me. No one slept near my billet in the bunk house, no one ate with me in the mess. Even the factor's men understood that something was amiss and avoided me, though they knew not the cause. For there was no cause, *madame, ma'mselle*. I had done nothing!

With a long, confining winter ahead of me I chose to go into the wood and trap for my own profit. The practice was not uncommon among the experienced *voyageurs* and all of the half-breeds and sundry natives of the fort did so. The friendly Indians considered it an honor to shelter a white man when his bivouac became too lonely. So with my pack and traps and well-oiled gear, into the wood I went.

As I tramped the sodden undergrowth I heard the faint chorus of a chanson rising from Fort McGhee and a great anger was kindled in my breast. Why should those men be warm and happy and drunk, while I ventured alone into the cold?

My wrath rose and I walked through the night, for the moon was full and I had my thoughts to keep me warm. At the first glimmering of dawn I stopped to rest and fell almost instantly to sleep where I sat against a great fir. When I woke I saw that the skookum had visited me while I slept.

The evidence was the same as at Toussaint's grave:

---

splintered trees, churned up earth, and a kind of rank smell that filled the close space between the trees. Not bear, not skunk, but something in between. I walked about and touched the jagged branches, sniffed a clot of leaves, went here and there and saw that the thing had followed me through the wood. I looked down a trail of scarred forest. Did it go back to Fort McGhee?

I made haste now, not looking for beaver dams or foxes' dens or any places to set my traps. I looked instead for a trail, anything to lead me to a friendly lodge, anywhere with human faces.

It was another day before I spied a game trail. Soon after that I met an amiable fellow named Teheyowey who was hunting deer with a musket. Upon seeing me he cheerfully abandoned this enterprise and led me back to his lodge where I shared out some tobacco and surrendered my brandy. Teheyowey went off to drink without delay but left me in the care of his sister Temenowhe, who I quickly christened Tem-Tem.

I spent pleasant days at the lodge. The lingering rank odor in my clothes was replaced by the smell of wood smoke. The place was known as Kamin's Lodge, for he was the headman of that band. It was a typical plank longhouse, dark inside but cozy around the fire pit which cast a glow on all the homey things of the place: the kettles and spoons, the mats woven of tulle, the painted screens that separated each *berth de famille*, and the bold ancestor carvings of red and black that climbed the columns.

The people of Kamin's Lodge had much to say about the skookum. It stinks of blood, they told me in the Chinook Jargon, the trade tongue. Others said, it smells of sage. One grizzled old man had heard it wail like an infant. The thing has no voice, another said. It's the size of a small bear, said one. It's the size of a shadow and can grow and shrink at will. You may kill it on the first night of the new moon, they said and also, It cannot die. They said prayers against it and then told me, no such thing exists. I gave up asking. I spent the last days of autumn fishing in the lake with net and spear and brought my catch home to Tem-Tem.

Dear, lovely Temenowhe. When she invited me to share her berth there was only one among Kamin's people who disapproved. His given name I could but ill pronounce, though his jargon name was Paul. He was the best hunter for miles around, celebrated in all the lodges on the wide lake's shore. And yet Tem-Tem chose me over him.

This fellow Paul pretended not to care but it was not long before he became unendurable. When I set my basket of fish at the hearth, Paul had something better to set beside it. A fat squirrel, a pair of geese, a deer – *ah la vache!* – all dwarfed my offerings to Tem-Tem. Though she said nothing I could see her delight with Paul's gifts and my ire was roused.

One morning when the snow had begun to fall, I rose up with my musket and set out after game. I knew that Paul was some hours ahead of me in the wood and I was determined to snatch his kill out from under him.

The air was cold but I hardly felt it. How dare my woman belittle my contributions? How dare Paul force me out into the snow? My face burned with the insult. A groan rose from the underbrush at my left.

I whirled about. Brindle fur over a hunched back, a thick, hairless tail sliding out of sight into the bracken. Judging by the tail, the skookum was as big as an elk but moved as nimbly over the frozen ground as a weasel. I slung my musket over my shoulder and chased it. I can see by your face, *ma'mselle*, that you wish to know why I committed such a foolish act. I can only say it compelled me somehow. Of course I was afraid of it! How could I not be?

What was it, *Monsieur*, this skookum? I can tell you no more than what Kamin's people told me, though they are none of them left now to say more…

Alors. As I said, I ran after it. I followed the great welts of its talons in the earth, the low moan that soughed through the boughs like a grieving wind. It led me through the dense tunnel of trees that is the deep wood, ferns slapping my thighs, thorns catching my sleeves. I saw no more than a glint of its claws, a blur of bristling fur just out of sight ahead of me. And then it disappeared. Vanished. Gone. And I stood face to face with Paul.

He gave a shout and ran, surprised to see his rival before him. My hand reached out to stop him but closed on a strand of shells he wore around his throat. In his panic he tore free and I stood clutching no more than his jewelry. Why did he run, the *imbécile*? I called out and chased him, searching until the threat of dark forced me to turn and trudge back to Kamin's Lodge. And though I arrived late, my dear maiden Tem-Tem sat up waiting by the fire and had ready for me a steaming bowl of fish stew.

There was no sign of Paul until the next day when some Chinook from a neighboring lodge came to visit Chief Kamin. They had found my rival's tortured body in the wood. The skookum had claimed another victim.

This caused a great uproar, for Paul was greatly favored by the people who lived on the lake. Kamin came to question me about all that had happened in the wood, for I had showed Tem-Tem Paul's necklace and I was now suspect. I tell you, good people of Fort Vancouver, I am no more guilty of what happened to Paul than for what happened to the people of Kamin's Lodge, to *ma chère* Temenowhe.

The chief would not listen. Tem-Tem's brother Teheyowey bound me to one of the lodge poles, my wrists at my back, and he drew the leather cruelly tight. He had watched my contest with Paul from a distance and had not interfered, despite his friendship with the hunter of the lake people. Now he let wrath assuage his grief, though I tell you again, I was blameless. Then Teheyowey and all the other men of Kamin's Lodge went out to hunt the skookum.

Where before I had been a source of great amusement to the women and children of the lodge, it was now as if I'd become invisible. I was as loath to them as the skookum. After some hours of great discomfort, my woman brought me a little to eat. I begged her most piteously to ease my bonds and when she relented, I got myself loose. She tried to keep me from the low, round doorway and raised a hullabaloo, but I found my way outside with some rough shoving, of which I am now ashamed.

It was not difficult to follow the path Kamin's men had made through the wood. And why should I not follow? It was my task to hunt the skookum with them. Was I not also a man of the lodge? They had no right to exclude me, no right to suspect me, and absolutely no right to bind me like a slave! I heard a deep, rumbling growl coming from somewhere close and whirled about in a circle. The path I had just traveled was rent and torn. The skookum was tracking me.

Se montrer! I cried, *Diable!* or some such thing, but my voice was lost by the great roar of the beast as it bounded into the open. It howled its fury to the trees and the branch-hidden sky as if its anger could never be slaked. One by one Kamin's men erupted from the underbrush with their muskets and hatchets. The skookum's mangy fur stood on end like a fighting cat's and its twisted body writhed in an ecstasy of fury. Yellow tusks tore into the boughs to the left and the right, loosing a great wind into the fir trees. The men of Kamin's Lodge, Teheyowey himself, could only stare at the skookum in shock.

A Micheau does not hesitate! I drew my knife and leapt to meet it, for I had come away without my musket. Again and again I struck and felt my good blade hit bone. I grew sodden with gore but kept my grip in the rank thing's fur and feared the moment fatigue would slacken my hold. *Par degrés* the mad thrashing calmed and the horrible tail gave a death rattle and lay still on the churned earth.

I stood alone with the dead thing in the clearing, for all the men had run off in fear. I looked down at the skookum. It was ugly, *mon Dieu*, was it ugly. But in the end it was just a carcass and I, Jean-Batiste Micheau, am a trapper of the St. Lawrence. I skinned it and draped the raw hide over my shoulders, the rank fur pricking through my coat. I cut off the verminous head for a trophy and wove through the trees full of pride. Who now the best hunter of Kamin's Lodge?

When I came to the longhouse on the shore there was no one about. I stopped before the door and called to my woman. *Come see, Tem-Tem! Come see what I have done!*

The door flap waved and my dear maiden stepped outside. She took one look at me and fell to her knees.

Do not fear, ma chere, I told her cheerfully. *It's not my blood. Stand up and take the trophy. This skookum will trouble your people no more.*

But Tem-Tem did not rise. She covered her mouth with her hand and her eyes grew round as saucers. Her other hand rose up and she pointed her fingers at the head I clutched in my fingers, the head I held out to her as the prize of victory. I turned the battered thing toward my face to see it better.

Her brother Teheyowey's dead eyes met mine and he grimaced back at me.

With a shout I dropped my trophy to the ground. I shuddered so hard the flayed skin slid from my shoulders. My woman began to keen. She pointed her fingers at me. Skookum, she wailed. Skookum! I turned my back and ran.

For many days I ran. *Par miracle* some oystermen picked me up on the other side of the lake. They were white men, a Mr. Swan and a Mr. Trimpey, who traded their harvest with the miners and panhandlers of California in exchange for gold. The story of the skookum was well spread by then. Kamin's men had been found mutilated in the forest and the women had abandoned his lodge. My dear Tem-Tem had fled. The Americans urged me to present myself to Factor MacLaughlin here, to profess my innocence.

So I have come and so presented myself and I tell you good people now as I told *Monsieur* McLaughlin, I am innocent. There is a creature in the wood who feeds on misdeeds and petty anger, one who can cause a glamour of confusion, so that a man may mistake his friend for —

What's that, *monsieur*? No, I cannot explain it. I cannot explain how Teheyowey's head became my trophy. I tell you I wrestled with a beast. It was a beast I slew and not a man.

Oh, how you look at me! I am innocent! Innocent, *oui*? I beg you, good people—*Monsieur* McLaughlin, I beg your mercy. Have you no—? Hark! Do you hear? It comes, it comes!

Do you not hear the scrape of that rough hide against the palisade, the blood hunger of that moan? Hark the splintering of the woodwork. The monster has breached the gate. Leave the cravat, sir, take it from my throat and flee! Save yourselves! Run, I say! Do you not see it? The beast is loose among you!

Me, you say? I am no skookum, *madame*! Would a man not know if a beast lived inside of him? *Mon Dieu*, you are all mad! Would you not know, *monsieur*? And pretty *ma'mselle*? And you, priest? And you there, yes, you at the back, who has yet to utter a word. Would you not know if a beast lived inside your skin?

After wandering the world like a restless ghost, Barb Siples is a permanent citizen of The People's Republic of Portland, Oregon. She shares her life with three classic cars, two worthless cats, and one incredibly charming industrial designer. In between planning for the imminent zombie apocalypse and keeping an eye out for Wraeththu, she writes horror, fantasy, historical fiction, and the occasional freaky sci-fi story. You can read more of her stuff at barbsiples.com.

THE DIG

MATTHEW WILSON

Cairo 1922

"What do you mean the men won't work? I'm paying them more than the others make on any dig site!" Richard Canning threw his maps up against the wall and strode out of his tent like six feet of thunder.

Maron had been a good scout. For what he was being paid, he'd assured Mr. Canning the tomb would be unearthed at utmost speed. There would be no problems and within a summer, there would be riches for all. But Maron couldn't take on forty disgruntled diggers alone.

"Mr. Canning, going out without a hat invites madness," he called. "Please don't anger them. They have pickaxes and mean bellies."

Richard took no notice; he had worked two years to get his grant from the University to visit these Egyptian sands--hotter than the hells of younger days on Blackpool beach--and find the lost treasure of old pharaohs. The constant delays were sucking his funds dry and it was getting humiliating to write those letters home begging for money after his long-winded speeches telling everyone how easily and under budget he would succeed here.

"What the hell is this?" Richard asked the men, who were sitting on the ground in protest, willing him to move them all. "Have you come here to take a holiday, or work?"

"The men are scared to work, sir," Maron explained,

fixing his turban in the awful heat. "There have been a number of murders recently."

Richard shook the matter away. He had seen the bodies carried out of the dark, barely explored subterranean passages. The worried workers had spoken of traps and warnings on the walls. They had spoken of the stale air down there and the constant threat of cave-ins.

Yet mostly, they spoke of the monster.

Richard couldn't afford to burn money on superstition. That fame-hogging swine Howard Carter had set up his own dig site less than three miles away and, daily, Richard had to waste resources sending men to shoo away his snooping scouts relaying reports of his own progress back to Carter.

That old Eton boy would be laughing in his morning tea if he knew Richard's men had gone on strike, downing tools. Could Richard control nothing? He was supposed to be the manager of the site but had proved himself an amateur. Unlike Carter, he had no place here.

Richard would show him. He leveled his rifle and asked his men what the problem was. Make a line; he had bullets for all complaints.

"The men want no trouble, sir. They just want to work in safe conditions." Maron translated their grumbles.

"These men will work in hell itself if they expect payment," Richard said. "Give me a torch. I'll go down there myself and show them there's no bogeyman."

Maron didn't have the confidence to lay his hand on the boss' pale sweaty arm, but didn't step out the way as he was accustomed to. Maron didn't agree with Richard's hard attitude on the men, but he considered himself a good and loyal worker. His reputation would go to hell if word got round to possible new employers that the last guy who had entrusted his life to him had ended up crushed in a mummy's rotting hand.

"I wouldn't recommend that, sir," Maron said quickly. "You've seen the condition of the dead bought up. Crushed by inhuman strength--"

"Cave-ins are a terrible thing," Richard interjected to kill the conversation. The heat had brought on a headache and the sooner he was in the darkened catacombs, the more grateful his strained eyes would be. Ever since he was a boy, he'd disliked how the sand had moved like water--like he could fall through it.

Into the bandaged arms of the barely breathing beast below.

Richard shook his head, unwilling to be infected by silly superstition. Besides, he had his weapon.

"Sir, that thing was a bloodthirsty warlord while a pharaoh; now, thousands of years of hate have built up his strength enough to fold a man into a cardboard box."

"A cave-in will do that." Richard looked away from Maron's eyes, disliking the dedication and belief to such mad ideas as monsters. Richard turned his back on the man. If he was worried this nut could stick a dagger in his back for the remains of his expedition, then Richard might never sleep again. Didn't he have enough to worry about?

He had to show some sense of power. He had to go in that damn tomb.

"Get me reliable men."

"But sir, they will not dig."

"I only need them to walk in the shade. Tell them I'll pay a year's wage for each."

"You can't ask for scabs to cross the picket line, sir. These men's wives cook for each other. If one went against the group, who could say one wouldn't add poison?"

"Rope," Richard said, tiredly. "Lots of it."

Maron gave a resigned nod and went to work. Sometimes, one had to see the monsters to believe them. But Maron would do his best to retain his work ethic and stay loyal. Even to a fool.

The rope burned Richard's hands, despite taking the

precaution to wear his thickest gloves. He thought of his mom baking cookies in the kitchen and the terrible heat that had come from the oven. Richard shook the smoke from his digits and found his oil lantern. It was too hot to fasten to his belt; he found it strange he had a need to keep his hands empty.

To defend himself?

Keep breathing, Richard. As a boy on those damn beaches, he'd always known what he wanted to be. An unveiler of things that times had buried. An archaeologist. He had sought out caves and stood in that darkness. Mom had told him it might warp him, but Richard was determined to prove her wrong.

Until he had fallen over the body. No one discovered who had killed the poor boy or why anyone had stuffed him in that rocky crevice, but Richard had been terrified of small dark places since. Even though his digging desires had remained. The need to drag things buried for centuries back into the sunlight and show the world how brilliant he was.

He didn't want to be down here any longer than he had to, imagining those still staring eyes of the dead boy. But if he failed here, he would be destitute back home, more than a laughing stock; he would be cast out onto the kerb to starve to death.

There had to be treasure down here. He had to succeeded.

"Stop poking me, man," Maron whined when one of the two men he had talked round let go of the rope and stood on his toe.

"Let's give ourselves some room now." Richard stiffened, his voice cracking with dust, trying to keep control of the situation. The three diggers laughed when Maron translated the orders. There was no way the men were leaving the circle of sunlight pouring down the hole they'd cut in from the ceiling.

Richard squinted, wary of reaching skeletons. He could just make out the faded scratched images of long dead pharaohs cut into the walls. "We can't stand here all day. Who's gonna go first?"

Maron tried to swallow the ball of iron that had somehow caught at the back of his throat: "You're joking. Right?"

"I'm paying a year's wage each here."

"To be your guides, sir. Not your human shields."

Richard blinked when he saw a dead boy's face etched into the floor. When he closed and opened his eyes again, it was gone. "You gotta do everything yourself," he moaned, and carefully moved forward. "This room has been cleared of traps?"

Maron tried to follow in Richard's footsteps, literally. "Too much credit is given for the old kin's safety measures, sir. All the ropes connecting the spikes and death pits have rotted over time. This dust will kill us faster than any booby traps."

Richard had heard of mummy curses, he figured Carter's luck would steer him clear of it. Lucky--

Richard stopped thinking when he heard it. A single word in the darkness. "Maron?"

"Voice throwing is not one of my skills, sir."

Richard cocked his father's service rifle. "I paid for men to guard this place at night... have you let tomb robbers sneak into my tomb?"

"To be fair, sir, the tomb belongs to the old king--"

"You men. Show some support and move up front," Richard demanded. If someone was making off with a gold coffin as he spoke, then his employees would have more to worry about than some damn mummy.

"Show yourself," Richard made his final demand as Maron informed him old kings couldn't understand English. "I'm talking to the grave robbers," Richard seethed. Something moved to his left - 9 o'clock - and Richard smelt the rot of the sea, the mold of a cave, and he started coughing. By instinct, he released the trigger before he blew his foot off. Again he was that scared little boy at the base of a body. He felt his cheeks burn and pricks of white lightning course up his spine.

"Stay with me, Martin. We're friends, right?"

"Maron, sir," Maron reminded his employer. Did his services matter so little that Richard could not remember his bloody name for five minutes?

Richard remembered now, the dark was total and had eaten away the sanity of the sun. His friend had been called Martin, but he hadn't wanted to be Richard's friend any longer. Richard had gotten mad and struck out. The poor lad had hit his head and cracked his skull. Now the darkness called him murderer and the absence of light was always right.

"There, there he is!" Richard yelled, following the flash of movement. There was a brief flash of gunfire, and Maron screamed in a greater sense of terror than he had ever known.

"Sir, that's Karik. You just killed one of your workers."

"There he is!" Richard yelled and fired again. One of his men screamed, woman-like, and headed back toward the circle of light. Though Richard put three large slugs into his back, he couldn't quite get the dead boy's face from off his back.

"Stop, you bloody maniac," Maron said but Richard's madness gave him strength; he wrestled the rifle free and shot Maron through the eye. Richard was determined to be done with monsters. There would be no more goblins or ghosts. There would be no more bloody Martin!

At last, silence reigned beside the rapid thump of his heart.

"This tomb is mine," Richard told the mute images of dead kings. There was no argument on that matter - nothing but the low groaning of a once chained thing that had broken free from the supports of its coffin.

Richard reloaded. "Martin? You can't hurt me anymore. You should have stayed in that damn cave."

The dragging footsteps hurried in excitement,

breathing heavy, making the room stronger with the stench of summer bog-land. The outline was definitely too big to be a boy. Richard tried to open his mouth, but for once, his authoritative voice didn't seem to travel.

The dead king seemed to be heading right for him.

Matthew Wilson has had over 150 appearances in such places as Horror Zine, Star*Line, Spellbound, Illumen, Apokrupha Press, Hazardous Press, Gaslight Press, Sorcerers Signal *and many more. He is currently editing his first novel and can be contacted on Twitter @matthew94544267 .*

THE SHRINE OF SAINT SALONIUS

BY GUY BURTENSHAW

I never knew my father, for he died when I was too young to form lasting memories, but my mother I knew well, or at least thought I did until her dying words cut any notion I had of trust to ribbons.

I had cared for my mother to the end. I do not know why she told me, but I suppose some secrets can weigh heavily on a person's soul, and when one knows the end is near and there is no turning back, there is a need to unburden any darkness before you face your maker; to seek absolution, if not forgiveness.

I did not have any uncles or aunts, and so no cousins. My mother had been the only family I had ever known, but now I knew that I had not arrived into this world alone. I had a brother who was identical to me in almost every way. A paradox maybe, but I truly believe that nothing on this earth can form a perfect symmetry. Imperfections exist to remind us that there is only one maker, all things created unique and nothing on this earth can deceive one that can see clearly. Whether my brother still lived or not my mother did not say, or did not know, but the moment the truth was revealed, I knew that I had to find him no matter what the cost.

His name was Louis, and he had been taken away following my father's death. There had been little money before the death, and less following. I had been told that my father had been ill and had quietly passed away, but I had my doubts. A priest by the name of Father Pippin had been passing through the village and had offered to take Louis to a monastery called *Piaculum Sanctus* in the foothills of the Black Mountains, where he would be well looked after in return for his devotion to the faith.

I was in no place to judge my mother's actions. I have been poor. I have been knocked in every which direction the wind blows, but I had never truly known the lowest depths of despair that she must have reached to have let a stranger leave town with my brother. The year was 1881, and though my memories have clouded over time, some memories have remained lucid enough to know that beliefs were once more honoured.

My mother was buried in the far corner of the churchyard where the light of the sun never seemed to touch, and the following day I set off. I knew the journey would be difficult. I had little money and what I wore was my only possessions. I had a name, *Piaculum Sanctus*, and that was all I had by way of directions. It was located in the Black Mountains, but those mountains are large and I am small in comparison.

I started before dawn to ensure that I had covered as much ground as possible before dusk, and I managed to reached the town of Tuchan before the sun set; thirty-five miles. My feet were sore, and as soon as I stopped walking I felt as though my legs would buckle beneath me if I did not sit.

A local innkeeper took pity on me and let me sleep in the stables. The smell was not good, but it was warm and my aching limbs just wanted to rest. I slept through until dawn when the horses became restless, and I was on my way again heading towards the mountains.

It took me five long days to reach the foothills. I ate fruit from the trees, berries from the bushes, drank water from the streams, and on one occasion I came across an encampment of gypsies who let me share their food. What they cooked over the fire looked like rat, but beggars cannot be choosers and I was grateful for the warm meat. If I was to reach the mountains I had to stay strong, and berries and fruit can only take you so far.

A small town stood at the entrance to the valley that led into the mountains. An old church sat on a hill at its centre with small stone houses crowded around it like disciples, and around the town was a solid stone wall rising thirty feet and lined with crenellations and towers.

The gate to the town had been open when I arrived, which I had been glad of. The last thing I wanted was to be explaining myself to anyone. What I did want, though, was to ask if anyone had heard of the monastery of *Piaculum Sanctus*. If they had, they could point me in the right direction.

The town seemed peaceful. People going about their everyday lives scratching a living the best ways they could. As I made my way along the narrow street heading towards the church, people stared at me as though they had never seen an outsider before. I know now why they regarded me so strangely, but hindsight is not helpful.

The church seemed like the obvious place to go. Every church had a priest, and if the monastery were in the region, the priest would surely know of it. I assumed that the priest that took my brother would have passed by the town. I had travelled straight, and surely they would have trod the same path as I.

When I entered the church I shivered. The air inside was cold, but more than that, the atmosphere felt sterile. I was reluctant to close the door behind me, but I felt compelled by a deep sense of respect.

"Is anyone here?" I called out.

My question was not met with any response, so I ventured towards the altar stopping as I passed a shrine. It had been carved in the whitest of marble, the writing chiseled along its side and gilded with gold telling me that it was the shrine of Saint Salonius.

I pressed the palm of my hand against its surface and

instantly recoiled. It was as cold as ice, possibly colder if that is possible.

"The church is closed," a strained voice caused me to turn around.

"The door was not locked," I responded.

"It is never locked and nor shall it ever be, but it is an empty shell and while it remains so it is closed to prayer."

"I did not come here to pray," I told him as he slowly walked towards me.

As he neared I was shocked to see that he was blind; his eyes grey with streaks of red as though they had been bleeding. He was dressed in a simple grey cassock and, whatever state of mind he was in, I was certain that if there were a monastery anywhere in the hills, he would be the man to know.

He reached out with his hand and I stepped back, afraid that he meant me harm.

"You can see me," the man said. "It is only fair that I know whom it is that I am addressing."

I stepped forward again and allowed him to touch my face and, as he did so, his expression seemed to sink.

"Why have you come back?" the man asked.

"I have never been here before," I told him. "You must be mistaking me for someone else." As the words left my mouth I thought of my brother. "My name is Armand Villeneuve."

The man was pale as though he never left the confines of his church, but I would have been prepared to swear that what little colour there was drained from his face as I said my name.

"Do you know of a monastery by the name of *Piaculum Sanctus?*" I asked, my heartbeat quickening.

"You cannot go there," the man said. "You must not go there."

"Do you know of a man that went by the name of Louis Villeneuve?" I asked fearing that if I did not keep pushing, I would learn nothing from the encounter.

"Saint Salonius is at peace," the man said.

"He is my brother, and I have come a long way to find him," I explained, not that I thought any explanation would bring even the faintest of colour back to his face.

"How did you know?" he asked.

"My mother confessed with her last mortal breaths," I told him. "And before I breathe mine, I will see my brother."

"He is dead," the man told me. "As dead to this world as Saint Salonius. He died long ago. Your journey is wasted, so there is nothing for you at the monastery."

I knew that it could not be true. If my brother had died long ago, how would he have recognised my face, and why would he have asked me why I had come back?

"You are Father Pippin," I told him. "It was you that took my brother."

"It was my duty to try to save him," he told me. "He was cursed, as was your father."

"You knew my father?" The atmosphere within the church felt as though it was closing in on me, but I was not leaving that building until I had answers.

"Your father was marked by the *Mullo*, and he in turn marked your brother. I had no choice in what I did. My hand was guided by God."

"You killed my father?" I asked hoping I had misunderstood what he had said.

"Your father could not be saved, but your brother was within redemption. Saint Salonius watches over his disciples. He binds them to the path of redemption."

I looked at the cold white marble of the shrine and then back to Father Pippin, but before I could say anything, he said: "Saint Salonius was a good man. He died fighting Childeric in 463 and his body was brought here to rest. The shrine, the church and the town built up around his body, but he would not rest. Two men opened the tomb, and the man that survived told a tale that sent him to the asylum near

Carcassonne where he died."

"What was in the tomb?" I asked.

"Saint Salonius rose from his grave to walk the night. The gates to the town are locked an hour before dusk every day, and they do not open again until light has returned. He went to an old Roman fort in the mountains that had been taken by the Order of Saint Benedict. There he found the solitude and isolation that he swore would remain his home until the end of time. The building sits in the shadows on a plateau five miles up the valley. The walls are three feet thick, the windows blocked, the door locked to all but the innocent marked. He ceased being your brother the moment he was marked. Leave him be."

I turned and left the church, the light from the sun intense on my skin after the coolness of the church. I felt that I had heard all that the priest had to say. There was nothing that he could have said to me that would have deterred me from finding my brother.

The walk back down the hill through the town felt different. What had seemed like quiet reflection on the way up now felt like passive oppression on the way down. I did not feel threatened, but I did not feel welcome either.

I did not want to spend the night within the walls of the town, but I knew that the gates would be closed before dark and, however magnificent the mountains might look, I had a feeling that once the sun set the land outside was not a place to be found wandering alone.

I slept in the stable behind an inn and woke with the sun to be on my way as soon as the gates opened.

The valley floor remained in shadow as I headed away from the town, and the sense of loneliness was almost overwhelming. I imagined Columbus and the crew of La Santa Maria must have had similar emotions as they left the coast behind and headed for the horizon not knowing whether they would ever see land again.

My limbs ached, but I was driven on with a

determination that I had never before experienced. While I could not see the monastery, I knew that it was ahead of me. I did not know how I would introduce myself when I arrived, but if my brother was there, and he was well, he would be sure to recognise his own likeness.

There was a trail, but it was rocky and the weeds had completely reclaimed long stretches as though the way was seldom beaten by the wandering feet of the town's people, although still visible enough to tell me that it was walked by someone. I kept walking and I kept an eye on the slopes ahead, looking for the outline of the monastery to appear, and when it did reveal itself to me, it was not what I was expecting.

The building was the colour of the surrounding granite on which it was perched, the plateau looking more like a ledge. It appeared as though it was part of the mountain looking down on the valley below, stern and unwelcoming.

I found the start of a rocky trail heading up the side of the valley. It was steep from the start, but I would not have given up even if confronted by a sheer cliff. Determination willed me on, but as I drew nearer to the walls of the monastery my will faded.

The walls rose a hundred feet and looked solid. There were no windows, and where there had once been an opening for a large door, there was only stone. I had never been to a monastery before, but it was not the image that I had formed in my mind. There were no crenellations along its top, but then I suppose its position was its defence. What would anyone gain by attacking a windowless block of black rock perched on the side of a valley?

The building looked like a tomb from without, and without windows I could not see how it would resemble anything else from within, but I had not walked for six days to be defeated by a wall. If there were a way in, I would find it, although I felt that I was being observed, and if the observer wanted me to enter, then I would be shown the way.

I walked along the wall and found a crack at its base. It was small and uninviting, but I was sure that I could force my way through with determination. I was determined, and I squeezed through, my shoulders scraping across the rough surface of the stone. I feared that I would become lodged between the stone and remain trapped within the wall forever, but I found myself inside a dark space.

I stretched my arms out and turned without touching any walls. The space felt large, and then a bright light filled my vision. A candle appeared, and behind the candle was a face. The features were gaunt, the skin pale, the eyes sunken and dark, the nose pinched thin and the lips as black as the stone I found myself within. I should have felt fear, but what I felt was awe. He turned and I followed.

From what I could see by the limited light, there were no passageways. There was just a series of rooms, one leading into the other, and I did not think that I would ever be able to find my way back out the way I had come in. One darkened space looks very much like another, especially when each space has no features that I could see.

When he finally stopped he pinched the flame out with his fingers, plunging me back into darkness, although I had an overwhelming sense that more eyes than those of the man I had followed regarded me standing in the darkness and, the longer I stared into the darkness, shapes started to form.

I became aware of figures standing around me, although I could not make out any features. My eyes gradually grew accustomed to the darkness, and I realised that I was in what resembled a chapel. At the front was a table. It was not covered with a cloth, but did have something lying on its surface.

I walked towards the table keeping my eyes off the figures around me, and looked down at what I could see was a skeleton. Intuition told me that the bones were those of the once venerated saint from the empty church on the hill back in the town. I had expected his remains to be whole as though he had stood and walked from the shrine, but these bones were old and I had no doubt that they would have crumbled to dust if I had dared to touch them.

When I turned to the figures I came face to face with an image I knew well. My brother stared back at me. It was as though looking in a mirror, his face the face I had seen in my reflections, but there was the imperfection. While I saw myself, others more observant would see the subtle chirality of a mirror image.

His cheeks were sunken, his clothes hanging loosely from his frame as though he had been fasting, but he was unmistakably the brother I had recently known nothing of.

"Louis," I said, my voice barely above a whisper.

"Why did you forsake me?" His voice was weaker than my own, and crackled as though being spoken through dried petals.

"Brother," I said. "I did not forsake you, but I have found you."

"Before me things created were none, save things eternal, and eternal I endure. All hope abandon ye who enter here."

If the place I found myself had ever been blessed, then it had been cut down to the ground as Lucifer was brought down to Hell. There was no goodness within the walls of the monastery, and when I looked around, the dark figures were nothing more than shadows. If they had ever been, their cursed souls clung to the world they had created hidden from the world of light.

Father Pippin had said that my father was marked by the *Mullo*, and he in turn had marked my brother. I had heard stories of the *Mullo*, the undead of the travelling people, buried without service or ceremony, and I wondered whether the walls of the monastery were where they were confined.

My brother raised his arms towards the altar, and said, "The shrine of Saint Salonius must be venerated. I came here as a child, and I can never leave unguided. Saint Salonius was marked, as am I, as was our father. I am the last of my kind, and soon I will be no more, for all who enter these walls are cursed and even Father Pippin has abandoned us, blinding himself with the red hot iron of his knife should he be drawn back."

I learned to live within the walls. Within the rooms dwelt the cursed souls, and I feared I would dwell with them until Judgment Day. I felt completely alone as though the world outside had ceased to exist, but I knew time continued to pass by, the world turning from light to dark as days became months and months passed into years.

I suffered lucid dreams of returning to the town with my brother where we beat our fists against the closed gates begging to be let in. I felt like Prometheus, the god of old, being tortured every night only to start the cycle again with each passing day, waiting for Herakles to release me from my torture.

I do not know how much time passed, but I do know my soul was close to being lost to me forever when those gates opened. I walked side by side with my brother up the steep hill, the buildings keeping us concealed in shadow until we reached the door to the church.

We entered the church and slowly walked towards the altar where Father Pippin knelt. I put my hand on his shoulder, and I knew that life had left him, but lying on the altar was his knife; the knife he had used to take his own sight. The knife that I knew would release me from my own visions of hell.

Father Pippin had told me that my father was marked by the Mullo, and he in turn had marked my brother. I was the same as my brother, and I was different in some way. I was cursed, but I was also still human. Where he had been marked, I had kept my freedom. I do not know if my hand was guided by God, but I took the knife and I forced the iron through my brother's heart.

The look in his eyes as he left this world was not one of

fear, but of relief. While the bones of Saint Salonius rest uneasily on the altar of *Piaculum Sanctus*, I laid the body of my brother Louis Villeneuve to rest within the white marble shrine of Saint Salonius.

As I left the church and walked back down the hill towards the open gates, I knew that we were both free at last.

Guy Burtenshaw lives in a small town in southern England and has been writing horror stories for many years. He has published several horror novels and his short stories can be found in various magazines and anthologies. He also writes murder mysteries under the pseudonym G D Shaw.

—

IT PAYS THE BILLS

BY S.L. WILLIAMS

"Ace. The Americans are here." I had but a moment to even acknowledge Chauncey's words before he ducked out of the tent on his way to the trucks that were starting to pull in on this grey day. The weather was promising a storm, and it looked like it would deliver on its word.

I put my pen down and stretched high above my head. Our infantry unit was getting a small segment of the 369th Division. It was one of the *Afro-Américaine* units that Pershing had negotiated for, as we needed more men. Apparently we were killing several birds with one stone. Least of all being the racial tension that seemed to fill the American Army. I shrugged, and looked out of the tent at the barracks and the barbed wire that had been put up to ward off the Germans. At this point, I'd take rabbits with slingshots if I thought it would stop the advancements the Germans were making into France.

I came out of the tent just in time to watch our new recruits pile out of the back of the trucks. Men of every shade of brown conceivable moved into formation and awaited their first set of instructions. I put my hands in my pockets, and walked up beside Chauncey who had already begun debriefing the men.

"Hello gentlemen. Welcome to Manicourt. My name is Marshal Chauncey Dubois. I wish we had time to show you the beauty of our lands, but alas we do not. We are at war, and with that comes a very heavy price. Whom, may I ask, is your leader?" Chauncey looked around, and one gentleman stepped forward.

He didn't bother making eye contact. Something I was sure he learned in the American camps. "I am Private Oliver Brown. The men here call me Obie."

I stepped forward, still looking the men over, trying to gauge what we were given to work with. Something was hovering just outside of my attention, but I fluffed it away. I had more important things to worry about. We didn't have time to rewrite years of bad racial relations. Germany was a wolf that was howling at our doors. "I see. There is no one here who is higher than a private?"

"No sir. Everyone here is a private." Obie looked over at me out of the side of his eye. He didn't look very impressed with me, either.

My lips tugged in amusement, but once again I would have to talk to him in length later. I had a report to give on the new troops. "Very well then. My name is General Acel "Ace" Forgey. We will start with training you in our style of fighting and policies, and we will go from there. It's going to have to be a crash course, I'm afraid. We will be off in about two days to head for Argonne. The men will take your company to their barracks, and we will see you at 0500."

Chauncey called them to attention, and began marching them to where they would be laying their heads while they were our guests. I was about to walk off, but suddenly what had been bothering me earlier finally registered. Obie had been speaking to me in French. I turned sharply, and watched the men go off. For the first time that morning, I felt like this could actually work.

Later that evening, our sirens started to go off. I grabbed my gun, and pulled on my uniform. Men were running around the camp calling out orders and getting into formations. The rain was coming down in sheets, and lightning was filling the camp with this odd greenish light. I stopped to watch with a frown. In all of my thirty-four years, I had never seen the sky do anything like this before.

Chauncey ran up to me waving his hands frantically. "It's the Germans, they are here! We have to evacuate! We..." Chauncey was abruptly cut off as I shook him sharply.

"Get hold of yourself. If they are here, we don't have time to evacuate! Get our new men ready. We have to fend them off tonight!"

"Your new men are here, and ready." The slightly accented French let me know it was Obie speaking. He sounded amused, but as I looked over his men, they were in fact up and ready.

Chauncey ran off to see where we were with the preparations for attack, and I turned to Obie. "My apologies. It seems we won't have time to get you properly acquainted with the area. It looks like tonight is the night."

"We're ready, sir. We didn't come over here to just sit back and relax. We knew what we were signing up for. Isn't that right, men?" Obie asked the rest of his regiment, and nodded.

Undoubtedly some of them looked scared, but that was normal. War was not a walk in the park for soldier, service, or civilian. I nodded and waved them forward. We would be moving to the front lines. Obie called them to order, and we marched to the end of our camp where the Germans had been sighted.

Once there, we spread all of our troops throughout the trenches that had been dug. There were four to five in each, waiting to fight. I could hear our chaplain praying as we went by. I wasn't a religious man myself, but for some it might be the last prayer they heard. I didn't begrudge them the comfort of their last rites. We waited, watched the spotlights wave above our head. It was insanely quiet. There was no movement. I started to believe it was a false alarm. I stood, about to give the order to break formation, when it finally came.

Our spotlight caught one of the planes, flying through

the darkness. I could hear the roar of the engine despite the rain. It was a German airplane, but something about it was odd. I only saw it for a moment, but there seemed to be a set of symbols on the side of the plane. If my eyes hadn't quit working, it was an inverted star with five points. I blinked and the plane disappeared, but in its wake was a sky filled with parachutes.

The spotlights were trained on them, following their descent. Something about the soldiers was off. They seemed to be jerking and twisting in their harnesses. I could hear groans following the howls of the wind, and I couldn't figure out where it was coming from. Obie, who was standing next to me, was saying something in English to his friends, and they all began to nod slowly. I turned to him, and his eyes met mine solemnly.

"General, I can't tell you how to handle your business, but if I were you, I would keep my distance from any of the Germans that came out of that plane." Obie once again spoke to me in French, and I remembered that I was going to have to find time to ask him where he learned it.

The first of the German soldiers landed, and I realized that the groaning was coming from them. They landed and started moving towards our camp. They didn't bother to release the harnesses that connected them to the parachutes. They just seem to shamble towards us in this slow gait.

"Surely the Germans aren't bringing us their wounded soldiers for help…" I murmur to no one in particular, but Obie looked over at me with a shake of his head.

"No, they surely didn't." He looked at me out of the side of his eye, and turns to his men once more to say something else to them in English. They nod once again, and I hear one beginning to pray in earnest.

The Germans came within firing range, and our spotlight trained on them. I laughed and stood up to get a better look. Those were our soldiers! The Germans must have released them to us for medical care. And to be honest they all look like they needed it. Some of them were barely keeping their insides from being outside. I and a few others crawled out of the trenches to speak to them. The Americans grabbed some of us as we crawled out, shaking their heads emphatically. Couldn't blame them; they didn't really know one of us from the next, but it was peculiar that they didn't recognize the uniforms.

I walked out to the gate that we allowed supplies through, and I heard someone come out behind me. I could only assume it was Chauncey with his clipboard and pen. Ready to process the soldiers into sickbay. "Welcome back men! We're glad to see you are none the worse for wear. We will get you patched up and back home as soon as possible!"

I heard more groans, and one stopped to look at me. I tried to be patient because I knew they must be shell-shocked, but it was damned hard. The soldier shambled to me, and I saw that his face was deathly pale, and he was completely riddled with bullets. I frowned, and looked at the other soldiers coming our way. By all accounts none of them should even have been able to breathe, let alone walk.

The one who was coming towards me stopped for a moment, and I shook my head in amazement. "How are you men even alive?"

The soldier groaned, and slowly looked up at me, and started to shamble faster. Startled, I took a few steps back as he started to reach for me. Suddenly a storm of bullets rained past a few of the other French soldiers from our camp. I turned and saw that the Americans had come out of the trenches and began shooting. I turned to Obie, enraged.

"Is this what they teach you in America? Shoot first and ask later? Stop them! They are killing our men! Tell them to stand down now!" I was incensed; I was going to send them back to their original camp at once.

Obie grabbed me around the waist and began hauling me back to through the gates. Some of our soldiers made it, but others don't. Some of the Americans went down, and I saw their friends turn to them with tears in their eyes and shoot them through the head. I had never seen such barbarism, and it took my breath away. Were they really that much different than we were?

Once back in the trenches, Obie began to give out orders in English and French. My soldiers were so shocked that they weren't sure what to do. His, however, were setting up barricades, and taking over spotlights to shine out on the fields. I ran up to Obie and grabbed his shoulder, pulling him around to look at me. Obie looked slightly annoyed, but that was just really too bad.

"Who do you think you are, coming into my camp and giving orders?" He was struggling and finally got out of my grasp. I was seething with anger, but I was not too far off from starting a fistfight.

"The man who is saving the lives of you and your unit." He turned from me, and started giving more orders, ignoring my outburst.

I followed him, and continued to berate and shout at him through the rain. He continued to calmly move about the camp. My soldiers were stock-still; they had no idea what to say or do. They were in as much shock as I was. "Those were our soldiers, you idiot! You and your men killed not only ours, but yours as well! You're acting like a pack of savages!"

Obie stopped to look at me then. I thought he was going to slug me, and that was fine; I was ready for it. I could feel the anger inside like it was a living-breathing thing. "General, they are already dead. They just don't know it."

I stopped and looked at him incredulously. I looked to my men who didn't know what to make of it either. I looked at his soldiers, and they were all in the act of doing something. Whether it was putting up defenses, praying, or talking amongst each other, I realized that Obie was serious. They all believed that those soldiers were dead.

I forced myself to calm down, and softened my voice. Clearly they were not well. They were too traumatized by life events or they were sick from not being taken care of. "Look Obie, I don't know what lies the Americans have told you about the soldiers here…"

"I'm sure they are nothing compared to the lies we got when we signed up, but that does not negate the fact that those men who were dropped off were not alive. Who do you know could sustain those types of injuries and still walk around?" Obie turned to me, and also softened his voice, speaking to me as if I was a small child.

I was starting to get angry again. "Look you, our soldiers are specially trained to…"

Obie laughed in my face and continued to move around to his men who were smiling and shaking their heads as well. "Come back from the dead? Unlikely, sir."

I raised my gun at him, and the air around us got very tense. Something was happening, and I could feel it, but had no explanation for it. Much like most of the events that just occurred. "You listen here! I am in command of this camp, and I am telling you to stand down now! I will have you court-martialed for this!"

"That's fine, General, because that means we survived long enough for you to start the process." Obie continued to move around the area, ignoring the setting of my gun. He moved about with purpose, and his men carried out each order without question.

"Obie, get up here quick!" Another of Obie's soldiers, by the name of Percy, was on the lookout with Chauncey. He was frantically waving out to the field, and Chauncey looked ghostly and horrified by what he saw.

Obie ran up to the top of the barricade, and I followed him. I was still in charge, and this argument was not over. We made it to the top, and another of his soldiers gave him some binoculars. He handed them over to me, with a grave look on his face. I snatched them away, but something told me I really didn't want to look through them. I took a deep breath and pulled the glasses to my eyes, and what I saw out in the lightning I knew I would never forget for as long as I lived.

The soldiers that had not been shot in the head, and the ones that had landed, started to reanimate themselves. One arm reached to the sky while another pulled itself up. One that had been cut in half by the spray of bullets began using its elbows trying to make it to the camp. One of my soldiers began to scream, and another began to join Obie's soldiers in praying. I stood in grotesque fascination of the way the dead soldiers had begun to pull themselves together. Suddenly, I heard a human scream out for help. One of the men had been injured and left on the field. There was nothing we could do for him. The dead soldiers heard the scream, and they all converged on our fallen comrade. The sheer ferocity that the dead tore into him with made my stomach churn. Limbs were torn, and skin shredded apart by bare hands. The soldier screamed until there were no screams left, and the zombies feasted on his organs.

I brought the binoculars down and handed them to Obie. He took them, and I didn't see a look of superiority--just one of sad resignation. I could tell from the look on his face that he didn't think we were going to make it out of here. I looked to my men, and they didn't seem to think we would make it either. I turned away from him, and headed back to my quarters to write up a report to send to our department head. They must know about this immediately. I left the other soldiers out there to make peace with whatever heaven they knew.

Obie came in later. I assumed he was seeing to what I could not. I had poured myself a glass of Chartreuse. When I saw him, I immediately poured him a glass as well. He watched me, and I was glad of the silence for a few moments. I was praying to the only deity I knew that would get us through this, and the only way I knew to get to him was through the bottom of a liquor bottle. Obie watched me for a few moments, as if trying to figure out what to say to a rabid animal.

"Your men need you, General," Obie stated flatly.

The Chartreuse was making my mood infinitely better. The world was calm, and there were no human flesh eaters outside our camp. But there were, and no bottle was going to change that fact, no matter how good the year was. "Your French, sir, is perfect! Where did you learn to speak so fluently? And please, call me Ace! No need for formalities now, is there?"

"My grandmother was from Louisiana. There are a lot of plantations there owned by the French as well as a large French community." Obie sighed and looked up the sky as if asking for patience. "General, your men are scared."

I laughed and waved the bottle, indicating myself. "No Obie. I'm scared. My men are pissing themselves, because we are going to have to go out there tomorrow and take care of that… problem!"

"My men will not go out there." Obie slowly shook his head, and I poured myself another drink. Only heaven knew how many drinks I'd had in the span of one hour.

"They have to! They are the only ones that seem to know what we are dealing with. Speaking of which, how do you know?" I waved the hand holding the glass as emphasis, ignoring the way the wind began to pick up again.

Obie places his hand on the chair I motioned him too, and remained standing. "Negro history in general is passed by word of mouth to each generation. A lot of it is lost to us due to various events, but there are some that are collectively in our consciousness."

I downed my drink, and coughed for a few minutes, trying to get my nerves to steel themselves. "What are those…things?"

"The walking dead. The picture shows call them zombies. Humans who are trapped inside their head, and only know how to eat. They crave life, and since they cannot have it, they take it." Obie looked a little far away as he spoke, as if remembering something from the distant past.

I shook my head and poured myself another drink. "How do we stop them?"

"Shooting them in the head or with fire, but since we are in the trenches, fire would probably not be the best idea." The sky opened up again, and more green streaks of lightning savagely arced across the sky. "My men want to march out of here at first light."

"Your men will have to help us!" I was shocked. Was he seriously contemplating leaving us here with this problem?

"No, my men signed up to protect our country despite our treatment, so that we could show America that we are a part of them. We did not sign up for a suicide mission involving dead folks." Obie shook his head, and continued to look at me as if daring me to make some sort of mistake.

I was a little confused with what he was saying, and the liquor wasn't helping. He was a soldier; surely he must feel that pull to defend his country. "Why are you even here, if you don't care?"

Obie laughed, and took his cap off to run a frustrated hand through his hair. "It pays the bills."

I almost fell for what he was saying, but something in his voice stopped me. I could see past the bolster, and at that moment I felt sorry for him. He signed up, and he had far too much honor to desert his post. It was why he was so angry. "But it is your duty...."

He cut me off with a shake of his head. "Duty to who? A country that can't stand us, or French soldiers we don't know? Ain't."

"Ain't?" I blink and try to run through my mental dictionary of American slang.

"Ain't is short for: 'No, I am not about to go out there and get myself or my men killed by zombies.' I have a wife and three kids to get back to." Obie crossed his arms and watched me steadily. He was used to being used as cannon fodder for other soldiers, and he wasn't about to put himself in that position for us. Not that I could blame him.

Unfortunately, it wasn't up to or even about him. I took a swig of Chartreuse, and looked up at him, my gaze never leaving his. "If we don't kill those things, the Germans will eventually send them after your wife and kids on your home shore. If we stop them now, we can keep them from doing any more harm to all of our people."

Obie cursed and turned away for a moment, but turned back long enough to take the drink I had poured. I pulled out a cigarette and offered him one that he turned down at first, then shrugged before accepting it. Might as well, after all. "Fine, but we have to have a plan. My men will not just go out there."

"Fair enough. Everyone is afraid to die." I waved this off as normal, and looked at our supply lists. We had a large amount of explosives we were to take with us to Argonne.

Obie shook his head solemnly. "No, General, none of my men are afraid to die for the reasons we signed up for. They are afraid of turning into zombies. It's one thing to have trials and tribulations, and then you die. It's a completely other thing to have trials and tribulations and you're still walking around, trapped in your head, hurting those you are here to fight for."

I nodded slowly, and started running ideas through my head. The one that I came up with was indeed a suicide mission, but it would save the lives of many of our soldiers, and the rest of the soldiers we were to meet in Argonne. "Do you know if any living thing will do, or do they only eat humans?"

Obie thought for a minutes and shrugged. "I guess any living thing will do. I'm sure they can't be too picky about the lives they take, as long as it's living."

I stood up, and motioned with my hand at nearby farm on the map where we got supplies from on occasion. "We have a farming community not too far from here. If we can draw them all to one spot, we can slip most of our camp out through the back. Once they are gone, we can open the front, then blow the zombies away."

Obie thought about it and nodded. "Not too many casualties, and it beats trying to kill them all one by one."

"So you're with me?" I stared at the bottom of my empty glass for a moment before looking back up.

"Looks like, but if anything happens to me, you find my wife and my kids, and you tell them what happened. Don't let some reporter come knocking on my wife's door with some cockamamie story about how we worthlessly died, and they can't get any of my benefits." Obie wasn't looking at me, however. He was looking out at the rain, and the greenish lightning streaking across the sky.

"I assure you, that your family will be taken care of." It wasn't a question. I would make sure that his family and those of the men who died here tomorrow would be treated fairly if it was the last thing I did.

Obie nodded, but due to his experiences he didn't seem to believe it. He stretched, and made his way to the door of my tent. "I'm going to get the men ready."

"I'm going to send in this last report, then I'm coming." I turned and begin tapping out my demands and concerns to our leaders. I would be heard before I even bothered opening the camp's gate to those things outside.

Obie nodded again and walked out of the door. He probably thought I was hiding, but that was okay for now. He would see that I was a man of my word, and least of all a coward. I could see in his eyes that he knew, as well as I did, that the chance of any of us making it out of here was very slim. I started to construct my report to our leaders, and I would make sure that my last moments would not be spent in vain. Every soldier here would get what he deserved, even if they couldn't get it in life.

The next morning was not only grey, it was dark. The sun was out, but a thick blanket of angry clouds hid it. We had taken the cattle from a nearby farm a few kilometers off and evacuated the people. We couldn't promise them that they would see their farm again, but they would have their lives. We had gotten a team of volunteers. We didn't want anyone to stay against their will. By the end there were only 12 of us; the rest were sent on to Argonne. I had gotten word back from my superiors that my demands would be met. I was ready for the day's events, and whatever it would throw at us.

By this time, the horde of the undead was rattling our gates. They knew that there was live meat behind the doors, and they were determined to get it. Obie looked over at me, and I nodded. It was time to get started. I looked over to Chauncey and Percy, and waved them off. They had the instructions for the families of the troops who were going to stay here, and I wanted to make sure that they were followed. Chauncey and Percy were perfect for the job. The troops started to file out. Once they had evacuated, I settled down in my tent, and put my feet up on the table and relaxed. It would be over soon enough.

Obie came in and I waved to the other chair and he sat down with his helmet in his hand. Though looking far more dignified then I did.

"I thought you would have left with the rest of the company."

"Someone has to make sure that if you fail, the explosives go off. I sent the rest of the men to the outskirts to pick off any that get away. They may have a chance of escape if they are lucky." Obie hand was a little shaky as he dusted off his helmet. I didn't say anything. My hand wasn't exactly steady on the cigarette I was holding, either.

I nodded and looked at the watch given to me by my grandfather. A memento that brought me comfort despite the day's events. "Well it's almost time. Why don't we go out and see what our friends on the other side are up to?"

Obie rose and I followed him out. There wasn't any real reason for rank at this moment; we would all be judged the same soon enough. We got closer to the gates and we could hear the despairing groans over the winds that had begun to pick up. It was like the earth was crying in lament of what it could not stop. One of Obie's men had started to sing a gospel song, and though none of my men knew the song, they joined in with parts of the high harmony. The sound was starting to break my heart. We got in position, and we motioned for two of the men at the gate to let them in. The barricade was lifted; the zombies began to shamble in, some tripping over themselves to get to the cattle in the center of camp. We stood in the center waiting for them to come. We were going to set off the explosives and take them out all at once.

I didn't look over at Obie as we walked, but I felt I owed him an explanation of what was taking me so long to some out of my tent. "Your family will be taken care of. They will receive a pension from our army. If they should choose, your family, and those of the soldiers that are here, will have the choice of becoming citizens of France. "

I could see Obie looking at me out of the corner of my eye. He looked no less than amazed, and I hoped that it was some sort of consolation for dying here today. "Thank you, Ace."

I shook my head and kept staring forward. If these were my last minutes, I didn't want to miss all of them. "No, thank you. If you and your men had not warned us of this danger, we would have taken them to Argonne as sick patients. I apologize for not listening."

"Don't worry about it. I'm just glad that my life is not being given in vain. It's a cold world that will let you die for it, but not truly live in it." Obie handed me a gun, and I moved to the explosives that were set in the center of the camp where the cattle had been placed. Where we would be standing when they went off.

I heard the zombies getting closer, and I watched as the sky started to clear up some. I believed I could even see the first rays of the sun. The zombies got to the first cow, and it screamed. The other cows began to run around, trying to get away, but the zombies were too fast and far too hungry to let them go. I closed my eyes from the biting and tearing of flesh. I heard some of our men fall, but at least they fell bravely. They screamed, but were dying on their feet, and it was the most we could ask for right then. The world seemed to slow down and stop around me. The sun broke through the clouds and a gentle rain began to fall around us.

My heart stopped, and I vaguely heard Obie start to pray. I heard one of the men tell me that we had all of them inside. The gate shut, and I sent up a prayer of my own. Not for me--I knew where my journey led, but for the men in the camp with me. The hair on my arm stood on end, and I felt one of them breathing near my ear. I opened my eyes, and looked at Obie as I pulled the lever. He smiled, and then suddenly the world went orange, then white, and faded into blessed darkness.

It kind of goes without saying that Sheena Williams loves to write! She can't tell you when it started. She just knows it's something that she's always loved to do. She loves different types of stories, and different types of writing, and nothing makes her happier than hearing when someone has enjoyed something she's written. She writes a lot of fantasy and horror, and maybe a smattering of sci-fi. She loves monsters and mythological creatures of all types, and they appear in her work pretty often. Along with writing, she loves to read. Her personal library is silly with books of all sorts. Travel, romance, murder mysteries, how-tos, art, biographies, and graphic novels have all found a way of filling up her shelf space.

Sheena's creative writing work has previously appeared in magazines like Gothic Fairy Tales for Melancholy Children *and* Mirror Dance. *Her non-fiction work includes her book* Computers 101 *published by Adapt Companies, and her contributions to* CampusJobXpress.Com *and* Zombie Guide Magazine.

WHAT THE PRODIGY LEARNS

BY MORGAN CROOKS

Marius watched the figure hurrying towards them and felt for the dagger concealed beneath this travel cloak, making sure it was still there. Tiberius was correct; the stranger was wearing centurion armor, as well as an Iberian short sword sheathed at his belt. From his speed and grace over the rocks, Marius judged him as military age, in other words, a threat.

"Maybe he's from a camp nearby?" Marius wondered out loud. "He could be foraging."

Tiberius shook his head. "The nearest garrison's back in Myra."

"A deserter then?"

"Possibly, but then why would he be running towards us?"

Marius watched the soldier round the final switch-back with growing unease.

"Are you in trouble?" the soldier shouted as he reached the Lycian ruins. He removed his helmet and Tiberius gasped. The same young soldier with the sure-footedness of a mountain goat bore the face of a septuagenarian. His head was entirely bald except for a fringe of white hair, his face wreathed in deep wrinkles. Peeking out from over his collar, Marius saw a deep white scar around his throat.

"Who are you?" Tiberius asked.

"My name is Cornicen," he said. "May I have the privilege of knowing whom I'm addressing?"

Tiberius gave a proper introduction for himself,

Marius, and then gestured at the unconscious bulk of Flaccus, propped up against a crumbling Lycian wall. "Our friend, Valerius Flaccus, had too much sun today. We'll need a wagon or something to get him back to the village."

"He appears to have had too much of a great many things." Cornicen frowned. "Has he been like this long?"

"Not long," Tiberius said and then with just a hair too much finality, he added, "We already have a boy running down to fetch help."

"So you'd like me to see where the boy's gotten to? What's the boy's name?"

"Groki," Tiberius lied.

"Groki? I've not heard of him before. Are you sure that he comes from Tal Podek? The village below? I confess that is a new name to me."

Marius' grandfather said deception didn't come easily to the equestrian order, reflexive and servile honesty bred into their very natures. Marius sighed. "To be sure, we wouldn't know. Would you perhaps be able to help us out?"

The old man smiled and adjusted the fold of his collar. "These mountains are no place to linger. I'm thinking it would be best to bring your friend away from here ourselves."

"Ourselves?" Tiberius laughed. "I nearly threw out my back dragging him to the wall. Do you expect to just sling him over a shoulder and carry him the whole way? Atlas couldn't carry him to the village."

The old man shrugged, swooped one hand beneath Flaccus and hoisted him to his feet. The cords of the soldier's legs and arms bunched and strained, but Cornicen's face remained as untroubled as Phidias' Zeus.

"I would take that wager," he said. "But if you help me our trip will go faster. Dark approaches."

Marius shrugged at his friend. "Every step closer is another coin we don't have to pay the inn-master for his wagon."

Tiberius gritted his teeth and rolled up his sleeves,

exposing the old fencing scar curling up his left forearm. Cornicen linked arms with Tiberius beneath Flaccus' shoulders and knees, each man gripping the other's wrist tightly, forming a cradle for the unconscious man's weight. When they were ready, the two lifted Flaccus into the air and set off, leaving Marius to stuff their belongings and cloaks into a sack. By the time he had started down the path, the two of them were already past the third switch-back. A blistering pace - one it appeared Tiberius struggled to maintain.

"Don't tire yourself," he heard the old man tell Tiberius. "I've got the issue well-in-hand. Just balance him out and we'll make it to Tal Podek with plenty of time to spare."

The route down the slope was tortured and winding, the path folding back on itself a number of times as it passed through the broken terrain. It had taken them most of the morning to reach the ancient Lycian ruins; it'd take well into the evening to return.

"It's lucky that you happened upon us," Marius asked when he caught up with Flaccus and his transports. "What were you doing out here?"

The old man turned his head slightly, eyeing Marius. "I live here."

"As a guard? For the town?"

"No, sir. I am no guard."

Tiberius was sweating freely at this point, straining to keep up his half of Flaccus, but he caught the general drift of Marius' questions. "Well, we owe you a drink at least."

"I do not drink."

Marius noted the flicker of displeasure on his friend's face. Letting the old man's help go unreturned would technically render all three of them clients to the soldier, obviously a distasteful scenario.

"Then perhaps we could add some weight to your purse?"

"I would not take money for such a light imposition."

Marius couldn't see how it could get much heavier.

"Then perhaps you'd care to dine with us, back at the inn. You could tell us tales of your service."

Now the old man's eyes twinkled. "Ah yes, young sir, that would be a welcome gift. I do have a few stories to share."

Cornicen proved only too happy to regale them with tales of the XV Corps, supporting the First Citizen's drive southward, chasing the whore and his shameless slave, Antonius.

"You were in Egypt, then?" Tiberius huffed.

"For a time, but I found my thoughts were always returning to this part of the world, Lycia and the pirate coast."

"Why in earth's name would you come back here?"

"I felt a pull," he said. "An attraction I can't explain. Some men are born in their homes and others have to search the world to find it. For me, home came quite late."

How late, Marius wondered, the dates not quite lining up in his mind. The Battle of Actium had occurred twenty years prior, which meant their companion had fought under Octavian's banner as a 40- or even 50-year-old man.

"And what about you three?" Cornicen asked.

"We're here to see the sights of ancient Lycia," Marius said.

"There are plenty of sights along the Lycian Way," Cornicen said. "Why are you in Tal Podek? Seems rather far afield."

"A little," Marius said, clutching his satchel with the wax tablet closer.

The old soldier grinned, his smile crooked and discolored but surprisingly full. "Perhaps you have heard of the legends of the Taurus Mountains? They're very amusing."

Tiberius laughed out loud, ignoring Marius' glare. "Oh, you're in the company of the grand satrap of near east legends, my aged friend. A regular Herodotus of Rome."

"Oh, how so?"

"He wouldn't be interested in my hobbies, Tiberius."

"Hobbies? Obsessions more like. Do you know what he is researching right now?"

The old soldier raised an eyebrow, shaking his head.

"Lyngurium. Have you ever heard of it?"

"I'm not sure, where do you find it?"

"According to Marius, right here. Well somewhere around here at the very least. Near Troy, or Pergamum or perhaps Damascus. He's always been cagey about its exact location. But rest assured, it's a fantastically wondrous substance, lyngurium. It's created, now get this, by a certain kind of cat which-"

"Lynx."

"What?"

"It's a solidification of male lynx urine."

"Whatever kind of animal it is, you told me this cat pisses on the ground and makes this rock which has all sorts of magical powers."

"Not magical, merely unusual. Theophrastus ascribed a number of beneficial properties to lyngurium. It would be a great achievement to see if the stories concerning its properties are factual."

"Magic kidney stones!" Tiberius said merrily. "Can you imagine it?"

The old man shook his head, but the look in eyes suggested anything but dismissal.

"Have you heard of this legend?" Marius asked when his friend's laughter died down.

"No, I've not but I know others you might enjoy."

"Trust me," Tiberius said. "If some Greek wrote it down, Marius wants to hear about it."

"Then perhaps you'd like to hear of the *chimaera*," the old man said.

"The what?"

Marius scowled. "You never finished Homer."

Tiberius and Cornicen had to pause while the young equestrian adjusted his grip. "The only part of Homer that's good is the part where Achilles finally starts slaughtering everyone. I don't go in for any of that kids' stuff."

"More's the pity," the soldier said. "A *chimaera* is a kind of monster, the front quarters of a lion, the body of a goat, and the tail of a cobra."

"If I remember the *chimaera* was supposed to spring from the hot springs of the Taurus Mountain."

The old man smiled.

Marius was about to ask the soldier more, but at that moment Flaccus' head lolled forward. Cornicen gestured for a nearby rock as their friend began groaning and mumbling to himself.

"What's he saying?" Marius asked.

Tiberius brought out his water skin but other than a few drops, it was empty. Fortunately the soldier's skin was full and he gently poured some of it into Flaccus' mouth. The senator's son murmured something to Tiberius and then fell unconscious again.

Tiberius grinned, "I think he's going to be okay."

Cornicen looked bewildered. "Did he just say something about finches? Does that mean something to you?"

Marius scratched the back of his head. "It's a sort of fad cure among the *nobiles*. I doubt it has any basis in fact but our friend swears by it."

"Then he's in luck," Cornicen said. "I just happen to know of an acquaintance a little bit farther down the path. As long as you paid for them, he wouldn't mind the sacrifice of a pigeon or two. He's a bit of a collector of rare birds."

Marius raised an eyebrow. "What sorts of rare birds?"

"All sorts," the soldier said. "Some for eating. Some for admiring. My friend has a few that might even interest a budding Herodotus of Rome."

Marius looked at Cornicen. "How so?"

Tiberius snorted. "Oh come on, Marius. Are you really that dense? Cornicen has a few *chimaera* running around that farm, don't you? A few coins and we'll even get to see a goat with a rug sewn over it."

Cornicen's expression darkened. "That is not the case."

"No? So maybe a hydra then, or a minotaur?"

"Nothing quite so extreme."

"Nothing we'd pay a few *denarii* for? What's the scheme then?"

"Tiberius Camillus!" Marius raised his hand in the air. "Will you drive this man away on account of a few coins?"

The soldier laughed. "Who's driving anyone away? The young sir was having some fun at a foolish old man. Quite understandable."

Tiberius was having none of it. "It was no accident we encountered you today."

"I am unconcerned with remuneration," Cornicen said, and Marius noted that the sour rusticism of his voice had dropped away, revealing a very precise and noble Latin not too far from what was uttered on the Senate floor.

"Lead the way," he told the soldier. Tiberius grumbled and then resumed his burden.

Finally, they reached the crest of a hill, perhaps only a mile outside of Tal Podek. Below stood a small farm house with mud-brick walls and a thatched roof. To the left was a simple barn with a low wall beyond marking off a pasture. The evening's first stars shone down hard on the fields of Lycia, and Marius's rubbed his arms vigorously to ward off the chill.

"What you want to see is in a cage within the barn."

"What I want to see is a table with food on it," Tiberius said.

"Of course, of course," the soldier said. "Let me rouse the farmer."

When the soldier was gone, Marius felt his friend staring at him. "What?" Marius asked at last.

"You're looking at the barn."

"So what?"

"So, I'm wondering if you think you're going to see

some real live *chimaera*. Because after you're not quite satisfied with that, he's going to mention this little valley out there in the hills. Some place really isolated that he just happens to know a path to. Then we're going to get robbed and-"

"Have a little faith."

"Faith? That this whole countryside would like nothing better than to rob, murder, and bury a bunch of Romans? Yeah, I've got plenty of that."

"Cornicen is a Roman."

"Then he's gone native. Which is assuming he's even Roman, which I'm not so sure of."

"He's helped us this far, the least we can do it humor him."

At that moment Cornicen shut the door of the farmhouse and began walking back up to the two of them, carrying a lit lantern. He informed them that the farmer had agreed to put them up for the night, even letting them have their bedroom. All he asked was that they help bring some bedding out to the barn to make their stay more comfortable.

Approaching the barn, they saw a number of farm animals dozing in one corner of the pasture. A few of them turned their eyes to watch the trio pass by and they heard a cow breathing roughly.

"A fine horde of monsters we've got here," Tiberius said.

"These are not the *chimaera*," Cornicen said.

The soldier lead them to the back corner of the barn, raising his lantern to reveal a large wicker cage suspended from the rafters. Marius stared at it for a moment, trying to understand what he was seeing. Tiberius leaned forward, causing one of the creatures to flutter its wings. Tiberius jumped backwards, his face suddenly pale.

"What is wrong with those birds?" he said.

"Nothing," the soldier said, untwisting the latch on the cage's door and plucking out one of its captives. Its tiny feet stuck out from the bottom of his fist and its furry head swiveled around in fright, a tiny wrinkled nose trembling, fox-like ears swiveling.

"Don't get too close, Marius."

"I've told you, they are not dangerous," the soldier said.

"They are not natural!"

"It is entirely natural," the soldier insisted. "It was through natural means they were created."

He used his other hand to gently pull back the ruff of fur on the creature's neck, exposing a pale line, a mushroom white scar, between the fur of the head and the feathers of its breast. "As you can see, the substrate is applied at the splice. As the grafting process takes hold, all of the veins and humors of the two creatures meet in the substrate and continue on as before. I'm told that this is actually quite crude work. In the ancient days, such joins were made with such delicacy, the splice couldn't even be detected."

"Grafts? Splicing?" Tiberius looked like he was going to throw up. "You've taken a bat and a bird and made some kind of perversion."

Marius put his hand on his friend's shoulder. "Calm yourself, Tiberius. This is not witchcraft. I've seen the slaves on my family's estate produce pears from quince trees with nothing more than a pair of shears and some-"

"I think we've seen quite enough for tonight," Tiberius interrupted.

Marius was about to protest but the lines on his friend's face were set, implacable.

"As you prefer," Cornicen held open the door to the wicker cage so the 'bird' could return to its roost. As Marius pulled his hand back from the cage, the animals began to screech, thrumming their wings. Through the slats of the barn, Marius caught sight of a figure standing up on a rock. He bent back down, trying to catch sight of him, but the figure was already gone. He guessed he had seen a shepherd, wearing some kind of fur hat to protect against the cold. With so much to consider, Marius put it from his mind.

The next morning, Marius awoke with sounds of uproar coming from the next room. He sat upright in the cot, recognizing the bellows as coming from Flaccus. Pushing the door to the farmer's tiny bedroom, he found his patrician friend sweeping clay pots off of a rough wooden table while the farmer cowered along the wall.

"Flaccus! What are you doing?"

"You! What are we doing here? Where did you two drag me last night?"

"Drag you?" and suddenly Marius found it difficult to maintain an even tone of voice. "We didn't drag you, Tiberius and I carried you here. You were passed out drunk!"

Flaccus' nostrils flared out and his eyes threatened to pop right out of their sockets. All at once, a change came over him and he began to squeal with laughter. This alarmed the farmer more than the shouting and he edged closer to the door.

"Oh my," his breath whistled through his mouth. "I thought I had been kidnapped! I thought you had sold me into slavery!"

Marius began picking up some of the pots and vases Flaccus had knocked over. "Who on earth would buy you?"

"I wasn't sure," he wheezed. "It just seemed like something that might have happened. My gods, I am famished. My head is splitting apart. Could you do a favor for me and find the person who hit me with a rock and brain him for me? An eye for an eye?"

"If you stop scaring our host half to death, I'm sure he would be willing to heat up some of the stew from last night." Marius looked over at the farmer who seemed about ready to bolt like a rabbit. "It was very good, Deru," he pantomimed enjoying another bowl of the soup. "Could you perhaps heat up some more? We can pay-"

"A stew? What are you trying to do to me, Marius.

Starve me? You know what I want."

His cure. Hadn't Cornicen told them the farmer had a few chickens on the farm? With luck they might have a few chicks to fry. He tried to make his request intelligible to the farmer but succeeded in only further confusing him. Marius felt a faint twinge of shame, one more Roman invading a home for pillage. This would not do. Flaccus would not be placated without his morning-after meal, but he couldn't calm the farmer down enough to get what he needed.

Fortunately, even as he started hunting around for his sandals, the door opened, producing Tiberius, a freshly butchered bird in each hand. He had a wild expression on his face, and blood splattered on his arms past his elbows.

"Breakfast is ready!"

Seeing Tiberius, the farmer's eyes went large and he produced a stream of foreign invective. Not a word of it was comprehensible to the three Romans, but its meaning was clear when he pushed past Tiberius to run out into the morning fog. Tiberius had probably slaughtered his prize hens. Marius made himself remember to leave an extra coin for the man before they left.

"Who's hungry for fried canaries?" Tiberius said, still grinning.

Afterwards, the three of them producing a stream of impressive belches, Tiberius and Marius began telling him of their adventures from the day before. They had just reached the point of introducing Cornicen when Flaccus broke in.

"And where is this new friend?" Flaccus asked. "I seem to owe him a debt. A Valerius must repay his debts."

Marius confessed he didn't know. Tiberius said when he had woken up he heard the farmer and the soldier talking together.

"Then he went out."

Marius thought about this for a second, something not quite jibing in his mind. "But before he went, he must have spoken to you?"

"No, why do you ask?" a strange fury entered into Tiberius' face, almost like he was daring Marius to press the question. Marius felt a slow sinking feeling.

"Then the chickens, how did you know where they were? I didn't see any last night."

"Who said I found any chickens?"

Marius felt the blood drain from his face and hands. "You didn't."

Flaccus looked back and forth between his friends, bewildered. "Am I missing something? Is something wrong with the food?"

Again Tiberius looked at his friend, daring him to tell Flaccus the truth. A lethal truth because they both knew that Flaccus would not, could not, permit Tiberius to travel with them if he knew what they had just eaten.

Once more it fell to the patrician to manufacture the convenient lie.

"Ah, no. They are fine. I just thought we were supposed to wait for our friend to come back with chickens from town instead of raiding this poor farmer's coop."

Flaccus smirked. "What's the big deal? Are you afraid you ate their sacred chicken gods? They tasted fine, a little bland perhaps. Don't get me worried."

Tiberius' face was a careful mask. "Like he said, what's the big deal?"

That night, back at the post-house, Marius worked in the dark of the night, writing down everything he had seen. At some point the noises of debauchery below faded but the expected return of his friends to the room never happened. Perhaps they had gone out. He started to head out of the room when he heard a tap against the shutters of the window in his room.

The old soldier crouched against the shingles of the house, a dark shape pressed close to the window. His eyes bore into Marius', his mismatched teeth grinding together.

"You have made a serious mistake," he told Marius.

"I awoke too late, I couldn't stop him."

"Then you should have waited for me at the farm house, explained what your friend had done. It may have gone a long way to avoiding misunderstandings."

Marius thought quickly, unnerved by the stern expression on the soldier's face. "We will leave the village tomorrow; you'll never see us again. If it's a question of restitution, I will pay any reasonable fee you name."

"Yes, restitution must be made," the soldier said and as he pushed open the window, Marius noted an old, familiar scar running up his arm. "But a restitution in kind."

"I'm not sure where we could find birds like those you showed us. How can we pay in kind?" He suddenly felt like he didn't want to know the answer that question.

"Your friends found a way," the soldier said. "Flesh for flesh."

The soldier was in the room now, and Marius backed away from him, his hands feeling for the latch of his door. He didn't start to panic until he discovered it was locked from the outside. "It was a mistake. A simple mistake."

Cornicen plucked at the collar of his tunic, revealing once more the thick white line encircling his neck. For the first time, Marius noted how very different the shade and texture of his chest was from his neck. The soldier smiled and drew his sword from its sheath. "And do you think my mistake was so large? More serious than yours? More serious than your friend, Tiberius, and that fat sack of shit, Flaccus? I assure you it was not. And yet you'll pay all the same."

Morgan Crooks grew up in a hamlet in Upstate New York and now teaches ancient history in Massachusetts. His story, "What the Prodigy Learns," is his fourth published work, although more of his stories are available on the Daily Science Fiction *website and in* Dark Hall Press Ghost Anthology.

Reviews and other essays are available on the Ancient Logic *website (www.ancientlogic.blogspot.com). He lives with his wife, Lauren, near Boston with one professional cat and one amateur dog.*

LAGUNA DEL ESPIRITU SANTO

BY DAVID BERNARD

The western sun will soon begin its daily voyage behind the mangroves, offering a brief respite from the oppressive humidity before the mosquitoes began their nightly assault. The moon will again rise languidly over the shattered turrets of the *castillo*, a sight I have never grown tired of watching. The shadows will almost hide the scarred stonework. The view does not inspire fear as much as it evokes empathy. For as the moon casts the shadow of the ruined *castillo* across the endless swamps of the *Laguna del Espíritu Santo*, it appears as if the skeletal fingers of the very darkness itself are reaching out to find an escape from this hellish miasma called *la Florida*. I too know that feeling of hopelessly seeking a way out.

Castillo de San María de los Dolores was my father's "reward," a vast estate in *la Florida*. At least that is what we believed when we set sail from our beloved *España*. What my father did not know was that the *Reyes de España* was trying to strengthen his claim to *la Florida*. The French king Louis XIV had begun to cast a greedy eye on the territory and his Spanish Majesty was granting large estates to reaffirm his claim to the lands. Unfortunately, many of these grants were in places that had not been explored, such as *Laguna del Espíritu Santo*, which as far as I could tell, was composed of a never-ending wasteland of swamps as far as the eye could see. To refuse a gift from the King was a fatal insult to crown and country. So, in the accursed year of 1653, my father built a fine *castillo* on the closest thing he could find that passed as solid land – a small hill surrounded by stinking swamps, razor sharp plants and the voracious demon *cocodrilos y caimanes*.

My sainted mother died almost immediately of fever. My brothers fled soon after, seeking the coast and passage northward to *San Agustín*. We have heard from neither of my brothers since, and I can only hope they survived the trek and are safely living once again in the fertile hills of *España*. That left but the two of us: my father, who is all but mad from grief and guilt, and me, a *mujer soltera de la nobleza*, with no prospect of marriage save the occasional miserable suitor braving the swamp to inherit Father's title. They certainly do not covet our lands and I have forever given up on marrying for love. This is my wretched existence, thanks to my father's "good fortune."

In 1656, the Timucua savages rebelled across la Florida. My father's workers joined the rebellion, destroying the dikes that kept the glade water out of the crops, and setting fire to the *castillo*. This was more than my poor father could bear. Now Father is bedridden in his room, a helpless invalid. I dwell in the few rooms that are still habitable. Without the slaves, we are unable to repair the damage. Since my father is ill, I must work like a common villager, farming and cooking to survive. In some ways, I believe that the *castillo* reflects my father's decline. Both are, at first glance, ready to collapse at any moment, but both have an inner strength that belies their outward appearance.

A horse whinnied in the distance, breaking my reverie. Soon, gaily trotting down the trampled muck that served as a path came a strutting peacock. I sighed to myself. It was another *señor soldado*, a plump dandy pretending to be a military man. I did not need a perfumed fop from the old country - soft hands were useless for rebuilding the *castillo* and ceremonial swords could not stave off Timucua warriors.

He gracelessly dismounted and doffed his hat in an overly grand bow. "*Doña* Maria Ana Reyes y Lucientes, I am *el*

Capitán Juan Bautista Suáre. I have come to rescue you from these dreadful swamps by asking your father for your hand *en santo matrimonio.*"

Not only was he pompous, he was brazen. I took an immediate dislike to him, but a noblewoman must play the part of hostess, even in a Godforsaken swamp. "Welcome to *Castillo de San María de los Dolores, el Capitán.*" I forced a curtsy. "Please come in. I shall tell Father of your arrival. He has been ill, but I am sure he will be delighted to learn of your arrival."

I ushered him into the main hall. I saw his eyes narrow in distaste at the fire ravaged walls, my crude repairs to the furniture and the water stained tapestries. I was equally unimpressed with him, short and portly, reeking of fine scented oils. He said nothing as he surveyed the hall, which told me I was right – I was mere chattel to be acquired so he could assume my father's title. The moment Father died, *el Capitán* would drag me from our battered *castillo* to someplace even worse, perhaps even among the cannibals in the Caribbean.

I offered him a decanter of wine. He poured far more than a polite amount into a goblet and guzzled it down, belched contently, and then refilled it. I turned toward the stairs to mask my distaste.

I ascended the stairs, preparing to give Father a full report on the swine befouling our threshold. I paused, "Please make yourself comfortable, *el Capitán.*" I hoped the irony in my voice was not too obvious. "I shall inform my father of your arrival."

I turned at the landing to glance down at the pompous ass. "I should advise you that Father already knows I shall refuse all suitors while he is an invalid. He cannot travel nor can he live alone in the *castillo*. Our agreement is that I will wed, but only if my suitor will dwell here with us in the *castillo*." I saw the look of greed momentarily replaced by dread at the thought of living here in *Castillo de San María de los Dolores*. I knew the look well. There have been other suitors and yet I still remain a single woman.

I knocked on my father's door. Before Father could answer, the oafish *el Capitán*, goblet of wine sloshing in his hand, charged up the stairs and pushed me aside. With all pretense of civility evaporated, he entered my father's quarters uninvited. One does not ignore niceties when meeting a scion of conquistadores and I eagerly waited for my father to belittle the preening magpie's lack of manners.

Indeed, as expected, *el Capitán*, shrieking like a frightened infant, came running from the room. He looked at me, his eyes wide with terror. I assumed he was about to apologize for his inexcusable rudeness, but the poison in the wine was beginning to work.

He collapsed, foaming at the mouth. I ignored the twitching form and rushed into my father's chambers. As I feared, he had greatly disturbed poor Father. The loathsome toad had tossed the goblet of wine at my invalid father. I sopped up the wine as best I could and then carefully picked up my poor, sick father's skull from the corner where it had rolled after the goblet struck him. Carefully placing it back on the pillow above his spine, I kissed him goodnight and reassured him I would not be leaving with this poor excuse of a suitor.

Tonight, the moon again rose over *Castillo de San María de los Dolores*. Unfortunately, I missed the night's spectral scene for I was intent on dragging the corpse of my former suitor, *el Capitán* Juan Bautista Suáre, into the swamps so that the *cocodrilos y caimanes* could dispose of his carcass before the heat began to bloat his body to match his ego. Father said he is pleased I have decided not to leave.

David Bernard is the pen name of Dave Goudsward, a native New Englander who now lives (albeit under protest) in South Florida, a paradoxical place where, when temperatures drops below 60,, locals break out parkas to wear over their shorts and sandals. His most recent works include short stories in anthologies such as

Once upon an Apocalypse, Strangely Funny II, *and* Mortis Operandi. *His newest book is* A Horror Guide to Massachusetts *from Post Mortem Press.*

THE CURSE OF GLAMIS CASTLE

BY COLUMBKILL NOONAN

Allister Sheehy, gentlemen-usher to the sixth Lord of Glamis, was both excited and sad at the same time. Excited, because today he was to be promoted to become Lord John Lyon's head steward, a position for which he had been training all of his life. Sad, because his promotion meant that the man beneath whom he had trained, Lyall Coburn, Lord John's current head steward, was dying.

In truth, this was not unexpected. Lyall was quite old, and had been feeling unwell for some time. For the last year, he had been forced to take to his bed more and more often, leaving Allister to unofficially assume the duties of head steward. But this time was different, for Lyall was not expected to rise from his bed again, and, indeed, few thought that he would last out the month.

From the time that Allister had come into service in Castle Glamis, Lyall had acted as a mentor to the youth, teaching him all of the subtle nuances involved in servicing the temperamental Lord John. Through Lyall, Allister had learned to anticipate the oft-times unreasonable and sometimes maleficent whims of the sixth Lord of Glamis, and thereby be prepared to either satisfy or tactfully circumvent the caprices of his master.

Because of Lyall's attentions, Allister had been able to rise from a mere apprentice gentleman-of-the-chamber to the exalted position which he was now about to take. As the young son of a cobbler from the nearby town of Forfar,

Allister had never expected to rise so highly in the world. In his entire life, he had never even left the valley of Strathmore, within which both Glamis and Forfar were situated, but now, as head steward, he very well might be expected to occasionally accompany Lord John on his frequent trips to Edinburgh.

More often, he would be left in charge of the castle during his master's absences. The disposition of the castle servants, the ordering of finances, and the procurement of the enormous quantities of supplies required by a castle of such a grand size as Glamis; all of these things would be his domain. Allister was much pleased with his success, and his humble parents were very proud indeed.

However, Lyall had been more than just the superior who had trained the lad. Over the years, he had also become a friend. When Lyall took to his bed for the last time, loyal Allister, knowing that his mentor's active mind would chafe at the confinement made necessary by the infirmity of his body, made certain to spend some time every evening with him to help him pass the time. Allister would help Lyall to sit up in his bed, propping his back against the bed pillows, while he himself sat upon the bedside chair in the old steward's small chamber. The two men, the old and the young, would sit thus together in the dim candlelight, reading or talking quietly.

And so it was that, one evening, as the darkness of night deepened over the castle, Allister, finished with his duties for the day, made his way to his friend's bedchamber as was his custom. This night, however, he found Lyall's manner to be agitated and distracted. Concerned at his friend's strange mien, and fearing that Lyall's health might be deteriorating to such a degree as to cause this odd mood, Allister fussed over him, fluffing the pillows behind Lyall's back and ordering the blankets repeatedly until Lyall impatiently waved him away.

"Sit, will you?" Lyall barked with uncharacteristic brusqueness.

Startled, Allister obeyed, and sat heavily on his

customary chair. Chastised and taken aback by Lyall's abrupt manner, he remained silent, and simply sat blinking at his old friend in some astonishment.

"You mustn't be so sensitive," Lyall scolded. "I've told you a hundred times, to serve a lord your skin can't be as thin as a dry leaf, can it?" Then, seeing Allister's chagrin, he softened. "Ah, lad, but you must excuse an old man his crankiness," he said by way of apology. "It's just that there is something that I must tell you, and it weighs hard on me."

"What is it?" asked Allister, eager to ease his friend's burden. "Don't fear to tell me, Lyall. I can handle it, whatever it may be."

Lyall smiled ruefully. "Don't be so quick to say so, my friend. You will feel differently once you hear what I have to tell."

"It cannot be so terrible," said Allister. "Tell me, I beg you! The anticipation must be worse than the tale itself."

"You'll wish it was, son, that you will. I am loath to bequeath this burden unto you, but it's something that the head steward must know, and since I'll be gone soon, you must take responsibility of this thing. That is the way of it and there's nothing for it but to tell you," said Lyall.

"Does this have to do with the secret of Glamis?" Allister asked, his curiosity much piqued by the old man's cryptic words. All of the castle servants, indeed everyone who lived in the countryside surrounding the castle, had heard something of the terrible secret hidden within the castle walls. Some believed in the secret, others thought it a mere tale to frighten babes. But whether one believed or not, all those who dwelt near to Glamis had grown up hearing the whispers about the castle. Some said that there was a secret room hidden within the castle, some claimed that a dreadful curse had been laid upon the place, and yet others said that it was haunted by the ghosts of the many who had died by various nefarious means over the centuries. "Please, Lyall, I am ready," said Allister. "Please tell me."

"No, you are not," said Lyall. "No one could ever be ready for this. For I am indeed going to tell you the true secret of Glamis, and it is a tale so monstrous, a burden so cruel, that only two people in the world must ever know it: the Lord of Glamis and his head steward. Once I tell you there is no going back. You must never tell another living soul, save for the man who will take your place upon your death. The secret will be yours to keep, until death releases you from its dreadful burden. Are you sure that you still want this?"

Allister, sensing that his friend was of the utmost seriousness, and that he was about to be entrusted with a matter of the gravest importance, nodded with solemnity.

Lyall nodded, a gesture that somehow conveyed a sense of momentous finality. "So be it," he said. "I hereby impart the secret of Glamis unto you. The burden is yours now. Bear it well, my son." And, so saying, he began his tale, as Allister listened raptly.

"A hundred years ago," began Lyall, his voice becoming deep and entrancing as though he were a very bard from the times when druids held sway over Scotland, "the whole of Strathmore valley, including Glamis Castle and Forfar, were ruled by the second Lord of Glamis, Alexander Lyon. Tales of Alexander's cruelty and iniquity were whispered of throughout the valley, and all of the people lived in fear of the thought of his wicked eye falling upon them. Of course, Lord Alexander's greatest act of vile atrocity, in which he murdered his mother's own kin, the Ogilvies, within this very castle, had yet to occur. No, the tale that I tell now occurred nearly half a century before that foul deed, whilst Alexander's father, Lord Patrick, was still the Lord of Glamis. But, although Alexander was still little more than a boy at this time and had yet to realize the full potential of his sadism, his qualities of callous spitefulness and vicious brutality were known and feared throughout the land. It is from the evil of Alexander that the curse of Glamis was sprung, a bane to plague Alexander and his heirs until the end of time.

"It so happened that when the young Lord Alexander was but eleven years old, his father granted him his own page. This page, a lad of nine years named Colin, was an earnest, kindly youth. His mother, Elspeth, was the widow of a local laird, and a lady-in-waiting to Alexander's mother, the Lady Isabel.

"Elspeth saw well the malignancy that blackened the soul of young Alexander, and warned her son that he must always be careful in his dealings with the young lord. She observed the vicious punishments that he ordered upon the servants for the smallest of transgressions, and she also saw the ways in which he abused the youngest of the castle maids and scullery girls. Though he had the barest beginnings of a man's beard upon his chin, still he was known to grope and fondle the girls, whilst they, fearful of his angry reprisal should they reject his advances, were forced to suffer this mistreatment in silence.

"In truth, Elspeth was far from pleased when the Lord of Glamis ordered that Colin was to serve Alexander, and she worried always for his safety. But one in her position did not lightly refuse the gifts of a lord, and so she was forced to feign gladness at the honor bestowed upon her son. Still, knowing the consequences that could come from drawing the ire of the young lord, she admonished her son to give Alexander no reason, however small, for displeasure.

"And so it was that Colin strove always to be the perfect page, faithfully completing his duties properly and without delay. Never did he allow his friendly, respectful manner towards his master to slip, even for a moment. When Alexander and Colin played at games of war, sparring with wooden swords or testing each other's skills of horsemanship or jousting, Colin never allowed himself to best Alexander, whilst always maintaining the illusion that he was indeed trying his best to do so. In this way, Colin avoided offending his callous young master, and indeed, the boys became friends of a sort.

"One winter's evening, however, everything changed. Lord Glamis and his family were sitting down to dinner, and Colin, as was customary, was responsible for serving Alexander. He was bringing a pitcher of mead to refill his master's cup when a hound, eager to snatch up a piece of meat which had just fallen, darted out from beneath the table directly into Colin's path. Colin, not seeing the dog until too late, tripped over the beast and stumbled. He managed to regain his balance quickly, but was unable to prevent a small quantity of mead from spilling onto Alexander's sleeve.

"Conversation stopped as everyone in the room fell into silence, steeling themselves for the fit of rage that they knew was to come. Colin himself froze, terrified to see the look of cold malice upon Alexander's face, that look which he had all too often seen directed at others, now aimed, for the first time, at him instead.

"'You buffoon,' said Alexander softly. 'You've wetted my sleeve.'

"'I am terribly sorry, my lord. The hound came out, I tripped, I never meant to...'

"Alexander raised a hand to hush his erstwhile friend. 'Enough excuses,' he said. 'I pronounce that, in punishment, you will go to the sitting room, dressed only in your nightclothes, and sit on a stool in the corner, for your embarrassment and disgrace to serve as amusement for the rest of us. You will stay thus until I release you.'

"Both Colin and his mother heaved a sigh of relief. The punishment was not so dire after all.

"'Yes, sir. Thank you for your mercy, my lord,' effused Colin.

"Alexander dismissed him, saying, 'Hie you now to the sitting room. You'd best be on your stool when I arrive, or it shall go ill for you.'

"Colin bowed and hurried away to his small chamber to change into his nightclothes. Once so dressed, he hastened to the sitting room and pulled a stool into the corner to await his humiliation. The fire in the hearth burned low; since the room had been unoccupied for most of the day it had been left for the most part untended, and would only be stoked moments before Alexander arrived. The frigid wintery wind outside probed its icy fingers into the old window casements, searching for any cracks of ingress, of which it found many, chilling young Colin where he sat covered only in his thin nightdress. Furthermore, the stool upon which he sat was hard and unyielding, and Colin shifted uncomfortably as he waited for his lord and the other young men of the castle to arrive and begin his mockery.

"However, Alexander and his friends did not come. One of them brought up the idea that it would surely be an entertaining diversion if they were to take themselves with all subterfuge into the chamber to which the ladies were to retire after dinner, hide themselves, and see what feminine mysteries they might uncover. Alexander thought this a splendid idea, and the youths left the table with all haste to make for the ladies' chamber, in order to stow themselves away unseen before the women arrived.

"So it was that Colin was left to wait, forsaken as Alexander, stuffed in a small side chamber with three other castle lads, giggled with the headiness of their game. After several hours, of course, the game became dull, and the boys tired of watching the women as they played at cards, plied their embroidery needles, or simply sat talking quietly to one another. The hidden boys, crammed tightly together into a small space, became restless, and shifted about uncomfortably. In truth, they were relieved when the ladies retired and they could emerge from their hiding place to stretch their cramped limbs.

"Tired from their long night, the boys congratulated each other on their cleverness at remaining uncaught, and each went off to his own sleeping chambers. Alexander, in his selfishness and narcissism, had completely forgotten about

Colin and the fact that he had been ordered to sit upon the stool until released, and so he made for his own nice, warm chamber and fell into bed, there to sleep soundly until morning.

"And so Colin waited. As the hours stretched on, the fire eventually sputtered and died entirely. Thus was Colin left defenseless to the chill tendrils of winter winds that found their way through the cracks in the window casement to dance about his barely clothed body, tormenting him with the cold.

"But still, he dared not move, for fear of arousing Alexander's anger. So he sat, uncomfortable and cold on the incommodious stool. As the night wore on, and the cold became more insidious, his discomfort turned to misery, his misery to wretchedness.

"Eventually, exhaustion overtook him, and despite the pain in his legs and buttocks and the chill that bit into his very soul, his head slowly drooped down towards his chest and he fell into a woeful, tormented sleep.

"Sadly, Colin would never wake up from that sleep, for just before dawn, the cold won out and the life was frozen from his sad, young body. He was discovered in the morning by a maid who had come to clean the room. She saw him, still sitting rigidly upon that stool, his chin resting upon his breast, his pallor the terrible grey color of the tomb. Screaming, she roused the castle and all gathered round to see what they could see.

"Elspeth shrieked in anguish when she saw her son, and fell to her knees before him, trying to revive him. But alas, her efforts were to no avail, for his soul had long since departed his icy body. Disconsolate, she was led, sobbing, out of the room by the other ladies-in-waiting.

"As she passed by Alexander, she looked up, beheld his countenance, and was shocked. For upon the features of his face, she saw no remorse, nor even regret at the death of the boy who had been his friend, and her son. Instead, incredibly, she saw nothing but boredom writ upon his petulant, fleshy features.

"Indeed, he spared her not a glance as she was pulled out of the room, and instead seemed to idly consider his fingernails with lassitude. He sighed, and said, "Well, that's done. Who's for hunting today?" She quivered with outrage as she pulled away from the other ladies and fled to her chamber to consider the cruelty of her loss, and the wickedness of the youth who had engendered it. Quickly, her anguish turned into a cold rage, and her grief screamed for reprisal."

"Oh!" interjected Allister, unable to contain his enthusiasm. "You're talking about the little boy whose ghost haunts the sitting room upstairs!"

"Yes, yes, that's the boy," agreed Lyall, a bit annoyed at having been interrupted.

"I have heard of him before," said Allister, "but I never knew the real story of how he died, or why his ghost lingered there in that room. Is that the secret that you wanted to tell me?"

"It's part of it, boy," grumbled Lyall, lowering his eyebrows to glower at Allister. "But it's just the beginning. Listen now, and don't interrupt."

Allister bowed his head, and folded his hands in his lap meekly.

Satisfied that his young charge was sufficiently chastened, Lyall continued with his story.

"Anyway," he began, "as I was saying, Elspeth was distraught not just by the untimely and senseless death of her son, but also by the grievous negligence of Alexander which had been the cause of young Colin's demise. Such grief and outrage can easily turn to hate, and so it was with Elspeth, who vowed to have her revenge upon the heartless young lord who had killed her son so cruelly.

"Therefore, after lying in her chamber alone, weeping

and thinking, for some hours, she sat up, having decided upon a course of action in which she would avenge Colin's death upon Alexander; indeed, upon the entire cursed family that had spawned such a monster.

"Her tears dried upon her cheeks, and her face was as cold and implacable as stone as she made her way out of the chamber, along the hallway, and down a narrow winding stair to the main floor. Other ladies, seeing her pass by, tried to waylay her, to offer her comfort, but she would have none of it, and merely passed by any who tried to stop her without giving any indication that she was aware that anyone was there.

"In such a way, she eventually came to the dining chamber, and passed through it to exit through a small side door that took her out of the castle entirely. Purposefully, she strode across the wide, manicured castle grounds. At the edge of the soft grass that framed the castle, where the dark, old woods met the civilized, open space, was a path. Elspeth headed unerringly for this path, and set foot upon it with no hesitation. For she knew where she was going, or, more precisely, to whom she was going. She was going to a woman as far removed from the polished and elegant people in the castle as the dense trees of the forest were from the clipped lawns upon which the delicate shoes of those people trod.

"The woman to whom Elspeth's determined steps were taking her was an old crone named Segna. Segna lived deep in the woods, betwixt Glamis Castle and Forfar. Segna lived alone in her small wooden house in the forest. This in itself was enough to breed suspicion amongst the superstitious townsfolk, but the fact that Segna was also an accomplished herbal healer and behaved in a confident, independent manner that was considered most indecorous led to even more distrust. Because of this, shocking rumors about Segna had been whispered for as long as anyone could remember. Indeed, most of the inhabitants of both Forfar as well as those in the castle believed Segna to be a witch.

"Regardless of the rumors, however, Segna's skill as a healer, and her proficiency with the various herbs of the forest and tinctures of the cauldron, was such that the townsfolk were willing to grudgingly overlook the old woman's eccentricities in exchange for her services. And although the Kirk taught that all witchcraft was of the devil himself, and that those who practiced magic were of the utmost evil and should be reviled and rebuked unto death, there was enough of their old Celtic heritage in the people to be a bit more accepting of her than their holy bishop in Dunkeld might like. Even the parish priest had been known to sneak off of an evening to avail himself of her healing herbs.

"But it was for no herb that Elspeth now made her way through the dark, forest track to the home of Segna. No, Elspeth was in search of vengeance most foul, and only the ancient magic of the druids would suffice. For Elspeth wanted to supplicate herself to goddesses of the Celtic Otherworld, and beseech them to aid her in her quest for requital against the Lords Glamis.

"Like most folk of the time, Elspeth had grown up hearing tales of the religion of her Celtic ancestors. Indeed, despite the best efforts of the Pope and the archbishops, the pagan Celtic religion had never been completely eradicated. Beltane fires could be seen burning in the ancient sacred oak groves each spring, and at Samhain, or All Saints Day as it was now called, it was not uncommon for the people to set out empty dinner plates to honor their dead ancestors, in spite of the Kirk's official stance against such heathen practices.

"So it was that Elspeth was quite familiar with many of the gods and goddesses of the Otherworld, and she knew exactly whom she desired to contact. To feed her black hatred, to accomplish the vile vengeance that would appease her seething outrage, only the three dread Battle Sisters, Mor-Rioghain, Badhba, and Macha, would suffice. But these were powerful beings, and not to be trifled with. Summoning them would require skill, and knowledge of magic and of rituals, that Elspeth did not possess. For such a feat, she needed a witch of powerful, druidic magic. A witch such as Segna.

"At last Elspeth's determined footsteps brought her to the doorstep of Segna's ramshackle, dilapidated wooden house. No more than a hovel, the hut, built in the circular fashion of the old days, leaned precariously. The thatching on the roof needed patching, and the wooden planks that led up to the door groaned alarmingly when Elspeth stepped upon them. But she was not to be deterred, and resolutely marched up to the door and knocked loudly without delay.

"No one answered. Elspeth knocked again, even harder this time, to no avail. Uncertainty entered her mind for the first time since she had embarked on her mission. It had taken all of her courage, fueled by her grief and rage, to propel her down the wooded trail to the home of Segna. But Segna wasn't home, and in the face of this unforeseen delay Elspeth's resolve to pursue this course of action began to waver. She stood conflicted on the doorstep, looking this way and that, her anger demanding immediate action, her fear begging that she leave off this business and retreat back to the castle.

"As she stood thus, vacillating, a wrinkled, stooped old woman emerged from the woods behind her. Moving with surprising stealth for her age, she crept up unseen behind Elspeth and watched her for a moment, trying to ascertain what this fancy creature from the castle was about. This was Segna, and long years of abuse at the hands of the townsfolk as well as from the people in the castle had taught her a prudent suspicion that had served her well over the years. Many an unsuspecting visitor, deemed by Segna to have spurious motives, was left to wait on that doorstep until at last the supplicant gave up and left, thwarted. But Segna saw honest anguish and desperation in Elspeth's face, and decided to see what she wanted.

"'What can I do you for, dovie?' she said from behind Elspeth, her clear voice belying her great age.

"Elspeth jumped, startled, and let out a small scream. She turned and saw Segna. Tiny, bone-thin, and fragile-looking, Segna did not appear to be the frightening witch for whom she had steeled her nerves. The only feature that was remotely disturbing about her was her eyes. An icy, white-blue, they shone from her sagging face with a preternatural brightness. Elspeth had never seen eyes like that, and couldn't decide if she found them entrancingly beautiful or eerily frightening. Perhaps, she thought, a little of both. But aside from Segna's eyes, she seemed nothing more than an aged old lady. Elspeth breathed a sigh of relief, and hurried over to the old woman.

'"I need your help," she began. "With a matter of some delicacy."

'"And why do you come to me?" asked Segna. "Is there no one else who can help you? One of your fancy friends in the castle, perhaps?"

'"No, no," said Elspeth. "You are the only one. I need someone who knows…that is, someone who can…" She hesitated, afraid now to confess her plan. Practicing the ancient arts was a dangerous business, and if caught she could easily end up burnt at the stake, or worse.

'"You need someone who knows the old ways," sighed Segna, "and someone who can keep your secret for you. Am I right?"

'"Yes! That is it!" cried Elspeth, grateful that Segna had been able to glean her mission from her so easily. "Will you help me?"

'"We'll see, dovie," said Segna. "But first you must tell me everything. Best to come inside." She paused, and peered about her, looking with keen eyes into the shadows beneath the trees. "You never know who's listening."

'"Thank you, oh, thank you," said Elspeth, and so saying, she took Segna by the arm, as if to help the old woman to the door. Segna, who was fully capable of walking on her own, shook her head and smiled, but allowed Elspeth to lead her inside nonetheless.

"The two women thus entered the house, and Elspeth found herself in a dim room that was lit only by one small, wax-paper covered window. She blinked her eyes, trying to see in the gloom, as Segna extricated herself from Elspeth's grasp and busied herself with lighting a candle, which she placed on a rickety wooden table at the other end of the room.

"Now that the candle was lit, Elspeth's eyes had enough light to better see her surroundings. In the center of the room stood a hearth fire, which, though cold now, would, when lit, be vented out through a narrow smoke-hole that exited from the peak of the badly thatched roof. A straw sleeping pallet was off to one side, and a rough wooden trestle, stacked high with baskets of herbs and flowers, on another. Two wooden stools sat near to the hearth, and Segna motioned for Elspeth to sit.

"Once they were both seated, Segna began.

"'Tell me your business," she said. "And be clear about it. I don't want to waste my time trying to guess what it is you want." She laughed wryly. "As you can see, I'm old, and I have little enough time left."

'Elspeth took a deep breath and let it out slowly. At last, she mustered her courage and decided it was best to just get it out, and quickly. "I want you to summon Mor-Rioghain, Badhba, and Macha," she said simply. "I need them to smite Alexander Lyon. I need them to avenge the death of my son."

"'The Battle Sisters?" gasped Segna, aghast. The old crone, despite her many years of life and her depth of experience within the legends of the Celtic Otherworld, was shocked to hear those names uttered. Many people had asked Segna to summon Otherworld guides for them, to ask for the favor of gods and goddesses on their behalf. Deities of health, money, and love; these were the beings that Segna was accustomed to dealing with. Spirits who might bestow upon a person some small gift that would improve of the meager life of a poor peasant, or who might enact some petty revenge on a cad who broke a castle lady's heart.

"But the Battle Sisters were another matter entirely. Ancient, primeval beings that held sway over men in battle, inspiring them to deeds of ferocious courage or striking mortal terror into their hearts so that they quavered beneath the killing blade, the three Sisters gloried in death and blood and mutilation.

"Never had someone asked her to summon creatures of such dark, angry power. Never had she dealt with beings possessed of so much evil and hatred. She shivered with fear at the mere thought of the fierce and terrible Battle Sisters.

"Elspeth saw Segna's hesitation, and pressed on. Now that she was begun, she refused to be turned aside. "I will pay you handsomely," she said, pulling a large emerald ring from her finger, placing it on her outstretched palm and offering it to the old woman. Segna's eyes widened at the sight of the expensive bauble, which was clearly worth more money than she had ever seen in her entire life, and considered Elspeth's offer carefully.

"True, the Battle Sisters were dangerous, but what of it? Their wrath would be directed towards the little lordling of Glamis, and Segna wasted no love on the Lyon family. The Lyons and their courtiers sat safe and secluded in their castle, wearing their fine clothes and glutting themselves on the richest foods, whilst the people who were ruled by them labored themselves into early graves, whilst being forced to pay onerous taxes to the Lyons while they themselves starved. And hadn't Lord Patrick himself ordered Segna's own cousin Simon to be publicly flogged, when the only offense of the poor man had been hiding a small amount of his grain crop, the grain that he had sown and tended and harvested with his own hands, that his little children might not go hungry? Oppressive and thoughtless were the Lords of Glamis, yet they were no more and no less cruel than any other noblemen of the time.

"But young Alexander was different. There was

maliciousness in the boy, a hint of heartless sadism that would be the bane of all of the people whose very lives depended on the whims of their lord. Yes, the world would be a better place without a spiteful monster such as Alexander. And the ring...well, that ring and the security it represented swept away the last of Segna's moral qualms about summoning three such vicious beings as the Battle Sisters like so much dust in the wind.

"Slowly, Segna reached out and took the proffered ring. She tucked it carefully into the pocket of her apron, and grinned sardonically at Elspeth . "Shall we begin?" she said.

"Elspeth smiled and nodded. "What should I do?" she asked.

"'I will mix an elixir for you," said Segna, as she stood and set a kettle of water on the hearth. While the water heated, she busied herself with her various jars and baskets of herbs. Efficiently, she gathered leaves, powders, and strange twigs and dropped them all together into a wooden bowl. Finally, she dropped the contents of the bowl into the kettle of water and stirred it slowly with a large ladle, muttering strange words over the brew in a language that Elspeth did not understand.

"A dreadful smell emanated from the kettle, and soon permeated the entire cabin until Elspeth gasped and choked on the foul stink. "Almost done," said Segna, lifting an eyebrow. "You didn't expect vengeance and death to smell sweet, did you?"

"Elspeth shook her head, and held her lavender scented handkerchief to her nose while Segna continued to stir the noxious brew. The old woman sniffed her concoction, wrinkled her nose, and added a pinch of yet another herb, and a splash of a viscous, yellow-brown liquid that she poured from a clay jug.

"Satisfied at last, Segna ladled the evil-smelling, puce liquid into a cup. She handed the cup to Elspeth. "All that you must do," she directed, "is steal a lock of Alexander's hair.

Burn the lock, being careful to catch the ashes in this cup. Mix the burnt hair thoroughly into the potion with a twig plucked from an oak tree."

'"Where shall I get that?" interrupted Elspeth.

"Segna sighed. "Any oak tree will do. There's one just at the beginning of the path there, if you like. Anyway, stir the mixture carefully with the oak twig, and then pour the contents of the cup into the well inside the castle. The Battle Sisters will come that very day."

"Elspeth took the cup, thanking Segna effusively, but Segna waved her away. As she created the potion, and thought of the dreadful beings that it was meant to conjure and the terrible havoc that they would wreak, her conscience had begun to trouble her. But then she had thought of the emerald, and had pushed her guilt as far down as it would go, telling herself that she merely brewed the potion, that any evil deeds done by the Battle Sisters would be on Elspeth's conscience, not hers. Now, she just wanted Elspeth to go, so that she could be done with the business.

'"Go now," she said wearily. "You have your revenge. Now, trouble me no more."

"Elspeth nodded and hurried from the hut. She stopped at the edge of the wood to pluck a twig from the large red oak that marked the beginning of the trail, and then walked quickly back to the castle, carefully holding the cup in both hands so as not to spill it.

"Her heart was still heavy with the loss of her beloved child, but her lips curved into a nasty smile as she contemplated the horrors that would be sure to befall Alexander once she poured the contents of this cup into the well. She laughed aloud, a grim, bitter sound that echoed in the silence of the woods. Soon, she made it back to the castle, and quietly let herself in by the same back door from which she had left.

"Elspeth hastened herself to her chamber, where she sat upon her bed, doing nothing but waiting for night to fall over the castle. And even then, she waited still more, until the moon had risen and nearly set again. Then, once the deepest darkness of night covered the foul business that she was about to perform, she took the cup given her by Segna, and crept in all quietness to the kitchens, from whence she took a small, sharp knife, and then made her way to Alexander's chamber.

"Once there, Elspeth did not hesitate, but took the knife and leaned over the sleeping form of Alexander. For a moment she thought that she might take her vengeance there and then. She could plunge her little knife into Alexander's neck, again and again, until he joined her dear Colin in death. But no, such a death would be too easy for a monster such as this. Her grief demanded more suffering than that. So she took her knife, and carefully cut a lock of hair from the nape of his neck.

"Once she had the lock of hair carefully grasped in her hand, she made her way quickly through the castle, dread purpose driving her steps. Near the main entrance, she stopped to take a candle from a lit wall sconce. Holding Alexander's hair above the elixir, she held the candle to it, until the acrid smell of burnt hair permeated the air. She held on to the lock as the ashes from it fell in little clumps into the cup. She held on until the flame of the candle burned her fingers, until every last part of the monster's hair had been turned to ash, and then carefully stirred the elixir with the knife that she still held. When she was satisfied, she turned to the spiraling staircase of stone that led from the left of the main gate down into the bowels of the castle.

"Down and down she went, until she came at last to the well. Wasting no time, she took a breath, and, with steely resolve, held the cup over the well and upended it so that the elixir fell with a splash into the water far below.

"At once, a strange blue light rose up out of the depths. Elspeth stood looking at it for a moment, frightened, and for the first time began to wonder if perhaps she had gone too far, was toying with forces beyond her ken. Then a terrible keening sound came from the well, echoing against the stone and piercing her ears. The scream erupted from the well, and it seemed as though a cold, foul wind carried it forth. As Elspeth watched, peering into the well transfixed, her hair blowing roughly in the wind, the water in the well turned a deep red color, and the air surged up and blew past her to screech its way up the stairs and out of the castle. Seeing this, Elspeth knew it to be Bahdba, the first of the Battle Sisters, who turned water to blood and portended the imminence of a violent death to come.

"Terrified, Elspeth fled back up the stairs, through the castle and to her chamber. She dove into her bed and cowered under the bedclothes until morning's light woke the castle.

"In the clear light of day, Elspeth could almost forget all that she had done in the night, could almost believe that all was normal. But she had done what she had done, and nothing was normal. Nor would it ever be again. Not here at Glamis, at least. Not now that she had unleashed Mor-Rioghain, Bahdba, and Macha.

"Elspeth waited anxiously that entire day, wondering what form her vengeance would take, hoping that it would happen soon, and hoping that it would not happen at all, by turns. Finally, in the late afternoon, Alexander and a group of his pages set out to go hunting in the twilight. Elspeth went out upon the castle grounds to watch the youths as they rode off, shouting and laughing with the ebullience of youth. She felt a dagger of sadness stab at her heart as she thought that her son should be amongst them, should be laughing and joking like the rest of them. She narrowed her eyes as she watched Alexander, carelessly laughing over his shoulder as he led the group into the woods, and hoped with all of her soul that the Battle Sisters would avenge her now, would strike him down from his horse while Elspeth watched.

"As she watched the boys ride towards the edge of the woods and disappear within its shadows one by one, a strange vision caught her eye. There, on the edge of the lawn, there seemed to appear before her eyes a stream. Now, Elspeth knew that there was no stream there, and so she knew that some strange sorcery was afoot. Her heart quickened with excitement at the thought that this might be a manifestation of the curse she had cast when she tossed the elixir down the well.

"But her excitement quickly turned to fear as she beheld the woman that kneeled at the water's edge. She leaned over the stream, and seemed to be washing a garment in its waters. She looked up at Elspeth, and she was beautiful yet terrible to behold. Her eyes seemed to be fathomless black pits that led to hell itself, with no white showing around the edges. When she saw Elspeth watching her, she smiled, her face contorting in a rictus of careless malevolence. Then she turned back to her work, and Elspeth saw that she was rinsing a tunic in the water. The tunic was bloody, and the water was stained red from it.

"Then, Elspeth knew her for Mor-Rioghain, the Washer Woman. Despite herself, her desire for vengeance wilted at the sight of that horrible smile, and those depthless eyes, and she knew that she had wrought an evil that far surpassed that which she sought to avenge.

"Sickened, she turned to go back into the castle, to hide herself from the hideous creature she had summoned. But she was stopped by a shout of dismay that came from the woods where they young men had entered just moments before.

"A sound of pounding hooves erupted from the woods, and soon enough a lone rider came into view. He rode hard, fear and horror etched upon his face. People from the castle gathered round, attracted by the noise, wanting to see what the fuss was about.

"Soon enough the rider reached those anxiously waiting on the castle green. "Ogilvies!" he cried. "They fell upon us in the woods. They came out of nowhere…some of us have fallen already…they are killing us!"

"'Did Alexander fall?' barked Lord Patrick. "Is my son

yet alive?"

"The youth nodded. "Aye," he said. "He saw that I was clear, and sent me to get help. Save them! Oh please, hurry!" At that, he began to weep openly, and could say no more. Elspeth stared open-mouthed. Her vengeance was meant for Alexander, not still more innocent young boys.

"Quickly, Lord Patrick and the other men called for their weapons and their mounts, and rode to the rescue of the beleaguered boys, quickly disappearing beneath the same tress that the boys had ridden under just minutes before. At that moment, a black raven sounded a wailing cry from high above. Everyone looked up, and there, on every roof, on every turret, sat hundreds of ravens. As one, the birds joined their voices to that of their leader, and took flight. The sky was blackened as the huge flock circled the castle before streaking towards the woods. The sound of their piercing calls filled all those present with dread, but only Elspeth knew the true horror of what was to come. For she knew this to be the manifestation of Macha, the most terrible of the Battle Sisters, who made men weak in battle and took the heads from the bodies of the slain as grisly tokens of her madness.

"The sound of clashing steel soon sounded from the forest, and Elspeth knew now that she must undo what she had done. So thinking, she raced down the wooded path until she reached the house of Segna. Quickly she told her all that had befallen the castle, and begged for help, offering all of her jewels to the old woman if only she could send the evil sisters back from whence they came.

"Segna thought a moment, and then agreed. Indeed, she had expected just such a thing. "I can call on the *Daoine Sidhe*," she said, "the fairy folk of the Otherworld. But the price they ask will be high indeed." The old woman quickly gathered her materials. "Take me to where they are," she said grimly.

"Elspeth and Segna hurried through the woods, and soon enough found the place where Lord Patrickand his men were fighting the Ogilivies who had attacked Alexander and his friends. Alexander, terrified but as yet unharmed, stood behind his father, trying to appear brave. The men of Glamis fought as though drugged, and were clearly close to being overcome entirely. Dead and dying men littered the forest floor, whilst the ravens cawed raucously above them in anticipation of the grisly feast to come.

'"Lord Patrick!" called Segna. "We must call the *Daoine Sidhe*! They can deliver you from this evil, but you must agree to pay whatever price they ask."

'"Yes, yes, I will pay anything they wish!" screamed Lord Patrick , "if only they will save us!"

"So saying, Segna summoned the fairies. Beautiful and gossamer as though made of light, they swept through and chased the ravens from the trees, and set about harrying the evil Battle Sisters who had beset the men with weakness. Chilling screams were heard as the Battle Sisters were driven back towards the castle. The fairies encircled the evil beings, and pushed them into a room high in the castle. They then caused great stones to be moved, blocking up the door, so that the Battle Sisters were trapped, walled up forever.

"Once the Battle Sisters were gone, Lord Patrick and his men recovered their strength as though by a miracle, and quickly beat the enemy back. When the last of the Ogilvies had been killed or fled into the woods, Lord Patrick reached for his son and held him to his chest in great relief that his son and heir had survived, where so many of the other boys had perished.

"The people cheered at their deliverance, but the fairies were not done. They came before Lord Patrick, and demanded their price.

'"Yes," he said. "I will give you whatsoever that you wish." And the fairies smiled, and whispered in his ear. His face went pale as they spoke, but he nodded gravely nonetheless, and gave his word.

"And so it was that the *Daoine Sidhe*, the fairy folk,

exacted their terrible price. In exchange for their help, the Lords of Glamis were forever bound to the promise made by Lord Patrick. Because of his vow, if the fairies desire to take a newborn babe from a Lord of Glamis, that Lord must give over the child, and accept a monstrous changeling in its place. If the child is not freely given, the fairies will undo their help, and let loose the Battle Sisters upon the castle, to complete the revenge of Elspeth. Elspeth herself, seeing the evil that her rage had wrought, said not a word, but walked silently into the forest, never to be seen again.

"That, Allister, is the burden that I now bequeath unto you. And if you are unlucky, and the fairies ask for a child in your lifetime, it will be your duty, as the head steward, to sneak the child from its mother's care, and replace it with the deformed creature that they give you in the child's stead. And you must do all of this without the mother's knowledge. Only the Lord of Glamis and his Head Steward may know the secret, for it a woman were to ever know, she would never consent to marry into the family, or to bear children for a Lord of Glamis.

"This is the Curse of Glamis, lad. It is with a heavy heart that I pass it from myself to you, but now you must keep it, and never tell another soul until death arrives to free you from it. And if the fairies come, you must do your dread duty. Though it would seem wrong, though your conscience will rail against it, you must give the *Sidhe* what they've come for, else all will surely perish."

So spoke Lyall, and, having passed the dreadful secret of Glamis Castle on to Allister, was free to breathe his last. Allister hung his head, mourning his friend, and felt the weight of the heavy burden that he must now carry to his own grave settle into his soul. Had he known the secret to be so evil, so foul, he did not think that he would have wanted it. But, unknowing, he had accepted it, and now it was his to bear.

Columbkill Noonan has an M.S. in Biology, and teaches Anatomy and Physiology at a university in Maryland. An avid history buff, much of her writing, which could be best described as "supernatural historical horror", combines historical events with elements of paranormal fantasy. Her first novel, Night Woods, *is available as an e-book. She is currently working on her second novel, which was inspired by a trip to Scotland, particularly by the grim castles and spooky underground alleys of Edinburgh.*

In her spare time, Columbkill enjoys hiking, scuba diving, and riding her horse, Mittens. To learn more about Columbkill, and to hear breaking news about her latest works, please feel free to visit her at www.facebook.com/ColumbkillNoonan.

REPORT ON AN INCIDENT DURING THE BATTLE OF MALVERN HILL

BY KEVIN WETMORE

Colonel Robert O. Tyler, Commander
First Connecticut Heavy Artillery
3rd Brigade, Second Division, V Corps
Army of the Potomac

July 15, 1862

Dear Colonel:

I write this report from my hospital bed in the hospital outside Washington, D.C., where I was transferred from the field hospital on the peninsula after the Seven Days campaign. I thank you, sir, for your good wishes and your letter of July the 11th requesting information on what happened during and after the battle at Malvern Hill. I deeply regret to share of these incidents, Colonel, but I can tell you every word I set down is accurate and as it happened.

As you may not know, sir, I was born the fifth of nine children in West Stafford, Connecticut. My grandfather had fought in the Revolution and we Grimhands are proud Yankees. When war broke out last year, I bid farewell to my mother and siblings, my father having passed two winters before, and rode my horse to Hartford to join the 4th Connecticut brigade. Like many, I wanted to defend the Republic. I was a simple schoolteacher from a simple farm town who had risen through the ranks to become a Lieutenant. When the First Heavy Artillery was formed, Captain Stevens asked that I follow him to your unit, Sir. I respect the boys and, with due modesty, I believe they respect me. If I may flatter myself, I have proven a competent officer and a worthy member of the First.

On July 1, 1862, our brigade was two miles from James River at the top of Malvern Hill. We had just finished giving Johnny Reb what for in the days previous when the guns of Armistead's brigade opened up on us right after noon. Well sir, you know our Nutmeg boys - they can give as well as they get. So we started firing off our cannon, raining artillery down on the Rebs. We saw Armistead's men begin to move forward around 3:30 in the afternoon. All they got for their trouble was cannonballs and grapeshot.

For much of the battle, I was astride my mount, running orders back and forth from General Porter to the boys and pushing the boys to push back Johnny.

Around 4:30 I noticed a group of Rebs coming up the west side of the hill. After sending a messenger to inform General Porter, he had our boys turn some of the guns to face them and we used canister shot to soften them up before the infantry went down with muskets to finish the job.

As the sun began to set the fighting began to die down. I suspect, Sir, that I was one of the last to be injured. Some ordnance was being sent in our direction by the Army of Northern Virginia. I was riding from General Porter to one of the forward batteries, which is why I suspect none knew where I was once I was injured. Grapeshot hit right near me as I rode to the foremost position. The boys surrounding the gun that was the target were all lost. My horse also was hit and collapsed. My leg caught some, but the real injury was caused by the fall of my horse. Xerxes had been an excellent mount, with me since my days in the 4th, and it was a damned shame to lose him. Still, my only thought at that moment was to get him off me. I could tell the leg had been broken under the horse, and its death rattles were only injuring me further. Like most men, I fancied I would face injury with the bravery and stoicism of Leonidas and the Spartans at Thermopylae. I must confess to my shame that my initial reaction was mostly to scream and cry for help. In light of the incoming fire, many of the boys withdrew to further up the hill, leaving me and the dying gunners to the battlefield, and I spent several hours trapped under my horse, slowly working my way out from under it by maneuvering my body and leg back and forth. Upon occasion the pain would cause me to lose consciousness, regaining it only to continue working the leg out.

As I lay there, hoping my leg would be worked free of the horse or that men would come to help before I passed away, I could hear the wounded and dying. Colonel, I do not mind telling you it was the most piteous and horrifying sound I had ever heard. Both Union and Reb could be heard, as the lines had been so close throughout the day. Men screaming and crying. Screaming in pain. Crying out for wives, mothers, water, anything that their fevered brains thought would bring them solace or respite from the pain and horror. My heart felt more pity for them, as I was now in their company, fearing for my own mortal life and soul.

I do not mind telling you Colonel, the most fearful hours were the ones right before dawn. I could feel my strength fading and the pain in my leg had dulled to a foggy numbness. Being from New England, I am used to heat and humidity in the summer, but I was not prepared for the weather in Virginia in July. The fog rolled in a few hours after the sun set, which left me alone with the body of my horse and the cries of the dying.

As the sun rose, the fog melted and I had a much better sense of my surroundings. I know now that in the mile of woodland on the side of that hill, four thousand dead and dying from each side lay there. Colonel, if the sound of them was the most horrific thing I have ever heard, the sight of them nearly drove me mad. I hope, once recovered, I return to fight on, but I hope far more to never see anything like the sight that greeted me that morning again.

The fog drifted away and from my position on the hill, under the horse, I saw what looked to be thousands of dying and dead bodies close to each other. So close were they and so intermixed were the already dead and the now dying and injured that it appeared as a singular crawling entity. I saw a squirming mass of bloody arms, legs, torsos and heads, undulating as if a solitary mass of human body parts melded into one giant casualty of war. I realized what I was seeing was the injured attempting to free themselves from the limbs and bodies of their dead companions and move to safety.

Colonel, here is the first moment I fear you will not trust me, nor would I blame you for not doing so. I am still not certain I believe it myself, though my head was clear enough as I experienced it. Looking at that writhing mass, as the sun rose, I swear I saw two or three dark figures emerge from the bloody carnage and shrink into the darker areas of the woods. I bring this up as at the time I thought them dogs or carrion scavengers. I know the pain and exhaustion may make some men think I hallucinated or fell to horrible imaginings. Later events, however, confirmed what I know I saw.

Men from the Third found me and lifted the horse off my leg. They carried me to the nearby field hospital. It was there the doctor confirmed the leg would need to go, crushed under Xerxes and further ruined by my attempts to pull it from under him. They gave me a bottle of whiskey and I took three long pulls. The doctor lifted the saw from a tray. It was covered in blood and bits of flesh. The doctor himself wore an apron also blood soaked and caked in bits of flesh and bone chips. His exhaustion was obvious and though I dreaded what was to happen, I found a scrap of pity in my soul for him, for I knew mine was the latest of hundreds of limbs taken that day by him. They then placed a piece of wood wrapped in leather in my mouth. Five men held me down on the bed, really a wooden door lain across two saw horses. I felt the saw placed on my leg just below the knee. The doctor looked me in the eye, I bit down harder on the bit in my mouth. As his eyes shifted from mine to my leg I saw the muscles in his arm tense for what seemed like an eternity, then I felt the saw rip across my flesh, biting deep. The scream that burst forth from me was short, and I managed to hold the bit in my mouth. My memory of the next few minutes is hazy. I am told I passed out several times, only to awaken screaming, vomiting the whiskey once. Every time I awoke to this nightmare I felt the saw drawn across the bone once again, drawing fire from the limb. I commend the men holding me down for their yeomen service, but clearly I struggled. Days later in my bed I found bruises where they held me, so strong had they to grip my limbs to keep me still for the old sawbones to finish his work.

Colonel, I must confess, the greatest horror of all this was not the pain of the saw but awakening to hear a thud as the now separate limb was dropped into a bucket already containing several other arms and legs.

It is here where the true horror begins and for which you asked me to write this report. I once again drifted into morphia's realm. When I awoke again my leg was thoroughly bandaged and I lay in my bloody uniform on a makeshift bed next to a window of the farmhouse made field hospital, a concession to my rank. The enlisted men lay on blankets on the ground outside. I was informed I had been drifting in and out of sleep for four days.

The sun was setting and the heat was unbearable. Sweat caked my face and remaining limbs. As I lay, possibly dying, I thought, I looked out the window and saw an orderly carry out a bucket full of limbs. He took them towards the barn behind the house. I thought perhaps he would take them into the woods behind the barn and give them some kind of Christian burial. I must confess, after a year of war I had not given much thought what happened to the limbs of the injured. Now that I was one, it concerned me greatly.

Instead, he simply upended the bucket over the fence

and a number of hogs came running and began consuming the flesh thrown to them. In my haze I wondered if one of those was my leg, now gone from me. Was my flesh the food of pigs? In the fading light of sunset as I began to turn from this sight, I saw one of those brown dog-like creatures emerge from the woods. It crawled towards the gathering of hogs. With a low hiss it frightened them away long enough to grab two or three limbs and scurry off again. The hole it caused in the gathering of swine quickly collapsed and the pigs returned to their meal.

I called over to one of the Contraband serving as a nurse of sorts. I do not know any Negroes back home, but this one seemed a decent, intelligent sort. I asked him to help me stand. He said nothing at first and I could tell he did not wish to do so for the sake of my own health. I ordered him to help me and to serve as crutch. The Contraband helped me out of bed and I swayed. Were it not for his strength we both would have gone down.

"To the barn, boy. Take me now," I gasped and jumped with my good leg towards the door. I believed, correctly, that if I began moving he would keep up with me rather than risk my further injury. It is just as well. I lost any strength or even the ability to stand after that first jump and the Contraband all but carried me outside.

"To the treeline, boy," I told him and he obediently carried me over. I heard the sounds of gnawing and rustling within the brush. I had the Contraband set me down. The odor there was unthinkable. The smell of death was everywhere.

"Back to the house, boy. Fetch me my pistol and get yourself a stout stick. Double time!" I barked and the Contraband, with a look to the woods, jogged back to the house.

While waiting for him to return, I heard something just within the treeline sniffing. The light was almost fully gone. Needles and leaves cracked as whatever it was moved closer.

If it consumed the limbs of the fallen, it must be drawn to the odor of my stump, and yet how could it smell that over the reek of all the death in this area.

I pulled myself into the treeline. Bodies of the fallen rebels had been thrown there. The corpses were the most horrific thing I had seen, even after all this war. They were swollen to twice their natural size, black as Negroes in some cases, and in most cases, not complete. Here lay a head, there a trunk without head or legs, yonder six or seven arms and a leg, further, a head and trunk with no limbs with fragments of shell sticking in the oozing skull, brains leaking out the side. These were battle remains, almost one week gone, unburied and now serving as larder for these creatures. If there is a place worse than Hell, Sir, I was in it.

It emerged low from a set of bushes about eight yards from me. It looked human. What I thought initially was fur in the dying light, was a grey Confederate army uniform. It saw me looking at it and froze, as an animal would. The hair on my neck began to stand up as I realized that it had realized I was defenseless. I looked back to the farmhouse hospital, hoping to see my Negro trotting back with weapons, but he was nowhere to be seen. When I turned back the man beast had cut the distance between us in half.

He was sniffing, growling low and looking right at me. I kept my eyes on him, knowing from my hunting days in New England that you never take your eyes off a predator. I felt about me for a stick or rock or something with which to fight when I realized the growl had turned to a low laugh.

"I've had you," it said.

Steeling my courage, I said, "Don't come any closer. What do you mean? Are you a man?"

It sniffed again and crawled another step forward. "I have eaten your flesh, oh yes, so sweet, too much metal, bite flesh, spit out, oh yes, but sweet." It inhaled deeply and smiled. I saw that its teeth had been filed to points.

Thinking that the uniform may be a tool by which the

beast might be brought to heel, I said in my most commanding voice, "Soldier, what do you think you're doing?"

He stopped, perhaps in confusion. "Hungry," he said then. "So hungry. Hurt. Ran away. But no food, no food. Now food."

I took it to mean he was a deserter from some unit of the Army of Northern Virginia and now followed them, looking to steal food.

He leaned back, closed his eyes and smiled. "Ate piggies. Sweet piggies. Tasty piggies. But piggies had eaten manmeat. After Manassas, they fed the limbs to the piggies. Ate the piggies after. Man meat make ham sweeter." He looked into my eyes and took a step closer. "Now don't bother with piggies. Just eat man meat. Sometimes the flesh cut from them. Fresh meat is best, though," and he pulled back as if to jump on me.

In my haze and in the darkness I readied myself for combat. I would be damned if this cannibal would get more of my flesh. I lifted my torso to meet him when a large stick came down and struck him between the shoulders. He shrieked and I looked up to see the Contraband had snuck up behind him quietly through the woods as he and I talked. The Contraband smashed him a second time and then pulled my pistol from his belt and threw it to me. Checking the chamber, I saw that the bullet I had loaded before I was shot was still in there. Saying a silent prayer I placed the barrel to the head of the cannibal and pulled the trigger. I suspect the sound of the gun would bring men running, but we are too used to the reports of muskets to be too worried about a single shot. Regardless, I slipped from this world as the revolver fell from my hand.

I have been informed the Contraband carried me back to my bed. I wanted to thank him for his assistance and rescue, but he was gone from the hospital by the time I awoke and never returned. I assume, in the manner of his kind, he sought to avoid any attention because of these events. Nevertheless, I am grateful to him. I do not know his name and so cannot recommend him for commendation.

I have also been informed that no body, wearing a Southern uniform or otherwise, has been found behind the barn, before the trees. There was some blood on the grass there, but I have been told the soldiers believe it is my blood, leaking from my bandages and in my delirium I imagined it all.

I do not think so, Colonel. Since I have begun to recover and gather my strength I was moved to this hospital in Washington. I have had some books brought to me by a clergyman friend. In the Orient there are a race of men called "ghuls" that are cursed to feed on the flesh of dead men. I fear me this great war is making a race of ghuls here in the States. I fear their taste for human flesh will grow and will be fed by this war.

It is for this reason, Colonel, that I file this report and beg you, Sir, to prepare and train a group of men to find and fight these ghuls, or I fear they will follow our troops. For now they are content to feast upon the limbs taken from the fallen. But I saw them out there that morning in the dawn after battle. They feast on the battlefield as well. Colonel, there is nothing more abhorrent than to be hurt in defense of the Union and wake to find one's self being devoured by a Reb cannibal. I beg you - beg you, Sir - hunt them, find them, kill them. Upon my return to service, once my damned leg has healed (the doctor assures me a wooden leg can be made to fit), I will return to service and fight these beasts as surely as I have fought the rebels.

They were once soldiers. They had eaten pork and ham and bacon made from hogs that had eaten limbs. Now they were ghuls and they were following the Army of the Potomac. Every time we engaged the enemy, every time limbs were sawn off, they emerged from the dark to consume our flesh and grew stronger. I beg you. Hunt them. Stop them. This is not fancy or nightmare on my part. Last night I heard one of them outside the window of this hospital, sniffing, growling and laughing. I fear for myself. I fear for my fellow wounded soldiers. Most of all, I fear for the Union. I beg of you, call me mad if you must, but know that when you cut the limb, you feed the enemy. That is what I have to report, Sir.

Yr. humble and obedient servant,

Lt. Gideon Thorne Grimhand
First Connecticut Heavy Artillery
3rd Brigade, Second Division, V Corps

Kevin Wetmore is the author of over a dozen short stories and several books, including Post-9/11 Horror in American Cinema *and* Back from the Dead: Reading Remakes of George Romero's Zombie Films as Markers of Their Times. *He lives in Los Angeles where he also acts, directs, teaches and does stunts.*

THE *LORELEI* OF THE TRENCHES

BY DAVID W. LANDRUM

Nurse Tilda Pennington had seen her again last night. First she heard the song. Going outside of the bunker, she spotted the figure and knew what she saw was no hallucination. Thirty-six hour shifts ending with her soaked in blood, having endured hour after hour of torn, shattered bodies, men screaming in pain, choking from gas, shot to pieces—it could certainly bring on hallucinations. Madness grew here like the slimy mold that coated the walls of dugouts, bunkers, and of the hospital itself. Since the establishment of the hospital two of her women had sunk into the refuge of catatonia and had to be returned home. At least three (she had not named them and probably would not) stole morphine to inject themselves so they could endure the sight of gaping wound, limbs blown off, bodies torn and maimed in every imaginable (and some unimaginable) way. Undoubtedly they were addicted. When the war ended, if it ever ended, and if they survived, they would carry the wound of dependency back home with them.

The other night, when the ward had quieted down, she had stepped outside for a breath of fresh air. The air was never very fresh outside the hospital. The fetid smell of standing water, of corpses rotting in no-man's land, of filth, offal, and guncotton tinged the air. Still, it was better than the suffocating inside of the hospital with its smell of blood, ripped open bodies, disinfecting alcohol, sweat and fear. She breathed in the generally clear air, which was, thankfully, cool, and lit a cigarette. She had taken up smoking since coming here. At the end of the trench, where it turned from the salient close to the infirmary, a woman stood.

You never saw women in the trenches except for the occasional nurse. Now and then wilted-looking clusters of French whores would trudge toward their rides home after servicing hundreds of men. This woman was not a nurse nor did she look like exactly like a prostitute. She stood tall, taller than many men, and wore a long, starkly white dress. She had a pale face that contrasted with her abundant black hair. The nails on her white fingers were long. From where Tilda stood, they looked like talons.

She stared, puzzled. The woman raised her arms.

A swirl of red light swished through the trench. Tilda froze in terror, thinking it might be artillery fire or, worse, gas, but this did not look like the discharge of any weapon she had seen. Steams and eddies of it rolled silently in the murky space of the diggings. Tilda felt buffeted with energy, though she sensed no pain. The streams of dull red (like dried blood) converged on the woman. For a moment she glowed red and then her previous coloration returned. She dropped her arms.

Tilda gaped. The woman noticed her and smiled. The smile made her shudder. Then—this made her blood run cold—the figure opened her mouth, hissed at her, and vanished.

How long she stood there she could not be certain. She looked at her hand. Her cigarette had gone out. She lit it again. A bullet whizzed by and hit the mold-encrusted doorpost of the field hospital, missing her head by inches. One of the vigilant German snipers in the opposite trench had seen the flame of her match and taken a shot at her. She scurried to the safety of a bunker, sat down, and recovered from the fright and shock of almost being killed. She had had brushes with machine gun fire and artillery, but never anything as near-fatal as this. After she had calmed, she finished her smoke. Her hands shook from the vision of the woman in white and from the brush with death. She tossed away the butt of the cigarette and leaned against some large sacks of beans stored in the bunker. She immediately fell asleep.

"Nurse! Nurse Pennington." She opened her eyes. A group of three nurses and two military men stood around. She saw the concern on their faces. "Can you hear me, ma'am?"

She came out of the haze of sleep.

"Yes, I hear you."

"Are you all right?"

She sat up. "I'm fine. Sorry. I just fell asleep. I sat down, leaned back. . ."

Captain Carr, the commander of the unit to which the field hospital was attached, puffed his pipe. "After working thirty-six hours with no sleep, it's understandable. You need to take a rest, ma'am. We value you too much to let you ruin your constitution by constant work. I'll have Captain Taylor escort you to your quarters. These ladies will supervise the hospital in your absence."

Candice Ames and Felicia Cummings were junior nurses (and a couple who shared a Sapphic relationship — they did not know she knew this). Tilda did not think they had the experience to operate the hospital. She also saw that Captain Carr was adamant in his resolution.

"Of course," she said. "Let me confer, though — "

"Nurses Ames and Cummings are quite capable of functioning, at least temporarily, in your absence. Go on now. Captain Taylor . . ."

Taylor, the hospital's ranking physician, and Tilda's lover, smiled, took her arm, and escorted her through the maze of trenches to a waiting vehicle. As they drove away, she fell asleep once more. Taylor drove her to an installation far enough from the lines that shell fire did not endanger it.

"I'll be back tomorrow," he said. "I have some leave coming."

Tilda risked a good-bye kiss, gathered her bags, and

settled in, marveling at the small room assigned to her, the clean sheets, the smell of flowers and fresh linen, and the grass and trees outside the window. It seemed to her as if she were a soul slogging out of the mud or filth of purgatory and arriving at the outskirts of heaven.

Richard Taylor and Tilda Pennington had carried on a discreet liaison throughout the war, managing to see each other during their times off and when they were given leave to see families. Tilda had been raised in a family that followed traditional morality and would have waited to have sex, but the war had changed her perspective. She lived only moments from death. The ancient slogan carpe diem said it all for her. You seized the day; you lived life to the full because it might instantly be taken from you.

Richard arrived in the afternoon the next day. In the morning light, after a night of love, she rested in his arms. Birds sang in the trees outside. A breeze carried the smell of blossoming linden trees through the window. For the first time in many weeks, she felt secure. She wondered if he would live through the war—if she would live through the war. The destruction she had seen in her years on the front defied description. Millions must have died if you added all the units of all the armies involved. She made a determined effort to not think of such things. Why let such things enter her thoughts when she was snug with the man who loved her? She pushed memories of carnage, death, and pain to the recesses of her mind and enjoyed the warmth, the refuge of a lover's nearness.

In the morning they had breakfast at a table outside the compound. She reveled in grass, trees, flowers, blue sky, and a clear, fragrant wind blowing over them. Tilda asked Richard if he ever heard singing in the trenches. "It would be high singing," she said, "in a haunting female voice. It might be ringing in my ears from the shells—tinnitus; or it might be auditory hallucinations from stress and fear."

He laughed. "Don't be so analytical, Nurse Pennington. I've heard it too. So have most of the men. We think someone on the German side has a gramophone and likes opera."

"I'm glad I was not imagining it."

"You know the war will end soon. Now that the Americans are in, the Germans won't be able to hold out."

"I'll believe the war is over when the shooting stops."

"It won't go on for much longer."

"Let's hope and pray."

Four days later, Tilda arrived back. The line of engagement had shifted. The French, bolstered with fresh American manpower, had driven the Germans back. Headquarters assigned a garrison of troops to guard the field hospital, but no attacks came. Artillery exchanges had ceased. A silent agreement that neither side would try to overrun the other had evolved somehow. Shots rang out now and then and no one with any common sense failed to exercise caution when outside. Conditions still demanded stealth. One soldier got a bullet in the shoulder for being careless. The war, Captain Carr reminded everyone, had not yet ended.

All the same, the lull was refreshing. Tilda's work load diminished. Soldiers were brought in, but their wounds were the type that responded to treatment more easily—not so serious or life-threatening as to prevent transportation long distance. Tilda and the doctors and nurses removed bullets, set broken limbs, stitched cuts, and irrigated the eyes of soldier temporarily blinded by gas. Her life, and the lives of her other nurses, grew less harrowing when the fighting moved further off.

Tilda saw the woman again. She turned her eyes and met her gaze. Tilda went back into the dugout. Felicia noticed her expression.

"What is it, Miss Pennington?"

"They've brought one of those French whores into camp again," she bristled. "I know the men here are deprived, but for the love of God I can't see how any man would want to cohabit with such a. . . hideous female."

Hideous, she reflected, described the woman perfectly. She might have been attractive at one time. Her height (she was unusually tall for a woman) might in the past have endeared her to the eyes of men, but now it made her look freakish; her long limbs and fingers lent a witch-like appearance to her body. She had large eyes and full lips, probably ravishing in her youth, now watery and bleary; her mouth twisted so that Tilda shuddered seeing her. Long black hair hung in thin, lusterless hanks about her rounded shoulders. The white frock she wore made her look like a madwoman wandering an asylum.

"You would think," she continued talking to Felicia, "if they were going to pay money for a prostitute, they would at least find one who is young and just slightly attractive."

Felicia laughed. "They probably have to take whatever they can get. I don't imagine many women, even the ones most fallen from grace, would want to come here. I sure wouldn't if I didn't think being here as a nurse was my calling."

"At least our calling cures disease rather than spreads it."

Tilda and her associates spoke freely and even quipped on a subject most women of the day blushed to mention. They examined the whores who occasionally came to camp for obvious signs of venereal disease. Still, soldiers caught the diseases, no matter how much lectures and posters warned them to be careful.

"I don't remember that woman coming in for a check-up."

"The tall one? I know who you're talking about. My God, she is ugly," Felicia said. "Maybe she comes here without authorization from command. We ought to bring the matter to Captain Carr's attention."

Tilda did rounds. The patients were quiet or asleep. She and Felicia emptied bedpans, checked medication charts, swept, and laid out clean bandages. After three hours of work, Felicia asked if she could go outside and smoke. Tilda nodded.

"Be careful," she said as Felicia left. She busied herself folding clean linen. They would change the sheets tomorrow. When she had stacked her third pile, she heard the singing. She had not heard it in some time. She listened while she worked.

Tilda jumped and screamed when a gunshot broke the song.

The trench in front of the hospital exploded into chaos. Troops surged out of their quarters and took up positions left unmanned in the recent lull. Tilda and her nurses initiated attack preparation protocols. Fear and tension hung in the air like storm clouds.

The attack never materialized. Silence fell over the dark, war-scarred landscape. Captain Carr called Tilda out to the trench. Walking into the cool spring drizzle, she saw Felicia lying face-up in the mud, a gaping hole in the center of her forehead.

Tilda vomited and crumpled. A soldier caught her before she fell. Reaching inside for strength, she breathed deeply to stabilized herself.

"I'm sorry, Tilda." She raised her eyes. It was Richard. "It appears she was standing on the steps."

She looked at the set of eight wooden steps that led out of the trench and into no-man's land. In the dim light Tilda could see the blood.

"Why would she have done such a thing?" she asked, shaking her head. "She knew better. She was a sensible woman."

"I don't know. Someone needs to tell Candice."

"I'll tell her," Tilda murmured.

By the time she got to Candice's quarters, she had found out and was incoherent in her grief. Richard gave her a sedative. Tilda and the other nurses took Felicia's body to the morgue, washed her, put on a clean uniform, and tagged the corpse for transport to a burial site.

Tilda lamented with the other nurses, though decorum and considerations of the wounded soldiers dictated they mourn silently. Everyone expressed bafflement that Felicia would do something as utterly foolish as exposing herself to an open line of fire. Tilda sat and listened to the talk. As she listened, she knew what happened was linked to the tall, ugly woman she had seen from time and with the singing that periodically filled the still air in the desolation between the trenches.

The next day they found Candice in the room where they kept medical supplies. She had hanged herself from a support beam. Tilda and Yvonne stumbled upon her suspended corpse, head twisted to one side, eyes bulging, mouth open, tongue hanging out. She could not have been dead very long. Her body felt warm. Later that day an ambulance took her corpse, and the corpse of Felicia, away for burial. Tilda hoped the two would lie side by side, though she realized such foolish sentimentality would not reinforce the mental fortitude it would take to survive the war.

Tilda had heard the song at the very moment Candice must have been slipping the rope she had made of twisted sheets over her head.

Two days later, she saw the woman. Approaching her angrily, Tilda demanded, *"Qui êtes-vous et qu'est-ce que vous faites ici?"*

A reply rang, not in her ears but in her mind. Tilda knew the reply was not her own thought and not the voice she heard in her mind. It was a different voice.

You are a lovely woman. Come to me. Come to my song.

The song began. Tilda had heard it so often she almost could sing it herself. It was not English, not French. It resembled the Welsh tongue she had heard household servants speak when she was a child — or the language of

Brittany or Ireland. The words stole into her body, weaving in a heavy, beautiful swirl that left her weak and lethargic. Her eyes grew heavy. She felt her body droop. Why, her mind asked, though in a different voice, did she persist in standing here in this filthy trench surrounded by death, stench, and filth, why be content with vermin and the smell of unwashed men of blood and antiseptic when the moon summoned the stars blazed and all around meadows of flowers blossomed thick in the soothing light of Artemis the huntress why linger here climb out flee from the squalor and find love see beauty once again its but a step up then another then another…

When the word *love* came through the song she thought of Richard. Her head cleared. The spell that had enraptured her faded. She saw the earthen walls of the trench, the wooden supports holding it up, the huts and buildings where she lived and worked. She smelled the wet earth, the damp breeze—the scent fetid for certain but so familiar a soothing sensation came from smelling it. Her vision returned. Her eyes focused on the woman she assumed was a prostitute.

The woman stared back at her, smiling. All at once, though, a look of nausea came to her face. Sick and horrified, she swayed on her feet.

Tilda's ethics demanded she attempt to heal anyone in any sort of infirmity—enemies, criminals, the most reprehensible of peoples. She tried to step toward the woman but could not move. Her body seemed made of lead. She could only stare. What she saw filled her with astonished revulsion.

The woman made a move as if she were about to fall, but her legs did not fold under her so that she crumpled; she seemed to diminish as if her legs had dissolved or she was sinking into mud or quicksand. At the same time, her upper body trembled and her flesh began to rot, then putrefy.

Tilda watched as the woman's skin liquefied and ran off her bones. Her hair fell off in long, black tails. The outline of her skull appeared as her cheeks, lips, eyes, and scalp dissolved and ran over the bones of her face in a sluggish stream. The bloody flux pooled at her feet, the loss of her flesh transforming her to a skeleton. She collapsed then, a heap of bones and a loathsome mass of liquid flesh. Tilda felt her knees go weak. She tried to keep her balance as a swoon rolled over her. She seized the railing on the ladder that led out of the trench, steadying herself. Managing not to faint, she lowered herself to her knees.

The smell lessened. Her senses rallied. As she tried to get to her feet, voices sounded. Richard, Captain Carr, and two nurses came for her. They helped her up. As they did, a shot rang out.

"Keep your heads down," Carr snapped. "The Germans are still over there, trigger-happy as ever."

Keeping low, the four of them helped Tilda to the hospital and put her to bed. Though she protested, the doctors gave her sedative. She awoke. Light came through the door. Morning had broken. All was completely calm and still.

Richard sat by her bed.

"Feeling all right?" he asked, he had an almost comical smile on his face.

"I think so, yes."

He took her hand. "You'll feel even better when I tell you the news: the war is over. All hostilities have ceased. The Germans have surrendered."

She felt too weary to react much. She said, "Thank God," and, after a trip to the privy, paused to send up a prayer of thanksgiving (something she had not done in years) before she returned to Richard. He gave her bread, boiled eggs, and tea for breakfast and then poured her a glass of brandy.

"Where did you get that?"

"They passed it out—a gift from the French. The locals are thankful we've liberated them from the Germans. Drink."

"It's too early in the morning to be drinking alcohol," she said. Then she caught the scent of it, nodded, and accepted the glass. The brandy burned luxuriously down her throat. She went to light a cigarette but stopped.

"Not good for you," she said. "I'm going to quit." She crumpled the cigarette and cast it away.

"Did you faint last night from the smell of that corpse?" Richard asked.

She hesitated, remembering, and then said, "Yes. It was a corpse?"

"Strangest and most ghastly thing I've ever seen. Flesh had liquefied and run off the bones. I've never encountered the like of it. It was a woman's corpse. She might have been one of the prostitutes who used to come here. She wore a white smock and had on jewelry."

"Could have been," Tilda muttered.

She automatically reached for a cigarette but stopped herself. She would break the habit. She would put everything that reminded her of the war far away. Tilda knew it would be a long fight. She had seen things no one should see. Horrors lurked in the corridors of her memory. The war to overcome remembrances of the four years she had spent on the front lines would be more formidable than surviving the conflict itself had been.

She steadfastly resisted the urge to smoke.

Tilda married Richard. They had four children. He established a practice in London and did well. She raised her sons and daughters and, when they got older, went back to work as nurse part-time.

She battled post-traumatic stress syndrome (they called it shell-shock back then). Nightmares, anxiety attacks, depression bedeviled her. She was a strong woman, though, determined, and not afraid to seek help. She weathered the storm. After 1926, she felt herself free of the effects the war had wrought in her.

She never told anyone the story of seeing the wraith-like woman, hearing her song, and watching her melt before her eyes. Tilda was not certain it had not all been hallucinations or she had imagined it. Interested in the new science of psychology, she wondered if her mind had created the creature as a way of focusing her imagination away from the terrible sights she saw each day in the field hospital. Perhaps the thing she saw who sang such an enticing song had only been an illusion.

One day, while helping her daughter study for a test on *The Odyssey*, she felt the icy hand of realization touch her as she read a question from a list the teacher had given his pupils for test preparation.

"Who were the sirens?" she read.

"They were women, sort of like mermaids, who lured men to their deaths."

"How did they lure them to death?" she smiled. "With their good looks?"

"No. They lured them with their singing."

Just for a moment, Tilda's mind returned to the mud, mold, filth and stench of the past she has spent four years in. She quickly remembered Elaine, smiled, nodded.

"Yes. Their song. Very good."

That afternoon, she went to the library and looked up sirens. Cross-references took her to other female monsters: *succubae, lamia, lorelei*. *Lorelei* were a European version of the Greek harpy and siren. They lured men to death through a song and fed on their souls. She sat in the tiny wooden carrel at a library until it closed at six. A librarian told her she would have to leave.

Stepping out into a foggy London night, she walked in the general direction of home. She had stopped smoking right after the war but wanted a cigarette to calm her. She might have wandered hours in the fog trying to sort out the thoughts racing through her brain but did not want to alarm her husband and children. She caught a bus and got home in time to cook supper.

For the next few days she turned over possibilities.

After concluding she had not grown delusive, she weighted the chances of the supernatural being real. Tilda had concluded she was more or less an atheist, though she did go to church for appearances and because she thought children should have at least some religious education. Yet science could not explain everything. Perhaps there were parasitic creatures of some sort. Perhaps they lived off the energy of other beings. She remembered the first time she saw the woman and how she had absorbed what looked like streams of blood and momentarily glowed red. Had she witnessed one of these beings glutted with the lives of the men who had been killed in battle that day? If creatures like this had always been around, stories of harpies and vampires would come from peoples' encounters with them. This idea went against everything progress and civilization had elucidated, yet she could not entirely dismiss the explanation.

And the song. She could never forget the song. When it came, men got up and went outside, exposed themselves, and were killed. Poor nurses Ames and Cummings had died when the eerie paean had overcome them. She had heard the strains, grown careless, and almost took a bullet herself. At first, when combat was heavy, the *lorelei* would not have needed to lure people outside and into the line of fire so she could absorb their life energy. After the lull in fighting, though, she used her song as a device to lead them to death. How had the woman suddenly dissolved? This had not been an hallucination. Richard and others found the loathsome mass of what had been her flesh. And the song—many others had heard it, not just she.

Two weeks after her trip to the library, Tilda came across an article in an encyclopedia of mythology that said the way to destroy a *lorelei* was to resist her song.

The memory of that night flooded her mind. She had been ensorcelled by the song. She had started to climb the ladder. The Germans in the opposite trenches would have seen her and shot her. The word "love" had reminded her of

Richard. It had broken the spell. It had returned her to reality. It had destroyed the *lorelei*.

Tilda stood at the window and looked out at the sun setting red over the rooftops of London. It had always set red in on the battlefield because of so much smoke and dust in the air from artillery fire. Here, it glowed red from coal smoke.

She watched the darkness gather until Richard asked her if she were coming to bed. It was Wednesday night, their usual night to make love. Love had saved her. Its song had drowned out the siren song of a spirit dead now. She turned and walked into the bedroom, smiling at him as she undid the buttons on her frock.

David W. Landrum teaches Literature at Grand Valley State University. His speculative fiction has appeared widely. His novellas The Gallery, Strange Brew, *and* The Prophetess, *and his full-length novel,* The Sorceress of the Northern Seas, *are available online.*

THE CELLAR

(THE STORY OF BLOODY BESSIE)

BY D. ALAN DUNN

Prelude

One October evening when the north wind swept down from the Rockies like the frozen breath of a ghastly beast, the sky was filled with thunderous lightning, and the moon was blotted out by dark looming clouds. Inside their warm home up Cripple Creek, two young girls waited for their treats as the smell of sweet cream, and apple dumplings tickled their noses from their mother's kitchen nearby.

Grandmother rocked the twin sisters on each knee as she told tales, on this All Hallows' Eve, of witches and goblins, and of things that go bump in the night. Grandmother was a good storyteller. Her voice crackled with age as she whispered out the stories of headless horsemen and haunted castles.

"Tell us the story of Bloody Bessie, Grandma," one of the girls asked.

"Yes, tell us again," the other agreed.

"Oh, darlings, it's a long story and grandmother is tired."

"But grandma, you tell it so well, please."

"Come now, girls, the dumplings are ready. Let grandma rest," mother yelled from the kitchen. "Aww, okay, Mother," the girls crooned together.

After the girls had finished their treats and their hair

was brushed out, they were dressed in their nightshirts, and allowed to play for a few more minutes before bedtime. The girls giggled as they ran down the steps to the root cellar, the spookiest place in the house.

They knelt before each other in the center of the cellar. Light from above shown through the cracks in the floorboards that illuminated the dirt floor with parallel stripes of dim yellow light. They dug a hole in the cold damp dirt, and chanted together this chant:

> *Bloody Bessie, Bloody Bessie.*
> *Face all red and hair all messy.*
> *Chant her name twice and one,*
> *And you will see what she has done.*

The girls held hands as they chanted Bloody Bessie once, twice and on the third, lightning flashed, and thunder rolled drowning out their young screams as something warm, thick and dark red bubbled up from the well they had dug between their knees — it was blood. The girls screamed as they ran from the cellar, "Grand-------ma!"

"What's the matter, dears? Oh, what have you gotten on your nightshirts?"

"It's blood, Grandma. We dug a hole, and called Bloody Bessie's name three times, and now she's going to chop us up in our sleep!"

"Oh no, dears, Bessie is long since dead and buried deep in the cold, cold ground. She can't hurt you."

"Mother, what was all that screaming about? Are the twins all right?"

"Yes, they are fine. They were playing in the cellar again and just got a little spooked. Storm's gettin' worse. I want to have the girls stay here with me in the main room for a while. Girls, go let your mother clean you up, and then come lay here by the fire. I will fix ya'll a pallet, and tell you both the truth about Bessie."

234

"Yeaaaa! Oh, thank you, grandma."

Shortly, the girls returned, and eagerly snuggled into their warm quilts. Their mother sat nearby doing some knitting while grandmother rocked in her rocker. The girls had never heard the story in its entirety, and their grandmother reckoned that they were of age enough now to hear the truth, as gory as it was.

The old woman rocked back and forth letting her little feet come off the floor as she told the story. Outside the thunderstorm added an eerie ambiance.

Grandmother's Telling

"In the year 1859, in an area below Pike's Peak in the western Kansas Territory during the days of The Great Pike's Peak Gold Rush, Thomas Church, his wife Bessie, and a young Cheyenne Indian boy named Chapal--that means 'one who is quick'--came to the foot of the Rockies in an area 44 miles southwest of Old Colorado City, and took up residence in a mining camp later known as Cripple Creek. The story of Bloody Bessie may have never been told if not for that young Indian boy who barely escaped the cruel and torturous captivity of his caregiver."

"How old was the Indian boy, Grandma?" one of the girls asked.

"Oh, he was prob'ly about 12 or 13 when he first told his story before a judge and jury in a crowded courtroom over in Old Colorado City. Old Bessie's witch-like face bitterly twisted, and mocked the Indian boy's words as he told all he knew," Grandmother said as she twisted her own tired old face to mimic Bessie's.

"Aaaaaahh! Grandma, stop you're scaring us. Tell us more."

"Well now, Thomas Church didn't have gold fever like most fellers did back then, but being a good businessman, he realized that men would be coming by the thousands to mine for gold in the vast mountains above, and they would have need of a warm, dry place to stay.

"The daring entrepreneur quickly purchased land, felled trees, and began construction of a three-story boardinghouse . . ."

"Grandma, what's an en-tre-pre-neur?" one of the girls asked.

"It's someone willing to take risks in a business venture. Okay, now where was I? Now the first years were quite prosperous, when many a mining company high hatter used the place as a base of operation, but the place fell onto hard times when a merciless blizzard shut down operations all over the region one long winter.

The boardinghouse might have recovered if Thomas Church would not have taken sick and died that winter. Left alone, Bessie and Chappy, as he was called, kept the place going as long as they could, but supplies and food quickly ran out.

Chappy was forced to hunt for wild game, and steal provisions from the mining camp's trading post. Winters were the hardest times for them since boarders were few and wild game was difficult to find, but Bessie would soon discover a way to not only to feed her and the boy, but most of the miners as well. Do you remember me telling you two that there is no such thing as monsters?"

"Yes, Grandma," the girls crooned in unison as they lay on their bellies and popped their heads on elbows. "You said it was just made up stuff to frighten children," one of the girls added.

"Yes, well, Grandmother wasn't being completely honest. You see, there are certain kinds of people whose actions are monster-like, and sometimes even a snowstorm can be monstrous like the blizzard that trapped Bessie, the boy and a poor old fool named Toby. That storm was so ghastly that it would eventually drive old Bessie crazy."

Just after twilight, a late December wind blew down sheets of snowflakes, some the size of handkerchiefs, which covered everything in a blanket of cotton ball white. Now, the western Kansas territory had seen its share of winter snows, but this phantom storm was like the breath of hell conjured up by the devil himself. The wind screamed like a banshee, and sliced through night like the blade of the reaper's sickle.

Now, somewhere up on ol' long mountain, a poor prospector inched his way down from his makeshift mining camp. He was nearly frozen stiff, and the already knee-deep snowfall bit at his toes like the razor sharp teeth of a rabid timber wolf. The tried and tested fellow was stricken with fear, because at times, the mighty wind blew so strongly that he was forced to hang on for his very life. The whiskers on his face covered with frost, and his snow-laden buffalo coat gave him the appearance of a snow creature.

He mumbled prayers as he struggled to take another step. Just as he was about to succumb to the storm's unrelenting might, a faint wisp of chimney smoke appeared below. With a new determination, he pressed on step by precious step.

Just after candle light, a knock came on a pair of huge oak doors as a traveler, so cold he was barely able to stand, bid entry. "Hel--lo the house!" he called as the bitter wind howled through the window frames.

"Chappy, go and see who is calling at this late hour."

"Yes ma'am," he said as he ran obediently to the doors.

Bessie braced as a gust of wind blew in drifts of snow through the opened doorway. From out of the whiteness a tall masculine form appeared like an apparition. "Ma'am, oh, praise the Lord. I need room and board. It's just too cold up in them hills."

"C'mon in there, mister, you're letting the storm in. Close that door, boy!"

"I'm Toby Coffey . . . thank yah kindly, ma'am," Toby tried to make his words sound manly, but his shivering gave him away as a frightened child.

Now, Bessie was a comely woman in those days. She was tall and big-boned. Her thick dark raven hair resembled salt and pepper with streaks of natural yellowish gray intertwined in the long blackish locks she normally wore in a big bun. Her face was barely beginning to show her age and hardships. Dressed in her nightdress, she quickly gathered the collar together at her neck, and covered her breasts modestly. "Excuse me, Mr. Coffey, while I fetch an apron, or something. I'm not decent. Are you hungry, sir?"

"Oh, please ma'am, call me Toby. No, ma'am, but some hot coffee would warm up my bones. For all that's good in the world, I'm about frozen plumb stiff. Sign out front says Bessie's boardin' house. Are you Bessie?"

"Yes, that's me and the boy's name is Chappy, and yes he is an Indian, and no he won't scalp you in your sleep," Bessie answered from another room as she dressed for company. "Hang your coat there on the hall tree, Mr. Coffey, and then get over by the fire there. I'll be out in a minute."

Coffey and the boy's eyes met. Playing on his mother's words, the boy stared through slanted eyes, devilishly. Coffey's eyes widened as he looked away. "How'd you come about having an Indian boy, Miss Bessie . . . ifen yah don't mind me askin'?"

"My husband and I adopted him when he was nearing his ninth year. His tribe raided our wagon train and killed some of ours, so the men raided their village in the middle of the night, and massacred them all. He was left for dead. My husband felt sorry for 'm and bought him to me to rear up. He don't talk much, but he's good at his chores."

In the foyer, Coffey pulled off his heavy buffalo coat, and shook off the snow. His reflection in the hall tree's mirror revealed the first look at himself in quite a while. The frost

238

that had formed in icicles on his beard and mustache was beginning to melt. Coffey rubbed his hand down his long beard as if he wasn't sure it was really his. It had been nearly three years now since he had stropped a razor; otherwise, he was a fairly good looking fellow.

Just then, Bessie emerged from an adjacent room. She had redressed herself in a bustled cotton print evening dress that clung to every curve of her voluptuous body. Her hair cascaded over each shoulder and down her back like the waters of Seven Falls when the snows melt in spring. Coffey could do little, but stare as he stood gentlemanly rigid, watching, waiting. "Mr. Coffey, please come, sit by the fire, and dry your clothes. It has been a time now since I have had the pleasure of a man's company. Come, let's talk for a spell. The boy will fetch our coffees."

"Thank yah kindly, ma'am. What's your terms?"

"Oh, bed and board is a dollar a day, or five dollars a week. The boy fetches wash water, and wood for the bedside stove. Breakfast is at first light . . . corncakes and molasses with coffee or tea. Supper's served at six o'clock, consisting of beans, put-up vegetables, and whatever the boy can hunt up. Don't worry, Mr. Coffey, I'm a good cook. I can make just about anything taste good."

"That sound's a right better than freezing to death up on that rock. It's bad up there. I didn't think I was gonna make it down. I seen yer chimney smoke and used it to guide me down."

"Are you a miner, Mr. Coffey?"

"Naw, I'm just a freelance prospector. Them miners are all hunkered down in the mines up there. If this storm keeps up, they liable to wind up like them Donners."

"Donners?"

"The Donner party, ma'am. It was a group of pioneers who set off from Missouri in a wagon train headed to California back in '46. They got stranded by snow up on the Sierra Nevada and when food runned out they went to eating each other."

"Oh, my word. You mean to tell me that a body can live on the flesh of a human being?"

"Oh, yes ma'am. It's called . . . can-ni-ba-lism. I read about it in one of them there en-cyclo-pedias. There's some jungle monkeys over in Africa that eat people. They call 'em can-ni-bals."

"Oh, my word."

"Oh, by the way, ma'am, I don't rightly have any paper money. I've got some nice nuggets though. Do you mind trading for 'em?"

"No, I don't mind. The man at the trading post will weigh them out and trade for supplies, so whatever puts food on the table."

The conversation died down as they each avoided eye contact. Coffey eyed the woman peripherally as he reverted from her to a portrait of Thomas Church that hung over the fireplace mantel. She smelled like spring flowers, and the way the firelight danced in her speckled tresses brought back memories of his last visit to Madame Genevieve's parlor house.

"Your husband is a good looking fellow. I look forward to meetin' him," Coffey said as he started conversation again.

"My husband passed on last winter, Mr. Coffey. It's just me and the boy now."

"Oh, I'm terribly sorry, ma'am."

"It's quite all right . . . ah . . . What is your given name, Mr. Coffey?"

"Oh, Tobias--Tobias Uriah Coffey. It's a dickens of a name. I guess that's why most folks just call me Toby. I mentioned it before. I guess you didn't hear."

"It's a lovely name, and it fits you well. How old are you, Toby?"

"I don't rightly know, Miss Bessie. Scrounging around up in them mountains tends to erase a man's memory. I figure I'm about two score and a couple of extra-rees."

"So you're forty-two, then."

"How 'bout yourself, Miss Bessie?"

"Oh now, Toby, you know a woman never reveals her age. Let's just say that I have seen a few less sunsets than you."

The conversation dropped off again and the only sound was that of a backlog crackling in the fireplace. "Well, Miss Bessie, my clothes are all dried now. I'm mighty tired. I hate to leave good company, but could you see me to my room?"

"Yes, Toby. The boy put your things in room ten, upstairs, second floor. It's just across the hall from mine, so if you need anything you just call."

"Thank you, Miss Bessie . . . Goodnight."

"Goodnight, Toby . . . Oh, there's a tub down the hall from your room if you wish to bathe. Also there's a razor and a shaving mirror. I can have the boy heat up some water," Bessie hinted.

"Oh, no ma'am. These whiskers tend to keep my face warm on cold nights. I plan to go back up there when this storm lets up... goodnight."

Outside, the blizzard raged. It was to be the longest snowstorm in the western Kansas Territory's history. It was to be a long, lonely winter as well. Up and down the hallways empty rooms lay in testament of the uncertainty of this godforsaken country.

It was on the second night that a man's presence had graced the halls of Bessie's Boardinghouse, and after another fireside chat with Coffey, that Bessie stood before her full length dressing mirror. She untied each bow down the bodice of her chemise and opened it. As she stood admiring her reflection, she moved her fingertips slowly down her upper torso in a soft gentle caress. She closed her eyes, and laid her head against her shoulder.

It was hard being a woman in such a disorderly territory. Men here had their minds on gold, and not on the delicacies of a woman. It was lonely without the company of a man. Toby had escaped her advances all evening with small talk and subject change. He would be leaving soon when the storm subsided. If she were going to share his bed, she would have to make the first move because Tobias was a goodly man.

Bessie's face smirked as she lowered her bloomers to the floor. Stepping out of them, she leaned down, and blew out the lantern. Bessie lighted a single candle, and walked toward the hallway. She stood outside Toby's door for a moment reluctant to enter, but with a sudden breath of courage, she went in.

Toby must have been expecting her because he was positioned on his side with one leg bent. He raised his head, and propped it up with his elbow in a manly fashion. His eyes caressed her completely. Nary was a word spoken, yet they spoke the language of love until early morning.

Bessie visited Coffey's room several more times that disastrous week. Winter blizzards were known to be severe, but never as ruthless as this beast. Strong, bitter winds blew mercilessly, day and night. A thick blanket of cloud had settled over the land, making visibility nearly impossible. It was as if the mighty Sun had abandoned the whole of the Earth.

Coffey and the boy had donned snowshoes earlier in the week, and trekked off to hunt for food, but unfortunately they came home empty handed. With the weather worsening, hunting had become impossible. Food stores in the cellar had run out as well.

An attempt to trek the five miles to the trading post would be suicide. Normally, folks would store up for winter knowing the history of this region, but Bessie had already exceeded her promissory note limit. The flour, cornmeal, sugar, and all the put up vegetables were gone; however, there was plenty of wood for the stove, plenty of water, all types of spices, pots, kettles, and everything needed for cooking except meat. That first week became two.

As Bessie lay in her bed, her stomach growled with hunger. She pondered on what Toby had said about the Donners and her mind began to squirm like a bullfrog. She began to plot an evil, but desperate plan, and when she was certain that her plan would work, she decided that she needed food more than she needed a man.

Bessie laid there in the dark, and schemed every detail. Toby was a big man, so hauling his carcass down to the cellar would be no easy task. He would have to be lured down, and killed. That part was easy enough; killing for food was nothing new to Bessie. She had pulled the head off many a chicken, and even butchered a few hogs, but how does one go about cutting up a human body? she pondered.

She would need to make use of every piece, so as to not have anything left over to deal with. The skin could be stripped off, and boiled in hog fat to make cracklings. Deeper chunks could be spiced and smoked. Sausages could be made from the tender pieces like ears, lips and nose. She and the boy could live for months with the amount of dried meat a 200 pound man could yield.

Early the next morning, Bessie went to wake the boy. "Boy, wake up! Hear me now. Go out to the shed and fetch me a saw, the block and tackle, the axe and hatchets and take it all down to the root cellar… and don't wake Mr. Coffey. Hurry now or I'll take pappy's razor strap to your backside!"

The boy obeyed without question, even as he carried the tools through nearly 50 inches of snow and icy wind, and down the steep steps of the cellar, he never queried. It wasn't the fear of the razor strap, but Miss Bessie's raging temper that drove him like a buggy horse with blinders. He had seen a side of her that her guests rarely saw.

By noon, they were both busy hammering nails, and sawing planks savaged from an old shed. It had taken the boy over an hour to dig it out, and the blinding snowstorm was no help. In a corner of the cellar, an old kettle stove for a smokehouse. In the center of the cellar, the block and tackle was hung from a floor joist. Toby had only come down from his room once, and hadn't asked what they were up to. If he was going to starve to death, he preferred to die alone.

That evening Bessie, tired, and covered with dust and spider web, climbed the stairs to her room. As she passed Toby's door, she could hear his snoring. "Dreadful man," she spat out in disgust. "If he's going to snort like a hog, then a hog he shall be."

Bessie washed and dressed for bed. The long day of hard work without food had made her weak, but she only needed to wait one more night, for on the morrow they would have plenty.

Murder at the 13th Step

The dawning of the next day came in a veil of secrecy as the black-hearted blizzard shrouded the sun's arrival. If not for the chiming of a mantel clock, and the screams of her empty belly, Bessie would not have known it was morning.

The house was eerily cold and damp as Bessie's form glided down a long hallway to the stairway. A spray of vapor escaped from her mouth with each exhale. Her sunken and despondent eyes, sleep-tangled hair, and hunger-stricken face gave her the appearance of a character from a Charles Dickens novel.

Downstairs, she woke the boy, who occupied a small room on the first floor, and set him about his morning chores. "Chappy, up now! Fetch wood and stoke the stoves and fireplace. When you're done with that, light the stove in the cellar, and wait for me there. Keep quiet, and out of sight. We have some cooking to do today." The boy was oblivious to her wicked plan. He trustingly obeyed.

In the kitchen, Bessie put on water to boil. She carefully unwrapped some well-strained coffee beans and prepared them for another futile straining. When the kettle started to boil, she mounted the stairs, and moved toward Coffey's room. Knocking lightly on the door she called, "Toby, would you come down for a coffee? I apologize that I have no more to offer."

"Sure, Miss Bessie, I'll be right down. I feel like a fly in a cobweb anyhow."

Bessie returned to the kitchen and poured boiling water over a swatch of gossamer cloth filled with mushy coffee beans. The product acquired was little more than weak tan water, but it was, at least, something hot on a cold morning.

It wasn't long before Toby came to join her. "Good morning, Mr. Coffey, sit and have some coffee. Do you think the storm will pass soon?"

"I'm a hopin'. It sounds like it has already lost some of it kick."

"Have you ever seen a blizzard this bad?"

"Well, naw, I can't say that I have. The winter of '62 was pretty bad, but this one has lasted longer than any blow I have ever seen."

"That was the winter I lost my dear Thomas. He took to the fever after going out hunting."

"That's a shame, Bessie. As soon as it lets up, I'll go out, and see if I can muster up something for the pot. Everything, and everybody has been holed up for so long now that just like us, them critters are gonna be wantin' to stretch their legs. I'll find us a nice fat buck or a rabbit of something."

"Oh, that sounds nice, Toby."

"What was all that hammerin' down in the root cellar yesterday?"

"Oh, it's a surprise."

"A surprise? For me?"

"Yes," Bessie said, straight-faced. Behind hungry eyes her perverse brain plotted ghoulishly. "Come and I'll show you."

Toby followed blindly as Bessie led him to the cellar

door. "Mind the steep stairs as you go down, I'll come behind you," Bessie said thoughtfully as if she really cared for his safety.

The cellar was dark. The only light was lantern light from the rooms above that shone through the cracks in the floorboards, and the flickering of firelight from the old wood stove. In the center of the room, a deep hole had been dug in the dirt floor, and above it was the block and tackle. A large boiling pot steamed on the old stove, and nearby a long wooden table held knives, saws, and cleavers. In a darkened corner the boy crouched, hiding himself as he had been instructed.

Toby stopped at the thirteenth downward step and as his eyes adjusted to the poor lighting, he glanced about the room. Behind him and unnoticed, Bessie picked up a hatchet she had premeditatedly placed under the top step of the stairway. "Well now, you have built a slaughterhouse. Has the boy yielded us some meat?"

"Yes… can you see it there in the corner?" Toby leaned in. His eyes were wide with anticipation. "Um… but that looks like the Indian bo… oomph!"

The downward swing of the hatchet spilt the back of Toby's skull open and blood splattered out, covering Bessie's face. Toby dropped to his knees, dazed, terrorized, and dying. "Oomph--umph--oomph--arrg!" Bessie whacked him again and again violently until his limp body sprawled flat out and gave up the ghost. The boy stood in shock as he unbelievingly watched. "Quick boy, help me drag him around, and string him up. We gotta bleed him out," Bessie said casually and matter-of-factly. The boy was frozen with fear and disbelief. "Did you hear me, boy? Don't stand there gawking with your teeth in your mouth. There is work to be done!"

The boy did not move. His eyes bulged, and all he could do was shake his head--no. Bessie's face raged with anger. She looked about for a stick or switch--something to beat him with, and then remembered the bloody hatchet in her hand.

Holding it out in front of her, she lunged at the boy. "Do you want me to whack you like I did that man? He is not a man anymore, boy, he is food now… do you hear me, boy?-- food! Now get over here and pull him around!" The boy complied.

Bessie and the boy repositioned the corpse, and Bessie pulled off his boots. She tied his ankles together, and fastened the hook of the block and tackle. While boy pulled the cadaver up, she cut off his clothes. As Toby's naked body hung upside down over the hole, Bessie slit his throat, and blood gushed out by the gallons.

Bessie never realized how much blood was in a human body. She had spent several nights in the library of the house studying through some old encyclopedias. She had learned much about the human body, but the new knowledge did not prepare her for the morbidity of death, yet her intense hunger determined her.

As blood oozed out, Bessie massaged the carcass from the feet down as if she were milking out every drop of blood. She showed no remorse as she went about her work. Her warped mind rationalized her actions, and she justified it not as murder, but survival. The horrified boy looked away and cowered nearby.

"You see, boy, we must bleed out every drop of blood. It is too rich in iron, and will poison the meat. We will wash and boil every cut and soak it in spices. We'll smoke some nice strips and make jerky meat. Do as you're told, boy and your belly will soon be full."

The slow trickle of blood had begun to dwindle, so Bessie kneeled, held the head by its hair, and sliced it off, dropping it into the hole. After a short wait, she and the boy lifted and repositioned the cutting table over the hole, and lowered the body down.

Next, Bessie fetched a bowl of wash water and soap. She washed the body thoroughly, and used a straight razor to shave it clean. With saw, hatchet, and clever she started at the feet, and butchered the carcass into workable cuts of meat.

The internal organs and undesirable pieces were dropped into the blood pit and covered with lime. The two of them worked all day, and long into the night cutting, chopping, stripping, washing, grinding, stuffing, and boiling.

By morning, the first batch of cracklings was cooking in a pot of boiling hog fat upstairs in the kitchen, and the make-shift smokehouse was full of specially seasoned strips of meat. In a span of 24 hours, they had dressed out enough protein-rich meat to last for months, and the unprocessed parts were wrapped and packed in snow.

Bessie Church slumped in a table chair immodestly. Her flower-print cotton dress and apron were covered in blood. The blood splatter on her face had mixed with sweat, turning her whole face crimson in color. Her uncombed hair encircled her head like a thicket of briars growing around an oak stump. The twinkle in her tired eyes was that of selfishness and greed. Her once lovely face had turned witch-like and her life would be forever altered.

The Feeding

A night and a day later, the blizzard finally ended, and a single ray of sunlight broke through, and shone through Bessie's bedroom window. Snowdrifts, some as high as her second story window, nearly encapsulated the house. From an attic dormer window, it appeared as if the whole world had been buried alive in deep thick snow.

Bessie wondered if anyone had survived, but a part of her knew that they would be coming down soon, and they would be hungry. In the dining hall, she and the boy, who had escaped into his own private spirit world, pushed two oak tables together, and set out plates for a large number. The boy never spoke another word after his horrible ordeal, and he responded to her commands mindlessly.

Privately, he had recovered a medicine bag and feather from under a loose floorboard, and had performed a ceremony that gave him courage to stand without fear. His body was present, yet his soul was safe from Bessie's wickedness.

Many Indians believed that eating the heart of their prey would give them great strength as a hunter, but never before apologizing for taking its life. What his caregiver was doing was a great abomination. He only ate to survive, and apologized for every bite.

"Chappy, dress warm and go fetch buckets. The well has frozen over and we must melt snow and replenish the water barrel." Saying nothing, the boy went without hesitation. "Why if that don't cry yah a handkerchief full of tears. I swear that boy is moodier than a hound dog with a tail full of cockleburs. You'd think he was ailin' from cabin fever or something," Bessie spoke out loud as if she were speaking to a room full of boarders.

Bessie moved through the house opening shutters and pinning back drapes. She checked each of the twenty bedrooms, fluffed pillows, and straightened the bedcovers in hopes that the house would be full by sundown. Catching a glimpse of herself while passing a mirror, she observed her face for the first time in days.

The mirror reflected the reality of what she had become. Using her hand, she tried to straighten her tangled hair. The eyes in the mirror accused her so she turned away from the image self-consciously and withdrew into a world of secrecy.

With much work still to be done, she found time to wash, fix her hair, and change into a clean dress. "Chappy, stoke the fire in the fireplace . . . build a big one . . . use wet wood, I want lots of smoke to lead their way."

By late afternoon Bessie was beginning to fear that no one had survived. Surely someone would have seen the smoke by now, she asked herself as she peered out windows.

The view was the same in any direction, a sea of pure white sparked with dots of diamond.

Through half-opened windows nary a sound could be heard for miles. Bessie sat down hard on a settee in the great room still hopeful that men would be coming soon. Bessie laid her head back against the plush Victorian fabric and closed her eyes.

The warmth of the sun was beginning to fade when she turned an ear to a faint distant sound. It was the sound of muffed voices. Men's voices, she decided. Rising quickly, she adjusted the hoops and bustle on her dress and ran to the great doors.

Stepping out on the veranda, she shielded her eyes from the bright whiteness as she searched the distance for the source of the voices. Just topping a nearby rise, she spotted first one hat and then another. Men were coming from the direction of the trading post. She stood at the edge of the veranda and waved her handkerchief. "Hel-lo thare, Miss Bessie," a man yelled out from a distance.

"Come, gentlemen and warm yourselves," she answered. There were six men in all each wrapped in heavy buffalo coats. Their faces were distraught with hunger. "We are sure glad to see that you survived the snowstorm, have you any supplies? The trading post and mining camp has been buried under an avalanche . . . poor souls. Women and children all."

"God have mercy," she said as the men tromped closer.

"We're miners from the high point mine. We're all that left. We lost six men up thar. Dreadful storm it was."

"Yes, siree, it was quite dreadful. C'mon in, boys."

"Miss Bessie, We'll be frank with you, we have been without supplies for some time now and there's nothing to be salvaged from the camp. Have you any provisions, ma'am?"

"Yes, take off your coats and warm up by the fireplace. I will serve you all in the dining hall." I'm sorry that I have no coffee or tea and nothing for the sweet tooth, but I have meat."

"Oh, praise God . . . Bessie you're a godsend."

Bessie frowned as she turned away to go to the kitchen. Under her breath she mumbled. "God did not have anything to do with it."

After a while, when the men were thawed out, Bessie seated them around the tables. First she brought out a pitcher of water and drinking glasses. Next a large platter of cracklings and then a platter of her specially made smoked jerky meat. The men filled their plates.

"Bessie, this meat is delicious. I don't believe I have ever had meat this good," one of the men said.

Another asked, "I can't make out what kind of meat this is. Is it venison?"

Bessie smiled as they tore off strips and chewed. "No."

"Is it mutton?" another asked.

"Gentlemen, it's a secret recipe and if I told you what it is it would not be a secret, now would it?"

"No, ma'am I guess not, but whatever it is it is very good."

"You men say you are all that is left of the miners?"

"Oh, from our little mine yes, but there are prob'ly hundreds still up there. Our mine is the closest to the mining camp and trading post. Others will be coming."

"Ma'am, you may have to feed them all for a while. It'll be a week or ten days before someone can get through to Colorado City. Word needs to be sent that we need supplies. Someone will have to rebuild the trading post when the snows melt."

Just then, Bessie withdrew into her own thoughts as the men filled themselves. Toby was a big man and had yielded much meat, but it would not be enough to feed the masses. Her brain squirmed like a king snake. "Did you men meet anybody else today?"

"No, ma'am. The avalanche is blocking the valley. The other will have to climb the ridge. May take a couple of days."

"Gentlemen, you must excuse me now. I have to rest a

bit. The boy will see to your needs. Make yourselves to home."

"Thanks, Bessie. You sure are a good cook. This is just delicious."

Bessie pondered as she lay on her bed. Tonight she must replenish her meat supply. No one would miss these men. Others would be coming and she must have enough to go around. The killing would be tricky and she needed to give it some thought, but first she must rest. It would be a long night.

The Slaughter of the Six

Once she had risen from her nap, Bessie made up six different rooms that were a room or more apart so that the men would not be awakened by any unforeseen disturbances. The men were gathered around the fireplace when she came down wearing her best corset and ball gown. Remnants of tobacco smoke hung over their heads as they told stories.

The men stood when she entered the room. Bessie watched their eyes. Now that their bellies were full and the jug had been passed round, there was only one lust remaining and Bessie welcomed it. As a matter of fact, she provoked it. Women have ways, seductive mannerisms which used cunningly can entice a man to do almost anything.

Bessie smiled as she sashayed over to a Pianola. Cranking the mechanism, the music began. Next, she held out her hand palm down as she batted her eyes. The men scrambled to be the first to dance with her. The room was full of gaiety.

Bessie smiled, laughed and bounced her bosoms as they each had their turn dancing her, holding her, groping her and kissing her. Bessie ensured each of them with a sultry whisper that she would be joining them in their chamber later that evening.

One-by-one the men trekked off to bed, save one. He

was a craggy-faced man no more than 40 years old, yet weathered by hard-work he appeared much older. Somewhat shyer than the others, he had only enjoyed a single dance before he retired to a quiet corner by the fire.

Bessie watched him as he puffed his pipe, seemingly uninterested in her flaunts. Precious time was being wasted with his reluctance to go up to bed. If using her charms to coax him off to bed with great expectations were unsuccessful, he would simply have to be the first to die. Bessie walked over and stood by him. "Will you be going up to bed soon, sir?"

"Oh, I'll be fine here for a while. I like watching the fire burn. See how the flame dances between the logs. It's sort of entrancing, reminds me of my home back in Texas. I have a girl there. I came up here to try to find enough gold to buy a ranch. Then I plan to marry her."

"That's wonderful," she said. Bessie did not care to hear his stories. She did not even care to know his name. It would make her task harder if she got personal with him. "Well then, here… sit here in this rocker and face the flame. You will have a much better view," she said dragging a rocking chair up to the mantle. He complied.

Bessie turned to the boy who had been watching all evening. Her face twisted back into her witch-like expression. She motioned for him to follow her out of the great room. When they were both safely away, she ordered him. "Go and build fires in the cellar, sharpen the knives and get things ready. Tonight we slaughter."

The boy's eyes widened with dread, and he wished himself somewhere far away—far away from his wicked caregiver and her murderous ways.

In a corner of the cellar, Bessie filled a washtub with heated water and removed all of her garments. Then she walked back up the stairs, hiding her hatchet behind her back. The great room was dark. In the glow of the fireplace light, she could see the craggy-faced man.

When she stood next to him, he immediately noticed

her nudity. "I have made us a bed in the cellar . . . if you want me," she said in a seductive voice. He stood. She stepped away from his reach. Giggling, she said. "Not here, the boy may see. Go down to the cellar. I'll follow you." The man obeyed. Her bobbles were hard to resist.

The man stopped halfway down the cellar steps. Something told him that the woman had lied. There was no bed. Pots of boiling water and all types of butchering implements lay in wait. Just as he jerked round to escape, Bessie, using the entire strength of her arm, sank the sharp hatchet deep into his skull. His eyes rolled back.

"Quickly boy, bleed him out and gut him. I must prepare for the next one!" Next, standing in the tub, she washed away the blood that had splattered on her bare skin and went upstairs to lure down her next victim.

One-by-one the men came down each being deceived by her tricks and each succumbing to her madness. Nearly noon the next day, Bessie finally collapsed into her bed, nearly exhausted from the night's work. The six had been slaughtered, bled out and butchered. Only one was cooked. The others were placed in snow-packed boxes.

On her dressing table lay the spoils of her labors. Along with the men's personal belongings like pocket knives and watches, tobacco sacks bulged with gold nugget. Later she would send the boy to the mine to retrieve other worthy implements such as pickaxes, shovels--anything that could be traded for supplies. With expectations of great fame for her delicious dried meats, Bessie slept peacefully.

Journey for Justice

"In yonder years," said Grandmother, watching little heavy eyes fight to stay open, "Indians were not accepted in white society. They had no rights and were treated worse than stray dogs. Chappy had quite a journey ahead of him, you see. He had seen enough. He felt obligated to make the long forty-four mile walk to Old Colorado City. He had to convince whomever would listen that his caregiver had gone mad."

The weather bettered the afternoon that Bessie slept. Chappy saw his chance to escape. Gathering his belongings and his hunting rifle, he donned snowshoes and slipped off toward the southwest. As soon as he was well away from the boarding house, he fell to his knees and put his finger deep down his throat until he vomited out every last remaining piece of human flesh. He would live on what he could hunt along the way now.

After a nearly a week of non-stop traveling through deep snow and treacherous terrain, Chappy arrived at Colorado City half frozen and half dead. He was first spotted coming down the street by some men who were loading supplies onto a wagon. "Look thare! It's a injun kid! Prob'ly sick with the fever. I'll put 'm down," the man said raising his rifle.

Then as a school teacher that happened to pass by yelled, the man held his fire. "Don't you see that he is civilized? Mister, don't you dare pull that trigger!"

"But, ma'am!"

"Look at his hair . . . it is cut short and his clothes are modern. He has come for help!"

The woman took him in and helped him regain his strength. A day later when his fever broke, he told her the story. At first she did not believe, thinking him still delirious by the fever. But he told the story with such passion that she decided it best to inform the sheriff.

The sheriff came and listened to his story. He was not completely convinced that the boy was sane. "He's talking gibberish. Nobody could do the things he said his keeper did. It's just insane, but I reckon I ought to ride over and look into it."

It just so happened that a wagon train was headed out that very day to rebuild the trading post and bring aid to the miners up Cripple Creek. The sheriff rode along. He had heard tell of Bessie's Boardinghouse, but he had never had the pleasure of meeting Thomas and Bessie Church. If nothing more, this would be his chance.

When the team arrived, the snows from the avalanche had melted and the entrance to the valley was passable. The men went about their work rebuilding and burying the dead while the sheriff rode on to Bessie's.

When he arrived, there were men everywhere. Some sat on the veranda while others chopped wood and did chores. Sheriff Stout went inside without hailing the house. Bessie was in the great room entertaining several men who sat around the fireplace.

He could tell by the look in Bessie's eyes when she saw his sheriff's badge that she was guilty of something. "You Bessie Church?" he questioned.

"Yes, I am. C'mon in, sheriff."

"Mrs. Church we have your Indian boy. He was mighty sick with the fever, but he's all right now."

"Oh, well . . . he run off last week . . . left me to do his chores until these men came along. That boy ain't all there, sheriff. I hope he was no trouble to yah."

"Mrs. Church, I need to see your cellar if yah don't mind."

"My cellar? What on earth for?"

"Well, let's just say that the boy told a pretty good story that couldn't possibly be true, but ifen I was to take a quick looksee . . . you don't mind do you, ma'am?"

"Well, yes sir I do mind. I've got some of my personals hanging to dry down there. You see."

"Ma'am, I've seen personals before. Is that the cellar door there?"

Bessie ran ahead of him and stood in front of the door even though it was well bolted and locked.

"Stand aside, ma'am!"

"No, sir. I can't let you down there!"

Suddenly, some of the other men had gathered 'round curiously. "Grab 'er, boys! I'm going down there one way or another." Bessie screamed like a banshee as they grabbed her. The sheriff shot off the lock and went down. The room smelled of blood and death.

Other men followed him down and when they all saw the boxes of frozen body parts, some of them vomited. "Get a rope! One man yelled. "Yeah, let's hang the witch!" yelled another.

The sheriff fired his pistol into the dirt floor to get their attention. "There'll be no lynching today, boys. I'm taking her back for a fair trial."

A week later, Bessie sat before a judge and jury of twelve men. Her face twisted as she mocked the Indian boy's words as he told all. There was much disorder among the crowd and jury. Several times the judge had to strike his gavel. Some of the women in the courtroom fainted and had to be removed, but after an hour Bessie Church was sentenced to hang for the murders of seven men. The execution was carried out the next morning at ten a.m. and that, my dears, was the end of Old Bloody Bessie.

"That was a wonderful telling, Mother."

"Look they have both fallen asleep. Bless their hearts," Grandmother said rising slowly from her rocker. "We should go and see what they have gotten into in the cellar."

"Yes, prob'ly an old can of paint or something. Here let me hold your arm. The stairs are steep."

Grandmother held a lantern as her and her daughter slowly descended the stairs. "Oh… what on earth? What is that, Mother?"

"It's blood red and it appears to be bubbling up from the hole the girls said they dug. You don't reckon they recited that old folklore chant?"

"The one I used to chant as a girl?"

"Yes."

"I could never muster up the courage to say her name three times. I don't think anyone has. It smells horrible in here. Like rotting carcasses. Let's go."

"Wait, dear, this explains it. Look there in the corner... the rain is washing through the timbers. The whole dirt floor is soaked. The rain has re-hydrated the blood from Bessie's victims!"

"Mother! Do you mean to tell me that the story is true? I thought it was just a ghost story, and why would you think this cellar is Bessie's cellar?"

"Oh child, Yes the story is very much true. You see, I have never told you this, but the Indian boy was my father. After Bessie's hangin' he came back here and burned the place to the ground and our house is built over the same foundation. So this is Bessie's basement."

"Oh, lordy, do you think the girls may have . . .?

"Pray no, daughter--Pray no!"

The ladies looked down at their feet. They were standing on the thirteenth downward step as a river of bloody mud flowed across the cellar floor. Behind them a noise. A quick turn to see. Above, an apparition appeared from a cloud of vapor. Just as it manifested itself, they saw the figure of an old winkled woman in a bloody white apron--her face all red and hair all messy. As it shot down the stairway, its skeleton teeth chattered, and in its hand was a bloody hatchet. Blood curdling screams shattered the silence of the night.

No one was ever sure as to what actually happened that cold stormy night, but some say a lightning strike burned Grandmother's house to the ground. Only two small bodies were found in the ashes. It was a great location, so it was only a matter of time before the house was rebuilt—right over the cellar.

D. Alan Dunn is a native south Texan retired from the building and plumbing trades after a bout with cancer. A longtime fan of crime mystery and horror fiction, Dunn's hidden talent for writing exploded into reality in 2007 when he wrote his memoirs for his grandchildren. Since then, his repertoire of author published works consist of The Moods of My Heart – *a collection of poems, sonnets and quatrains and* 5 After Midnight – *a collection of short stories in the psychological and horror genres.*

Dunn has also penned a series of western adventure novels and is currently writing Dead Bone Posse, *a crime/horror novel that blends the old west with the crime violent 1930s. Once having a story-telling father and a novelist mother, Dunn has a natural passion for telling tales. A bit of a warning: don't get him to talking; he never knows when to shut up, especially when he is talking about his writing.*

ST AYER'S GOSPEL

BY OLIVER SMITH

I sat in the public bar of 'The Turkish Reveree'; the jukebox was blasting out some rockabilly. Will Maurice, Jack Rackham and Pikey McKnight were gambling and knocking back a few pints. My granddad always said, "It's the way of the devil to betray men, draw them to ruin their good deeds in drink, and entice them to waste their lives in pleasure." Will Maurice, Jack Rackham and Pikey McKnight were very enticed that night. They danced to Jimmie Lloyd, rock-and-rolled to the 'Rio de Rosa' and didn't care whether they spilled their drinks on the flagstone floor or me. They all sang:

Down in San Antone where the Rio de Rosa flows
I'm gonna settle down, down in ol' San Antone

In between their drinking and dancing, they made fun of me.

Will Maurice, shouted, "Come on Captain Cyclops, have a jar, don't just sit there hogging the fire and fretting over Davy Jones's Diary."

Jack Rackham said "Have a tot of rum, Nelson."

"Won't you have a glass of grog and dance a jolly hornpipe to Billy Lee?" said Will Maurice, spinning on his heel, jerking and jiving around me like a madman.

"Johnny Kidd and the Pirates is the band for him", said Pikey McKnight "with his granddad and that."

"Looked a lot like you, did Old Wooden, what with the

eye," said Jack Rackham.

I answered them then. I said, "Old Wooden, that was the name his good brothers gave him when they pulled him ashore; they thought he was driftwood from a winter storm, him being so cold and sea-mauled. He should have been dead, but he was a fine man, a strong man, a wise man who saw more with his one eye than most men see with two, and too good a brother to the sea for the sea to kill him. Your own grandpa was there, Pikey; he was just about to saw through his frozen fingers to get this book off him, and well--your grandpa had his knife out and raised it to make the first hack. Then my granddad nearly gave Grandpa Pikey a heart attack because though my granddad had lain all night in the cold arms of the grey widow-maker and had come to them frozen stiff and solid, he opened up his mouth and said a prayer. Right scared them, I understand.

> *I was young when I set out on the endless ocean*
> *For a hundred years on those grey ways I toiled.*
> *I was crushed by the bitter home-longing in my heart*
> *until for nine full nights I lay bound in the weed*
> *Wounded seven times by the bites of Ran's Teeth*
> *a gallon of blood each night I bled, until, at last*
> *with these pages I stuffed my empty skull*

He was a lucky man. He was a pious man. The gods give the pious the luck. He taught me the skills of his elderfathers. He taught me to read the old prayers and sing them high and pure as a nightingale just like the old lidmen did. He could navigate the wily and treacherous waters of Granny Ran's Grounds like no one since the elderfathers. So don't you slander him, Pikey McKnight, they never proved the piracy."

Jack said, "Keep your hair on."

Will said, "Never heard you speak so much ashore."

Pikey said, "Sorry, Nelson."

But they were still laughing inside at the precious memory of my good old granddad. My granddad always said that 'cattle die, kinsmen die and even the gods will die, but the one thing that never dies is the reputation of each dead man'. If he could hear them talk and what in their talk they made of his reputation, he'd have skinned them alive, poked their eyes out and hung them upside down from an oak tree for the ravens. He did have a temper, my old granddad.

They downed their pints and shot their dice, they laughed at the book, the book of St. Ayer handed down from my elderfathers.

"Put down that Devil's Bible, Cyclops, play some dice with us, dice with us for a round," said Will Maurice.

You might think I should have joined them, loosened up, had fun, but it was the night of a fishing trip and Granddad always said, "If you're going on the sea, no bread should you take, nor slake your thirst with strong drink."

So I sat close by the fire and I undid the bronze clasps with the old key, the old key shaped like a twist of wrack-weed, the metal gone all green with saltwater corrosion and the turning of time. I undid the clasps, the clasps shaped like the clawed and grasping feet of ravens. I uncurled each scaly raven toe and although the hinges were reluctant with the ages, when they moved they moved smooth and quiet. I peered into the pages of the old book; it drew me down, down into the seven lines times seven of the hymns and the seven lines times nine of the prayers. It was as if I looked somewhere deep as the sea. What was written there I took up, I took it up though I screamed inside. Screaming inside I leaned forward, closer than ever to the fire, shaking from the chill of the elderfathers' memory; shaking with cold and knowledge. I saw the future with my one good eye and with the other one that ain't really there.

The future, we all want to know our futures. Well let me tell you how it looked. It looked just the same as the past:

the cattle died, the kinsmen died, and even the gods died. Just like my granddad said. Just like always.

I huddled ever closer to the flames, trying to get some warmth into my bones all frozen from being so near my elderfathers; my elderfathers who stand caught forever in the northern ice. My elderfathers who are buried in shallow graves hacked in the permafrost. My elderfathers who lie drowned at the bottom of the cold grey sea. I got too close to the flames and my coat started smouldering. I had to beat it out with my hands and then I cursed as my fingers flamed and sparked like distress flares.

That made them laugh.

"Get some sleep, Will Maurice and Jack Rackham," I shouted, quenching my fingers in Pikey's pint so it hissed and steamed "Get yourself sober, Pikey McKnight."

Will and Jack called me Killjoy and Grim-man.

Pikey said "Leave off, you old slave driver."

Although they laughed, they heeded me and left 'The Turkish Reveree' well before midnight.

At four in the morning they were back, back to follow me into Granny Ran's Grounds. They followed me with sore heads and scum-glued eyes, they followed me on unsteady legs, their hands still palsied from the beer.

Why did they follow?

They followed because I have St Ayer's Gospel.

Will Maurice, Jack Rackham and Pikey McKnight laughed in my face as they signed on for a share of the catch, put their marks in the Superstitious Book, annotated the Devil's Bible, and made their entry in Davy Jones's Diary.

"There" I told them, "now we have made us all goodbrothers,"

They found hollows and lockers to stow their gear aboard the 'Lindy'. Just a little boat, but they knew I would bring them a good haul. Bring them cod and pollack bigger than those the big ships can catch, bring the big wreck-eels that fight in the deep like you've got a sea serpent hanging on the line but turn limp as jelly aboard the boat. No other boat brings in fish of that size and quality and those fine fish would fetch a good price from the smart restaurants. From all those smart restaurants that send buyers to the quayside to welcome me home, all those fine restaurants that would never let the like of me through the doors.

I hauled myself aboard the 'Lindy', and they rolled her easily through the shingle, but she stuck on the strandline.

"Come on," I shouted, "Heave!" and they had to bend down and brace their feet in the slippery stones and force her through the weed and wreckage. As she slid free into the surf, Pikey went over, that Pikey went head first into the shallows, thrashing like a beached mackerel, the cold waves were hissing on the shingle and he yelped and howled like a startled dog.

It gave me the first good laugh I'd had all evening. Really lifted my mood.

"Are you sober now, Pikey," I said, "are you freshened up a bit?"

The other two helped him aboard and he sat cursing under a tarpaulin changing out of his freezing clothes before he caught his death.

So we set out, the little diesel motor chugging away nice and regular as we rounded the beacon on the headland groin with the dark still sea before us. The land was empty of light, just a dark silhouette of hills against the stars with the unending waters rolling beneath the keel's draught.

The cover felt smooth beneath my fingers, the ash-wood grown hard as iron with the years, the skin covering the ashboards turned hard as wood with time. That cover polished with the wax and oil of my ancestor's hands till it shone: shone like a flanks of a bass or a herring fish. I don't know what animal's hide it is that covers St Ayer's Gospel; at a guess I would say walrus. The cover has a picture on it. It isn't a painted picture, but an image pressed hard into its surface; blind embossed with a heavy punch. The picture is familiar; it shows my elderfathers in a boat. It surprises me how little boats have changed since the book was made; but then again, men haven't changed either. There's only one way to build a boat. There's only one way to make a man. Of course the tugs and liners and factory ships are a bit different, the crews too if you come upon them. But little craft that fish day to day, night to night, and men that scrape and scoop their living from the sea along the coast remain much the same. Perhaps I have a diesel engine inserted aft, so I don't need rowers, perhaps a radio under a bench so I don't need no raven to signal the land. All the same, the 'Lindy' looks much like the image pressed into the skin of that book. Very much like the little boat with my elderfathers rowing through the Stonegate at midnight.

Will Maurice, Jack Rackham and Pikey McKnight sat on the hard oak benches in 'The Lindy' drinking from a thermos flask and passing baccy and a little bottle of spirit between them. Combing Brylcreem into their hair and trying to mould and massage it into shape. I pretended not to notice; they may be my goodbrothers but I only need them for the muscle.

I sat watching at the bow's wake, St Ayer's Gospel clutched in my ice cold fingers. Straight through the night I took her, steering her clear of hidden reefs and those monstrous things that roll among the lonely lows of the grey seas. These things were all laid out in the prayers and hymns in the book. It was just the same as when it was written or maybe not quite the same. It would be strange if these waters were unchanged since the elderfathers navigated them all those years ago. I think the book must have altered since then. Though then again, if the book has changed that would be strange. Perhaps it's just that here the waters are as they were before the trawlers tore the life from the sea. Here just beyond the shore, among Granny Ran's granite teeth, sharp black rocks too close-packed and *wantij's* too shallow to admit a bigger boat.

We skulk and wind around the coast in shadow of cliffs where the motor disturbs the gannets in their shanty nests and alarmed whooper and curlew calls and mewling gull rise like white ghosts in the wind. We skulk with black scent of diesel fumes billowing from the motor, after the fish that the big factory ships can't reach, the fish on the wrecks and reefs caught with line and skill.

Through storm and treacherous calm.

I sat leafing through St Ayer's Gospel, rehearsing my part.

"See, Pikey, how the pages are so white? That's parchment, the finest parchment you'll ever see, do you know how they made it so fine and pretty and white? It's not rags or wood pulp like modern books. It's skin you see, stretched on a frame and dried and split thin and polished. That's why the covers have to be so stiff, so solid. That's why it has to have those big bronze clasps; to keep all the pages pressed in tight, to stop it going back to its old shape, it has to be. This parchment is so fine, the finest ever, not sheep you think, Jack, no not sheep.

"Pikey, you think it would be goat, this parchment, or perhaps kidskin? With your signature in red drying now to blackest black ink on fine white parchment like all those other names, thousands of them going back to the elderfathers?

"What do you think it is, Pikey? Well it's not goat that parchment, no, not even kidskin, the skin this is made from is too white. Can you see the marks of goat hairs? No it's too fine, too pretty. It's just too fair and pretty. You see the men who made this book weren't exactly Christian. No, they weren't kind men. They were hard, tough, and evil, but you had to be to be a sailor in those days. Given the sort of men that made it you don't want to know what it's made from and I don't want to tell, I'll just leave you to wonder.

"No, Pikey, you really don't want to know what it's made of."

Cold fetters froze my feet and hunger seared my heart with sore sea-weariness. We were following the old whale-road to the place where pollack, coley, and long greedy eels grow monstrous huge; difficult waters where the fish can only be dragged from the weeds and rocks with line and sinker. I sang the hymn of the star, and St Ayer cleared the sky of clouds for his light to lead us and guide us through the waters lost to the big ships; those waters where the real Whales retreated from the harpoons, spears, and lances.

I kept the boat hanging back though the tide tried to drag us through.

"What are you waiting for?" said Pikey.

"The man who stands at a strange threshold, should be cautious before he cross it, take his time. Who knows beforehand what foes may are sat awaiting him beyond the gate?"

Still I waited, the clouds rolled black wings over the starfields and starflows. Hail scoured my skin, and ice hung from my fingers but still I steered her steady to the place where a hoarfrost bridge seemed to shine between the low grey clouds and piled distant cumulous mountains like the last refuge of the old giants. Granny Ran's Teeth grew long and ragged here, keeping those other boats away. The guiding star shone clear at the end of the tunnel and the waves at last were stilled. Still the dark waters flowed trying to drag us through that darker mouth in the darkness

At last, the tide slackened, so we passed through the Stonegate under our own power; through the arched tunnel under the bridge of tempest-tested granite crags where the ice-winged tern would taunt and soar and scream.

We could tell we had entered St Ayer's Blessed Waters, Granny Ran's Ground; the sea was no longer churned with green mud and dead fish left by the trawlers. Below us great ribbons of kelp waved and swirled fathoms down in the clear dark waters, luminescent fish shot among them. There were the True Whales. I steered well clear of those great fish shaped like mountains of rough stone and covered with ragged coats as if sea-weeds grew on their hides. My granddad always said, "He lives forever, and his anger and hatred of man has grown huge from the slaughter of his goodbrothers these centuries gone."

You've been thinking on them white pages have you Pikey? Wondering how many died to fill St Ayer's Gospel? A few I reckon, a few, but that was a long time ago and they were honoured sacrifices.

"Pikey," I said, "if you think the paper is a horrible thing, what do you reckon the ink is made of? The ink that makes the prayers so black. They seem to have a life of their own; to run and change with the weather and mood of the sea. Sometimes the prayers are like naked birch and larch twigs silhouetted in the midnight sun. Sometimes they are like shrines of black burnt things on the snow lit up by the skull moon in the endless winter night. Sometimes they are fish-bones in the white sands, thousands and thousands of dead fish washed up and rotted on the edge of a dead sea."

Will Maurice, Jack Rackham, Pikey McKnight, my goodbrothers could not read, could not sing like a lidman, all they could do was drink and fish.

So as captain it fell to me to read the prayers of St Ayer's Gospel as we straddled the stay-bridled wave-horse.

The thin sun was rising over low black clouds in the morning haze, rimmed with anaemic bloodstains. I held St Ayer's Gospel tight and read the words as my granddad showed me. Will Maurice, Jack Rackham, Pikey McKnight lowered their lines with the shads, grubs, pirks and worms, to jig and lure, to tempt and trap the sly fish.

Pikey got a bite and hauled up his catch, the line weaving around the boat. He had to chase it lifting the short rod over the others lines

"Reel 'em in," he shouted, "give me some space."

He was hauling and chasing, chasing and hauling until a black and silver knot appeared far below us tangled with a streamer of the giant kelp.

"Conger!" he shouted.

Jack stood ready to tickle it under the chin with a gaff hook.

The eel was thick with slime; Jack couldn't get the hook in and had just gouged the skin on the back with the gaff's point. I cursed for the loss of cash on the spoiled eel. Will was trying to grip it but his hands slid off the mucous and blood. I cursed them again, put down St Ayer's Gospel, and jumped to subdue the eel with a yard wide piece of dry tarpaulin. I leant over the 'Lindy's' side and had him wrapped and got a good a grip on him behind the gills through the tarp'. A curse on them for distracting me from the hymn. We didn't notice the whale; its great fin reared up to starboard crusted and overgrown with barnacles and weed, an enormous paddle scarred with the marks of monsters and storms.

I saw the lines leaking from the book before my eye as the boat yawed.

I remembered my Granddad's words: "When he, skilled in treachery, feels the sailors settled firm upon him, encamped, enjoying the clear weather, then suddenly the ocean-spirit dives down with his prey into the salt wave, seeks the depths, and in the death-hall tries to drown ships and crews."

With the roll of the boat, St Ayer's Gospel flew open through the air and into the water.

Will Maurice, Jack Rackham, and Pikey McKnight tried to hold me back from getting it but I shook them off and dived after. Down I went after the Gospel. The weight of the clasps was sinking it. I swam down until I had it in my hands. Up I rose. Paddling with my feet as hard as I could to raise it from the deep and they hauled me aboard the wounded 'Lindy'. The radio beneath the seat sparked and smoked.

"We should have brought a raven," I said

I started the motor and tried to head for shore, but it sputtered out, I looked up and I saw the sky was smudged and grey.

"Get the oars out, then," I said.

I opened St Ayer's Gospel, expecting to find a prayer to take us safe to port; expecting to see that familiar strange writing crawl across a fine white page, but there were no pages.

The sky was filling with angry clouds, swelling and sweeping low, and the sun was gone. The boat listed badly with the timbers on the port side all staved in and crushed. Water was sweating and streaming through the planks.

"Bail faster," I said "Pikey, use that bait bucket."

The 'Lindy' was sinking, the sea seemed pale silver, filled with black fronds of kelp drifting to and fro. The sky like black marble veined with grey, she just fell away beneath our feet, leaving us floating in water turned white as milk; the seaweed took forms like the naked branches of birch and larch lit by the midnight sun. Black fronds like shrines of bound black bones on the snow illuminated by the bleached skull-moon of endless winter night, the black fern-like coils and curls of the kelp, coils and curls of the kelp like fish bones on white sand.

They wrapped around Will Maurice's legs. He struggled and yelped and tried to leap like a fish from the water. We tried to reach him, but a wave the colour of blood rose up to cover his head and he was gone.

That left three of us treading water; we were bounced upon the waves. A plain wave, then a big wave, a pitching wave; a surging wave tried to drown us and a wave that reflected the light of the sky dazzled us. We wrestled with the grasping wave, and thought the chilling wave would kill us with cold, but then came the last wave. The water was black, black as the raven's wing; a few white forms flickered far down beneath us. They flapped like paper in the wind, coiled like damp rags in a scupper, then they were there: a shoal of white girls swimming about our feet, at least they were shaped like girls; hollow white girls made of paper; fine and pretty paper.

My goodbrother Jack Rackham was dancing in the water with nine pale girls and he was singing with them:

Down in San Antone where the Rio de Rosa flows
I'm gonna settle down, down in ol' San Antone

Down, down he went with the white girls and I saw something else white in the blackness rising up to meet him; something that was once my goodbrother Will Maurice. Will Maurice rising up with his arms stretched out, and all over him was writing, writing blind-embossed on his skin where the weeds had held him, the writing washed out of my poor drowned book, black letters like naked birch and larch. Marks like shrines of bound black bones on the snow of endless night and his eyes were black as well, his eyes opened up wide and empty where the fishes had started on him, and his mouth opened wide as a whale, his mouth filled with ragged teeth like Granny Ran's, wide enough to swallow a boat, wide enough to drink down an ocean. With weeds whirling in a maelstrom around him, up he rose. The sky above us was whirling in a maelstrom too. I saw the thing that was once my goodbrother, Will Maurice, wrap his arms around Jack's legs. I watched as he pulled my goodbrother Jack Rackham down: down he went like a lead sinker. Down they went together. I could see both my goodbrothers rocking and rolling down, down into the darkness and the deep.

Pikey McKnight was screaming as the strangling hands of black waters lapped at his neck and white fingers of foam crawled upon his head, entwining his hair and leaving lumps of ice clinging wherever they passed.

He screamed, "Why don't you use the craft? Where is your elderfather's magic now?"

"It was all in the Gospel, Pikey, it's lost."

"But you know the songs."

The songs were in the ink and skin.

"What are we going to do?"

"Well Pikey" I replied "the elderfathers said that cattle die and kinsmen die and even the gods will die: the one thing which never dies is the reputation of each dead man. You and I will die bravely, Pikey McKnight and leave the world our fine reputations."

"I don't want to die."

"Then keep some iron in your hand, Pikey."

Around and around us they swam, circling beneath white water with the writing on their skin, around and around with hollow eyes and mouths as big as whales filled with terrible rough teeth.

With their terrible rough teeth, they tried to take my brother Pikey, and though he screamed in terror, he fought back. His clothes were torn to rags and each time they passed, they left a letter carved on his skin and each time he plunged the gutting knife into the water he carved a new one on theirs, writing their lives and deaths on each other, writing in blood and skin.

Still I held the empty book close, still the water froze my bones, still the sea and sky swirled in a black maelstrom, but I had a smile for Pikey.

I smiled for my goodbrother Pikey with the writing on his skin, and swam to him with my own knife in my hand. I held my goodbrother Pikey in the water, held him so I could read what the writing said,

"Pikey," I said "You have the prayer to Saint Ayer there on your stomach."

I cut a page from his body and placed it between the empty covers, and I sang. I sang like the nightingale in spite of the cold. My goodbrothers stopped, all my dead and drowned goodbrothers were basking just beneath the surface listening as I sang. I sang the seven by seven and the seven by nine, as I slipped into the cold sleep, I felt the hands of my dear dead and drowned goodbrothers bear me up.

The men that pulled me from the water had no earthly inkling of how I, a wretch wrecked on ice-cold December seas, lived through that night.

They found me washed up in their nets, blue but only cold–drowned and St Ayer's Gospel held tight in my hand. They took me to the hospital and revived me, but my goodbrothers, they never found them. I swore they were saints, and made the coastguards search in their helicopters and lifeboats, but they never found my goodbrothers. I reckon they are still out there somewhere, bless them, bless Will Maurice, Jack Rackham and Pikey McKnight; they brought St Ayer's Gospel back; see how the pages are so white, the finest parchment so fine and pretty and pale. It's not rags or wood pulp like modern books. It's skin you see, stretched on a frame and dried and split thin and polished. That's why the covers have to be so stiff, so solid, why it has to have those big bronze clasps, to keep all the pages pressed in tight to stop it going back to its old shape.

You don't believe me? I swear on St Ayer's Gospel; it's the truth. I wouldn't want to be thought a liar; my granddad used to say; cattle die, kinsmen die, even the gods will die, the one thing which never dies is the reputation left by each dead man.

Oliver Smith was born in Cheltenham, Gloucestershire. He is a fine art graduate and his writing practice developed from an interest in various surrealist techniques.

His prose writing has previously appeared in the following anthologies, such as Land's End *from Inkermen Press,* Transactions of the Flesh: A Homage to Joris-Karl Huysmans *from Ex Occidente Press/Zagava Press, and* Dark Hall Press Cosmic Horror Anthology *from Dark Hall Press.*

His poetry has appeared in S T Joshi's Spectral Realms *from Hippocampus Press.*

More short stories are due to be published in the anthologies Demon Rum and Other Evil Spirits *from Angelic Knight Press and* Techno-Horror *from Dark Hall Press.His Amazon page can be found at: http://www.amazon.com/Oliver-Smith/e/B00IHK049VV/*

———

COMFORT FROM LIES ABOUT HEAVEN AND HELL

BY T. FOX DUNHAM

"We expect results," snapped *Reichsmarschall* Göring. He whipped his diamond-studded baton under his flabby arm.

"*Ja, Herr Reichsmarschall,*" Doctor Josten said. "And we are working fast, but these are delicate procedures. The brain is a fine box of wiring, and we do not fully understand how the nervous system operates. We may never completely understand it."

"All things are possible with German will," he said, gripping his baton. His gray Luftwaffe uniform bulged at the seams, and his cape barely covered his round girth. Josten thought he spotted dark eyeliner along the *Reichsmarschall's* eyes, perhaps a hint of cherry-red lipstick staining his lips. He didn't stare and looked down at his pages of formulas and notes. His fingers ached from intricate surgeries and procedures, and if not for the dreams, he would have just put down his head to sleep. All men had a private war to fight in the war, and he steadied himself.

"My team is making progress," he said. "We have mapped out the lower brain functions." He held up a gray slice of nerve bundles in a dish of formaldehyde on the desk and pointed out the various morphology of the human mind. The *Reichsmarschall* feigned an interest and pulled back his airman's cap from his eyes. He stank of French perfume.

"Decay starts here in the frontal lobes and gradually

spreads through the higher functions of the brain: memory, personality, everything that separates us from the lower order, the apes and animals."

"From where did you procure these specimens?" he asked.

The questioned stunned Josten for a moment; usually, German officers didn't ask such questions, preferring ignorance to incrimination. The S.S. had developed new terminology to hide their programs in plain language: evacuation, special treatment. Doctor Josten informed the *Reichsmarschall* about the specimens. "These were dissected from Red Army prisoners after administering the treatment. Each prisoner was euthanized to avoid damage to the central nervous system, however lack of oxygen causes necrosis of the brain tissue."

"Perhaps a *Deutsch* brain or even Englander or *Amerikaner* would not decay as fast. Russian brains are genetically inferior."

"*Ja, Herr Reichsmarschall*," he said. The sadistic visions of his actions in the name of Reich broke free their mental bonds, and Josten felt under the sleeve of his white lab coat, then pricked his finger on the thorn chain, the wrist jewelry he'd woven from barbed wire plucked from the fence around the camp. The images of what he'd done—the Russian soldiers in rags, some screaming at the door, others standing solemn and at peace—flashed before his mind's eye. His stomach twisted, and he choked back vomit. The *Reichsmarschall* eyed him, and he pressed the barb into his flesh. Hot pain pierced the soft skin and muscle and distracted him from the visions, focusing his mind. He'd devised this device for a quick fix when the situation made it prudent not to shoot his bum full of morphia.

"Preservation is key," he said. "We need to preserve the memory if we are to extract intelligence. In their current state, the specimens are mere machines, missing all the essence of life and humanity. Lowering the body temperature just after death will preserve much of the vital tissue. We have seen this with aircrews shot down over the English Channel. If proper precautions were taken with recently deceased specimens, I believe we can initiate complete reanimation."

"The Luftwaffe funded this program to gain intelligence from down Englander and *Amerikaner* bomber crews, shot down over the Reich. The program has the potential to win the war. Are you sure your serum will make them vulnerable to interrogation?"

"I am entirely satisfied that my formula and the effect of death will diminish their will," Josten lied.

He led Göring to heavy steel door at the back of the lab that used to serve as a meat locker when this building housed a mess hall, before it had been turned from a troop barracks when the S.S. expanded the camp to handle the new influx of inmates from Poland and the east. His hands shook as he fed the key into the lock and threw off the bolts.

"We keep our . . . progress in here. If you would follow me." Göring wrapped his cape around his girth and waved to his staff to stay behind in the main lab. The temperature dropped, and Josten rubbed his hands to stir his circulation. He led Göring to the first cell—a cement cubicle. Violet ichor, blood, saliva and semen drained from the body and into a metal grate in the floor. "We chain them up for security, not that they try to escape. We have to keep them from damaging themselves."

The specimen hunched in the corner of the cell, cupping its hands and long fingers down in mock prayer. His assistant tattooed the designation R-1 onto its forehead in block letters. Its genitals sagged out from the loincloth's side, and it held no concern for modesty, or any other elements of human personality. Semen leaked out its penis in a constant stream, joining the viscous fluids pouring from its nose, mouth, ears and anus. The ooze hardened into a thick gel on the concrete floor.

The *Reichsmarschall* put a handkerchief to his nose.

"Communist filth," he said.

Doctor Josten extended a poker and pointed at sutured scars along the specimen's shaved scalp. "We vivisected part of its brain—though dissected perhaps is the proper parlance, since its heart does not beat nor can we detect active life functions. The serum reanimated sections of the brain, parts of the frontal lobe, but the specimen does not fully function—a vague shadow of the light of life."

"Spare me the poetry, doctor," he said.

"*Ja, Mein Herr*," he said and led Göring to the next cell. An emaciated body stood in the corner, hiding from the light. The body had nearly starved when it had been selected for the experiment and taken to be treated. The skin wrapped tight to its skull, exposing the curves and caves of the bone. Josten looked askance from the eyes— bulging eggs. If it still had voice, the specimen would be screaming.

"Its eyes," the *Reichsmarschall* said. "This specimen has seen something beyond this world."

Doctor Josten reached for the barbs around his wrist and punctured his skin, driving off the creeping melancholy.

"I do not believe such things," Josten said. "There is no consciousness beyond death."

"Then you are a small man," Göring said and chuckled. "I would like to know what it says when you restore its voice. It will tell of Germanic gods and the gates of Valhalla."

"*Ja, Herr Reichsmarschall*," Josten said. "I apologize." He moved on with his presentation and admonished himself for disagreeing with his superior. Göring had the power to dispatch him back to the Russian front, where Josten had lost a toe from frostbite before the High Command approved this project. "With the new preservation techniques I described, I believe the serum will be successful. We can glean intelligence from the minds of Allied pilots."

"I will make preservations for crews to be standing by with ice in our cities. We will find downed aircrews fast and transport them to your lab." He maneuvered his baton. "Does it eat?"

"It requires no food and only small amounts of water, though sometimes the specimens bite at the air when my staff gets too close. We think it is a reflex action."

"Impressive, Doctor. Now how about lunch?"

Doctor Josten followed *Reichsmarschall* Göring out of the vault, but he paused when he heard someone whispering. He turned to study Specimen R-2, still avoiding his eyes.

"Whispers?"

It cracked its lips, and ichor oozed down its chin, spilling down its ribs. "Have seen your son. Wife."

"What? What are you saying?"

"They are served on the Lord's table. His mouth watered. Opens jaw wide. The Lord of the Pit."

Then the specimen dimmed. Its mouth shut, and it gazed at the wall behind him.

"What Lord? My family? How do you know?"

"Empty belly." The specimen groaned then spoke no more. Doctor Josten smacked it, cracking its brittle jaw. It gazed through the concrete wall.

Doctor Josten shut the door to his private office, took off his shoes and lab coat then splashed cold water over his face and through the blond wisps of hair still clinging to his scalp. Then he opened a drawer in his desk and took out an ivory case—a gift from Gretta when he'd gained his new position at the University of Berlin. The syringe felt cool in his fingers, and he dipped it into the vial and sucked up a drink of morphia, then dropped his trousers and injected it. It rushed his mind instantly, and he lay on the couch while his mind floated so he wouldn't fall.

The opiate didn't change past events. They just stopped burning, so he'd stop laughing wild and soprano laughter as he did from melancholy. His father beat crying out of him in his crib, and Josten laughed now when the need welled in him to weep; so he generally avoided funerals, which had become harder as the war progressed.

They buried his family today. He'd asked his mother-in-law to attend to the funeral, that important business of the war kept him out of Berlin. The old crone had never approved of her young daughter marrying her old professor. The scandal had caused her a stroke, but she recovered and warmed to the family when his son was born — the child with such fair hair, the joy and light. He'd never serve the *Wehrmacht*. Josten swore it.

They closed two caskets at the funeral to hide the damage to their bodies — the truth of the war. Germany lived in a closed-casket state. He felt thankful he hadn't been there to see their bodies dug out from the bricks and wood of the crushed building. Gravity bombs dropped by Lancaster and B-17 bombers fell and cracked the ancient domains of Hamburg like eggs, with no regard for the precious life within. Josten threw himself into his work, and when the emotions peaked, he resorted to morphia — an old remedy for a shrapnel wound he'd taken outside of Moscow. If he couldn't fix the equation, the *Reichsmarschall* would send him back to that raw and unforgiving winter. There, he'd fall in the snow and freeze stiff, forever preserved like a statue.

Their burned bodies would be far from saving now — the brains destroyed and the bread of worms and bugs. He couldn't save them. Their life had fled, drained like a dying star. Stars died, and the universe darkened. What was life without their life? The suffering of the war, of the world lost its meaning, and he held to the work, to the pursuit of science. Now, it served as the only motivation to not just lay his head down and sleep forever. Maybe that was the key. The specimens had been reactivated, turned on again like a switch, but they needed more — not a soul but some essence of life, of spirit. His family had been his spirit, and now his body emptied.

He shut his eyes and watched the colors swirled, laughing as they danced. The voice of specimen R-2 whispered in his euphoria:

Open jaws wide.

The dark wolves howled in his heart. The war is lost. The struggle is meaningless. They died for nothing. He pushed away the doubt, the defeatism and released himself into the euphoria.

The Lord eats us all in time.

The Luftwaffe flew in three fresh specimens in special refrigerated Junkers 52 transport. The RAF and US AF bombed Münster the night before, and several Lancaster and B-17 bombers fell in the raid from German air defenses. The pilot assured him that only moments passed from their death in the air from flak and that they had parachuted to the ground, thus preventing concussive damage. Doctor Josten nearly danced while they carried the bodies, wrapped in ice, into his lab.

"Prepare the treatment," he ordered his staff—mostly old scientists or wounded students, no longer fit to serve in the *Wehrmacht*. Camp trustees, draped in striped suits and keeping their eyes to the ground, set the first cadaver on the operating the table. The rest they carried into the morgue to be kept cool in the freezers.

Doctor Josten read the body's previous name on his uniform. "Good evening, Captain Brightfield," he said to the corpse. He examined the first specimen—a RAF airman, still adorned in noble blue uniform, the fabric bloody and shredded—abdominal shrapnel wound. He must have bled out while floating to earth, making fall like an angel who'd lost his wings. He helped an orderly search the pockets before stripping the corpse. Normally the intelligence services confiscated all possessions, but they'd hurried to freeze it under special orders from Göring. He recovered a pipe from his top pocket and faded pictures of a pretty brunette and two sons. Josten slipped them into his lab coat pocket, then they snipped away the uniform and underclothing. Sans the uniform and trappings of rank—the divisions human create—he looked weak and vulnerable, indistinguishable from a German man. Josten's work had the potential to heal the world, to end weakness, and he focused on this vision to survive the dark days. The world couldn't go on burning, and he and his work would be venerated in peace.

"Assemble my device," he ordered. "Bring out my vision." His staff unlocked a closet by the specimen shelves and generators, and they lifted out the device—his creation, his vision. They set the iron sphere down on a table by the body and connected cables to the generator. The sphere hummed, vibrating the table, and Josten sensed the vibrations through his feet. "The stuff of life. *Aqua Vitae*. Prometheus come." He cupped the sides of the sphere in his palms. The vibrations suffused through his groin, and his genitals hardened. He peeled off four panels and screwed in the copper poles, then turned the crank below, connecting the circuits to the capacitor within the sphere. "Soon," he addressed the cadaver. "We will have you up and about and dancing. Such a beautiful family. I will bring their father home to them. No family should be without a father—and no father without his family." One of his staff shaved the airman's head, and Josten reeled out two wires attached to two copper cups then pressed them to his temples, driving the thin nail into the brain. Another assistant handed him a box of metal vials, and he plucked one out and fed it into a stainless steel syringe.

"It'll be terrifying, I'm sure," he said to the airman. "First life. Bright beautiful life. And flight. Then you slept. Your eyes closed, and you surrendered your burdens. Falling into the darkness. Nothing. A void. A vacuum. No dark lords and dinner tables." He scoffed and laughed at the Russian's primitive observations, probably a side effect of the process. He gulped hard against his dry throat. "Then light. Light so bright it burns your eyes. I apologize. It will be jolting. Back to the world. Back to this agony and war."

He spun the internal capacitor into the circuit, and the

sphere ignited and pulsed crimson light. "This is my child, my beautiful baby. For years I dreamed of electricity, the raw stuff of life. But it required finessing, dear Group captain. A current can kill or caress. It was a symphony, Beethoven, that inspired the rhythm, the code. I saw it in a dream. I saw the music made flesh. An angel flying for each note and become lightning. Lightning! Lightning bore life. And now I command it. The serum prepares the cells, a conductive fluid."

Josten turned the airman's head, exposing the back of his neck, then injected the serum into his spine. "Return. I am lightning's master." The fluid fed into the subject's brain. Its properties not only facilitated the reanimation, but in theory also changed the brain chemistry, extinguishing will and personality leaving the subject submissive. It had worked on test animals, though the human brain was far more complex.

Josten signaled to his assistant, and she threw the generator's lever. The engine roared, gaining speed, pouring raw power into his device. He adjusted several rheostats, and power fed along the conduits into the head of the airman. The reaction fired immediately, and the airman twisted and trembled. His eyes shot wide and scanned the lab with intelligent intent. Doctor Josten shut down the device.

"Welcome back, B-1," he said, petting his head. The airman's nose leaked magenta mucous, joining the saliva pouring from its mouth. His genitals dripped semen. "Speak to us. I order you." The specimen didn't respond, looking confused. Though alive again, or at least reanimated, the subject still lacked something, an element of esprit, of will. The airplane glided but without direction or purpose, no pilot in the cockpit. He slipped out the photo of the family and showed it to the specimen.

"Your family. Do you remember? They are here waiting for you. You are home." The specimen focused on the photo and its jaw moved, lips waving. It groaned, searching for words. The spirit in the dark water drowned and kicked, trying to break the surface. "Come on now. They are here. If you do not speak, you will not be able to see them." It groaned louder, and its arm reached for the picture. Then the specimen surrendered and fell back into its stupor. Doctor Josten recorded notes on a clipboard. "Good progress," he said. "Now let us treat the other specimens."

Doctor Josten moved off to assist, and specimen B-1 grabbed his arm and pulled him down with a giant's strength. Doctor Josten dropped the clipboard in surprise, and the specimen whispered something, though he couldn't discern all the words:

"Hungry Lord and the folly of man. We feed its appetite with war. Laughing when he weeps." The specimen jerked its neck and chomped its jaw, and Doctor Josten yanked his arm from his grip, nearly losing a chunk of flesh and lab coat. The body fell back to its stupor.

"Interesting," he said.

Doctor Josten recorded his notes:

We reanimated four more specimens. Two Englanders. Two Amerikaners. I have amplified my efforts to return the spirit to the specimens, and for the single men, I ordered that pretty inmates be brought to the cells and made to strip. The naked women — fresh and healthy, only recent camp interns, summoned some recognition in the specimens, but when it didn't prove enough, I ordered them to fornicate on themselves and each other, hoping to stir a deeper sexual desire. Though I found this most distasteful and had to remind myself that this was in the name of science. I hoped to reach their spirit by invoking sexual need, a biological desire buried deep in the oldest parts of the brain. The hypothesis proved successful. The corpses groaned and moaned and began to touch their own bodies or reached out for the women. Death melted from them, and the energy remained.

"Good morning, A-2," Josten said to the specimen. They'd found him in a field outside a ball-bearings factory in the Ruhr, the corpse still clutching a ten-gallon Stetson hat under his arms. They had to pry his arms away to get rid of the hat. They shaved his dark hair, leaving black bristles on his scalp and covered him in a white loincloth. The size and natural shape of his genitals made some of the staff uncomfortable, though the specimen, beyond such worldly concerns as modesty, cared little. Ichor, spoiled blood, and semen drained from the specimen, and they changed him three times a day. A-2 responded better to the treatment and the new process of fornication than the other specimens, and over the days, it had even formed coherent sentences and seemed to understand its environment, though the tone of its voice inherited a monotone sound from its time dead. It felt off, not entirely alive, like some puppet, and each night when Doctor Josten finally fell asleep in his morphia-induced euphoria, he dreamed of men wearing vacant visages and speaking sans mouth, watching sans eyes, and they ripped at his face, removing his eyes so they could show him a secret that only the blind could perceive.

"Hey Doc," A-2 said. "You got a smoke? I'm dying here. You understand me?"

"When I was a boy, I went to live with my uncle in California. I learned English."

"Well that's just swell, slick. The Lord of the Pit just loves a traveler. He'll toss that soul on the fire and lick you up all nice and crispy."

He jotted down the specimen's dialogue, underlining the word *delusion*.

The trauma of death and reanimation has left the specimen's brain addled and perhaps demented, and even though the specimen had been preserved, no current process could entirely suspend decomposition. Perhaps the mind translates the trauma as a nightmare, something the brain can understand. I should consult a psychoanalyst. The vision is similar to the one described by the previous subject when it obtained brief consciousness. I attribute this to a shared folklore, perhaps one of the Jungian archetypes, a common element in human psychology. The specimen has still not given any intelligence or information of military value. For hours, it sits in a fugue state then suddenly comes to life. In brief flashes of memory, it speaks of its previous life in Texas, its family and experiences of childhood.

"Are all krauts deaf?" it asked. "I could really use a smoke."

"Smoking is *verboten* in the lab."

"God damn."

It raised its arms and examined the manacles securing its wrists with puzzled eyes that leaked hoary juice. The eyes held barely a semblance of life the way light bulbs glow sickly just before burning out.

It has recognition of some remaining elements of world events, but concepts such as war, enemies or politics it does not understand or it no longer has any concern for such mortal trifles. I admire it. Though a mere echo of life, it has released much of its worldly burdens. Whether this echo-state of life has made the specimen vulnerable to interrogation techniques remains to be seen, but even if that part of the experiment fails, the process of reanimation of soldiers to even this diminished state holds military value.

"I am going to ask you a question, and you will answer," Doctor Josten said. "Do you recall your mission?"

"Sure, slick. To bomb the hell out of the Germans until they get on their knees to suck our dicks."

He jotted down the response, briefly shaking his head with dismay at the *Amerikaner* vulgarity. If only one of the Englander specimens had proven to be so communicative. He would have preferred talking with a civilized man, not some cowboy.

"At what altitude did you begin your bombing run?"

The specimen clicked its tongue, considering the

question. "As high as angels fly way up in the sky. The Lord has hosts of angels that ferry its food."

"Can you be more specific?"

"A good smoke always got my noggin humming in the morning."

Doctor Josten sighed and hunched his shoulders. "I'll see what I can do." It yanked on the manacles, pulling the chain bolted to the wall. The iron carved into his skin and stripped away layers, damaging it. "I can loosen that for you," he said and retrieved the bolt from his coat pocket. He reached for the slimy cuffs, and the specimen relinquished its civil behavior and chomped the air, biting for Josten's arm. The doctor lurched back, nearly tripping, and the specimen caught a sleeve with its teeth then tore a hole in the coat. It chewed on the fabric, shredding it. Josten calmed his breathing. "What was the purpose of that?" he demanded.

"Nothing personal, slick," he muttered with a mouthful of cloth. "My belly's growling, and your meat smells sweet."

Josten grabbed his clipboard from the pool of bodily secretions on cold concrete floor and wiped off smeared ichor with his remaining sleeve. He turned to leave, and a familiar child's voice cried out to him: "Papa."

"Your voice."

"Don't go. I am scared of the bombs."

"You bastard," Josten said and gripped the clipboard until his knuckles bleached white. "This is a head game. Nothing more. No lords in pits and dead children. My son is dead. My wife is dead. They feel no more."

Specimen A-2 watched him with bemused white orbs. "It's no dream, slick. Your son, Albert. Named after your hero. Your wife, Gretta. Cute family. They wait, set on the table. A real cookout. A fine clambake. They were next when I last saw 'em."

"You overheard some of my staff gossiping. I shall discipline them."

"Gretta read your son fables of the Brother Grimm

every night. When the bombers came at night, Albert recited the magical name to drive them away: Rumpelstiltskin. Rumpelstiltskin. Rumple—"

Doctor Josten aimed his arm to slap the specimen, but he held back after its recent attempt to eat him. "Impossible."

"Waited we did in the void—darkness. A black sea. Squid's ink. A thousand souls in the night and no light. We whispered. We sang. We wept. Some waited for Jesus to lift them to sit at His side in Heaven. Others hoped for oblivion. For the pain to end. Always the mouth slurped and chewed, gathering souls closest with claws and a hook. I knew your son. I knew your wife."

"Even if what you are saying is true—and it is a fantasy with no scientific backing—you expect me to believe that in all the thousands of dead, you knew my family?"

It nodded its head, and a glob of mucous dropped from its nose and stained its loincloth. "Sure, slick. We had ourselves a shared moment in life. Random. Of no meaning. No destiny. Just a fast eclipse."

"I don't understand."

"I'm the son-of-a-bitch who dropped a bomb on Hamburg, and it fell so happy and whistled and hit an apartment. It pulverized it and all inside, even killing those in the basement shelter. So pretty. Dang beautiful."

The vision of their death pierced through Josten's mind, and he pressed the barbs into his wrist, sinking three deep into the muscle. The specimen laughed dry like rubbing sandpaper and sang: "Rumpelstiltskin." Josten ran from the vault.

"Rumpelstiltskin. Rumple—"

Doctor Josten slammed the door to his cramped office, fetched out the syringe kit from under his desk then stripped off his soiled lab coat, his shirt, trousers, shoes and knickers. The syringe felt smooth in his fingers, and he sucked up several drams of morphia, far more than his usual recreational dose. He dropped on the couch, lifted his hip and drove the needle and opiate into his flesh. His bum pinched, and the pain drove through to his crotch. He plucked his flaccid manhood—now a shrunken old man. He always insisted to Gretta that they make love in the dark. She thought it romantic, but really he did it to hide his rotted body. When they made love, he used to pretend he was swimming in the ocean and going out with the tide. She sowed Eden in his body—pure beauty and light—and after she'd fallen asleep, he'd laugh and laugh in melancholy and suffered the guilt of a rapist, a monster poisoning her body with his decayed filth.

The opiate flowed through him, and he floated again, gliding through the darkness. A pressure weighed his lungs, and he hallucinated a black mare sitting on his chest and gazing through him with fire eyes. He struggled to pull in each breath, fighting the weight crushing his ribs and lungs. He'd overdosed on morphia, and it suppressed his breathing; however, he didn't care. Only a deeply programmed survival instinct pushed him to fight for life. He had to know.

Was this what they felt when the building collapsed on their fragile bodies? Did they struggle against the weight of the stone for air in their last terrifying moments? Gretta had pleaded with him to get her and Albert out of the city, to bring them to live at his lab. He'd refused. How could he let her see the necessary work he did? He could never let her witness the mission of Treblinka. He had refused, and they'd suffocated, choking on the dust of ground rock, murdered by a Texan. They remained dead while their executioner lived—or half lived.

Could it be true? Had he truly witnessed a banquet of souls? A ravenous Lord in his pit?

He breathed shallow now, and his mind slipped from his body, sinking into the black ether and absorbed by the midnight fabric of reality. He fell fast into a dark pit, and below he witnessed shadows—thousands of thousands of shadows waving and moving like countless ocean waves on a stormy sea. Mechanical claws, steaming and pumping, chains dangling from the fingers, scooped up the souls and fed them to a gaping boiler with grated teeth. Fire burst from the boiler with each mouthful, and steam vented from pipes as the burning pipe organ played.

Doctor Josten clung onto a slender tether to the mortal world, floating between both realms. The chimneys blew smoke and steam from the crematoriums out his office and lab. And the evil work of Treblinka progressed.

Doctor Josten threw the specimen a brown pack of *Sondermischung* cigarettes. He'd traded an S.S. guard for them. The guard had taken the tobacco off a Polish Jew arriving and stripping before receiving special treatment—the walk down the garden path to the showers. The specimen ripped open the envelope, and several cigarettes spilled from the package and dropped into the gunk covering the floor. It hung one off its dry lip and sucked on the end.

"Need a light, slick." Josten reached out slowly, handing him a silver lighter, also borrowed from one of his staff. The specimen took it, and Josten pulled his arm clear before he got bit. "Begging your pardon," it said. "I can't help it. Your heart smells so sweet, like ribs on the fire. I can taste your blood on the air, all salty. Don't know why. I ain't hungry for steak or thirsty for beer, but human fare makes my mouth water something fierce."

His staff had lost limbs, flesh, even noses and eyes because of accidents of proximity with the other specimens. Those wounded suffered infection, blood poisoning, and slowly died in the camp hospital.

"I saw them. My family."

"So the good doctor has seen the light? Hallelujah! Praise the Lord. Praise the Pit!"

"What will happen to them? I saw an oven."

"His Mouth. He is the all-after. He is inevitable. Not Heaven or Hell. Those are lies to comfort us. Only metal teeth chewing await us. This is the end of the soul."

He lit up the cigarette and puffed on it. The coal tip burned red, and he blew a stream of smoke from his nose. "God damn," he said. "Can't even taste it. Shit." He spit out the cigarette.

"Now tell me. My wife. My son. What will happen to them?"

The specimen grinned, and Josten shook with chill. Their positions exchanged: master and slave. The sly Texan got the better of the German scientist. "I ain't got to tell you shit."

"I will dissect you slowly," Josten said, suffering ruthlessness, a dark nature that had grown within him every time he blocked out the human suffering playing out around him. Each time, he'd sacrificed a mote of his humanity, and his soul had dissipated.

"Don't matter none," the Texan said. "I can feel no pain. This hunger gets worse each day. My flesh freezes. My blood is still. Your hot muscles would heat me up. Your burning blood would give me life for a few moments. Feed me steaming life. Feed us all."

Doctor Josten collapsed against the wall. "All of you? You want me to release the other specimens?"

"I no longer feel passion. But I want to murder and kill and eat." The Texan clawed his thigh, driving his fingers into the muscle, piercing the flesh. Clotted blood fell in clumps from the hole. He gritted his teeth in frustration then yelled and howled. "I don't feel shit! I can't smoke or eat or fuck."

"You promise to tell me if I release you?"

"Swear to God," he said, grinning like a child about to get what it wants after throwing a tantrum.

"You said there wasn't a God. Just a mouth."

"God is hunger. It is the Lord in his Pit. The pit has no bottom."

Doctor Josten fished the bolt to release the chain from his pocket and carefully maneuvered to the chains. The Texan mocked him: "What about your important war? Isn't this treason?"

"None of it matters anymore. There's only the mouth and the pit in the end." The Texan cackled and hit his knee, laughing at Josten. He released the Texan and stood clear. Once free, the specimen leaned down on hind legs and leapt through the vault, giggling and cackling and singing in a child's voice: "Rumpelstiltskin, Momma! I'm afraid of the bombs!"

With care, Josten released the rest of the specimens. Some collapsed in mindless stupor. Others ran for the vault door like anxious dogs, howling to be let out. They had the intelligence not to attack and devour their emancipator, and Doctor Josten unlocked the cell door, releasing his creations onto his ignorant staff.

The pack fell upon his lab assistants and the guards, first raking their faces and skin with claws. Any semblance of humanity bled from them as they raged and devoured, chomping down on muscles to bone. The guards fired into the pack with their MG-42s, but the specimens ignored the bullets and soon ripped them to kite ribbons. Two of the specimens jumped through windows and galloped on hind legs into the complex. They howled, and their keens echoed across the camp.

Josten poured petrol meant for the generator onto the tables and chairs of the lab. He returned to the vault, found the dropped lighter and set the facility on fire. The flames wafted, surging through the rooms, burning his equipment, his notes, and cremating the bodies of his devoured staff.

"Now tell me, demon!" Doctor Josten yelled at the Texan.

"There will be no more pain. The Lord in the Pit will grind your loved ones in his teeth, and their agony will end."

Beakers and glass vials popped. The windows exploded out. The flames burned Josten's legs, and he ignored the pain. It wouldn't matter in a moment.

"You lie!" he yelled over the roar of the fire. "You taunt me."

"Sure, slick," the Texan said. "The Lord just keeps on chewing 'till all our souls are in his teeth." The specimen tackled Josten and chomped down on his neck. His artery burst, squirting a stream of hot blood down its gray face. "You'll know soon enough."

T. Fox Dunham resides outside of Philadelphia PA – author and historian. He's published in nearly 200 international journals and anthologies. His first novel, The Street Martyr, *was published by Gutter Books this October, followed* Professional Detachment, *a literary erotica from Bitten Press and followed by* Searching for Andy Kaufman *from PMMP in 2014. He's a cancer survivor. His friends call him fox, being his totem animal, and his motto is: Wrecking civilization one story at a time.*
Site: www.tfoxdunham.com.
Blog: http://tfoxdunham.blogspot.com/
Facebook: http://www.facebook.com/tfoxdunham
Twitter: @TFoxDunham

ABOUT THE EDITOR

Sarah E. Glenn, a product of the suburbs, has a B.S. in Journalism, which is redundant if you think about it. She loves writing mystery and horror stories, often with a sidecar of funny. Several have appeared in mystery and paranormal anthologies, including G.W. Thomas' *Ghostbreakers* series, *Futures Mysterious Anthology Magazine*, and *Fish Tales: The Guppy Anthology*. She belongs to Sisters in Crime, SinC Guppies, the Short Mystery Fiction Society, and the Historical Novel Society.

Sarah is the Editor-in-Chief and co-owner of Mystery and Horror, LLC, an independent micro-press publishing speculative fiction. She and her partner really appreciate you reading this book! If you would like to know more her and the press, she is active on social media.

Here are our social media coordinates:

Follow Mystery and Horror, LLC on Facebook:
https://www.facebook.com/MysteryAndHorrorLlc

Follow Mystery and Horror, LLC on Twitter:
HTTP://WWW.TWITTER.COM/@MAHLLC

Find us on Pinterest:
http://www.pinterest.com/mandhbooks/

Favorite our Smashwords page:
https://www.smashwords.com/profile/view/mysteryandhorrorllc

Subscribe to our blog:
http://www.mysteryandhorrorllc.com/blog

Connect on LinkedIn:
https://www.linkedin.com/company/3635768

Visit our website:
http://www.mysteryandhorrorllc.com

www.ingramcontent.com/pod-product-compliance
Lightning Source LLC
Chambersburg PA
CBHW051242260626
47162CB00002B/561